# THE
# IRISH ROSE

# THE

# IRISH ROSE

## A NOVEL

## JOE HILL

**B. Jain Publishers (P) Ltd.**
An ISO 9001 : 2000 Certified Company
USA – Europe – India

# THE IRISH ROSE

First Indian Edidion: 2007

*Published in India by Kuldeep Jain for*

## B. Jain Publishers (P) Ltd.

An ISO 9001 : 2000 Certified Company

1921, Street No. 10, Chuna Mandi, Paharganj,
New Delhi 110 055 (INDIA)
**Ph.:** 91-11-2358 0800, 2358 3100, 2358 1300, 2358 1100
**Fax:** 91-11-2358 0471
**Email:** bjain@vsnl.com
**Website:** www.bjainbooks.com

Printed in India by
**J.J. Offset Printers**
522, FIE, Patpar Ganj, Delhi-110092
Ph.: 91-11-2216 9633, 2215 6128

B&T 23.95 11/07
ISBN 10: 0-9787294-0-4
ISBN 13: 978-0-9787294-0-0
BOOK CODE :BH-10901

*For*

*Lillian, John, Brian, Maureen, Denis*

# Acknowledgements

This novel could not have been published without the loving support and devoted editing of Anne C. Hill, my wife. Thank you!

I am grateful to Lillian without whom I never would have seen the beauty of life and the Emerald Isle. My appreciation goes to my son John and my daughter Maureen who typed the early stages of this novel before it was born after a 105-month pregnancy. To my son Brian I am indebted for naming this work of fiction, The Irish Rose. And to Denis I am thankful simply for being Denis, the baby of the family, as was his mother, Lillian, in her Dublin family.

# ONE

# Malignancy

"Malignant..."

"I'm sorry, Mrs. O'Malley," the doctor said. His acid-stinging words scarred her ears and heart.

Tara heard his voice, the nurse on the phone, the whisperings of patients...soliciting for her attention like clamoring voices from a literary agent's slush pile. *Is my life over? She thought. Not if I can help it. And I can help it!*

Blood rushed to her head. Her face flushed with fear. A nightmare...sitting opposite Dr. Stein. Her body froze in a fixed position, her hands tightening round the arms of the chair rest. Her hair shampooed and set the day before, settled closer to her head. Stroking her forehead, she felt faint. Her back and legs felt weak. A stressful spell came over her. Her heart pounded in her head, her ears, her fingers; it beat so fast she had difficulty breathing. She shot the doctor a look, but tears clouded her vision. She heard the word "malignant" and nothing else. A baseball-size lump in her throat made her cough.

His hand on hers restored the realism of the moment. *Lump.. malignant.* To herself, she repeated what he said: "I'm sorry,

Mrs. O'Malley." She felt cold. Strange, in this stressful situation, she should remember when she and John had attended the ballet last season. In a draft, she said, "I feel cold."

Once again, she needed her husband to hold and warm her to share her stress. Her worst fears had surfaced. Cancer! How could it happen? *How, at fifty-four, could I have cancer. It wasn't in the family. Death might be my partner. No, I will not die! I will not permit it.* Harold Kushner's *When Bad Things Happen to Good People* flashed to mind. She knew God would help. But according to Kushner, God did not interfere with the natural order of things, which meant God would perform no miracle on her left breast. She felt isolated. Desolate. Deserted. Discontinued. She needed God. *God might reject my prayers; he might not halt the natural development of cancer cells multiplying in my lymph nodes.* Her thoughts pitched at her like a dentist's drill without medication, unnerving every tooth in her mouth. She hurt all over. *Once on top, now at the bottom. How can I climb up?*

"Mrs. O'Malley . . .Mrs. O'Malley . . ." Dr. Stein voice startled her.

The oncologist spoke through partially opened lips. "Your primary physician is correct. Your tumor is cancerous."

Instead of saying, "It can't be. There's no cancer in the family." She stammered, "What?" She tried to smile. But her cheeks hurt like the leathery skin of an octogenarian in God-awful health. *An outcropping of cancerous cells growing in my body like an extraterrestrial embryo.*

"Nice to know you are in competent hands, if I can use the word *nice* in this sad situation."

Sad isn't the word for it, she reasoned. More like a death sentence. A swelling of emotions filled her lungs. She coughed.

She coughed again. She, a mother of four with a touch of gentleness, as soft as a summer breeze, had cancer. Cancer! Impossible.

"Relax, Tara. Here, take this water."

*You must be wrong, doctor.* "Thank you," she said, taking the glass. "It's a wonder my husband didn't feel the tumor."

"What?"

"He always has his hands on my breasts, especially in bed."

The oncologist smiled. "Men are interested in other things."

"My husband's a fine man. I love him and couldn't have a better husband and father to our four children. We're more than good together. We're one." *We're one and now he may be on his own.* "Well, I kid him he has a one track mind. Every time I look around he has one or both hands on me," said she.

Laughing, he said, "It's a wonder you didn't have more children."

She teared up. She told herself to be brave. With her inner strength she cleared her eyes. *My children. . I may never see them married nor hold my grandchildren!* Now more than ever, she'd have to be a leader for her children's good. To lead through fear is not to lead; she must be brave and courageous and lead courageously. To do so would help her family through difficult days ahead. *After all, everyone has difficulties from time to time.*

"I'm sorry," he replied. "You have much to offer the world and people."

"I already do as an administrator of a personal care home as well as owning my own facility," she answered.

"I know," the doctor noted.

She felt the need for a hug. "I love my residents. I love my job. I love my husband. I love my children. I love life. I don't want to die," she said. Courage mounted in her like mercury sizzling in a thermometer in a sauna. No wind blew outside. The world seemed calm. Before riding her sail, she'd first have to paddle her own boat in the days ahead.

She went on, "I want to live, but I might die. Some people are 65 but act like 25. Others are 25 and act like 65. I'm young in age and heart."

He tried to restore her confidence. "Wait and see what the surgeon says after examining your lymph nodes."

"Who's the surgeon?" she questioned.

"He is one of the best. He's chief of staff at the Cancer Institute. Dr. David Wiseman. He's about your age."

"And he will live."

"Don't be negative now, Tara."

"Negative is not part of my vocabulary. Determination is." She recalled St. Francis de Sales saying, "It is in giving we receive." She believed she'd have to give more to life and to her family than ever before in order to win a longer life. How? She didn't know.

"That's the spirit! Remember, you're not dead."

She smiled. "And I won't be."

"Of course, you won't. In cases like this, you need to be strong-willed."

"And I am."

"Your husband is supportive, I take it?"

"Always was and always will be." She had not asked the size of the tumor. "How big is the tumor?"

"Anything is too large," said he with understanding.

"Is it large?" she persisted.

Dodging a direct answer, he replied, "It is a fair size. Dr. Wiseman may recommend a radical mastectomy or possibly a lumpectomy if he feels it safe. How will John feel about this?"

Her glasses moist with her tears reminded her of the tide at Ocean City, the site of many good family vacations. "Probably tell me he loves me and he'll want what is best for me."

"Not all men would say so."

"You don't know John. He loves me and I love him – unconditionally." She felt like an old book, its pages ripped out and stripped of its title and ready to be food for the worms. She felt the need to risk all. She wondered, if she would ever win this battle with cancer.

"Look up there," he said, pointing to the nickel-steel sky. "Pretend it's dark and there's a star up there." She nodded approvingly. "Pretend the star is coming down…down…and here it is. "Do you know the name of that star?" She shook her head. "Its name is Tara."

"Thank you," she smiled as he held her hand. "Well, here is Dr. Wiseman's phone number. Give him a call. And do it today." Leaving the office, Tara noticed the sky clear and steel blue while an inky cloud of blackness hung over her life as if she were Dorothy in *The Wizard of Oz* fighting against the witch of Oz. *Like Dorothy, I'll win this fight, God willing.* She looked straight ahead into the bright sky, using imagery; she imagined the blue sky represented the Blessed Mother, beckoning her to fight for life. For a moment she froze at the car door listening to the whirl of cars. Her Grand Marquis stood shimmering and shining in the morning sunlight. She vowed not to dream of the person she might like to be, for that would waste the strong-willed person she was. She didn't want to be anyone else. She wanted to be herself. She didn't cause cancer. She couldn't control cancer. But she'd do her best to fight it.

Determined, she drove along Bustleton Avenue to Dr. Wiseman's office. *Hump off, cancer, I'll live.* She trusted

Dr. Wiseman. With Dr. Stein's recommendation she felt confident of living a long life with Dr. Wiseman's help.

The air smelled like a bottle of champagne gone bad with an odor of vinegar. She noticed a large billboard sign advertising women's nightgowns. The ad incited her to recall their first night, their honeymoon night in Waterford, County Waterford, Ireland. They left the reception at the Shelbourne Hotel in a rain of white rice, mostly thrown by Padraic, her brother in a devilish manner, which characterized his love for pranks—and him with his doctorate in chemistry.

She had driven the ninety-eight miles to Waterford on a June Saturday night. John had never driven on the left side of the road. She remembered what her brother-in-law, Paul, said: "We Irish drive on the right side of the road and Americans drive on the wrong side." His remark recalled to mind *The Wrong Side of the Tracks*, the memoir John wanted to write. She knew Paul offered the divvy remark to test the nerve of her American husband. As she continued on Bustleton Avenue, her attention shifted to the azure blue sky, puffed with a myriad of white clouds, which shaped themselves into geometric and abstract designs. One cloud formed into the shape of an embryo ready to be born. *Does this mean I must be born again in order to live again in a new body?* As the clouds moved from south to north, she too would not take this truculent battle with cancer standing still. She too would move forward, as she did with everything in life. She faced each day with acceptance, flowing with the good and tackling and charging through obstacles whether they be persons, places, things attempting to destroy her contentment with life and love of herself. She attributed her happiness to her parents who had a happy life together filled with love and respect. She recalled Maurice

O'Sullivan's book, *Twenty Years A-Growing*. It paralleled her happy childhood days in Dublin when like a little heroine, her life modified the life of Queen Maeve. *I must pick myself up, but I feel as lifeless as the toy wooden soldiers my children had once played with.* •

Her father had been a colonel in the Irish army. He fought the Black and Tans, as they were named in 1918, because they wore dark green and khaki uniforms. The colonel fought under the command of Michael Collins. Once she recalled, her father had been captured by the tans, who transported him in a lorry to prison. Collins had given the order to attack the British vans, but when he learned Colonel O'Shea was in one of the van, Collins rescinded his order and allowed the Tans safe passage.

She stopped for a traffic light. She recalled about the beautiful ride they had through Wicklow on their honeymoon. They had driven on N11 through the Bray seaside known as Greystones, where Charles Parnell had his home—Avondale. And on to N25 to see The Meeting of the Waters, the Avoca Mills, Arklow, Wexford, Waterford. In the states John drove, but in Ireland Tara drove, since she had the experience of driving on the left side on the road. They had arrived at the Waterford Arms with still an hour of sunlight left since dusk occurred in Ireland around tenish, and the skies did not darken until 11. It is a great country, which holds back the night allowing people to enjoy a long day's journey into night. *How strange, my homeland.. filled with sad stories for a happy people. The sadness stems from eight hundred years of English domination of Ireland until Padraic Pearse in 1916 wound the clock of Irish nationalism in the hearts of its sons and daughters and tolled the bell to meet English military strength with Irish nationalism.* They emerged from the car. Strong crisp winds nudged them forward. The air smelled fresh with no smokestack pollution experienced in the states. She remembered the fresh aroma of the roses planted in front of the hotel in rows of ten. She touched a pedal—soft and fleshy, like a baby's skin.

A red Cherokee jeep pulled out in front of them, cutting into their lane. It reminded her of the red tie John wore—British in design. It went well with his blue serge suit and accented her Sasson suit. They were a perfect couple for a perfect life with a perfect future. They checked into the hotel. A porter carried their luggage to the bridal suite. John cradle her into his arms, carried her across the threshold, and where else she thought would he deliver her but to the bed. He chuckled heartily, as did she.

"I hope your head's all right," said she, smiling with a glow in her pupils. She smelled the clear mint toothpaste, after shave lotion, and English Laver.

"It's not my head I'm thinkin' about," he quipped. "Oh, honey...honey," he stage-acted.

"Easy, John. Easy."

He hovered over her.

"You look good...very good," she said, her naturally tinted red cheeks glowed redder.

"From my angle, you look very good, too."

Tara chuckled. "And you told me you were shy once."

He bent down, kissed her lightly, and whispered, "Let's have a drink first in the lobby."

---

Two bluejays fluttered onto a Japanese Maple tree. A Philadelphia trash truck screeched to a halt. *Typical of Philadelphia,* she thought: *the city needed more money and lubrication to flow smoothly.* Birds veered from branch to branch. She delighted amidst the shining bright colors of the rustic maroon leaves etched with the mint blue and white colors of the ever-moving bluejays. She took inspiration from the birds' movements and told herself to move forward like the bluejays' efforts of looking for food. Talking to herself in preparation of dealing with many experiences in life and telling herself how to behave was her way of rendering self-psychoanalysis. She named one bluejay Tara and the other John. Lovers. Soulmates…one in mind, spirit and body…like herself and her husband.

She giggled aloud as she had remembered him saying "Let's have a drink," as a Fed-Ex van started up beside her new maroon, Grand Marquis. And she a pioneer, the same as her father and her brother Padraic. Her other brother Seamus, himself a pioneer and a Ph.D. in physics, was jovial and laughed often.

In the Waterford Arms cocktail lounge, he enjoyed a So Co Man Up, as she sampled a diet coke. How easy to have eye-to-eye contact with John. Like looking at herself. They had walked fleetly, hand in hand, to the elevator. As she passed through the door, he padded her buttocks.

"Well," he said, "I'm about to subjugate you to my trophy room."

"I like that!" she snapped, letting him know she allowed him to conquer her. An independent woman, she would give herself, and no man would ever take her. No one would ever *take* anything against her will. "Used to be *status quo ante*," said John. She remembered what her mother advised: don't give a man anything for nothing: marry him first. She glowed at John. "You had to pay for it first."

"Is the payment marriage?" he questioned. He speculated they were about to enter into a bacchanal of love.

"Of course. You sound like Yul Brenner in *The King and I*.

"Your mother talking again?"

"Of course."

"Let's see now. About how much has this nineteen month courtship cost me: a full summer of weekly music fair plays and musicals, two or three dinners each week, etcetera, etcetera, etcetera."

"Of course."

"That's the third time you said this."

"Of course," she said, playing with him. "That makes it four times and it's not explicitly a straight nineteen months. We dated ten months before you asked me to marry you." Two deeper red circles flashed across her already reddened cheeks and tempered her soft, fair, native-Irish skin.

"We were engaged for nine months." Her eyes widened as she peered through a window and felt Irish winds from the Irish Sea blow through trees, causing leaves to swing and sway up and down side to side, at times gently touching one another the way John touched her: gently, smoothly, deliberately. A garde car flashed by the window, the siren belching its bone-chilling clamor. She recalled what Tim Hilton said in a novel: "Relationship come down to men and women. There's no third sex. You have to make do with what there is." She had wanted to make do with the moment. Outside a skein of geese flew off in a northern direction. *Maybe they're headed for Dublin*, she guessed.

She had observed a young couple with an elderly lady leaving the lounge. The thin silvery-haired, lady reminded her of John's mother, a friendly lady who acted like a stereotype mother-in-law: pleasing her to hold family peace. She had married her son. Tara believed John's mother held her at a distance. No matter, Tara knew she had done the best she could to hold the peace.

"I haven't *had* you yet. I want to make love to you, Tara."

"You soon will."

"What about now!"

"Now is the time," she agreed.

John held her shoulders and steered her to the elevator. He had imagined himself the drover in poems of an Australian balladeer.

John said, "You are my *raison d'être*."

He made her atavistic. The ceiling light shone on her soft, fair skin.

He couldn't resist her look of approval. "The light reflecting on your red lustrous lips shines from you. It comes from your heart and radiates your hair."

"Another Blarney line," she said, her eyes gleaming, her body yearning, her desire intensified.

Again, John carried her through the doorway of room 303. Gently, he lowered her to the bed. How in the past she resisted she didn't know. Never again, she concluded, would she be a virgin. One of those life experiences that would end forever a way of life. She wanted him. He wanted her. Soon to be one.

At her apartment door when they had dated, they had kissed and kissed, filling both with desire. She wondered how she would feel when they had intercourse. Now, she would find out.

"You are beautiful, Tara. You are all I want in life."

"You are all I want, John." Funny she should remember what someone said to her before the wedding: something about being at the right place at the right time. And now, locked in John's embrace, she felt the importance of being at the right place at the right time, time for their world to begin. Her world, his world…of one flesh. She felt the sparkle of his faith in her love for him. She felt the magnificent desire swelling inside her. She descended into the depths of a gentle world as if in a trance and in touch with finding deeper truth in her sub-conscious. He put one arm around her waist, and eye-to-eye, they guffawed like school children.

She would give herself to him and he would give himself to her. There could be no taking, only giving as if they gave each other a wedding gift. Like O'Henry's "The Gift of the Magi." His athletic mustered body melted against her unmarked, pure skin, like butter melting on hot toast.

John melted onto her like snow instantly melting on days with above average temperatures.

"I love you, Tara. I've waited for this moment. I need you. I want you."

"I'm giving you, John, what I want you to have. I love you."

They caused each other total abandonment. They lay quietly in oneness, not stirring, not groaning, not thinking, exhausted. Perfection. United, combined, merged. One.

A car honking snapped her back to reality. *Now I have cancer, how long will this perfection last?*

# TWO

# Arrival in America

"All is perfect," she said aloud to herself as she parked in Dr. Wiseman's parking lot. "Yes, perfect all right. I have cancer." *With four children, two out of college and two others about to begin what is perfect. Life before cancer. Cancer cells trap me like a prisoner in a cellblock. But I'll fight like a salmon fighting rapids to get back upstream to lay its eggs. Determination. A positive attitude. I'll beat cancer. John will be here soon and I'll feel better.*

For a moment, she closed her eyes and felt in the brief moment the weight of carrying the cross of cancer, swelling and groaning in her body like an embryo implanted in her by an unknown source. A woman bicyclist rode on the sidewalk, as she unfolded from the car. A three-year-old daughter sat on a rear seat in the car next to hers. *That woman will dance at her daughter's wedding.. more than I can say.* The early morning sky formed an appealing three-tier formation: in the far distance, a yellowish-pink sky blended with pale blue cloudy rudiments. Overhead, two huge gray-blue cloud formations shielded the sun's rays as if the rays appeared to peek above ominous clouds, encouraging dreariness to dissipate. Beyond the dark make-up, she noticed puffy white clouds in a cheering, bright sky. She imagined these clouds to be mountaintops with her above the clouds, looking down on their magnificence. She imagined the radiant clouds represented heaven, and the threatening clouds, cancer.

Eighteen people sat around the waiting room.

After more than an hour's wait, the nurse called Tara into the doctor's examining room.

When Dr. Wiseman entered, he greeted Tara by name with prompting from the medical file set in the holder attached to the door.

"How are you doing today, Mrs. O'Malley?" Wiseman inquired in a tone of filial affection. A competent man, confirmed by colleagues, he was aware of his established reputation. He possessed strong bedside manners, a reason why people waited for him, long beyond appointed times.

"I'm Dr. Wiseman."

"I hope you can help. Dr. Stein said you can."

"I'll do my best. Dr. Stein has referred many of his patients to me." He admired Tara's black hair. "With beautiful hair like yours, you look Irish." She sat like a pilgrim at Lourdes, hoping to be cured.

"I was born and raised in Dublin. My husband and I married in Dublin in 1963."

"You've been married twenty-six years?"

"Twenty-five," she corrected him. His skin twitched beneath his eyes. He was unaccustomed to being corrected…for anything.

He placed the file on the examining table. "Let's see the tumor."

She exposed her lovely breasts. He examined both breasts carefully. "Well, the tumor on the left breast must be examined more closely. I'll do exploratory surgery to examine the lymph nodes and remove the tumor."

"What are my chances?"

"To be determined. I can't say now. I will examine the lymph nodes to determine how many are affected. Hopefully, the cancer cells have not spread far through the lymph nodes."

"And if they have?"

He avoided a direct answer. "Let's wait and see."

"I am a straight forward person, doctor. Tell me about my chances."

"The fewer the lymph nodes affected, Tara, the better your chances for survival."

"Give me numbers."

"Well, if more than four are malignant, you're in stage three and your chances are slimmer."

A knock on the door. Dr. Wiseman invited John O'Malley into the room. After introductions, Dr. Wiseman said, "We are discussing the pending surgery. Your wife pressed me for information about her chances of survival."

"What can be determined, at this point?" John asked, an edge in his voice, demonstrating his jealousy. He didn't like anyone touching his wife, including medical doctors.

"I said four or more malignant lymph nodes is a concern."

"When can you schedule the operation?" John saw his wife sitting half naked on the examining table. He looked at Doctor Wiseman to see where the man fixed his eyes. He felt at ease to find the doctor staring at him.

"As soon as possible."

"This week!" John requested.

"Wednesday?" asked Tara.

"That'll be fine."

Since John drove to the doctor's place directly from school, they drove home in separate cars. As she drove home, she imagined a strong Irish Sea breeze blowing across her mother and father's grave. She wondered if the small tri-colored flag remained implanted in the ground at the head of the grave. She recalled how, on Mother's Day in 1959, she had arrived in America.

She had come on an important day in American life…a day people saluted their mothers. Irish people didn't celebrate Mother's Day or Father's Day. Smiling to herself, she wondered why Americans did not have a Son's Day, Daughter's Day, Niece's Day, and Nephew's Day since they celebrated special days for about everyone else. *It's a wonder they don't think Irish have Pigs-in- the-Kitchen Day or some weird thing.*

One of her father's American contacts met her when she arrived in New York. He owned a large building contractor firm. The man offered to let her stay with his family. She refused. Independent and single, she wanted to stay independent – but not single all her life. She hailed a taxi to take her to her cousin's house.

The yellow New York taxi delivered Tara to Jackson Heights. The driver, an earthy Heathcliff character, opened the door for her. Not knowing the money value and paper denominations, she held out one hand filled with coins and in the other she had bills marked "1" at each of four corners.

"Ah, Gawd. Don't ya know how t' pay people?" he grumbled.

"Is this not enough?" she stated in clear English, with an Irish word arrangement with enough ambiguity to intrigue people.

He grabbled with the money. "Nahhh. Dis pays the rates. There's nuthin' here for a tip."

Sorry. Wait until I open my luggage. I have money there."

"Nahhh, you foreigners…all the same. You ain't able to speak right, are ya?"

She looked at him and he at her. She asked, "Will you help me with my luggage?"

"You gotta be crazy. No tip and you want me to help ya. No way, gal. Get it yourself. I'm outta here."

The temperature read 85 degrees, warm for May. In an Irish tweed suit, she felt uncomfortable. A brilliant, bright blue sky raised her spirits. People like the taxi driver would not ruin her day. Her new beginning, the road less traveled, unfolded before her like the growth of a spring daffodil reaching for the rays of the sun. Raised in a family that shared experiences and loved one another, she carried within her an inner peace and contentment of mind. She kept her eyes on the cab fading into New York traffic and observed the way sunrays gleamed on the yellow taxi.

She had dragged two pieces of luggage from the trunk and onto the sidewalk. She understood she would never see him again, as she watched the cab turn a corner and pass out of her life. But that's life – people come into one's life and exit as fast.

Tara managed to tug her luggage to Dora O'Shea's apartment door. Together they had journeyed to the Marriott Marquis on Broadway, between 45th and 46th Streets in the middle of Times Square. She thought of Frank Sinatra singing "New York, New York"

Dora had booked lunch at the Skyview Revolving Restaurant on the forty-seventh floor.

"That's a lovely, yellow suit, Dora. I'll have to buy a new wardrobe. These Irish clothes are too heavy for this weather."

The elevator stopped at the forty-fifth floor. An employee told them they had to return to the eighth floor, take the escalator to the ninth, and ride one of two special elevators to the Skyview Restaurant.

While waiting for the next elevator, they saw an assemblage of men with walkie-talkies coming at them.

"Who's coming?" she asked.

"The Prime Minister of Cyprus." the man's guard said.

A short white-bearded man, royally robed in black flowing garments came forth. His head covered with a turban and a long gold chain with a medallion draped at the navel area swung as he strolled with the support of an extended brownish-black cane.

"It's a wonder they permitted us to be here." Dora said. "He looks like a cloistered nun."

"My father guarded the president like this man."

"Yes, as aide-de-camp to the president?"

"My father has seen and shaken hands with popes, prime ministers and presidents. When he came to this country for St. Patrick's Day, he met President Eisenhower and stayed at the Blair House. He sent me a letter on Blair House letterhead. He liked Eisenhower but not Nixon. Eisenhower was pleasant, Nixon too indifferent."

"You come from a good family, do you not?" Dora suggested.

On the revolving platform, Dora explained, "This rotates once every fifty-eight minutes. There is," she said, motioning to the window, "the Empire State Building. Over there is the Chevrolet Building."

"Can we see the World Trade Center?" Tara asked.

"No. Unfortunately, it can't be seen from here."

They watched decorative desserts carried passed them: ice cream scoops with wings to resemble a flying horse and a small circular mound of ice cream made into a carousel.

"I have a surprise for you," said Dora.

"I love surprises."

"I have two tickets for *Phantom of the Opera*."

"Inter-resting. Thank you." Tara said the word "interesting" as if it were two words.

---

"It's around the corner at The Majestic on 44th Street. It starts at 2:00."

She looked at her watch. "We have time."

"But not a lot of time. Dessert?"

"Thank you, no."

"Tea?"

"Lovely," she said.

"Our tea is not the same as yours."

Her face shone like a full moon, beautiful. "I know. Dad told me they give you a cup of hot water and a tea bag."

"You'll get use to it."

---

After the performance, they saw two marines in droll uniforms. In a tick, she flashed back to the military formal dances she, the colonel's daughter, had attended. She had been one of the most attractive girls at the balls. She had black wavy hair, beautifully styled round, seagreen eyes, which turned hazel-brown according to the dress she wore, round eyes, a reclined nose with thin nostrils, and thin lower and upper lips that expanded to a satisfying fullness. At five foot six inches and 124 pounds, Tara looked smashing.

# THREE

# Stage Three Cancer

Dr. Wiseman and Dr. Stein darted into the room like bees looking for honey. They converged on Tara as part of a platoon ready to overrun the enemies' position. "Good morning," they echoed.

"Take care of me," Tara petitioned.

"That we will," said Dr. Wiseman.

"We're set for the lumpectomy," John said.

Dr. Wiseman said, "The procedure will be a right lumpectomy and axillary node dissection." John recalled their conversation after the doctor gave Tara the option of a lumpectomy or a mastectomy, and he reassured her it was her choice—he wanted Tara to live. Whether she had the breast removed or had a lumpectomy made no difference to John. With his reassurances, she decided on a lumpectomy.

"How long will it take?" John asked, clinching his fists.

"Less than an hour."

"I will make two incisions to determine the extent of the progression of the malignant cells."

"What is node dissection?"

"Removing malignant lymph nodes."

"Good luck, doctor," she said, smiling, her eyes flashing green like a cat about to chase its prey. Caught momentarily off guard by Tara's pleasant and calm manner, he said, "Good luck to all of us." *All is now as before cancer—silent and hopeful.*

"May our luck be better than good," John stated. "Be a Teflon Man...or Teflon Lady," he encouraged.

"What's that?"

"Like a Teflon pan: don't let all this stick to you, Tara. Treat this with the ease of washing a Teflon pan and all the grease will wash away."

"Easy for you, John...but I'll try," she smiled a smile that said "thank you."

An hour and one-half passed as John paced in a room near the recovery unit. He gaped out the ground floor window. *As Autumn leaves filter to the ground, I remember how Tara and I used to jump into a pile of raked leaves on our lawn to impress our four young children during the golden years of building boys into men and our daughter into a woman.* Burnish-brown and yellow and rust fiery leaves spotted the ground. Two bluejays flew in the wind like sacred gods, untouched by human hands. He observed the receptionist performing her duties oblivious to life and death situations all around her. Nurses entered and exited the sitting area with a professional manner of doing their jobs, like pawns on a chessboard, ready to be moved by the master player, the doctor, unconnected to the many people sitting in the room in anxious and edgy tension. A fleshy wife and a stout husband sat across from him. He noticed their wedding rings. A patient gave medical insurance information to a billing department clerk. *Well, no insurance, no operation.*

Buses, trucks, and a sea of cars moved slowly along Broad Street. Ladies with light fall coats flowed along the sidewalk. Men moved with quickstep determination towards the hospital, their faces fixed in worry. *Like me, they love someone and they're coming to see their loved one in this valley of tears, as long as they are passing through this valley and not living in it.* The scent of medicine cascaded throughout the room. He studied the white texture of doctors' cotton coats. He detected the odor of ethylene glycol and butoxethoxy-ethanol in the semi-gloss painted woodwork.

Finally, Dr. Wiseman came to him. With what seemed to be a personal interest in Tara as if he was treating his sister, he said, "We removed the tumor and twenty-four lymph nodes, John. Thirteen were malignant."

"What's the diagnosis?"

"Tara's in stage three of breast carcinoma." Fear swept over him like an arctic air. Fright filled his mind. He remembered what Dan Rather had written in *I Remember*: *"If we knew all the difficulties at the outset of a long journey most of us would never start at all."* He told himself he'd do it all over again to be with Tara. *Better to have known her one day than never to have known her at all.*

"She'll survive, doctor? When she believes in a cause, she'll fight for it."

"Good. She'll need the strength now and you will, too."

"She's a strong character, filled with perseverance. Obstacles are not obstacles to her."

"How many stages are there?"

"Four."

Dr. Wiseman watched John's face sink. The doctor realized the futility of mentioning the fourth stage.

"With Tara's strength and your support, John, she'll go up."

"Right," he said, faintly.

"And, up is life."

"I'll do my best. Remember, I am not God."

"None of us are."

"That being understood, I recommend you return to Dr. Stein who, as Tara's oncologist, he'll see her on a regular basis."

"What will he prescribe?"

Dr. Wiseman said, "He'll probably suggest chemotherapy and radiation."

"Will these guarantee success?"

"We'll see. Adriamycin will be used, but there are no guarantees here."

"Isn't that the red dye medication, which causes hair to fall out?"

"Yes, chemotherapy may cause hair loss."

"May?"

"Depends on the required dosage. In stage three, stronger treatment is often necessary."

––––––––––

Tara visited a radiologist a week later. After the first visit, Tara wanted to drive herself to her office. She didn't want John to miss his classes.

Tara walked into the office, registered with the secretary, and went to the changing room and wrapped a hospital gown around her slim body. She entered the radiation room and looked at the permanently marked black dots on her skin around the left breast area.

––––––––––

After several treatments, the technician directed her to the waiting room. "The doctor wants to see you."

An attractive woman with black hair, black eyebrows and tan skin, Dr. Johnson was a recent immigrant from Portugal. Looking at a report, the doctor said, "The treatments have helped. I see Dr. Stein placed you on Bactrim for the urine infection."

"Yes. I had a burning feeling."

"And you're also taking Prednisone, Decadron, Ativan and Compazine."

"The Prednisone didn't agree with me and Dr. Stein told me to stop taking it."

"To date," Dr. Johnson said, "there is no trace of malignant cells."

"Thank God."

"Your lungs are clear. There is no discharge from your nipples. There's no arm edema."

Interrupting, Tara asked, "Edema?"

"Swelling in the arm areas and your abdomen is soft."

"I am progressing well?"

"At this time," the doctor stated cautiously, "you are doing well."

"My left breast is red and my throat is sore."

"Yes, I see," the doctor said, examining reports, "all in all, you will received 23-treatments over 31 days."

She vowed all the more to fight. She couldn't go up the ladder of beating cancer with her hands down and doing nothing. She'd fight cancer. She assured herself, the way General McAuliffe fought the Germans in the Battle of the Bulge when surrounded and offered with surrender; he wrote his reply: "Nuts."

# FOUR

# Getting on with Life

Tara drove to Summit Personal Care. The administrator of the one hundred fifty-five bed facility, she recalled the time in June when John agreed to re-mortgage the house to buy their own facility—O'Shea Personal Care, which they opened a few months before the doctor diagnosed Tara with cancer and how she trained herself for the state inspection. Beginning as a part-time secretary and advancing to assistant to the administrator, Nathan Mountain, the owner, offered her the job of administrator. Mountain, a sympathetic man, supported her through her chemotherapy and radiation treatments by advising her to take time off and rest and let the assistant do the job, which she never did. She loved her work, working six days a week, ten hours a day, sixty hours each week.

Nathan Mountain cautioned against this as did John her husband. But Tara found comfort in going to work each day. Her working in a loving environment was reality-therapy for her; it kept her going, taking her mind off cancer. Her oncologist, surgeon and radiologist all agreed to let her work, if it made her happy. Work suited her and she accepted it as therapy to battle cancer.

She drove along Bristol Road, a country-like road with over-hanging tree leaves holding hands and hugging cars like God protecting his children. With few homes along the road, she loved nature along Bristol Road with birds chirping and a scent of honeysuckle. The air had a perfumed, Frangipani fragrance. The drive each morning gave a sense of undergoing a metamorphosis. She left her home as a mother and wife and in her office she changed into the role of administrator. Cancer and work, her *non-possumus*. She thrived on work. Work: profession, occupation, her salvation.

As administrator of Summer Personal Care, she managed a staff of 45 people and supervised the needs of each resident. She considered herself their protector. One day, an irate son demanded the immediate release of his father. Tara had reason to believe the father's finances are in danger of being confiscated by the son.

Fearlessly, face to face with this man, she refused. He threatened her. She did not back off. She stood her ground. In a calm voice, she replied, "If you hit me, I'll have you arrested." Like a policeman who, when challenged, readied himself for action, she assimilated possible danger into her real-life role of administrator.

Angered, the man stormed out, slamming the door with enough force, it broke loose from its hinges. The psychologist who observed the incident remarked, "You have guts."

A workaholic she went to work out of love for her chores. She loved her job. She believed in putting in a full day's work for a fair day's pay. Residents loved her. It was an act of love. On more than one occasion, she stayed overnight. Once, while eating Thanksgiving dinner with her family, a person from the home notified Tara the L.P.N. had called out sick. The elderly needed their medications. With John, she left dinner and went to Summit Personal care and served meds to all.

Her creed in life was to be a good wife, a good mother, and to be a person who helped individuals to be as happy as they could regardless of their color, religion, or nationality. Unlike many greedy people who made money their god, she sought personal satisfaction to help residents live well while approaching their final days. She encouraged individuals who didn't understand this, to understand.

Tara loved life with a passion. She loved John with every fiber in her soul. She and John fused together in love. Soulmates. And Tara's fight to survive cancer was not only her fight; it was their fight to survive, their fight to win life. Without her, John told her, his life would be unlivable. If Tara died, he believed he could not go on. To be reconciled to Tara's death...never. He realized he should never say "never," for he did not know what God had in mind for anyone's future.

In a quiet moment, she sat back in her chair and let her mind rest. Strange how, at this time, she recalled breaking her engagement to Martin O'Brien and how she met John.

---

At twenty-four, she had been engaged to Martin O'Brien, a hard working Dublin resident who had worked in the same office at the Permanent Building Society.

She thought Martin a good man, though she didn't like his size. She had an inch on him. With him, she couldn't wear heels. She had fine legs and liked wearing three-inch pumps to illustrate legs, which men admired. She liked him for his ease of manner, character, his handsome features and his glibness. He followed her everywhere. He kept asking her out and she said no until she grew weary and finally said yes. After she broke her engagement, she felt sad for him but knew she did the best thing for both.

Martin had reminded her of Billy Kwan, the Australian-Chinese dwarf press photographer in C.J. Koch's novel. He would do anything she wanted. He could have been a stand-in for Mammy, O'Hara's faithful slave in *Gone With the Wind*. When she met John, she fell in love. He chased her until she caught him.

On their last evening, he knew something was wrong.

He said. "You're too serious."

"This is serious," she said.

"What now!"

"Sit here on the sofa, Martin." She recalled his eyes bulging out of his head like soft-boiled eggs oozing from its shell, ready to hear the worse.

"You're giving me orders."

"Stand then. No sense playing verbal volleyball."

He sat down near her as he usually did. She inched toward the arm of the sofa, two feet away from him. It gave her moral support to have space between them.

"The two years I've been with you have been pleasant."

"And so they should be."

She had ignored the comment and continued. "But I feel I've not had time to think."

He leaned forward to kiss her.

"You crowd me with attention and kisses."

"What's wrong?"

"Nothing's wrong with it."

"What is this about, Tara?"

"Martin, I feel I can't meet your needs. I can't give you what you want."

"You know my needs?"

"I think I do."

She answered, "In lieu of this conversation becoming an academic one—"

Martin's facial expression grew portentous. "You're trying to tell me something I don't want to hear, is that it?"

She wanted to tell him to hump off, but she said, "During the last few weeks, I have not felt the same about you." Her eyes grew gray like a threatening storm. He blinked often, holding in his emotions.

She tried to tell him she wanted to return his engagement ring.

He said, "I feel as strongly about you as ever."

"I know. That's why this is difficult for me."

"Out with it."

She held his ring in her hand. His eyes widened. She recalled the sadness she felt when she told a previous suitor, Ken, when they were both students.

"Martin, I can't keep this." She handed him the ring. He made no movement for it. She continued to hold the ring in front of him as if her fingers froze in time, locked into an experience never to be repeated. A moment of truth. She had crossed over the line with no turning back.

Tears filled his eyes. Tara felt like Clytomnestra after killing Agamemnon. Martin's face twitched like a dying body taking its last breath. He lowered his head. His hand gripped the cushions.

"Martin, I'm sorry."

"To go on would be unfair to you."

He held the ring in both hands. His voice scratched like sandpaper. "How did it happen? We were doing well together."

"I suppose it wasn't to be," she quipped, avoiding a more detailed reply.

"But I love you, Tara."

"I thought I loved you, Martin…I did love you…when we were in Dublin. After I came here, I realized I didn't love you. Something…it's hard to explain, but we better stop—"

Standing, he asked, "Can I see you again?"

"Do you think it wise?"

"Yes. Of course. I love you."

She felt emotion swelling in her. If she didn't get away from him, tears would stream down her cheeks. And she didn't want him to misinterpret her tears to mean she would miss him.

"It would be disastrous for both of us."

"You mean," he remarked, "I will never see you again?"

The finality of the words: never again. Death-like.

"Sorry, Martin." Without saying another word, he knew what she meant. He saw it in her eyes. For her, a new beginning. For him, a shocking ending.

She knew he felt like a ship lost at sea ready to crash onto rocks. But she was responsible for herself. In time, he'd be fine. *I intend to live. I will live.*

# FIVE

# John O'Malley

John chased Tara until he caught her.

They met on a clear, crisp meaningful Sunday evening at the Drexelbrook Tennis and Swim Club in Drexel Hill, the other side of the city from where John lived. The wrinkly early November leaves mixed with an early evening rain, spreading the fragrance of freshly cut grass. A sign of what was to be…a clear and meaningful married life, always fresh and alive.

She wore a form fitting black dress. Standing with one of her roommates with her back to the crowd and facing the dance floor, she held a cigarette in her hand, holding it for a friend who went to the restroom.

She felt a finger tap on her right shoulder and turning she saw a smiling round face. "Like to dance?" he asked.

A magical spell fell over them. *A la mystique* she had yet to experience. Meeting John attests to a once in a lifetime *vis-à-vis* experience. The impact of this sudden, chance meeting swept over them like a soft dew spray from a soft fall rain, sweeping them into a mythical ride of natural peacefulness.

She felt the chemistry, like the two Scott Terrier magnets she played with on the top of her desk at school when the nun wasn't looking.

"I work for a brokerage office," she responded to one of the questions men ask in the getting-to-know-you process.

"What do you do?" he had asked.

"I am in the transfer department. I'm the manager."

"Stocks?"

"Yes. I oversee stocks as they are bought and sold."

She knew he had an interest in her. The interest was mutual. She laughed like a schoolgirl in braids at a cartoon movie. The cigarette smoke didn't bother her. Nor did people bumping into them on the dance floor. Nothing bothered her. Time froze in a maze of fluttering pulsations.

Tara liked John's directness. She imagined what he wants, he often gets. "You have beautiful hair and knowledgeable eyes."

*Knowledgeable eyes? Did this mean I have smart eyes or bookworm eyes?* She knew she had both.

"What do you do?" she asked.

"Teach. I teach English at St. Brendan Catholic High School."

"That's strange," she smiled inwardly. "I read a novel about that Catholic school. It's called *The Faculty Room.*

"Oh yes...I read it, too. The author knows what it's like for a layman to teach with bigoted and prejudicial clergy who think they're better than everybody else. And the two pedophiles were disgusting.

"Absolutely," she said.

*A point for you, John.* "My father was a teacher before he became aide-de-camp. Have you been to the Irish Center?"

"I go there all the time," he said.

"I attend the balls."

"I do, too," he said, looking directly into her eyes. "I can't do all the Irish set dances."

"Waltzes?"

"No. You'll teach me some day?" *As if he knew we'd have a future together.*

"It will be my pleasure," she smiled. Her face flushed.

"Soon!"

"My…are you not direct?"

"Most times," he said, still staring into her eyes. "What's your name?"

"Tara."

"Your full name?"

"Tara O'Shea. People call me Tara."

"Well Miss O…Meet Mr. O. My name is O'Malley." She noticed him staring at her.

She eyed him carefully. "You are from Philadelphia, are you not?"

"Yes. And with your clear, precise accent you are from Dublin."

"Very good. People think I come from Kerry."

"They don't know Irish accents."

"You're Dublin all right."

"I am."

"The phrasing of your words is native Irish."

"You mean the way I end my sentence with 'Are you not?'"

"Of course."

"That's why we Irish are excellent in conversation."

"Right. When answering a question you end your sentence with a question."

"And in this way, the conversation runs along."

The more they danced, the more she became interested in him. She could tell by the way he looked at her; he too had a strong interest in her.

*Two points for you John.*

"Well, Tara, I know your name – Tara O'Shea, a beautiful name, where you work, what you do there, something about your mom and dad."

The air smelled like a melting pot of fruit punch.

"You know it all," said she.

"No," said he. "Your dad and mom—where are they from?"

"Tipperary."

"Oh, I'm off to Tipperary in the morning," he sang.

"Well, that's not the correct tune."

He smiled and continued. "And your family?"

"I have two sisters and two brothers."

They had danced and, as time moved on, they talked and danced the rest of the night. Conversation with John lightened her heart. John found her a delight in intelligent discussions. "I have two brothers and one sister. I am third in line."

"I'm the baby of the family."

"Once the baby of the family…"

"Once the baby, always the baby," she ended the thought for him.

He liked her tender smile. His heart beat faster.

"My, what confidence."

"That's the way I am."

He held her a little tighter the more they danced. The sweetness in her eyes bewitched him.

"You know," he said, "I know all about you!"

"All about me?"

"Well . . . a lot."

"Then, there's nothing else to tell?"

"No. One important fact, I don't know."

"What's that?"

"Your phone number," he smiled and guffawed.

Tara grinned. "Pennsylvania 5-6000." The crystal ball hung overhead sparkling like diamonds and reflecting stars on the floor, reflecting the stars in their eyes and hearts.

He said, "Playing hard to get?"

She laughed, "526-1934." They both laughed. Strange how two people can laugh at nothing funny.

"I have it." He took a 3x5 card from his shirt pocket. "To be sure, though, I'll write it down."

As he wrote, she said, "A Hal Roach joke."

"Right. He always says, 'That's a good one. Write it down.'"

He had driven himself and she drove with her roommate. Saying goodnight, he pressed her hand firmly and held it awhile. The dawning of the rest of their lives together had begun. She left him with the thought that one crowded hour of glorious life with him verified the truth of their meeting. A seed of love germinated in their hearts. If she were Juliet and he Romeo, he would have told her as much.

———————

She had gone home that night and wrote her mother a letter. She told her she met the man she was going to marry. She was sure to state, he had not asked her to marry him at first sight in the light of the moonstruck night. She stated he would ask her. When…she didn't know. She told her mother he had dad's qualities–teacher, considerate, sense of humor, intelligent, caring – and her mother would like him when they met. She knew Vince

Lombardi had said: "Confidence is contagious. So is lack of confidence." *Confidence.. that's for me.*

John was a handsome man at five foot, nine inches and 154 pounds. Like her, he had black hair. He had a receding hairline, like her dad who lost his hair when placed in English prisons during the fight against England to gain Irish independence in 1918. A positivistic person.

While dating, John did not ask her what she wanted to do or where she wanted to go. She liked his decisiveness. He had a definite place in mind before he asked her for a date. Like a teacher, he didn't ask a question he didn't already know the answer to and he didn't ask her a question unless he knew how she would answer. He would say, "Let's go to dinner and then Playhouse-in-the-Park."

After they married, John had told her when he first saw her he had fallen in love with her. He knew he wanted to marry her at Playhouse in the Park, as they watched *Dark at the Top of the Stairs*. He said her face radiated like a clear, blizzard white sky, putting him in a whiteout and he couldn't see clearly, but it wasn't his eyesight that concerned him. She had captured his heart.

———————

John had dated her two months when he knew he wanted to marry her. Her eyes, hers embraces, and her kisses…everything about her he held in his heart. Nine months later, he took her to dinner at Drexelbrook, the place where they had met. John told her he selected Drexelbrook for dinner, a special place for a special occasion. What special occasion, she already guessed. Winners win their own games without mistakes; losers lose their own games with mistakes. No mistake, he won her heart, and in having the heart, he had everything. It was time to ask her an important question.

She wore a green satin Liz Claiborne dress to please John, himself half Irish. His grandfather came from Cavan but his mother came from English-German blood. Like many English settlers in Ireland in the nineteenth century, John was more Irish than the Irish. He wore "Ireland" emblemmed short-sleeved tops; an Irish sweater embroidered with the word "Ireland" and a hand-knitted creamy, Aran Islands woven Irish sweater. He had friends from the north side of Dublin, North Siders, who called him a plastic paddy, since he was half Irish, but acted like he was born in Ireland. North Siders had less money. Some South Siders called people living on the northern side of Dublin "burglars." South Siders enjoyed a more sybaritic lifestyle with higher incomes and higher priced homes.

"You look beautiful," John said.

"And you look handsome," she smiled.

"You have a fine figure and wonderful black hair, beautifully styled."

She smiled "Thank you!"

Secreting hormones from the pituitary gland into the bloodstream stimulated his thinking. "I like your waistline."

She snickered. "I like to accentuate the waist with wide belts."

"There's no fat on you."

"Did you bring me here to discuss my body?"

"No . . . yes." He chuckled.

"What is this – our ninth month?"

"Right. Our baby will be born soon," he teased, his face aglow and at peace with himself.

"Nine months."

"Nine years?" she kidded.

"What!" he gasped.

"Kidding," she smiled.

"Time to have a baby?"

"Not on your life," she answered.

"This is a special night."

"Because we met here nine months ago," she volunteered.

"Correct. I wanted to bring you back here to celebrate."

"But we often come here for a drink.".

"Yes," he responded, "but this time I thought you would like . . . I mean, nine months is a long time."

"Not long," she said sipping a soda. Back in Ireland, she had pledged with many Matt Talbot supporters to abstain from taking alcohol, a form of self-abnegation. Reparation for sins. The sins of Ireland. The Irish Catholic way.

He lifted his So Co Man Up, saluted her and sipped. "Well, it is and it isn't. Here's looking at you, kid." Love stirred in her like an embryo ready to come to term.

The waiter arrived with a second round of the same drinks. She studied the waiter who resembled Montgomery Cliff. *Another person who entered and will soon exit my life like the New York cab driver. People make their stage entrances and exits, don't we?* She wondered how many times does a person see another person for a moment and never sees the person again: thousands.

John directed her. "Put your hand under the table for a minute...do you know you're beautiful? Hey darlin' how'd like to be buried with me family?"

"What...?"

"Just jokin'." And besides, when you compliment a beautiful lady, it's not flirting... it's acknowledging your beauty."

They shared a moment of silence. She wasn't sure. She looked at him. Her eyes widened. She raised her eyebrows. She put her right hand under the table.

"No...not your right hand. Your left." Like a novice master knowing the inner workings of a novice's soul before the novice expressed his feelings, he knew she loved him as he loved her.

She did. "What are you doing, John?"

"You'll see. Give me your hand."

"My right or left?"

"Your left."

She giggled. "You want me to cut off my left hand and give it to you?"

"Playing semantics?"

"No," she said, giggling. "You said, 'Give me your left hand.' Meaning cut off my left hand and give it to you." In her playfulness, John noticed her greenish eyes glistening like the sun shining on a far-away sea, making it sparkle as if a giant light from heaven illuminated them.

He smiled, ignoring what she said.

"Give me your hand, please. Don't make a production out of it." In his right hand, he held a brilliant diamond ring with baguettes on each side, tucked between his index finger and thumb.

"Here is my left hand." She tried to reach his hand but couldn't. "I can't reach. People will think we're crazy." She felt like a schoolgirl at the senior prom.

"Let them. Who cares."

"I don't care either."

"Tilt your left shoulder down more and stretch your left hand out to me again."

She tried. "This table is too big. But let me try again." John took her left hand into both his hands. She felt him place a ring on the second finger of her left hand, the ring finger. He sat poised over her hands like an orthopedic surgeon prepared to reset her fingers in place.

They both giggled. She knew it to be an engagement ring. She had intended to pull away to examine the ring. He held her hand tightly. "No, not yet." He said. "I have something to ask you."

They smiled. "I must look silly."

"You look fine."

His face changed from a giggling smile to a glow of contentment. "Tara," he began, "you are beautiful. I love you."

She peered at him, her face beatified. Her eyes sparkled. She touched his hand—soft and warm she wanted him to hold her hand. Her eyes sparkled. "I love you, too, John."

"You do?" he sighed.

"Of course. I've loved you since we met."

"And I've loved you, since we first met. Will you marry me?" he asked, looking directly into her eyes.

Out it came—the question she wanted him to ask, the question she knew he would ask, and the question she'd say "yes" to. Her face felt warm. Shining. Shimmering. Scintillating.

"Yes, John. I want to be your wife."

"And I want to be your husband."

She had selected the ring a week earlier. John bought the engagement ring after considering her tastes. "This is a lovely ring."

"Only the best for you, Tara."

"I'll call my mother when I get home."

"And I'll tell my mother and brothers and sister."

He excused himself, got up, came over to her chair, and faced everyone at Drexelbrook. In child-like embarrassment, she sat in sanctified rapture. His boyishness clinging to him and as confident as a circus ringmaster, he announced, "Ladies and gentlemen," he shouted in a stentorian voice over the loud clamor of human conversation. "May I have your attention?" Everyone looked at them, "Please, ladies and gentlemen in the far corners. May I have your attention for a special announcement?"

The waiters stopped clicking knives and forks together. Voices grew silent. The room became as quiet as an empty church.

"Today, September 5, 1962, I, John O'Malley, have asked Tara O'Shea to marry me." Interrupted with the applause of everyone in Drexelbrook, he projected his voice louder. Getting down on his left knee, he held both her hands as she felt like a seagull flying to unknown heights.

"Tara," he said, "I love you. I am delighted you will be my wife. I will honor, cherish and keep you until death do us part."

Everyone applauded. The room vibrated with enthusiasm. People near them offered congratulations and best wishes, raising glasses in one united toast. People nearby voiced their approval. The band played the wedding march. Waiters arrived at their table with an arrangement of fresh-cut flowers in a vase. A theatrical production. John had orchestrated a play with more than sixty players and soon she would be Mrs. John O'Malley.

John huddled over her, raising her up. Hand in hand, they waved to everyone. Sitting, they blended into the night, a night of eternal remembrance. It had been the most perfect night in her life—and his.

I will have many more perfect nights. I feel it.

# SIX

# On the Job

*These autumn leaves look as beautiful as my daughter* She surveyed the leaves on the trees opposite the parking lot. Tara unfolded from her maroon Marquis, grabbed her attaché, passed through the black plastic fence, which gave the appearance of wrought iron. She watched a police car with siren sounding turn the corner at Parkland Avenue. A truck's brakes shrieked. She entered the four-story building through the kitchen. Dressed in a charcoal gray suit, she looked like an administrator.

"Good morning, Susan," she greeted a resident and to another resident she said, "Good morning, Henrietta. How are you?"

"Terrible," said the lady. "I need my medication. I don't feel right."

"You'll be fine, Henrietta," she replied, continuing to make her way to the office.

Tara thought if Henrietta had cancer she would have good reason to be gloomy. She studied Henrietta, eighty-two years old and going to live and she at fifty-four, going to die.

She rebuked herself for negative thinking. *No, I will not die – with the help of doctors, God, Mary. I'll win, yet. I'm embarked on a path to win. Who was it who said, "It's not whether you win or lose that counts... probably lost." And, give up, I will not.*

The cook ran to her. "We don't have enough chicken for dinner," he stammered.

"Go to the store and buy more," she said, shaking her head. "Oh, all right," he said, smiling and walking off, the lines on his face softening.

A man approached her. "I want to die," he stated.

"You won't die," she said. "You'll live longer than me." *And I might just be right.*

"Good morning," another man greeted her, his face aglow with a smile.

"Hello, Harry. You're your cheery self this morning."

As she entered her office, a woman took hold of her arm. "My sister won't give me any money." She gazed at the four pictures of her auburn-haired children who resembled herself, John and her father and his mother. She assimilated strength from their pictorial presence.

"Why?" Tara said, still holding her attaché.

"She hates me. She told me the money is about to run out."

An aide entered. "I wasn't paid right this week. I'm short two hours."

"Sarah," she told the lady, "wait a minute until I get settled. I'll ring your sister."

To the aide, she said, "It's not the proper time to discuss money in front of a resident. Please see Miss Martin in payroll and she'll adjust your pay."

The aide left, her face indifferent to Tara's needs. As Tara placed her attaché on her desk and still standing, she addressed Sarah's concerns. "Now Sarah. Sit down and relax."

As she reached for the telephone, another aide appeared in the doorway "Roland pulled the sink off the wall in his room last night."

"Why did he do such a thing?"

"He was annoyed. She said the maintenance man told him 'to go to hell.'"

"I'll page Bill," she said.

Tara picked up the intercom. "Bill Martel. Bill Martel. Please call the office. Thank you."

"By the way," the aide said, "How are you?"

"Fine," she said. "I take one day at a time."

"How are your radiation treatments going?"

"Finished, Janet."

"You're clear?"

"The doctors said there is no sign of cancer at this time."

"Good news," the aide said, coming toward Tara and hugging her. "You're a good woman. I want you to live."

"Thank you, Janet. Thank you for your concern."

As the aide left the room, Tara finally took her position behind her desk and sat down. *Finally.* From the outer office, she heard her secretary say, "What's the use of treatments. She's going to die anyway." She grasped both hands into fists. The maintenance man walked into the office. A short, bald man with glasses. "You paged me, Tara?"

Sarah grew impatient. "What about me, Mrs. O'Malley?"

Tara smiled, came around her desk, and gave the woman a hug. "Don't worry, Sarah. I'll take care of you."

Reassured, the woman smiled. "Okay, I know you will."

"Bill, I hear Roland got annoyed with you for telling him to go to hell."

"I said no such thing. I told him to stop acting like a child because he was angry at the owner."

"What did Nathan Mountain do to make him mad?"

Not a strong muscular man, Bill Martel's slight features proved sufficient to do maintenance work with skill instead of strength.

"He told me the owner canceled a fishing date with him and he was disappointed."

"Do you know about the sink off the wall in his room?"

"First I heard about it."

"You didn't tell Roland to go to hell?'"

"No."

Tara glared at Martel, studying his eyes. *A person lied with the eyes.* Guilt flashed in his eyes. Martel lowered his eyes. Tara surmised Martel did tell the resident to go to hell. But Roland's actions may be the result of both Martel's verbal abuse…a violation under state personal care regulations and cancellation of the fishing trip.

"Well, please fix the sink in Roland's room."

"Whatever your pleasure," he said, leaving the office.

With little time to relax, Tara entered the first floor sitting room. She said to Sarah. "Now then, Sarah, it's your turn."

"Thank you, dear," the resident said. "You're a fine lady."

Tara dialed Sarah's sister's telephone number. *No sense being disagreeable. The world is overloaded with disagreeable people. Anyway, every person in here is fighting a thorny battle.* Her priority: provide for residents' needs with love and attention.

Tara waited patiently for the sister to pick up the phone. She noticed Sarah studying her. *Whatever I can do to help my residents is what I want to do.* Tara considered the residents' families and referred to them as "my residents." She loved being of service to the elderly and treating them like family. Once, she and John attended the funeral of a resident who had no mourners attend services. They attended mass at Our Mother of Mount Carmel and went to Saint John Neumann's Cemetery for burial—a funeral director kindly offered to bury the resident at no charge.

The most unnatural funeral she and John had ever attended. St. John Neumann Cemetery, the place where she and John would be buried; hopefully, not until after their eightieth birthdays. She and John had openly discussed cancer. They hadn't feared it. They worked to defeat the tiny deadly cells with positive imagery and meds. John joked if she died first, and when he died, he would have himself placed face down in his casket so when lowered into the grave his casket would be placed on top of her with his body facing into her face. It would be one last death-long intercourse between them he kidded. *Thank God, we maintain our sense of humor while treated with chemotherapy and radiation.*

"Hello," she said into the telephone. "I'm Mrs. O'Malley at Summit Personal Care."

"I'm calling on behalf of your sister, Sarah. She claims you told her there was no money to pay for her care and she is rightfully worried."

She paused, listening to the person on the other end.

"Oh, I see. That will be a relief. A misunderstanding? Right ... Right ... Fine....I'll tell her. In fact, she's here now, listening to me."

She paused. "Thank you. Goodbye."

She hung up and faced Sarah, smiling with love and attention. "Well, Sarah, a misunderstanding. Your sister told you funds had been transferred from one account to another."

"You mean everything is fine?"

"Yes. Don't worry." Tara knew how to console the residents in the early stages of Alzheimer's. Robert Cohn flashed into her brain. He too didn't understand the Hemingway code in *The Sun Also Rises*, as the humble Sarah did not understand her sister. But she valued Sarah and all the residents who deserved to be treated with respect and dignity. She leaned back against the chair, smiling and remembering what her mother often recited to the family, growing up in Ireland: "Do not lead, for I may not follow. Do not follow, for I may not lead. But walk beside me and be my friend." She needed a friend. And had one in her husband, her best friend.

*This is my Calvary. But I will survive. I'm determined to change my Calvary into salvation and live to an old age with John and the kids.*

# SEVEN

## Calvary Continues

Wind whistled through trees. Large gray clouds formed. Velvet showery mist blanketed earth.

Tara made the usual daily tour of the facility, not like Nathan Mountain, who toured the facility on a few occasions, wearing a white glove and brushing over furniture tops, checking for dust.

She carried pen and notebook to record matters, which needed to be mentioned at the next staff meeting. She clutched the pen like a knife and she slipped it between notepapers.

In the Victorian styled waiting room opposite her office, she noticed Ellie playing the piano.

"What wonderful music you create, Ellie."

Ellie blushed. "Why thank you, Mrs. O'Malley."

"Not at all, Ellie. If you played all day, my day would be more pleasant."

Ellie smiled and continued moving her long, thin fingers across the keyboard. *Piano fingers*. "That's what she has – piano fingers," she said aloud as she turned towards a resident rising off one of two sofas facing each other. The resident lifted her dress to her face and said, "What beautiful underwear I have. Look for yourself."

Tara smiled.

"Don't you think, dear," the lady said to Tara. "Don't you think I have pretty underwear."?

"Yes, you do, " Tara said, humoring the resident.

"What kind of underwear do you have, dear? Let's see." The lady approached Tara as if to lift her skirt.

"No, no, Madelene. Let's not get inter-rested in what I am wearing."

"Well," Madelene persistent. "What color are your panties?"

"Madelene! My undergarments are not for discussion." Tara chuckled.

Madelene climbed onto the seat cushions and again held up her dress to her face. Tara calmly stated, "Madelene, it's time for your exercise period."

"Oh, it is. Well then, dear, I'll do my exercises." She walked off.

Tara smiled at the other residents and said, "Thank God, it's exercise time."

She passed through the dining room, straightening napkins and utensils and examined new bedrooms recently added to the main building. She reasoned, rooms and furniture were pleasant and comfortable with the off-white painted walls attractive and conducive to raising the spirits of residents. *If I owned this, I'd have better furniture and bedding and make the rooms more decorative.* This she did, when she and her husband remortgaged their home to buy O'Shea Personal Care in July 1987, fifteen months before diagnosed with cancer.

In room 103, she found George Nowak in bed...mouth open and staring lifelessly at the ceiling. The pale, white face she had seen several times on residents who died in their sleep. She closed his eyes, went to a house phone and told her secretary to notify the doctor about George's death. The designated payer, she told her secretary, will be notified later after the doctor certifies a death certificate. Strange she should remember an article she had read in yesterday's paper no one had ever drowned in the Dead Sea. Composed of 25 % salt, the water is heavy, making it practically impossible to stay submerged.

*Well, George didn't die in the Dead Sea.* Fully clothed, he lay on the bedspread. Death…a lonely sight. She examined his face, wondering if she died from cancer would she too look lonely. Would her face appear ashy? Would her hazel eyes and mouth be open? Apparently, they would, she speculated. The few who died in the home had one natural thing in common—their faces looked ash-gray and lonely. George's hair was disheveled. Did death cause the blood flow to cause hair to be upright and unkempt, she wondered? His eyes seemed centered in the absence of warmth and life…eyes once opened to see people and events around him. She hoped he found eternal peace. *Death, when the body laid completely still, completely at ease.*

*My face might one day soon be stone-like in death.* His hands seemed whiter in death. She didn't want to die. She remembered when the doctor first told her she had cancer. She drove home from his office. How, she didn't know for tears rolled down her cheeks, blurring her vision. They dropped from her lids like beams of bittersweet syrup.

"CANCER. CANCER. CANCER. *God. . .no. Cancer rhymes with "I can see." I dread being without John and our Four Green Fields– Sean, Enda, Maura and Thaddeus – and FiFi and Puff, my toy poodles and Persian cat, Daddle, and my midnight black cat, Pushky. I'm too young to die. And leave my love, John. How I love him. . .Where*ver she went without John, she felt his presence with her.

She judged her eyes too would be open, staring at the ceiling. Would they be looking into heaven? Seeking, searching, researching...for God?

Heaven she envisioned a great place. But heaven she did not yet need. She felt perfectly happy on earth. She was content to live her life on earth with her family and die when all the children were married with their children, her grandchildren.

She grew sad as she continued to stare at the resident's anemic face. Never again would he be the same. Death settled upon the man like the grayness of an afternoon rain. She thought she may never see any of her children married, never hold a grandchild as her two sisters and two brothers had experienced. Never would she grow old with John. Never again...Never again...Never again. She laughed at her morbidity. She could do better. She found lightness in the darkness of death. She may not live to experience the loneliness and isolation of old age. At least, she would not end her life in a personal care or a nursing home or having someone take care of her. She found something positive in having cancer and possibly her death. All people's talents are gifts from God. We can't be angry with God for what God does. She felt she had used her talents wisely. If she died, she'd be ready.

Tara used the stairwell to get to the second floor to inspect the stairs. She found dust balls and pieces of paper and wrote a reminder to herself to mention these items at the next staff meeting. She wrote a note to ask George's relatives for a copy of the death certificate to place in George's file in order to stay within the regulations of the Pennsylvania code, Title 55 of the Public Welfare. As a basketball official knew the rules of the game, she had memorized Chapter 2620, Personal Care Home Licensing Regulations. And she followed the "regs" explicitly – the reason why on the last yearly state inspections the facility received only a minor infraction, such as a dented food can.

On the second floor, she observed the bright orange, greenish, and ten-year-old Oak tree across the street from the facility. Leaves from a Japanese Maple had already turned colors from a spring green to a rustic fall. Leaves undulated in the fall winds. Fall winds pushed forward into winter. Nature's beauty reminded her of John and of his determination to create a rapturous body rhythm as he penetrated down into her as she moved up to meet his demand. She noticed how freshly cut the forsythia shrubs looked along the false wrought iron fence. The sweet odor of the mignonette on the windowsill reminded her of O'Henry's "The Furnished Room." *Bill Martel did a good job.* The side street appeared to be in an unfolding process of shedding leaves in preparation to welcome winter. The sun hung high in the heavens, like a giant stage light engulfing the main character in a play, casting silvery streaks of light around the home. *Might this majestic light signify my last performance?* She hoped not. She prayed not. It would not be.

She made a note in her padbook: resident in 203 rested in his bed, not a violation, but she wanted to be sure he didn't stay there all day. In 207, she walked in on Millie and Sheldon. Both were naked. Sheldon blanketed Millie like a bed comforter. He descended onto her like a dog in heat. In their pre-occupation, they did not hear the door open.

"Oh my," said Tara.

Sheldon breathlessly whispered, "Close the door. We're busy."

"Would you like a cup of tea?" asked Millie in the most ladylike voice. She had the mind of a child.

Tara understood the rights of residents for privacy. She recalled Frank Mc Court's book *Angela's Ashes* in which he mentions his mother's sexual "excitement."

"What's going on here?" Tara asked. The scene vibrated against her norms.

"I hope you're not *deirbfhines*," she laughed. She admired the bed sheets, as soft and pink as cotton candy.

"What the hell is deir . . . what?" Sheldon said, without losing rhythm in his abdomen movements.

"That's Irish for first cousins."

"Nice to see you dear, " grunted Millie.

*Poor Millie. . .with dementia.* Tara closed the door and while writing a note to observe those two closely, she heard their pleasurable moans. *Sounds like excitement to me.* She smiled. A simulacrum of John and herself. She and John making love proved holy. She noted an unmade bed in 208 and the hallway had not yet been vacuumed.

The third floor looked orderly. She returned to her office. *Well, this is my life. And, this is my light.* She understood people are forever breaking rules of every kind. The problem with people today, a staff member told her, is people think it is the "Ten Suggestions" not the "Ten Commandments."

———————

Tara sat opposite Dr. Johnson, the radiologist, at the Cancer Hospital. She waited patiently as she reviewed her notes.

"Well, Tara, the results are good."

"Encouraging, is it not?"

"When did you have the initial surgery?"

"After cancer was discovered in November, 1988, the tumor and malignant lymph nodes were removed in December 1988."

"Let's see," she said, thinking. "This is September 1989. Nine months ago."

She nodded.

"Our findings are…" she read from her notes, "the lungs are clear. The heart is not enlarged and the aorta is okay. There is no evidence the disease metastasized to the heart, lungs, or mediastinum!"

"All that is good."

"Yes," the doctor replied. "All good."

———————

Snow gathered on the O'Malley lawn early in the morning and, by the time John left work, snow had covered the street. Tara collected herself and drove off to Dr. Stein's office with deliberate caution. When she arrived, she waited a brief time. Stein, unlike Dr. Wiseman, rarely kept patients waiting.

Dr. Stein escorted her into his office. Tara sat in a chair in front of him. She knew he found her a courageous patient. He treated her like a friend.

Dr. Stein began, "The radiologist examined you in September 1989." He paused, studying the report. "You had a bone scan and you were given IV administration of a tracer dose of Technetium 99m MDP. No pathologic areas of localization in the bones or soft tissues are identified." To clarify these points, he said, "Means you're doing well. And the renal and bladder are fine. You know, Tara, you are one of my most determined patients. It is a pleasure to treat you."

"Thank you, doctor. Determined is what I am. Through all my operations and treatments, I have a positive outlook."

"Thank God. And you had your chest x-rayed. In the lungs, there are no localized areas of infiltration and your heart is normal. The mammogram revealed no evidence of a dominant mass or suspicious calcification in either breast. There is no evidence of malignancy."

"In 1951, I had an appendectomy, a gall bladder operation in 1964, hysterectomy in 1980, a Marshall Marchetti in December of 1984. In 1986, I had a blepharoplasty to restore peripheral vision and the lumpectomy in December 1988...I have it all here," she told him, handing him her typed medical history.

"That's what I mean. You are a strong soldier," he tittered. "And organized."

Smiling, and with eyes aglow, she said, "I am a determined Irish girl."

"None better," he agreed.

---

As she drove to Summit Personal Care after seeing Dr. Stein - a practice she established early in her cancer treatments. She didn't want to miss a day in a job she loved, supervising the proper care of her residents. She thought about the word serendipity. She knew it meant finding something without looking for it. She decided she would take one day at a time without looking for a long life while under treatments and in so doing, a long and happy life would find her. She remembered the remarkable dream she had the night before. On an operating table, when her heart had stopped, she clearly saw her spirit leave her body. She entered a dark long tunnel. Her spirit darkened, dark like a sun-tanned girl from a full summer of sunbathing. She exited at the end of the tunnel into a bright, glorious light. At first sight, she saw beautiful flowers growing in a wondrous garden. Off in the distance, she saw a beautiful man. He spoke to a large group of people and when he saw her, the man in a snow-white gown came over to greet her.

"I love you, Tara." The man walked as he talked. "I've been waiting for you."

She filled with immense joy. "I love you, too. But I didn't expect this would be the way it is."

"Come here," he motioned for her to sit on a park bench.

"I thought there might be heavenly spirits flying every which way."

"They are spirits waiting to be united to their bodies at the last judgment."

"But we look real...the way we are on earth."

He said, "We appear to be real. We're spirits."

"You look beautiful...I mean, handsome."

The man laughed. In all artists' conceptions of him, she saw him to be serious and thus she thought him too serious to laugh. How could she ever doubt a perfect man couldn't enjoy a laugh? Artists did this man an injustice, picturing him in a serious mood.

"You can now spend the rest of eternity with us."

*Eternity. I dread leaving John and the children at their young age.* "Is it possible to return to earth?"

"No one wants to return to earth once they see me and this lovely place."

"It is lovely. But I love my family."

"Do you feel your life is incomplete?"

"I do. I must complete my husband's life and the children's beginning a new life in marriage."

"Most unusual request, Tara. No one has ever asked to leave this state of perfect happiness."

"Please. You're the only one who can help."

"You have been a faithful daughter."

"I've tried."

"You have treated people with respect and dignity, a major ingredient to obtain heaven."

"May I return?"

"You may. I'll be waiting for you and your family. But remember, I can't wait too long. I don't have to wait," he said. He faded away before she could ask him how much time she had left.

Awakening, she sat up and blinked into the darkness. *My mission was to marry a man like John and have children. Now with cancer, the purpose of the rest of my life is no longer clear. Doctors might explain this dream as being the work of endorphins. I don't know.*

# EIGHT

# The O'Malley Family

She reflected on the day she met John's mother and two brothers, Daniel and Henry. His sister, Mary, had married and lived in Ohio.

His mother had an oval face with penetrating light green eyes and developed lips. She had smooth, unwrinkled skin and a round stomach. Hidden behind her radiant smile was a life of sorrow. Daniel, the oldest brother and happily married at 35 had five children. She met him briefly one summer night in 1962. Henry was the baby of the family like herself. He had an Elvis Presley hairstyle and crooked teeth. John's sister Mary, she met later after they had their first two children. Frank O'Malley, the father, went unmentioned in the family. The O'Malley's tried to avoid unpleasant topics and didn't mention the father.

Frank O'Malley, a lifelong alcoholic had separated from John's mother, June, twenty years ago. On occasion, he met one of the O'Malley children on street corners to give ten dollars he earned from caddying. Ten dollars? Did he expect his wife and children to survive on ten dollars?

At times, when she felt well, June worked at a factory, but most of whatever scant income she earned came from cleaning houses where once the builder offered her five dollars to go to bed with him. She refused for any amount of money. There would be no Frank Mc Court's "excitement" for her. Too often, John told Tara he saw his mother lying on the sofa in the living room, her right arm over her eyes. She was overburdened with debt while always loving her children. He considered his mother a saint. The room had one window and one glass door to emit light. John said sunlight refused to shine into their dark house.

John loved his family...with reservation about his feelings for his father who used money to drink instead of working and feeding his children's stomachs and buying their clothes. Twice the family went on-welfare for extended periods. John told Tara few welfare people succeed in life to become professional self-supporting and family-supporting citizens. How many succeed? He reasoned about ten per cent climb out of poverty with steadfast determination and perseverance—according to *Psychology Today*.

*Fascinating how the four O'Malley children did not follow in their father's path and become alcoholics.* Though scared emotionally by living with a father and in an unhappy environment, Daniel dropped out of high school in his junior year; Henry in his sophomore year; Mary dropped out at 16. *What a family history...all drop outs except for her John.* Mrs. O'Malley dropped out of school in the fourth grade and John's father quit in the eighth grade. John stayed in school, becoming the sole high school graduate and the only college graduate in his entire family. No one except John came near getting a master's degree – John had two.

Tara saw in him his ability to succeed through hard work, determination, perseverance, and persistence. His qualities of kindness, compassion, generosity, calmness, tolerance, concern, thoughtfulness endeared him to her; he was serendipity in her life. She had not sought him. He simply came to her. Neither tried to arrange it. Serendipitous. By happenstance, they met. John reached upward to touch people's lives and to influence them with gentle fatherly fingers. And that was why he had entered teaching—to be a positive force in changing children's lives as he had changed his.

Mrs. O'Malley had greeted her cordially. "Welcome, Tara, to our family."

"Thank you, Mrs. O'Malley."

"I wish both of you all the happiness, all the best."

"Thank you. I will be happy with your son." It eased the strain in the getting-to-know-you process.

"This is Henry," John said. "My youngest brother."

Henry had risen to shake her hand. He gave her a hug, which she graciously returned.

Motioning to Daniel, John said, "This is Daniel, my oldest brother who used to knock me off the bed in pillow fights."

"How are ya?" Daniel said.

"I've heard much about you, your wife and your children."

"All good, I hope."

"Of course," she said, noting paint peeling from the ceiling. The living and dining rooms she remembered as small and able to fit into half her drawing room on Circular Road in Ireland and the kitchen seemed smaller than her family's laundry room. The small three-bedroom row home had ten windows on a one way Philadelphia street in the Germantown section of the city. She loved John for what he was—a good man, not what he came from. She grew up diametrically opposite in social strata. *Weren't opposites supposed to attract each other according to astrology?* Someone once told her to hope for the best. Plan for the worst...never surprised.

She rejected the idea: planning for the worst is not a good idea. Too negative. She planned for the best, and, if it didn't happen, she reset her plans, seldom surprised, unafraid of the next challenge.

On television, Harry Callis gave the play-by-play of a Phillies game. "Mind if I turn this off?" John had asked. Everyone sat at Mrs. O'Malley's invitation.

"Not at all," said Daniel. "You'll have to meet my family." He sat there, leaning forward like a man conditioned by a world of determinism, a world driven to present one problem after another, without relief.

"You'll have to meet my family, too," Henry injected. His eyes had a bluish tint.

"Mrs. O'Malley laughed. "You don't have a family."

"Who knows, mom?" offered Daniel. "He may have a family on the side."

"If I do, my book binding job may not be enough to support you, Mom."

Tara delighted in their frolicsome conversation. She mentioned her father had been aide-de-camp to the President of Ireland. "You had much in life, Tara."

Mrs. O'Malley lowered her head and looking at the floor said, "Not like me . . ."

John Interrupted. "Now, mom...none of that. This is a happy occasion."

"Happy for you, John." Loneliness swept into her heart. She felt lonely and unnoticed like the large metal statue of William Penn atop City hall.

The atmosphere had changed. She sensed Mrs. O'Malley's discomfort. John's mother believed Tara had come from the "haves" and "all her life she had lived as a "have not." Mrs. O'Malley worried, even about yesterday. Her life never changed: money problems today repeated themselves the next day followed by the day after and on and on…one sorrowful day after another, without the loving comfort of a spouse, without enough money to give more than the bare necessities to her children and herself. She gave the most important thing: love. She sacrificed herself for her children, with loving attention. She worried about tomorrow and, when it came, she knew there would be no changes from the poverty of the day before. Always the same…another crown of thorns, problem drove her deeper into a bottomless pit of melancholy. She worried about the present; the present represented her state in life—deprivation and disillusionment. She had become, unfortunately, used to be being knocked down by life's sorrows and stayed down. What good was hope with never enough money to pay existing bills? All this for loving and marrying the wrong man. Her children loved her as a loving, caring mother.

Tara tried to change the subject. "Mrs. O'Malley, John and I would love to take you to dinner next Saturday."

"Delightful," she replied.

"We'll go to Beck's on the Boulevard."

"Oh that's a lovely place."

"Yes, John and I have had dinner there."

"You'll like it mom."

"Can I go?" said Henry.

"You're too young." John said, smiling.

Daniel asked Tara, "You came from Dublin?"

"Yes. Actually, a suburb of Dublin."

"And your father was a colonel?"

"Yes. aide-de-camp as well."

"Oh, you come from the aristocrats," Mrs. O'Malley said, sneering.

Tara wanted to make this a cordial visit, to make no waves. She swallowed. "Like anybody else."

"Not if you had servants."

"We had but they came with my father's job, Mrs. O'Malley."

"Oh, you had a good life in Ireland?"

"Yes. We had a good life," Tara stated with ascertainment. She had felt the present a good time to go to the toilet allowing Mrs. O'Malley a chance to unruffle her jealousy.

She walked up the thirteen steps to the second floor. At the top of the stairs, she saw an old scratched bureau, and, turning right, she noticed a small bedroom on the left and glimpsed into the front room with two double beds and three bay windows with paint peeling from the ceiling—John's bedroom. To the left of the doorway, she saw a worn bathroom at least fifty years old, probably never reconditioned.

The bathtub rested on four legs with chipped paint. The sides of the tub revealed its painted wrought iron, not an imitation iron like Nathan Mountain's fence at the Summit. A round bar hovered over the tub, covering half of it with a plastic curtain clinging to snap clamps. She pulled the chain to flush and as she did, she heard the neighbor's toilet flushing through the thin wall adjoining the neighbor's. Like sitting on a public toilet with a partition and seeing the other person's shoes. Living this close to neighbors people went to the toilet together gave her a laugh. She vowed John and she would not live in the city when they bought a home. Tara had lived in single homes all her life and she hoped to have a single house in the suburbs.

At the other end of the hallway was the back bedroom where her mother-in-law slept. It contained a double bed, bureau and two windows. The bed size allowed no room to walk near the outside wall. *A compact house John lived in for sure.*

When she came down the steps, she heard John's voice.

"Where's John, Mrs. O'Malley?"

"Oh, he's playing one of his games."

"Games-s-s-s?"

"He's hiding on you."

"Hiding?" she questioned, standing in the middle of the living room.

"He does silly things," Henry told her.

"He's still a boy," Daniel said.

"Here I am, Tara."

She heard his voice coming from the kitchen. She walked to the kitchen and peered into the small square room. "Where are you?" She felt lightheaded.

"Here." His voice came from behind the kitchen door. She nudged open the door.

"Here, I am," said he, kissing her cheek.

Daniel prepared to leave. "Well," he said, getting to his feet, "I must go. I hope to see you soon."

"Nice meeting you, Daniel…does everyone call you Daniel?"

"No, my family does. Friends call me Dan."

"Inter-resting. I'll call you Dan."

He clutched her hand like a car clutch stick, ready to swing it into gear and gave her a bear hug, causing her to gasp for air. John and Tara had waved goodbye as Daniel disappeared off the porch flanked with a faded awning.

"Know how I got the name, Henry?" Henry asked.

"How?"

"Dad named me after Padraic Pearse…Padraic Henry Pearse."

"I know Pearse."

"He started the rising in 1916. And, without his motivation, the Free State of Ireland may not be free today."

"Henry knows his history," John injected.

"Michael Collins got too much credit for saving Ireland."

"He doesn't deserve all the credit. Without Pearse, there would be no Collins."

"I agree. I attended a private school and we studied Irish history in Irish."

"Interesting."

She winced. "Try studying history or French in Gaelic and speaking Irish in those classes. Then, see if you'd like it."

"You don't like the Irish language?"

"I do...to a point." "Do you know how Ireland got its named?" John asked. They looked, observing him...waiting. "Since you seem interested, I'll tell you." He studied their faces. "The Milesians did. They controlled half of Ireland. They called the land Eriu – Erin. It is a Scandinavian word. Someone added 'land" to form Ireland. The evening flowed. Dinner was a tasty home-styled Irish stew, which she seldom ate in her household in Ireland: pigs in the kitchen, that sort of thing.

John and she drove to Tara's apartment in West Philadelphia. He told Tara once he understood alcoholism as a disease he could understand his father's need to drink, but, at the same time, since his father made no serious attempt to stop drinking. John didn't respect him. "Alcoholics must learn to deal with their urge to drink," John said. "They can do this if they attend meetings with alcoholics anonymous groups and share their feelings and cravings with other alcoholics." John understood tolerance of other people's shortcoming and respected their viewpoints. John sought out good in people and to be forgiving of himself and others. He dealt with reconciling with his father's neglect and alcoholism. Tara and he knew he still had a way to go.

---

She parked the car in the Summit parking lot, near a rocky stream. The babbling brook reminded her of babbling people in the business world. Too many airheads. She followed a twig in the stream as it swooped around a rock, avoiding collisions and in a matter of three seconds it disappeared forever from her life. That's how quickly one passes through this life. Tara studied the autumn leaves at the tree top level in the valley. Built on a hill in the distance, the ground sloped sharply so in the distance tops of iridescent trees could be seen! *A deck should be built at the point of the incline so people can study the foliage and birds flying.* Many beautiful leaves, orange-red with brown spots; brown with rust, yellow, pale yellow with faded green lines; withered brown ready for a walker to crunch them into splinters.

Off in the distance up an elevated hill, she noticed many trees had yet to change colors. A winding road appeared to be a long asphalt ribbon, under the haze of a warm autumn day.

As usual, she gained entrance to Summit Personal Care facility through the kitchen.

"Everything's fine today, Mrs. O'Malley," said the cook. "No complaints yet."

*Thank goodness. I deserve a break.*

"How are you, Martha?" She asked passing the sitting room sofa.

"Terrible! I ache all over."

*Here it comes – a normal day.* "You'll be fine, Martha."

"Think so?"

"I know so."

"I hope so, " said Martha. Helen, irate the last time she saw her, blocked the doorway. "I wanna see you."

"Good morning, Helen. Come in."

"You better do something about these residents."

"What's wrong?" she said, sitting at her desk. "Please, sit down."

Helen ignored her and waited near the door. "I hate this day shift. There's too much to do."

"I told you, Helen, when an opening occurs. I'll place you on the second shift." She smiled.

"If I don't get on that shift next week," the aide threatened, "I'll quit."

"We don't want you to do that Helen." Tara tried to humor the agitated employee by listening and being respectful.

The aide fumbled a set of keys in her hand. "I want to know. Will I get the job or not?"

"Helen, at present, there are no openings. Please be patient."

"You bitch. You're not doing anything. One aide told me somebody's leaving."

She ignored the contumely remark, and wanted to tell the aide to hump off, but she said, "If you talk like this, the conference is over," Tara said, her lips held rigidly. "No one told me anyone's leaving."

I told you," the aide shouted.

"Helen, don't raise your voice at me. I hear you."

"But you're not listening."

Helen held keys in her right hand and raised the keys to eye level and flung them across the room, aimed at Tara's head. Tara moved to the right and the keys jangled into the wall, denting the drywall and nicking the beige paint.

"I quit," shouted the aide, hurrying from the office and jostling the secretary who had rushed to the doorway when she heard shouting.

Tara sat still, collected. She took a deep breath. In her head, she recited Theresa of Avila's prayer:

*Let nothing disturb you,*

Let nothing frighten you.

All things are passing.

God never changes.

Who has God wants nothing.

God alone is sufficient.

"What's this all about?" Eleanor quizzed.

"She demanded to be placed on the second shift and there are no openings."

"She shouldn't do this to you, Tara. Not with what you're going through."

Tara smiled. *That's what you say now and you're the one who said: I'm going to die anyway.*

Tara performed her duties as usual the remainder of the day. She prepared to leave for the day when six aides entered her office.

She stayed calm. She told herself to be calm. In a conundrum of difficult time, she silently counseled herself how to behave or what to do.

"We want an increase in pay, starting in two weeks," demanded Joan.

"Two weeks is it? This is a surprise." *I can't believe it: two battles in one day.*

"It's due us. We deserve more money," Joan said.

"We all do, I suppose, but raises are not due until January," said Tara.

"Now," Joan demanded.

The other five aides remained silent. Joan, Tara knew, acted as their spokesperson, a probable instigator of this demonstration of power. *Beat down, Joan, and I've beaten the others. Stand my ground.*

"If we don't get what we want, we'll quit."

Tara sat calmly, surrounded by six aides in a half circle. *As Abraham Lincoln once said in one of his cabinet meetings, "How many nays are there and all hands went up. And how many yeas are there and his hand went up, and Lincoln claimed victory, saying, the yeas have it."*

"Well," Tara stated with deliberate composure. "The first one who wants to quit may walk through the doorway and, if desired, the others may also follow her out."

What had she done! She took a risk. *But, if they call my bluff and walk out, how in short notice can I replace six aides?* She had gone to the literal summit: win or lose. She had risked all, but she knew she was right. *Mite makes right.*

In what seemed like minutes, Joan relented, "We better get a good raise in January." Aides smiled as if they admired Tara's courage as they quietly left the room to return to work. She won both the battle and the war.

*Short and sweet. Time to go home to John, Sean, Enda, Maura and Thaddeus – and peace. Thew. . ..*

On the way, she greeted people with relief and hearty smiles. Untouched. She thought it a victory. She didn't seek victories; she sought respect and dignity demonstrated by all who served in the facility.

*Victory in this cancerous sea? Victory while seeing a sea of doctors? What will Dr. Roth have to say?*

# NINE

# More Doctoring

Tara sat in Dr. Roth's waiting room, watching other patients as they waited to see the urologist. Ever since she had cancer, her life seems to be spent in a doctor's waiting room, doctoring. Sky blue painted walls made this office more home-like. John had painted their living and dining rooms sky blue. Blue raised her spirits and matched John's eyes.

The receptionist ushered her into a small cubicle where she disrobed and put on another hospital gown—one that her arms went out the front while the rear remained open for easy examination by the physician.

Dr. Roth, an officious man, had little bedside skills. He reminded her of Demetrius Doboobie—the bold, adventurous practitioner in *Kenilworth*.

"Now, this is your fourth visit to us, Mrs. O'Malley, " he said, hovering over her.

She nodded.

"You have had two episodes of recurrent congestive heart failure since cancer treatments began in 1988. You are 149 pounds.

Your blood pressure is good at 140 over 88. And you're taking Novadex, Lasix, Lanoxin, Synthroid, and Keflex for the bladder."

"I am still having a great deal of trouble voiding, doctor."

"MMnnnn," he sighed, looking up from his file. "And, today, you are entering the hospital for interstitial cystitis treatments."

"I am unable to void, except for small amounts. I go frequently about every hour or have a sense of intense urgency. Along with what you told me, the pain in my left leg may be associated with my urgency to void."

"Tell me more about the pain."

"It is a severe arching pain in the left calf. It extends into the left ankle and to the left toes. The great left toe involuntarily quivers and my left foot may turn in. The pain lasts about one minute and returns once in a while."

"How often?"

"About…a few times a day."

"Do you smoke?"

"No, nor do I drink."

"The pains could be caused by all the radiation you have received."

"What treatment will you give me to stop this constant need to void with a few drops every time I urinate?"

"Insert a chemical into your bladder. It has proven successful in a large number of cases, but not all."

"Let's try anything."

"It's called DMSO. I'll do it next week at the hospital."

She observed a picture on the wall of spring flowers, which eased her mind. Nature scenes like those in doctors' offices helped mollify her mood. "My husband is supportive of me."

"Fine. If all goes well you should be able to go home not long after the procedure is finished." His words fluttered through the room like an electric current flashing through the wire to create light.

*The light is for me. To encourage me.*

———————

A nurse wheeled Tara away from the recovery room. The nurse waved John O'Malley to follow. Another medical procedure caused her to forget making an appointment with the hairdresser. She said to John, "I must look terrible".

"You look lovely," he told her.

"I bet," she whispered, encouraged with his lie, still sedated.

"I love you, Tara. He centered his attention on her kissable lips, bent over her and kissed her gently.

"I love you, John."

"Do you see that star up there?" he said, pointing to the ceiling light.

"Sure," she said.

"Well, that star is coming down and its called Tara."

"Dr. Stein told me that awhile ago. It's good to hear."

She smiled and held his hand. "Always newlyweds. Remember our first night?"

"How could I forget," he said. "And every day after."

"We were better than Robert Redford and Nancy Sinatra in *Breakfast at Tiffany's.*"

She pressed his hand. "You're a fine man, John."

"Mushie. You have made my life glow. You have given purpose to my life."

"You've not burnt out, yet?"

"From last night's adventure, rolling around in bed, you know I haven't. I love being with you," he said, ignoring the rumble of something rattling in the hallway. "My whole being exists in your eye...doesn't it seem love is everywhere?"

An answer was not needed. She smiled. "Kiss me."

"Wasn't that delicious?" he asked. "You have an *idee fixe* about me."

"You're always showing me something."

"And other things, I show you, too."

"I've always said you have a one track mind."

"Absolutely. You rouse me to action. But let me tell you this: a lady called school today and she had the wrong number. But I have your number, Tara," he said with devilment in his eyes. "There's one number one—you."

Dr. Roth interrupted their teetering. "You're having trouble breathing, Tara?"

"A little."

"For safety, we're going to keep you overnight." To John he said, "You might as well go home – or, if you, want you can sleep in a chair."

Near midnight, she developed shortness of breath. John called the nurse. She paged the resident doctor. They decided, for Tara's well being, to place her on a ventilator. He inserted a tube into her mouth, which caused gagging. He held her hand. Unable to sleep for a long period, she slept in brief spans. John slept on the chair.

Tara remembered the poem "Footprints." She had the poem memorized. Why did it contain a man? A man must have written it, she concluded. She considered the part where the man noticed one set of footprints along the path of life. He also noticed it happened at the lowest and saddest times in his life. Tara contemplated what the man asked, "Lord you said once I decided to follow you, and you'd walk with me all the way. But I have noticed during the most troublesome times in my life, there's one set of footprints. I don't understand why, when I needed you most, you would leave me."

*Why, Lord, have you left me on this ventilator? Where are you?*

She imagined the Lord's reply. *"My precious, precious child. I love you and I would never leave you during your time of trial and suffering. When you see one set of footprints, it was then I carried you."*

*How can you carry me now, Lord? I am in a hospital bed, on a ventilator, unable to move. Well, you left the Apostles, all married but John, and the Twelve apostles were the first run-away fathers and husbands in recorded history since they left their families to follow a rebel. I hope you don't leave me, too.* She glanced over at John...asleep in the chair. He looked uncomfortable. Like the disciple in Gethsemane where Christ prayed while his disciples slept. *Weren't you able to stay awake for one hour?*

She mentally recited Luke: "Ask, and you will receive; seek, and you will find; knock, and the door will be opened to you. For everyone who asks will receive, and he who seeks will find, and the door will be opened to anyone who knocks."

*Well, Lord, I have asked since 1988 and I have knocked and I have sought. Still, I am not cured. Forgive me, Jesus. Like Tibia, I don't mean to complain. But please continue to help me win the fight against cancer. I want to see my children marry and have children and to stay here through John's retirement when we can spend more private time together. Time. Time.. something I'm running short of. Well, God, any good I do, you can do a greater good. Help me!*

The next morning, Tara had improved enough to go home. She wondered if her improvement should be accredited to God or to Dr. Roth's expertise? The ventilator? Or all three?

———————

The following week She went back to work. She left Summit two hours early for an appointment with her oncologist. She managed to usher herself out of the building without any late day interruptions, for whenever residents or aides saw her, they opened up their mental boxes of sorrows and complaints and unloaded. Not always, of course, for many people respected her as a fellow human being, not a problem solver. A shrieking wind ripped through her hair. *God! I look a fright.* As she opened the car door, a white paper blew away. *Like my life. . blowing away bit by bit.* Dead leaves tossed about and crunched against the windshield along with a black candy wrapper. She liked the taste of the cherry lipstick on her lips as she drove off, hearing the American flag snapping and crackling against the flagpole to the left of the entrance.

On the way to Dr. Stein's office, she read a sign on the lawn of a Lutheran church:

If you're looking for a sign from God…

HERE IT IS!

She greeted Dr. Stein's receptionist with a pleasant smile and took a seat in the waiting room. A picture of yellow tulips hung on the wall, as soft and light as cotton candy. She imagined the bright yellow tulips squeezing nutrients from the soil like an abortionist doctor squeezing life from an infant in partial birth abortion. She was directed to Dr. Stein's office.

"Hello, Tara. You look good today – as always." He held her hand.

"It is good to see you, Dr. Stein."

They sat opposite each other. "I'll examine your heart and blood pressure as well as your breasts."

"Okay," said she, thinking of John's jealousy when he didn't like any doctor touching her breasts. "How am I?" she asked, with him examining her breasts. Her sudden question surprised even herself.

Dr. Stein smiled. "What?"

"How do I compare to other patients?"

"For an Irish girl," he giggled, "not bad." They both laughed. "Your sense of humor is the best," completing his examination, he made notes. "You're 152 pounds today and your blood pressure are 150 over 92. The brain scan is clear."

"I have quite a file, Dr. Stein, with all the tests I am getting."

"That's part of it, Tara," said he. "We want to be sure you have every possible means to keep you healthy."

"Never ending?"

"Right. I'm ordering another breast x-ray, an MRI of the cervical spine, an MRI of the lumbosacral spine, and a CT scan of the pelvis."

"I am a marked woman, am I not?

He smiled. "In the near future, I would like you to have MUGA and an echo-cardiogram."

"Can I do this early morning or late afternoon?"

"These tests may take a fair portion of the day."

"I don't want them at this time. I don't want to lose time from work." Suddenly, a sharp darting pain raked her like the sting of a cat's claw.

"These tests are, as all the others, helpful for your diagnosis." He knew her to be a strong-willed woman. "All right," he hedged, "we'll discuss this another time."

"You see," she said, showing him her left arm, "my left arm has swelled a bit...."

"I see. There is lymphedema in the left arm. I don't like it."

"Why?"

"Swelling indicates fluids building up in your arm. This happens with some patients."

"But I don't want the patient to be me."

"I see here," he said, referring to his notes, "Dr. Wiseman has taken two biopsies and there is no evidence of metastasis carcinoma present. "That's wonderful news."

"I need good news."

He prescribed a topical steroid cream for the eruption on the right inflamed chest.

"But this was my right side? The swelling is on my left."

"I am not certain why, but we'll watch you closely. In the meantime, take this prescription. It's an ointment that may keep the swelling down."

She wondered if he had received Dr. Roth's report. "After Dr. Roth treated my bladder, I feel relieved. Did you get his report?"

He searched through the file. "Oh, here it is. Sorry about that."

"Well, I can void now, but I still don't feel normal when I urinate as I did."

"Is it better?"

"Much better."

"We'll watch it."

"Well...I know all this is to keep me alive. I wonder will I stay alive."

"We'll do our best."

*But will the best defeat cancer?*

# TEN

# Trying to Stay Alive

On Bustleton Avenue and turning onto Byberry Road, Tara thought of Ireland, her home for her first twenty-four years. Passing over the train tracks, she decided to telephone her sister, Una, and ask her to go to Mary's shrine in Lourdes where St. Bernadette Soubirous received the vision of Mary, the Mother of God, and promised great cures would happen if faithful people pilgrimage there.

The holiday would be her eighth trip home since her wedding. Doctors could only do so much and she would leave the rest to Mary.

"Hello, I'm home," she announced, entering the center hall. The house was as silent as a church mouse. "Anybody here? Oh, there you are, my little ones," she said to her four pets—the dogs FiFi, Puff and their cats Pushky and Daddle—who greeted her in the hallway.

In the kitchen, she saw pots and pans on the gas stove. The aroma of flavored foods incited her taste buds. The aroma of skinless over-cooked chicken made her hungry. "All right, John, where are you?"

With no response, she said, "I know you're here."

From behind, she heard, "Good afternoon, my bride," John slid his hands under her arms and squeezed her waistline "True complexity is in simplicity."

"Hiding again?"

"I hid behind the wall in the living room," he said, holding her tighter.

Ignoring his hold, but enjoying his strength and affection she continued, "I've decided something." Marriage can be such—talking while in a love hold without showing verbal awareness of touches, but all the time excited about the touches.

He held her tighter. "Don't hurt me."

"And what have you decided, my love?"

"I want to go to Lourdes."

"Go."

"You're a good man, John. Just like that…you say, 'Go'."

"Why not! You give me the "excitement" as Frank Mc Court calls sex and I give whatever pleases you."

"John," she whined, wiggling to set herself free.

He released his hold, turned her toward him, and kissed her passionately.

"John, the children.…"

"Don't worry about them. I must have you," he panted.


"Where are they?"

"Forget them," said he, breathing heavy.

"The dinner will burn. Your mind…you always want me!"

"And why not? A quickie…"

They made love. Their energies expelled, he raised his head and said, "With whom?"

"What…oh…you mean Lourdes?"

He nodded.

"I'll ask Una and Margaret to go with me."

"Your sister and your lifelong friend."

"I think so."

"That was a quickie all right; it took a few minutes."

"That's because I love you," said she.

"Again…tonight," he teased.

"Oh God, what a sex fiend."

"Love fiend," he corrected.

"I need you."

"You always need me."

"Of course." He suggested an analogy. "I am an automobile and you are my fuel. I fill up with your love as I fill my car."

"You want me every night."

"What else is there in life," he laughed. She joined his laughter.

They washed themselves. "This could be the beginning of a beautiful friendship."

"Casablanca," she said, "Bogart told Claude Raines at the end."

"You know," he said, "you're a little rich girl compared to me."

"We weren't rich."

John whipped the potatoes with butter and added a pinch of milk.

Tara saw how well he learned from her. "They look good, as if I prepared them myself."

"I have a good teacher," he said.

"In Ireland, you might be called *ollam*."

"What's that, my beautiful bride?"

"A chief poet. He was equal to a bishop or king of a *tuath*."

"A *tuath*?"

"In ancient Ireland, a *tuath*, a political unit or a small kingdom."

"*Comme il faut*. But I still cannot figure out why you married a man like me."

She gave a look, as if she pulled out a weapon and clobbered him…. "I loved you," and with a shine in her eyes, she added, "and still do."

"What do you see in me? You could've had any man."

"I've already told you."

The two oldest boys entered the house. "Hi mom, hi dad," they echoed.

"Maura and Thaddeus should be here soon," John said.

"Where are they?"

"Next door with Chris."

"Time for dinner," Tara said.

"Looks delicious," Sean responded.

Maura and Thaddeus grinned and greeted their parents.

"Let's eat now," ordered Sean, the oldest child.

"Hey who's in control in this house – we or you?"

"We are," replied Thaddeus, the baby of the family.

"You are, huh," wondered John.

The family sat at the oval kitchen table, each in a captain's chair.

"Wait now…Grace."

The children moaned.

"Bless us, O Lord, for these thy gifts through thy bounty. Amen."

"Good grace, Mom...short, Ma Ma." Maura said, using her pet name for Tara.

"Don't be irreverent, Maura," Tara urged. "Must be reverent, you know."

Sean said, "We'll be out of college soon. I suppose this family dinner scene is coming to an end."

"Like all of us at one table," responded Enda, "and don't forget FiFi, Puff, Pushky and Daddle."

"Yes, it is coming to an end," said John, "but there'll be times when we'll have dinner together."

"Probably not too many," offered Thaddeus.

Tara wondered about her end days. *Anyone who has cancer must think the end. Yet, we live and try to make each day a new beginning. We psych ourselves by taking one day at a time. We seek reconciliation with cancer to make the rest of our days livable.*

They ate skinless chicken covered with barbecue source, string bean casserole, and whipped potatoes; the conversation flowed among the O'Malley family.

"I shouldn't tell you this, but you're all old enough...I will."

"Tell us," the children suggested.

She grinned. "This man came into the home and he wanted to see his father. First, he asked an aide the whereabouts of his father and the person told him his father had gone to the hospital since he had a slight fall. Now, this is what happens in a home, the size of ours – people have accidents . . ."

"Com' on, Mom, this is exciting," Sean mimicked respectfully.

"Well, I'm telling you since this incident is a freakish example of what I deal with on a daily basis."

She laughed, placing her hand to her right cheek. Her face reddened. "This man came to me and told me he had located his father. This I knew. But he demanded he have his father's bank account books. This same man caused a previous raucous, but this time he cursed."

Enda stopped her. "But how can he have what's not his?"

"I suspected he would do this, I reported him to the Area Agency on Aging, and they had the books. I told him he couldn't have them." He said to me, "'Fuck you' and jumped up and down."

"My God, " the two oldest boys joined in unison.

"Never thought I'd hear *that* word in this house," Sean grinned.

"I'm not cursing. I'm telling you what happened."

"But you did curse," said Thaddeus.

"Go on, Tara," John encouraged.

"Well," she said, "he wouldn't stop. He came up to my face with a clinched fist. I said, 'If you hit me I'll have you arrested.'"

John said, "I've never heard my Irish wife say such a word. He looked straight at Tara and snickered. The children joined in the frivolity. "What kind of example are you giving our children?" he teased.

"As if they haven't heard it before."

"It's in our way of life," Thaddeus said.

Playing out one of his pranks, John swooned to the floor and lay motionless.

"Dad's dead again," Maura said.

"Look at him," Tara said. "Ignore him and he'll get up, if we pay him no mind."

John stirred, moaning. "Call an ambulance," he groaned.

"Get up. Dad," said Tara, "and wash the dishes."

"I get no respect round here. Always working. No respect."

He resurrected himself and began washing dishes as the children went off to their rooms to do homework.

---

After the six o'clock news, John went to the living room where he prepared for classes, read and wrote a first draft article on Irish history. John had been writing for several years. Some day, he knew he'd be published. Determined, he sent articles and stories to magazines, and had them returned with a printed rejection note such as: "Sorry this material does not meet our editorial needs. It is not possible for us to comment on individual works. We wish you good luck in your endeavors to find a publisher. The Editors." Tara read the paper and watched her favorite television programs: "Maud," "Dallas," "All in the Family," and "The Jefferson's." Quiet time, a time to lock out the outside world and enjoy family living inside. A good time for conversation, involvement with family members and inner peace the outside world could not give. The exterior versus the interior; the external versus the internal.

At nine in the evening, the family regrouped to watch television together. Either the children or Tara set the program to be watched. John went with the wishes of the family. He did not enjoy television watching. "No greater crime than waste of time," he told his family, "and television viewing," he declared, "a waste of time."

But each week, they watched "Cheers" together.

"This is a great program," Sean said.

"I like the mailman," stated Maura. "He has a dry sense of humor."

"No, he doesn't," John interjected. "He memorized the script well. The script character has a sense of humor."

"Oh, be quiet," Tara said, "You're tearing the actors apart. "Let's enjoy this." She peered at John with a tantalizing smile.

Enda scolded his father. "You do the same thing with movies, Dad."

"He's a nuisance to go to a movie with," said Tara.

"Movies are not real. Often, they make no realistic sense," he said, ceiling-gazing.

"Be quiet," said Tara.

He ignored her. "And they can correct any mistakes by refilming parts. And the movie plots are incoherent. Events happen in movies that could not happen in life."

"Watch this," she pointed towards the screen and laughed.

"That's another thing – when you hear laughter, it's a recording."

"Dad…" Maura moaned.

"It's true. When the producer wants a laugh, he turns on the record and you hear people laughing."

"Cheers is performed before a live audience," said Thaddeus.

"Where's the audience? You never see them."

"John…" Tara warned. "Why watch this, if you don't like it?"

He smiled, "My son, reprimanding me?"

"Be quiet."

"I can't ask you."

She lay stretched across part of the rap-around sofa where on occasions she and John made quickie love. "Ask me what?"

"I have tickets for *Les Miserables* at the Forrest. Go with me?"

"Yes," she said, staring at the screen and not at John. He endlessly told her he had tickets for something or other…his way of asking, her way of responding. But she enjoyed his choice. He had her interest in mind as well as his when buying theater tickets. She never felt irritated about this when they dated; he was definite about where they went...and this she liked. He was never wishy-washy like many men who asked her where she wanted to go. She liked his take-charge attitude; he had confidence and direction. He had confidence, and she knew when a person's confidence goes up, so does the competence. But now, watching TV, she grew impatient with him for interrupting her TV stories.

As administrator, her workday centered on making decisions. The social part of their life, she left to him. Thus, she wanted John, who still had the old fire of their younger days, to steer their social life.

She remembered back to 1962 when engaged and they saw such plays at the Playhouse in the Park as *The Crucible, Sunrise at Campobello, Inherit the Wind, Gideon, Picnic, Look, Homeward Angel, The Dark at the Top of the Stairs, Death of a Salesman*, and *Detective Story*. She remembered the musicals they saw at Valley Forge Music Fair, the Camden County Music Fair, and St. John Terrell's Music Theater in Lambertville, New Jersey. Such glorious musicals: *Music Man, My Fair Lady, West Side Story, Bridgadoon, Annie Get Your Gun, Oklahoma*, and *Guys and Dolls*. Like her good health, all those theaters were destroyed.

At night in bed after they had made love for the second time in a day, he said, "I should take all of us."

"What?" she murmured.

"Maybe, we'll all go to see *Les Miserables*."

"All six of us?"

"It'll be a fine night. After all, we want our children to appreciate theater."

She looked at him. "We've taken them to many plays and concerts."

"That's what I mean."

"Get tickets."

"It'll be expensive," he said, "and I want us to go to dinner first."

"Where is it?"

"Forrest."

"There's a fine Italian restaurant Portofino's on Walnut Street . . . The Forrest is on Walnut?"

He nodded. "The owner's a good man. He gives the homeless a free turkey dinner on Thanksgiving—with all the trimmings."

"I didn't know that. Remember what I said about the first three letters in 'assume?'"

"Sure...a-s-s. Ass."

"That's what you are," she added playfully.

"You cursed," he teased.

"I did not. I never curse."

He smiled at her playfulness. "I'll make reservations."

"Fine."

"Tickets will be $360; dinner about $140 - a $500 night."

"But we'll enjoy it."

---

She lay in bed awhile. John slept beside her. The house spoke to her with its moans and creeks in the stillness and peace. She listened and the house addressed her needs to be peaceful. Then she listened to the silence. Silence...peace... not a perfect silence like the weekend they spent in Killington, Vermont. There, climbing the mountain ride on a lift chair, she looked out on mountaintops, with no noises except the swishing of the wind. She in one chair and John in another, she felt the presence of some omnipotent being to cause such magnificence. Viewing the world above the mountains in a bluish-gray afternoon with no human voices, no sounds of automobiles, no disturbing sounds from the world below. Silence. She felt in the silence, she could live in this solitude forever.

As John rolled over and put his arm around her, she felt his hand under her nightgown, moving upwards where he cupped his hand lightly over her right breast. *In his sleep, he has sex on his mind.* She heard cars moving on the roadway, the grandfather clock chiming, creaks from house settlements, euphoric splatter of rain on the roof. She thought about mammy's letter to John in response to him writing to her telling her he and her daughter would be married. Mammy wrote, "Thank you for your nice letter. Needless to say, we are all looking forward to meeting you in June. I hope it will be a happy time for you and Tara and you'll both have a long and happy life together. Her father and I had 43 years together. And when I look back on it I think it much too short. When people are happy and contented life seems too short. God favored us. I hope you and Tara will be able to say the same in the years to come."

She sighed when she repeated the line: "When people are happy and contented life seems too short." She remembered another letter, responding to Tara's telling her mother she had received a beautiful engagement ring. She missed her mother. *If I read mammy's letter, I'll feel better.* She got out of bed and switched on the light in the corner. Her eyes raced back and forth over the page as if she had been given a speed-reading test or like a cat waiting to pounce on its prey.

"I got your letter today and am happy for you. I'm sure the ring is lovely. I hope to see it, please God. I don't know what to say about the wedding arrangement yet. Do you think it would save money if you got married over there and came on to Ireland for your honeymoon? The money for a big wedding would be more useful to you to start a home. It would also be nice to tour Ireland and stay in good hotels and let John see the country. Think it over. A nice wedding breakfast here would cost about 25 pounds or more per head. You'd have to have all the family and relations. If you got married quietly over there and come on here you'd both have a nice holiday for the price of the eats to everyone here. What do you think? That's what your father and I did from Templemore the morning we married. I think it would be wise and save a lot of bother. But please yourself. Is John the kind who would prefer a quiet wedding? If he has a priest friend he'd do it for him. Talk it over with him. As I'm still in bed, I intended to send the card but I thought I'd write those few lines and let you know I'm delighted you are happy. May God bless you!

Love, Mammy"

Yes…I'm happy mammy, thanks be to God…and you and daddy.

# ELEVEN

# The Wedding

She recalled their wedding day, June 15, 1963, the best and happiest day of our lives John had called it—with each day following, confirming their wedding as the best decisions of their lives. A day of love. A love of someone who had consented to give everything to possess the love of a loved one. A love of hope. A calling of new life. A new love upon the world. Love…the answer to making people better and the world a better place.

They left for Ireland June 8 on Aer Lingus. On Saturday night, six of their friends had seen them off. John's former principal was on the plane along with friends from the Irish Center, the group sponsoring the trip.

In Ireland, they stayed in her mother's home in Rathgar, a Dublin suburb. She slept in her old bedroom, John across from her on the second landing. She hoped she and John would have a long life together with children and grandchildren. She feared she would never experience those dreams now that she had cancer. *We seek what we want. But it's not what we want but what we get. We don't always get what we want. And once we get it, we move on to another want. But what I want is life. And life may leave me.* Tears swelled in her eyes.

She recalled the time her sister and husband Paul, her mother, John and herself had seen Hal Roach at Jury's Café in Dublin. The famous Irish comic told joke after joke, using such names as Murphy or Flanagan, playing an important part in his delivery. Some of Roach's jokes had a hint of age and needed to be revised. However, he purified his humor.

Her wedding day had been most memorable including John's dress adventure. A *tour de force*. John had taken an early bus—an impulsive—act into town to buy her a dress as a wedding memento. Her mother had thought he had cold feet and fled the scene. Mammy had friends whose daughter married her groom and, in a Kafkaesque twist after greeting guests in the receiving line, left with the best man and together they flew off into an irascible honeymoon. The mortified parents had to accommodate the numerous guests who had come from out of state, had everyone sit down to the wedding meal, without music, without the bride, without the bridegroom, and without the bride's and groom's parents. Her mammy recalled the dinner as somber as a post-funeral luncheon.

Mammy experienced another most unusual wedding. The girl, a snob of the first class, said she would only marry a professional. When the girl made that possible by getting engaged to a doctor, wedding plans had been made. On the day of the wedding, as she prepared to walk down the aisle, a telegram came from the doctor telling her he had changed his mind and intended to marry someone else. She ended up marrying a sanitation worker many years later.

Mammy did not want this to happen to her daughter. They married in the Church of The Three Patrons, Saturday, June 15th by Father Sean O'Shea, no relation to Tara; John invited his friend from Greenland to be best man. She had a beautiful wedding gown embroidered with silvery pearls with a full train and John wore a formal long black coat with gray stripped pants and carried a grayish top hat. Her pink and white eighteen roses cascaded in the form of a triangle. The headdress gave meaning to her wedding day, an Irish 2000-year tradition symbolized a fruitful marriage between the bride and groom that celebrated continuity of life and ensured fertility.

A friend filmed highlights of the day. The limousine took them to the Shelbourne Hotel, rich in Irish history when, in the rising of 1916, British troops fired from knocked out windows onto Irish volunteers in St. Stephen's Green across the street. She remembered the menu card as if it were yesterday. Yesterdays can be like that – long ago past events easily recalled. They had grapefruit Maraschino, Petite Marmite, fresh salmon Bellevue, roast stuffed spring chicken and ham, bread sauce, creamed cauliflower, roast potatoes, and the special soufflé surprise Milady Tara, tea or coffee. The conversation, the wedding guests, the music, the speeches, the dancing...all heavenly.

Tara remembered her mother playing a practical joke on them after their honeymoon to England and Ireland. In her mother's house, they occupied a bedroom with two single beds. Her mother began to open the door and as she heard the rustle of John going to the other bed, she giggled. She heard herself giggling when she remembered their farewell cocktail party given by her mother.

They were to be up by 8:30 A.M. The night before, Mrs. O'Shea, in jest, handed Tara a note: "See you at 8:30 A.M. – if you're up."

*Thank God, mammy.. .we had a happy family life with plenty of laughter.*

She thought about her pending trip to Lourdes. *I wonder how many people mispronounce the word Lourdes in the plural?*

# TWELVE

## Sean Black

Plans set for Lourdes in August, she bought a ticket on *Aer Lingus*. She planned to fly to Dublin and stay with her sister, Una O'Day, then journey to Lourdes with her sister and friend, Margaret White.

John took her to the General Wayne Inn in Merion for dinner as a bon voyage treats. She liked the General Wayne. It had a formal atmosphere where most men wore suits, a fading custom in the 1990s of casual dress. The long English-styled bar at the entrance presented an imperial image, which matched the dining room with its oversized fireplace, always lit on wintry nights. Fiery flames danced on logs, casting mysterious configurations on the stucco ceiling.

An elderly man scuttled across the black street after we drove into the parking lot. He used a cane as a crutch to help him through life, his face drawn tight, fixed in emptiness. He wore dark clothes. Pitched in darkness.

John opened the door of Tara's Grand Marquis and handed the keys to the valet, a young energetic man who sprung out of the darkness like an explosion of the Sulfur Springs on the island of St. Lucia in the Caribbean. As Tara turned her legs to the asphalt, John said, "You should do this."

"Do what?"

" Look the gentleman in the eyes upon getting out of the car."

She smiled, for she knew what he would say next.

"You know your skirt goes up when getting out and if you capture my eyes, I must look at your face and miss seeing your beautiful thighs.

"As if you've never seen them."

"I can't see enough of them."

The waiter escorted them to their table. Tara ordered a cup of tea and John his usual. "So Co Man Up Rocks Back, Two cherries, please."

"Sounds like a menu," a man at the next table said. "Here's lookin' at you, kid."

"Here's looking at you, kid," she said.

"That's a switch, Bogey," he said.

Her glass of water clinked with his Manhattan, sealing their toast.

"When you get to St. Stephen's Green, be sure to sit by the circular mount of flowers in the center of the Green and remember me."

"Yes, I will. It's a gorgeous place...so flowery, so green, so rich with nature."

"Unusual, isn't it, for a city to have a floral garden park in city center. It's much bigger and greener than Rittenhouse Square."

She said, "Not only that but the pond and the water fountain."

"And young toughs..."

"They only come to the gate near Grafton Street...and in the evening."

"Rittenhouse Square is pleasant, but it's not St. Stephen's Green."

"Nothing is. In August, the flowers will be purple, reddish, and white," she responded.

The waiter served their dinners. They often ordered the same entrees.

"Ah, this looks delicious," he said, admiring flounder stuffed with crabmeat.

"It certainly does," Tara echoed, sucking in breath before taking a first taste. This time, she decided against her ordering, the traditional calves liver with fried onions, her favorite dish.

"If we hadn't sent our children to Catholic grade and high schools," said John, chewing, "we would have saved...Let's see...I estimate about $50,000 net dollars."

She could hear hot water gurgling through overhead pipes. "A lot of money, but this we had to do – our religion."

"And we had to earn $75,000 gross."

"Our religion," she repeated.

"And college has and will costs us another four to five hundred thousand." With religion, Tara reigned as the dominant one. With educational values, Tara reigned as the dominant one. With matters of business, Tara reigned as the strong one. Tara got what she wanted, with a mixture of undertone strength and kindness. John wanted the children to attend school in their suburban school district to save tuition. Tara would not hear of it. John wanted her to take a pill or use a devise so he could make love to her whenever he wanted. She abided by the Catholic Church's teaching on the use of rhythm. Its restrictions drained his libido. An "x" marked on the kitchen calendar had guided their sexual appetites for fifteen years, thanks to men who call themselves theologians and believe they had direct communication with God.

Straining to satisfy his concupiscence, he painfully consulted the calendar when he craved Tara's body as a cigarette smoker desires a cigarette or an alcoholic yearns for a drink. John was lovingly addicted to her tender, soft body, her spirit. As he savored the flounder, he desired her as she sat there in all her beauty. A beauty, he chided himself for not acknowledging more often.

"I want you," he said suddenly.

"Again? You had me last night."

"Thank God for hysterectomies."

They laughed. "Since then, you've haven't had to wait, have you?"

"Thank God, no. Sex on demand."

"And you're wearing me out."

"No way. You've much energy in your body, no one could wear you out."

"You do," she said, smiling, kicking his shoe lightly.

He responded by placing his hand under the table and holding her thigh. "Let's do it here," he stammered, his eyes glowing with a devilish tint..

"You're crazy," she said, her thigh quivering from his touch like an emissary from heaven ready to do whatever he wanted of her.

"Don't climb across the table at me."

"I have before."

"No, you haven't," she said.

"Sure?"

"Yes. When did you do it?"

"Now," he said, getting up and with arms outstretched

"Don't you dare," she chuckled, thinking he may try it. She could never be sure with a prankster for a husband.

He sat down. "Now is the time."

"Crazy. Where do you get these ideas?"

"From you...being with you gives me these thoughts – all the time. If I could, I'd spend my whole life in bed with you."

"We have to eat."

"Have someone bring in our meals and we'll eat as we lay together."

She sipped water. "Here, take this and cool off."

"Whenever I'm with you, I need a cold shower."

Thrilled, she still excited John; she smiled but said, "You're a sex fiend."

"I'm a love fiend. I told you."

"You need restraints."

"Not anymore. The church ruled by single men placed restraints on me by having people like you adhere to rhythm."

"Can't argue with a person's conscience," she said.

A moment of silence followed. "No, but I can argue with single men who do not know married life telling other people when to have sex in marriage. Inter-resting" he said, mimicking her use of the word *interesting*. "They claim to be following God's will. God never said anything about rhythm. Men did. Single men. SINGLE MEN."

"Isn't this supposed to be a bon voyage dinner and not a lesson in sexology?" she said.

He smiled, "In loveology, you mean."

She giggled as he removed his hold on her thigh. "Hope you didn't bruise me," she said.

"When you see your sister, Una and Paul, tell them I asked about them."

"I wonder how they'll like their new home on Circular Road."

"From the picture you showed me, they must be happy with it."

"Yes, it's a beautiful home. Mammy would have loved it."

"Your mother was a fine lady. I remember the time in her house she opened the bedroom door when we tangled ourselves in the sheets. I thought she'd come in."

Tara smiled in agreement but avoided the issue. "It's a big house, red bricked, four large windows, a large green door with two windows. The gray stone wall...."

"What else in Ireland – either stone upon stone or cement, but a wall in either case...and most of them gray."

"The wall has a four foot hedge behind it."

"I know. I was there. Remember?"

She blinked her eyes, laughing.

The waiter removed their plates. John had eaten every morsel. Tara left vegetables and a partially eaten baked potato.

"John," Dr. Stein said. "There's a spot on my lungs."

He gave her a look as if she were a little girl crying out for someone to help. "When did this develop?"

"They're not sure. He said x-rays showed a dark spot."

"And what does that mean?"

"Cancer's back."

"Why can't God cure you?"

She dropped her eyes, and smiled. She felt a burning sensation in her neck, from the radiation. She spared her husband anxiety and ignored the ache. "The Rosary Novena may help."

"God cured the crippled woman on the Sabbath, and he won't cure you. He called out to the woman, laying his hands on her and said 'Woman, you are free from your sickness. And the woman straightened up immediately.' And he won't cure you."

"That's your seminary days talking. Have faith. Keep praying."

He peered at other waiters moving about the room and other healthy looking couples having dinner. "Is God like Harold Kushner's God – one who doesn't interfere with the natural order of events?"

"I'm not sure that's what Kushner meant."

"Well, not interfering with natural order leaves out miracles and, as Catholics, we believe God performs miracles."

"May not be," she said. "What he meant is God will help those who help themselves, but he will not deal with a physical need. He will help in spiritual needs."

"Is Dr. Stein like Sinclair Lewis' Dr. Martin Arrowsmith?"

"No," she blurted. "Dr. Stein is a knowledgeable man who is interested and cares for his patience. He's not interested in the pure science as Arrowsmith."

He looked up to the ceiling and sighed. "For God's sake…God, do something. Cure Tara."

She patted her stomach. "I'm full."

Instinctively, without regard for people watching him, he patted her breasts. In total surprise, she could do nothing but laugh.

"Well…you said, you're full and I wanted to be sure. You looked full, all right."

He reached across the table and held both her hands in his. They found meaning in each other's teary eyes.

A young, handsome man delivered their car to them. The same young man who parked their car. Getting out of the car, the young curly haired man said, "Hello again, sir, I'm Sean Black."

Taken with the young man's friendliness and ease of manner, John said, "Hi, I'm John O'Malley. And this is my wife, Tara."

"Hi Tara," Black greeted her, extending his hand to shake her hand.

She found courage and comfort in the valet. Is this the meaning of life – to be courageous, youthful, and accept what comes your way…like parking cars? In that brief meeting, she adopted him as a role model, one who looked the world straight in the eye and went forward, no matter what. So shall she, she told herself. She held up three fingers to John who from past experience knew what Tara meant.

Black came quickly around to Tara's side of the car and opened the door for her as she folded into the front seat. "I'm a sophomore at Villanova," he said, hoping to get more than a dollar if she knew he was paying his way through college. She felt she had known Sean a long time.

"Inside the car, John said, "Villanova! I have my M A from VU and my son is a sophomore."

"What's his first name?"

"Enda…."

Sean smiled. His face radiated with warmth.

*At six feet, the young man has success written all over him.*

"I know him. He's a friend of mine."

"My goodness," remarked John.

"Where you from?"

"Massachusetts."

"Where in Massachusetts?"

"Brockton."

"The home of Rocky Marciano," said John. Sean's face opened like a morning glory greeting the sun at John's recognition of where Marciano lived.

"Great fighter."

"Sure." John's tip of five dollars led Sean to believe his working-his-way-through college line had paid off.

Another car pulled up behind them. "We'll tell Enda we met a success story when we talk to him," Tara said, smiling.

"Well, thank you, Mrs. O'Malley…and Mr. O'Malley. Good luck."

They drove off into the night. Tara wondered did Sean Black know she had cancer.

"Nice to know, there are fine young men in this world like Sean Black." Her thoughts wondered onto the message in a Hallmark greeting card, which praised mothers as the person to settle disputes…the family member to create and keep peace…to establish safe feelings of love…the one to cause a deep sense of security…the one to make everyone know they are understood. *Reminds me of a Nelson Rockefeller type. He'll have his face on the front page of Fortune someday.*" Mentioning a magazine prompted her to remember Dr. Stein giving her an article to read by a Dr. Wordsmith who wrote something like, "It's but little good you're doing watering last year's crops." *Exactly what I've seen my patients doing. Worry about things that can never be changed since it's in the past.*" *I better not worry about a disease I already have.* She fought it with modern meds. She remembered what John had told her: worrying is like rocking in a rocking chair and going nowhere.

---

An acorn dropped from an Oak tree, pinging off the Mercury's hood, leaving a pinhole mark. *The car marked for life like the radiation pinhole black marks on my chest.*

# THIRTEEN

# Grotto

She arrived in Ireland on August tenth. Una met her at the airport. After an emotional greeting, they went to Una's room.

A day later Tara, her sister, Una O'Day, and her life-long friend, Margaret White, flew to France, landed outside Lourdes and journeyed by bus to their hotel, the Saint John of Arc. Tara had come essentially to ask Mary to cure her of cancer. *And why won't you, Mary? Besides, I recite your Rosary Novena to honor you as the Mother of God and to request a cure at this place...Well, I'm only asking for a longer life to benefit my husband and children. Please do this for me, Mary? My mother gave me Bernadette for a middle name. I'm the first mother among my friends to contact cancer. I want to live like all my other female friends. But, then again, why should I be any different from the thousands who died in their fifties and sixties?*

The following day, they traveled to Lourdes.

After lunch, they walked along the river road. She marveled at the beauty of the area. The town of Lourdes squeezed between the foot of two mountains, one barren and desolate; the other filtered with a flirtation of greenery but mostly rock-covered. High at the top of a mountain, a symbol of what she carried in her cancer-celled body hovered over her…a cross devoid of the risen Christ. She didn't believe as John did: it wouldn't be long until one of their friends get cancer and dies. She hoped they wouldn't. Her cancer caused her husband to be bitter. She could face it. Her mammy and daddy had given her, brothers, and her sisters an abundance of love and therein happiness and contentment to be at peace with whatever challenges life offered. A Roman aqueduct, she noticed, went straight up one mountain. At the base of the second side of the mountain stood a Gothic white Basilica.

At Mary's Basilica, Tara admired four Gothic spires guarded steps and an elevated arched walkway, which lead into Mary's basilica. A hospital sat adjacent to the base of the walkway. Volunteers cared for the sick while they visited and prayed for a cure. Train tracks ran parallel to the river beside the basilica. In 1854, Mary instructed Bernadette to dig with her fingers. A spring flowed from the good earth and has continued to flow all these years.

The sea of humanity thronged the grounds. A life-sized statue of Mary rested inside a naturally formed opening in a large rock directly along the wall and beside the sanctuary of Mary's basilica. The statue stirred her feelings. Some days she felt like a high-flying hawk soaring into the winds and other days she felt frozen like a statute. Tara viewed crutches left by people who had been miraculously cured and walked away. Candles from an inch to fifty inches burned around the white statue. Mary wore a sky-blue cincture. *Be not afraid for God will strengthen me.*

She believed Mary would provide for her needs and cure her. She believed faith would move mountains. She prayed for an increase in faith and peace of mind. Lourdes had a hold on her, at least the Virgin Mary did. And if she weren't cured…who can argue with God?

Tara, her sister, and her friend went to confession. Tara's English priest advised reading scripture to inspire an increase in faith. She was appalled by the commercialism of Lourdes. So many shops, one duplicating the other, selling medals, statues, rosaries, holy pictures, holy water, mementos of various kinds of trinkets — all unsavory to her. She visualized Jesus casting them out, saying, "My temple will be called a house of prayer for the people of all nations. But you have turned it into a den of thieves."

Nonetheless, she bought a thirty-inch candle for eight dollars to be burnt at the grotto.

Is this what my religion has turned into? She speculated. The buying of holy water and candles to prove you believe? She shook her head in dismay. She whispered to herself a friend's philosophy: *There is so much good in the worst of us. There is so much bad in the best of us. It hardly behooves any of us to talk about the rest of us.*

John whispered, "It's a wonder they don't charge to get in here."

"Shhhh" . . . came the well-known sound of worshipers. Many of those people know the rule of silence.

Sounds of "Shhhh" they heard all over the basilica grounds.

At dinner in the hotel, Tara saw a little boy in a wheelchair. She thanked God no such illness claimed her children...one of her many blessings. She remembered Sean's birth, her first child. She worried he might not be perfect. After several hours of labor, she delivered a beautiful baby boy—in perfect health. She was amazed.

She remembered details of Sean's birth and the entire scenario. In the hospital, at five in the morning, the obstetrician told John to go to school; he didn't expect any activity until late in the day. She gave birth to Sean at 9:30 in the morning. When the doctor called, he advised John to stay in school for she wouldn't be ready for visitors until late afternoon. Twice the doctor was wrong and twice she faulted her husband for not staying in the hospital and for not leaving school immediately upon hearing of Sean's birth. His excuse: he had followed doctor's instructions. "Anyway you should have been there," she said to him occasionally during their marriage.

She studied her sister's face. "Una, did anyone have cancer in our family?"

"I never told you?" Una looked into the bright sunshine. Dropping her eyes in guilt, she wanted to say, "Never any cancer with us," but she said, "Mammy's mother died of cancer."

"What? You never mentioned this."

"We never thought you would get cancer."

"You should have told me. I would have had a mammogram." *How Irish of the Irish not to speak of disease and death. Detecting cancer sooner may have given me a better chance of survival.*

"It didn't seem important."

"Didn't seem important!" Tara felt warm; her blond pressure had gone up.

"I wish you'd told me," Tara said. She didn't want to embarrass her sister further. She changed the subject. Cancer was in the family. One more example of being the baby of the family in an Irish family. *The baby! What did I know? Tell me nothing, but the time of day. How cruel some Irish customs are.*

Walking back to St. Joan of Arc, she recalled Enda's birth. He came on July 21 at 3:30 in the afternoon with John in the waiting room. Labor pains had been fierce. Enda was a beautiful child as were all her children. He weighed seven pounds ten ounces. Having Enda in the middle of a heat wave gave her comfortable relief for her six-day stay in the hospital. *Nowadays, I'd be out in twenty-four hours with the new medical insurance restrictions.*

At night in room twenty-nine – the age when she married – she recalled Maura's birth and how she and John had tried to have a girl. Her doctor told her of a way she might conceive a girl and she wanted to try. John was willing; she knew John was ready at any time, without trying to have a child.

She had instructed John how to do it and one night on the eighty-eight inch sofa, they had intercourse. Elevating himself with his hands higher off her than usual, he penetrated half way. In this manner, the sperms had a longer distance to travel to the egg – the sperms that produce a boy – would die, and the slower moving sperms, the ones to cause a girl, might enter the egg. The procedure seemed to have worked. She became pregnant with Maura.

Maura was her delight, as were her three boys. Her first girl...Maura was marked at birth by forceps, which quickly vanished and far less hair than did Sean and Enda. But Maura was her girl—and she was beautiful.

During that time, life seemed more beautiful until the pediatrician told her he heard a clicking in Maura's hip. After an x-ray, his conclusion: Maura had congenital hip. She remembered how her heart, her spirits sank. The doctor re-assured her Maura's hip would be fine in about two years, if placed in a plastic splint, a diaper-like piece of light plastic with six straps to hold the femur bone in place until the hip socket formed around the femur, locking it in place. If not done, the femur would slide all over the hip joint and as the hip joint matured and grew round, the femur would not be held in place for the hip to enclose it, causing her great difficulties in walking. He told her the splint would immobilize the femur and hold it in a fixed position until the hip joint had fully formed over the femur.

She remembered when she told John. In fact, she didn't have to tell him. When John visited her in the maternity room, tears flowed over her round cheeks. Tara needed his love more than ever.

"The pediatrician told me Maura had congenital hip," she cried.

When she calmed herself, she explained the disease and how it would be treated.

"As long as we know what it is and what to do," John said, "we'll all be fine."

"I cried all day, John."

"I love you, Tara," he said, embracing her.

"I love you, John," she said, hugging him tightly.

"You are everything to me, Tara. Without you, I am nothing."

"With you, I am everything, too, John."

They held their embrace in the purest form as two married people could ever appreciate each other in the spiritual sense. Both John and she cried. They remained so in silence, a meaningful silence husbands and wives understood. She called on the Blessed Mother to help them.

Finally, he said, "Is the doctor sure?"

"He is."

"I mean – how can he be sure?"

"John, I heard the clicking in Maura's hip."

"Shouldn't we get a second opinion?"

"No . . . Well, the obstetrician called in Dr. Cardio, a pediatrician, not long before you came."

"He agreed?"

"Yes. He said congenital hip."

John looked at her in one of those understanding looks. "We will stand together in this." A look in which they had often communicated – not with words, but with their eyes. Their eyes spoke, reflecting their minds and hearts, one of the ways married couples communicate. Nonverbal communication they developed over the years. Open with each other, they often revealed their feelings through their eyes. They embraced again, patting each other's back. In his sorrow, he recalled someone saying, "Those in power, write the history. Those who suffer, write the songs." He didn't feel like writing a song.

During visiting hours, Peter Coulter arrived. Peter, a heavy man, let his once trim athletic body inflate to 250 pounds, one hundred pounds more than he weighed when he played for LaSalle University's baseball team. Solemnly, he said, "I expected you two to be overjoyed with a girl."

They looked up. Tara held her hand up to greet Peter's hand. He must have thought she needed a hug and he hugged her as John concurrently shook hands. A threesome of harmony in sorrow.

"You haven't heard. . . " Tara said, "No, how could you."

"Maura has congenital hip," John uttered.

"Oh my God...Paula's niece had that in her family."

"I know what it is. Don't be upset. Its' treatable."

They studied Peter's expression. He appeared to understand the diagnosis and treatment for congenital hip.

John had yet to know about the plastic splint. Tara explained briefly the procedures John had to follow in changing Maura's diapers.

"Simple enough," he said, trying to smile.

"Really," Peter encouraged. "It is treatable and correctible."

Tara felt relieved another human being understood. This helped to alleviate their emotional stress.

Peter sat in a chair at the end of the bed as John held Tara in his arms. Finding strength to continue with their lives, and to inject some humor to help them through this sad situation, John said, "See Tara's black negligee. The doctor told Tara by wearing a sexy thing, she'd be back here again."

"I think," said Peter, "you should remember great faith is often built during great trials." John and Tara looked at each other in disbelief that such profound advice came from Peter, a man, they suspected, of little faith.

Peter laughed. They joined Peter in soft laughter. Like a bee looking for its honey, Paula Coulter, Peter 's ex-wife, entered the room, carrying a small baby shoe ornament filled with flowers. When she saw Peter she said, "You'd think . . . oh... I followed you." She did not established eye contact with her ex-husband." Peter visited me today with my alimony and told me he planned to come here."

"And you followed me, " Peter commented.

"Did not, you goat."

Paula made her remark with a smile. They remained on cordial terms since their divorce and annulment, a Catholic synonym for divorce. Tara never understood annulments. What God has joined together let no man put asunder, was her belief.

Paula offered her sympathy and support when she heard about their child's hip. "Whatever I can do, I will do."

"We know, Paula. You've been a good friend."

"You'd think," Peter began, "after ten years, two children, and plenty of alimony, Paula would offer sympathy to me."

She said, "I'll take your money and give you token sympathy."

"Ah, at least, I get sympathy. Since you didn't say 'no sympathy' I still have hope."

"Don't hold your breath," retorted Peter's ex-wife. "As the O'Malley's might say, Peter: hump off."

The Coulters had been married for five years and had two children. She divorced him and gained an annulment. The Church Tribunal granting annulment circumvented the true issue, Tara believed. Besides losing an unwanted husband, Paula and Peter an unwanted wife, they grew apart.

Tara knew Peter and Paula had not slept together the last two years of their marriage when finally Paula decided to divorce him. Prior to the divorce, Tara heard both complain about their marriage and they tried to explain why it went sour. A complain and explain syndrome. *Funny, how people like us, never say how good their marriage is and how people in unhappy marriages are always complaining how bad theirs is. The good ones are silent. Bad ones complain.*

---

The second day at Lourdes, they again walked through the commercialized area of what she had imagined to be a completely holy place and not a place of employment for hundreds of native people. Margaret and she desired to enter the baths. Una did not believe in outward display of religious faith. To Una, religion seemed to be an inner journey through life. Her faith was personal and private. She did not believe a person had to go to Lourdes to seek a cure, rather a person should pray privately for a cure. But, if her sister wanted to go to Lourdes, she agreed to accompany her ill sister.

Una waited outside the bath while Margaret and Tara entered the enclosed room where they disrobed. Attendants placed a towel around them and they waited in a queue for their time to emerge into the elongated bath filled with dirty water, partially from other people's body oil. Tara marveled how people didn't get sick from the dirty water. An aide helped them into and out of the baths – all in about one minute. Dressing and leaving the baths, Margaret said, "Is that all there is?"

"Peggy Lee sang that song," Tara quipped.

"And the church frowned on it."

"Yes. It expressed pagan philosophy," Tara replied.

"People in the Church thought so. I didn't," Margaret said.

Rejoining Una on one of the many benches used by people to sit and meditate as they prayed to the Virgin Mary, Tara noticed a small boy in a wheelchair. The boy resembled Thaddeus, her youngest child. She thanked God for her four children's health, including Maura whose hip joint had completely encircled the femur bone and Maura walked like any other young person.

She recalled the day Thaddeus was born, Wednesday, January 23, 1974, wondering why at Lourdes she relived all four of their births. John had arrived at school around eight in the morning and the principal greeted him. "John, your wife called. She's ready to go to the hospital. She wants you to come home." John came home to find Tara throwing up. He took Maura to a neighbor's house. He tided the house, as Tara got ready. She had her first heavy showing of blood an hour earlier. Around nine, they went to friends' homes to leave clothing for Sean and Enda who had gone to school. Behind a snowplow for one half block, John grew impatient and swiftly passed it and traveled on Street Road, a main artery. They arrived at the hospital at five to ten, the same time Maura had been born, also on Wednesday.

John sat in the father's waiting room for a while. He saw Tara walking around, trying in her strides to bring on labor.

John went to lunch at 12:30 while Tara waited in the labor room. It was a bright, spring-like day with a blue sky. With a temperature of fifty degrees, an atypical winter day.

John planned to go into the delivery room with Tara, but when he saw the agonizing pain she experienced, he grew pale and began to sweat. "I don't need another patient on the floor, Mr. O'Malley," the doctor said, "You better leave."

He protested – weakly.

"You better leave and wait outside, You're not going to make it. Tara will, but you won't."

The encouragement John needed. He left the room and waited in the father's room. *If men had babies, there might be one child in each family. And men call themselves the stronger sex* he thought.

Tara was induced at quarter past one. She had severe pain on her left side. John wanted to re-enter the delivery room to console her but the nurse didn't permit it. Thaddeus was born at 2:19 in the afternoon. Both worried for Thaddeus' health, especially after Maura's congenital hip. Her lightest baby at six pounds, thirteen ounces, Thaddeus' birth, she fantasized, caused a weather change, for the sky became cloudy and threatened rain. The first person, John thought of ringing…God to thank him for a healthy baby. John then rang his brother, Daniel.

"Dan, congratulate me."

"What did you have?" queried Dan. *Imagine 'what did he have' as if I went through all the pain.*

"A boy. He looks like me."

"What else," Dan said.

John visited the chapel to thank God for the safe delivery of their healthy baby boy.

"Tara," Una interrupted Tara's thoughts. "It's a good time to start back for dinner."

"The meals are good enough," remarked Margaret.

"I'm ready. Let's go."

"You're pensive, Tara."

"Oh, Margaret, I thought about John and me – and the children."

"Now, don't think you won't be here."

"That's what I thought."

"You'll be here," encouraged Margaret.

In full view of the basilica, she jeered, "Don't hold your breath."

She feared she might not be here when John became a published writer. She remembered the good night prayer with the kids, "Dear God, let daddy be happy and successful" and hoped it would come true, but she wondered would she be around to enjoy it with him? She speculated if he would enjoy recognition without her. She hoped he would.

———————

Soon after Tara arrived home from Dublin and Lourdes, she rang Dr. Johnson and Dr. Stein for appointments.

Scheduled for five in the afternoon not to interfere with her work schedule, she ventured to the radiologist's office in the same building as Dr. Stein. The radiologist, Dr. Johnson, gave her x-rays to take to Dr. Stein.

"Congratulations, Mrs. O'Malley the spot on your lung has disappeared."

*Disappeared? Thank God. Thanks Mary.* "That's great news, Dr. Johnson. I'll go right up to show Dr. Stein. He'll be delighted."

The radiologist smiled and shook Tara's hand.

She burst into Dr. Stein's office. Her heart beat faster. She dropped the x-ray folder twice on the way to the second floor. Out of character for her to be emotional. *But why not, it's my life.*

Checking in with the receptionist, she said, unruffled, "I'm back from France and I feel fine. Dr. Johnson said my lungs are clear."

"Thata girl," uttered the receptionist.

Tara smiled. "Dr. Stein will be happy with this news."

"Sure will." The girl reached over the counter and hugged Tara. "We love you."

"Hello Tara," Dr. Stein extended his hand. "How was Lourdes?" He mispronounced the word in the plural.

Graciously, she ignored the mistake. "You'll see the results," she said, pointing to the x-ray copy.

They entered a small cubicle examining room. It had a polychromatic setting: fresh yellow and purple tulips in a mini vase, decorated in brown, white, orange, a small photo of Boathouse Row. Out the window on Bustleton Avenue, Tara viewed cars halted at a traffic light. A red pick-up truck dashing to make the green light and turning left on a red light edged pass a town car slightly bumping its front. The driver of the town car got out of his car and, though she could not hear his words, she knew he screamed by facial expressions and obscene gestures. Road rage, the newest rage in America. Why couldn't people know life proved too short to be angry over a simple thing as a near traffic mishap? *Are people like me, people dying from a disease like cancer, the only ones who understand the value of life?* She wished people would be wiser like the young doctor who experienced a life-threatening accident on the Schuylkill Expressway. His compact car crushed between two tractor-trailers, yet he was uninjured. He told the press, "Your time could be up in a second. Don't take it for granted."

"What have we here?" questioned the oncologist.

She handed him the x-ray and he placed it against the viewer.

"My...My. What have we here?" he repeated.

They looked at each other with joy in their eyes. He continued, "I should say what do we not have here."

"I thought you'd like it."

"I'm overjoyed. There's nothing on your lung."

"Absolutely."

"I can't account for this."

"I can," Tara replied.

"How's that."

"Before I left for Lourdes, I told you I'd take the matter to the Virgin Mary."

"And you did?"

"I know you don't believe this, Dr. Stein."

She paused. Her corneas enlarged. Dr. Stein noticed her beautiful seagreen eyes.

"Go on," he urged.

"I believe the Blessed Mother cured me."

"Something happened. If the spot grew, you might not be around much longer."

"Well, Mary did it."

"All I know is before you left for Lourdes, the spot was there. Now, there is nothing showing on the x-ray and how this happened I cannot medically explain."

"I told you how, " she said. "A miracle performed by Our Lady."

"Your trip did you good," he responded. "Your spirits seem higher."

"I will live after all," said she.

"You're a strong woman, Tara," said he.

Mary answered and gave me renewed energy. I hope it doesn't come back.

*And I thank you, Mary, for my Four Green Fields.*

# FOURTEEN

# Racism

The celebration of renewed faith for a longer life verified the importance of living. Tara decided to buy a new suit after work. At the Hallow Hills Mall, she parked at Strawbridge's, tried on several suits and settled on a Leslie Fay, sized petite eight. She selected a yellow jacket matched with a black skirt. A stylish suit for the fall season. A black sales girl assisted customers. The girl was amicable, knowledgeable, and serviceable. Two customers were discussing the sales girl in soft undertones. When people often criticize or character assassinate, they do it in undertones. They don't have the courage to ridicule a person to their face. They hide behind their own inferiority and blast another's character.

The tall lady said, "What do you think of that Black bitch salesgirl?"

"They shouldn't have hired her. This is a white store."

"I'm not prejudice," said the short lady.

"Nor am I," agreed the tall lady.

"I," continued the taller lady, "feel more comfortable being with my own kind."

"They don't. They want to move into our areas."

The salesgirl approached them. "May I help you?" she asked with a broad smile.

"No thank you, dear," the taller lady said with her best hypocritical smile.

As the pleasant salesgirl walked off, the same lady mimicked, "No, thank you, blackie." She spoke in a hushed voice. When Tara heard the lady, she knew the woman didn't belong in a store like Strawbridge's, nor in the human race.

The shorter lady giggled. "I lived in the city. I moved to get away from the Blacks."

"They used to be called Negroes."

"What's the difference? They're still Black and black is the absence of white."

Tara imagined them to be characters from *Mississippi Burning*. She fingered more suits, but could not be silent any longer. "You ladies should know my neighbors are Black and better neighbors I could not have." *These two ladies moved backwards in their journey through life.*

They glared at Tara. She noted their mouths and eyes wide open. Tara went on, "That girl is a pleasant person with a pleasing personality. What difference does it make what color she is?"

"We're talkin,' muttered the short lady.

"I didn't want to interfere, but someone should remind you . . ."

The taller lady interrupted her. "We weren't talking to you," she snapped, with hostility in her eyes.

"Someone," Tara continued, "should remind you of Christian charity."

"Well...of all the nerve . . ." the short lady began.

"Of all the nerve is right," Tara stated. "We're all human beings."

"Mind your own business, lady," the tall lady flared.

"Have a good day, ladies," Tara remarked, turning towards the salesgirl. Like shoppers in motion with the rhyming cash registers jingling up sales, people moved in unison amidst the pronging of "attention please" announcements, the pinging of high heels clicking across the tile floor, and the mumbling of shoppers' voices. The two ladies faded into the bigotry of white America's historiography. Outside, Tara admired the purplish-green and yellow-gold colors of the rainbow, a sign of hopefulness in a world too often filled with hopelessness. *Here, I'm trying to soar above cancer and its stresses, and, yet, these women are content to live inside their narrow-minded hopeless prejudices and descend into the bowels of Mother Earth.*

# FIFTEEN

# Humble in Spirit

With frigid temperatures outside and warm feelings inside her, she lay in warm water in the tub. She pushed the day's problems out of her head and, splashing water over her body, she began whispering to herself…a habit she developed in youth. Talking to herself gave Tara the opportunity to straighten out the day and ease herself into the family routine of peaceful night activities. She relished locking the world out of her life once she came home, opening the door to family life.

With the bathroom door locked, she guaranteed herself privacy – as long as John didn't pick the lock by placing a paperclip in the minuscule opening, breaking her moments of reprieve. She wished he would stop invading her privacy. She gave herself sound advice in her bathroom conversations.

On occasions, John would press his ear against the door and listen to her soliloquy – as he called her private conversation.

Out of the bath, she sat on the edge of the bed. She observed the sun's rays illuminating the blue sky and spotlighting fast moving and wind blown clouds. The sky opened up into a majestic child's fairyland of stately beauty and peace, a storyland that holds one in sacred inner peace, peace within one's self. Puttering through drawers, she found an old school autograph book. Having read one poem, she read through the autographs and read what her former classmates had written. One of those experiences in life, when, finding notes on photographs from the past, one felt compelled to continue reading and viewing pictures. Like eating cashews or Carmel-coated popcorn – once started, you can't stop.

That's what the notes were…poems…from classmates. She wondered what kind of lives they lead…and hoped they found happiness and contentment.

She began to read:

*Fun and carefree we were.*

*Irresponsible days were they.* One boy wrote in her autograph book:

"Folks would think it naughty.

But I should think it fine, if I could press my lips to yours, and you press yours to mine."

How giddy I was and I didn't like that boy.

Tara took delight in Roberta's work:

"Friends are like books. How e'er they are dressed.

The new ones are good, but the old ones are best."

Maeve's thoughts saddened her:

"When twilight draws its curtain and pins it with a star

Think of me, dear milady

though I be afar."

*I never again saw Maeve. She went to England, married, and died in her early fifties. Cancer.*

Padriac's poem brought back happy memories of her mother who died at sixty-eight with Sean at nine months sitting on her hospital bed in Dublin. Her mother was a strong-willed woman and she waited to see her first American-born grandson before she died. When she saw Sean on the bed, she said, "He's a lovely little fella." *A strong character, my mother, and that's what I must be.* "As you thinketh, so you are," said Earl Nightingale.

Her own poem refreshed her beliefs in her country's efforts and, in particular, her father's. She read aloud:

"De Valera had a cat.

It sat upon the fender,

and every time it wagged its tail, it cried out, 'No surrender.'"

*What a sense of humor.*

Another girl wrote:

"He kissed me on the garden path.

My mother heard the *smack*.

She said I was a naughty-girl, and made me give it back."

She picked up Aileen's poem. *An insight into my future:*

"A hundred years before today,

When wilderness was here,

The man with powder in his gun,

Went forth to hunt the 'deer.'

"But now also the times have changed.

They are on a different plan.

The 'deer' with powder on her nose

Goes forth to hunt her man."

*Instead of hunting for my man, I found my man at Drexelbrook — a serendipity experience, one that made all the difference.* As she remembered Robert Frost's "The Road Not Taken"—symbolic of John and all the differences that road made.

She humored herself by reading Shamus' good-bye wishes:

"There was a young girl from Paris who thought that her covers were too few.

She walked out of doors with a fig leaf – no more and now she's in bed with the flu."

John came upstairs to check on her health. Usually, by this time, they watched the evening news together.

"What's up, Tara?"

"Oh, you know what it's like when you find old school letters," she quipped.

"Must be good by the sound of you."

"Listen to this," she said. "Bridget wrote it."

"The night was dark and stormy
and the Billy goat was blind;
he bumped into a fence
and scratched his... never mind."

"We were all silly."

"Come on down. I miss you."

"I'll be there in a few minutes," she said.

She enjoyed the play on words in the next poem:

"A flea and a fly in a flu
were imprisoned so what could they do.
Said the flea, "Let us fly."
Said the fly, "Let us flee."
So they flu through a flow in the flu."

She giggled when she read Marie's poem:

"When Tara was a little girl,
she was fond of toys,
but now there is nothing in her head,
but boys, boys, boys."

*I couldn't wish for more. It's a wonder, I didn't have a dozen.*

She replaced the small book in the top drawer and went downstairs.

Before she fell asleep, she relived the sixteen consecutive years they spent on holidays for three to five days in Ocean City, New Jersey. They had stayed in motels like the Impala, StingRay (now the Beach Club), Port-o-Call and the Sands. Buying a home and furnishing it proved to be a heavy burden during their early years so they delayed their first vacation by four years.

During those family vacations, they ate in restaurants for breakfast and dinner and lunched on hot dogs or pizza on the Twelfth Street beach. Staying in beachfront motels allowed them easy access to boardwalk amusements and restaurants and therein John had an additional vacation of not driving from place to place, though he enjoyed driving.

Their early vacations were shared with Sean and Edna. In a short time, Maura and Thaddeus had arrived. John claimed it his vacation too – and his idea of a vacation with her was in bed. How typical of him. When possible, they sent the children to the boardwalk immediately after dinner and they stayed in the room and made love. John termed these experiences "quickies." She feared one of the children coming back and finding them.

Their routine, she remembered, with nostalgia: up early to ride bicycles, breakfast, beach, lunch, brief naps (more for them than the children), dinner, amusements on the boardwalk and exhaustive sleep. They had true family oriented holidays, not a lover's holiday. Whatever time they managed for lovemaking had been stolen moments in the late afternoon. Thoughts of the boardwalk reminded her of the time at the Jersey shore when she had told John he was like an alarm clock: once wound up he wouldn't stop.

One morning, biking on the boardwalk resulted in John's going to Shore Memorial Hospital. They rode individual bikes. John rode with Maura on a three-wheeler with a canopy. They steered into the railing and John gashed his leg. A four-inch opening required stitches. He grew faint and she notified the police who took him to the hospital for treatment. In Ireland, bicycling was a means of transportation for Tara during her school days. She liked to bicycle home for lunch on occasions and, when she did, she latched on to the side of the green double-decker bus and let it glide her to South Circular Road. Not to ride bikes in the morning at the shore was unthinkable. It was a vacation ritual.

One of their favorite breakfast places was Olga's Restaurant on Central Avenue near Ninth Street. Not cooking any meals was part of the vacation. The amusements had been the highlight of the night with the beach and ocean taking the essence of daylight. The merry-go-round their favorite, the operator filled a wooden 'arm' with large, metal rings and as the kids and John – in heart John was a kid – reached out for a ring as the merry-go-round revolved. The person who snatched the silver ring received another ride – free. They enjoyed it as Tara relished watching.

As the children grew up and left home, their special vacations ceased. Change is part of life. All things pass and all things change. Tara had hoped she'd be like her mammy and daddy and enjoy forty-three years of a happy marriage. In stage three of breast cancer, her outlook for a long life appeared dismal. *But I've had a happy marriage. For the unhappily married life had to be tortuous.*

The lady she met shopping related her happy marriage was too short. When her husband died, she had been married sixty-three years. *That fortunate woman will beat me by about thirty years.* She kept asking, seeking, knocking – and the door will be opened to her... please God. The Biblical woman who bled for twelve years had nothing on her. She came up from behind Jesus and touched His cloak. The woman said to herself, "If I touch his cloak, I will get well." And Jesus told her, "Courage, my daughter! Your faith has made you well." Tara's faith was as strong as that woman's.

*Funny thing about faith, prayer, God, and God's mercy.* Unlike John, she didn't question God.

Tara wondered what was the age of the bleeding woman when she finally died? She understood John wondered if life seemed worth living when after living happily with a person for years the wife dies and you end up lonely, depressed, and desperate for many years? *Better to have loved and lost, than not to have loved at all.* For John, she prayed for him to understand. Her remaining days would be easier if he could accept her death. She reasoned how she could murmur dejectedly because she had cancer, got a bad deal, when she was blessed with the gifts of a loving husband and fine children.

# SIXTEEN

# Under the Boardwalk

About to fall asleep one night, John said to Tara, "Let's go to the shore."

"Shore. What are you – a mind reader?"

"Why?"

"Reminiscing about our Ocean City days as a family."

"What?"

"Well, how's this sound?" he rolled over, his arm around her.

"That's good—hold me."

"I love you. To touch you is to love you," said he, coupling his left hand over her right breast.

"Here we go again."

"Tara, let's relive our shore days by going to Ocean City this weekend – the two of us, for old times sake."

"You want to relive what can't be relived."

"I know, Tara. But let's go to the Impala and . . .have a kind of honeymoon."

"You don't need to go to Ocean City. You have too many honeymoons in this bedroom."

He chuckled. "The Irish sense of humor. I mean, let's be adventurous."

"It's out of season and chilly."

"For us...always in season."

"Ugh, oh, something's up."

"You're right about that," he said, pressing against her. She felt him.

"What do you have in mind, if I didn't know," she snickered.

"Let's go to the beach at night, with no one there, hide under the boardwalk and make love."

"You're sick."

He chuckled. "No...I'll make a deal with you."

"Some deal, I bet...."

"Here's the deal," he stated. "Make love under the boardwalk and we'll go to the Showboat in Atlantic City and you entertain yourself at the poker machines."

"And you'll go to the Irish Pub?"

" Right."

"I can't wait."

The weekend arrived and they drove to Ocean City having made arrangements for their children.

Is it my imagination John seems to be driving extra fast?

They registered at the Impala and began to walk the boards. As darkness descended over the city like an angel of mercy, illuminated by the boardwalk overhead lamps, John nudged Tara toward the steps to the beach. Like kids, they looked for anyone watching them. Undetected, they slipped under the boardwalk with their blanket. John assisted Tara in disrobing.

"It's too chilly to take off all my clothes."

"Take everything off from the waist down. So will I."

"What if someone sees us?"

Breathing heavily he said, "No one will."

On the blanket, Tara complained, "Sand. There's sand on me."

"Forget it," John said. "We're on the beach you know."

He attempted to kiss her, but stopped abruptly. "There's sand in my mouth."

She repeated his comment. "We're on the beach, you know."

"Hurry before we get sand covered."

He cleared his lips of sand. Waves crashed on the beach. "Listen to the magnificent liquid thunder."

"Yes. It's simply mesmerizing." She smelled the salt air, tasting sand on her lips. A full moon and high tide pulled the water close to them. She touched John's salty lips with her finger.

"We're not here to listen to the ocean smashing ashore."

She uttered softly, "But doesn't it add to a romantic get-away?"

"Yes. Now concentrate on romance"

"We're also here to go to Showboat."

He became rough and aggressive. "Don't man-handle me. Take it easy."

"How can I take it easy when I'm excited, have sand all over my body . . . oh God."

"What?"

"I must have emitted. Sand's all over me."

She laughed, softly at first, then uncontrollably. Sand caught in the beams of the boardwalk fell through the board openings and sprayed on top of them. Caught up in the incongruity of the situation, he joined in the frivolity. They lay together sprinkled with sand, half-clothed, but without achieving his goal.

"Well," she uttered between out burst of laughter, "Let's go to Showboat and see if I can achieve my goal."

"Some honeymoon," he moaned.

She heard waves crashing onto the beach. *A wave once broken will never be whole again in the same shape, like snowflakes—no two are alike. Our lifelong wave won't break.*

---

As fall turned into winter, winter to spring, Tara continued living a scheduled life. *Life must go on.* She drove on Bristol Road to her job. Like any cancer patient, she longed to live. It made no difference where one traveled or how much money one had or the size or elegance of a person's home. What did matter: the state of happiness in which one lived. Happiness and health made all the difference in one's life. Happiness she had; health she didn't. She didn't mourn the loss of a dream; she mourned the lost of oneness they will lose. *Before 1988, I had both. But in 1988, I saw Dr. Stein several times for check-ups after the lump in my breast had been removed along with thirteen lymph nodes. In 1991, at fifty-seven, I have no sign of cancer and I feel good overall. My weight needs to decrease. At 150, I have gained twenty-six pounds over my wedding day weight of 124. But being tall, my body assimilated the extra pounds and I appear well proportioned.*

Under Dr. Stein's care, she continued taking medications: Voltaren, Przax, Synthroid, Lanoxin, Lasix, and Nolvadex along with vitamins and minerals.

Nonetheless, she planned to return to Ireland in the summer to visit her two sisters and two brothers. It would be her ninth trip home since her marriage. John encouraged her to go home to be around family and build up psychological and emotional strength. He thought it good therapy. Her sister Una didn't agree with Tara's working full-time. Una believed working gave unnecessary stress to Tara who would do better without the work environment. But

Una's thinking ran counter to her doctors' advice that working in a job she loved would aid her fight against cancer. John supported the idea of Tara working. And this caused friction between John and his sister-in-law, Una, who told John, "You should discourage her from working. You might be sending her to an early death." In every family, there is at least one thorn—and Una pricked him like a thorn.

Instead of causing a row, John had remained calm and quiet and simply stated, "Doctors believe that working will help Tara. It takes her mind off cancer. And she loves being administrator of Summit Personal Care as well as owner and administrator of her own personal care home."

Bloodlines are strong but marriage vows are stronger. Tara followed her own wisdom and decided to continue working.

---

John said to her about her frequent trips, "You get all the holidays and trips. It's about time I go with you to Ireland."

He spoke without malice. He wanted her cured and maintained going to Ireland advantageous for her health.

"You can come, too," she replied.

"How can I? I have school and my summer job."

"I won't go."

"No, Tara. I want you to go, but I'd like to go with you."

"You go, and I'll stay home." She didn't mean those words. She had tried to placate her husband with kindness. Like a woman far from her homeland, she longed to be in Ireland with her sisters and brothers. Ireland for her was what purring is for her kitties, Pushky and Daddle: her essence. *You can't go home again is not always a true statement.*

"What would I do in Ireland without you, and with your family?"

She loved him saying, 'without you.' "I won't go, if that's what you want."

"No, I'm sorry," said he, "you know I want you to go home. We can't afford the airfare for both of us."

# SEVENTEEN

# An Irish Story

Her weekday drive to her office along Bristol Road was a scenic wonderland—civilization hadn't yet destroyed it. A fence of mighty cloud formation surrounded a farmhouse high upon a hill. A wavy mountain of Evergreens and shrubs framed the house in its natural grip. She imagined it could be Heathcliff's house in *Wuthering Heights*. When she entered her office, a resident gave her a caricature of herself in action, his birthday gift to her as she turned fifty-seven this day, May 26.

The resident called it, "Birthdays are special. The colonel's daughter."

"Thank you very much. You've made my day," said she to the eighty-two-year-old artist.

She greeted Eleanor and remembered her secretary's thoughtless remark. *"She won't live long anyway."* Her spirits dropped whenever she unwittingly remembered those words. Strong willed, she dismissed the thought and told herself to brighten up.

Opening the mail, she had an encouraging letter from one of her resident's daughter who also battled cancer.

Leaning on the desk, she read: "Greetings and how are you? I think you will remember me. My name is Ruth Roisman. We have spoken on many occasions. On two of my visits to my mother, I noticed you were not present – unusual. I spoke to Eleanor who told me you had gone to your oncologist for late afternoon visits. Hope I am not intruding and you are feeling better. Thought a little encouragement might be good for you."

"You see, back in 1979, I had a bilateral mastectomy followed by radiation therapy and one year of chemotherapy at Sloan Kettering Memorial and continued to go there for semi-annual visits and checkups. That year of chemotherapy passed quickly and I worked four days a week. I know how tired you must be, but hang in there and, before you know it, the year will be over. If I can do it, you can."

"Tara, I hope you are doing well and I will see you soon."

"Take care and be strong. I know you will be."

---

After reading the letter, Tara felt more spirited. She knew from adversity came success. Cancer wasn't the problem. Attacking the problem was. And she felt comfortable in how she planned to defeat the disease. Many people supported her since being diagnosed with breast cancer in 1988, a year after buying O'Shea Personal Care. She whispered a prayer to the Virgin Mary for continued good health for Ruth Roisman. She vowed to include Ruth and her mother that night in her Rosary Novena prayers.

Harry, a resident, stood in the doorway and announced, "Mrs. O'Malley, have you heard George Bush is running again for President."

She looked up from her desk. "I've heard, Harry."

"He won't win this time. That younger feller will."

"Clinton might. But I don't like his stand on abortion."

"Well, to many people, abortion is not an issue," said the man.

"Inter-resting," she smiled. I suppose it's better to follow the advice of the friend, who said, "There's so much good in the worst of us and so much bad in the best of us it hardly behooves any of us to talk about the rest of us."

"I'm too old to take one side or the other."

"Never too old, Harry," she smiled.

As he walked away, he said, "Just the same, Clinton will win the White House."

The remaining mail sat on her desk. She needed a break. She advised Eleanor she would return after making her daily check of the facility. She made a mental note to go to O'Shea Personal Care after work to do the same thing and to re-assure an Alzheimer resident she lived in a safe environment.

On her tour, she encountered several residents. Henrietta mistakenly called her Marge. Sarah had wet the bed through to the mattress and Roland complained about the menu being boring – par for the course, a scenario in keeping with daily living adventures with residents at Summit.

Back in her office, she continued sorting the mail, returning telephone calls, listening to more residents' complaints. She had the humane capacity to deal fairly with situations that needed her attention with residents' concerns and needs. In their lonely lives, residents wanted someone to listen to their concerns and to give the feeling someone cared for them. Many of their children and relatives no longer cared. Placed in Summit and virtually forgotten. Once they had their own homes, families, health, freedom to come and go. Now, they no longer owned homes and had little contact from family members who occasionally brought them to their homes for dinner, only to rush them back to Summit or O'Shea's. They were in poor health. Many used walkers or canes and didn't know where they were. They had become shut-ins. Freedom…never again would they have. From all they once possessed, life reduced and downsized them to owning a few items of clothing for daily use, a comfort chair or a small television set. Tara tried to fill their modest needs with love and attention, a motto she expected the staff to fulfill as well. *Resignation to the will of God is best.*

At times in her work, she felt a tinge of guilt for she received payment for the work she loved. But residents received nothing but whatever love they could find in the facility. Her job was a mission; she made it her mission in life to make happy those unhappy or those who mourn the loss of a life they want to live again. A resident's pain of loss was never again seeing the lifestyle he or she once lived in freedom and health. She attempted to instill in residents a sense of inner peace, which she had in her personal life. Living an active life in good health and living life in poor health in a personal care home are heterogeneous to gender.

Eleanor excused herself and said, "Tara, there's a Mrs. Gail Riggs here to see you. Her mother is one of our residents."

"Of course. Show her in." Tara got up and as Mrs. Riggs came forward, Tara walked around her desk and greeted the lady.

"I'm Gail Riggs, Mrs. O'Shea. My mom is here."

"Yes. Your mother is a fine lady. She smiles a lot." Tara knew the mother as one of the most pleasant people in the home. Riggs told Tara her mother sold her home, didn't want to live with any of her children to maintain her independence and decided to come to Summit after meeting Tara. Riggs liked her clear, precise Dublin accent, a selling point.

"Mom is happy here, especially since she has her car and can go and come when she pleases."

"I'm glad of that. Inter-resting,"

Mrs. Riggs wanted to change the subject. "I came in to see you to tell you a story, which might interest you since you're from Ireland."

"Yes. I was born and raised in Dublin. Came here at twenty four."

They sat. Tara felt comfortable with Mrs. Riggs. After all, she started the conversation by mentioning Ireland. Tara's secretary served tea, a practice Tara instigated when she became administrator.

Mrs. Riggs noticed the four pictures on the administrator's desk. "Your children?"

"Yes, I have three boys and a girl."

"The boys are handsome and your daughter is beautiful – all with red hair."

"Thank you. This is Sean," said she pointing to her son in a full front view picture. "And this is Enda in the cap and gown. Maura is our daughter. Thaddeus is my youngest."

"Enda and Thaddeus look like brothers all right."

"They look like my father. Sean is a cross between John, my husband, and my father. Maura resembles Sean."

"A gorgeous family."

Tara smiled a thank you look.

"Well, I came in here to tell you a story you might find interesting. It is about my sister and how she met her husband in Ireland and fell in love instantly."

*The same as John and me.* "My husband and I had a similar experience."

Gail Riggs began her narration. She leaned on the desk, her face pinned to Tara's gaze as if transfixed by her radiance. "A friend of mine, Nora, went to Ireland, England, and Paris on her vacation last year. Ireland...her last stop. She had two days in Ireland. The first day there, the tour brought them to Limerick. Sitting in Dirty Nellie's pub, having a chardonnay with people on the tour, this man Ted came in, saw her and instantly felt strongly attracted to her. He told me he had fallen in love with Nora at first sight. Imagine, he hadn't spoken to her."

"Yes, with John and me, it wasn't love at first sight." Tara smiled. "But we had a lengthy conversation first."

"This man, Ted, told her he wanted to talk with her but she was in the middle of a crowd. His friends managed to tug him away as they had other plans in other places. He left knowing he would see her again. Later that night, Ted went to Ryan's Hotel and there she was."

"What's to be will be," Tara interjected. "Is that it?"

Riggs nodded approvingly. "Ted approached her, bought her a drink and spent several hours in conversation. He told her he loved her. Nora in turn said 'You're crazy.' She didn't know him. He told her the more he saw and spoke to her, the stronger his feelings."

She paused, tittered, and said, "It must have been like a love fairy sprinkling love dust over them, at least over him. He hadn't yet asked her to marry him."

"A surprise," Tara said, with a twinkle in her eye, "considering they'd known each other several hours."

"Possible," Riggs laughed. "It's possible."

"Ted told her again he loved her and she didn't know what to say. She saw him again the next evening, her last night in

Ireland. He escorted her to the airport. The attendant in the duty free section observed them saying goodbye. 'I must see you again,' Ted said, 'How can you?' Nora replied. He said, 'I can and I will,' his eyes beaming at her. Her eyes filled with wonderment."

"'You'll see her again,' the attendant said, observing how they looked at each other. Well, low and behold, didn't he come to America to see her. Nora had given Ted her address and phone number in Jim Thorp, where she was staying with her aunt. After ringing her twice a day for a week, he showed up at her house unannounced. When she saw him at the door, she wanted to run away, far away. Her aunt told her she was confused and didn't want to face the situation head-on."

"Good advice from the aunt," Tara said sipping her tea, as Mrs. Riggs extended her narration.

"In the first week in Jim Thorp, he asked Nora to marry him."

"And…?" Tara wondered.

"Nora wanted to say yes, but was fearful. She didn't want to make a mistake. But Ted persisted and after two weeks, she said yes. Ted wanted to play it the old fashioned way and visited her parents to ask for her hand in marriage. Her mother said, 'Whatever I say will make no difference. I see it in your eyes when I saw the way you looked at Nora. So good luck.' Her father wished them the best and the wedding took place nine weeks later."

"And why not? John and I have had great success in our marriage, but John never asked my parents for permission to marry me."

"He didn't?"

"No, my dad had died and my mother lived in Dublin. John wrote to mammy and said he loved me and would take care of me, but he never asked."

Riggs sipped tea and noticed a wall-framed picture of Dublin city. "I like this picture."

"Where I grew up," Tara responded.

"Eighty people walked from Our Lady of Help Church near her parent's house for the reception. They began their honeymoon...much later that summer."

"They cruised to the Bahamas."

"John and I," Tara began, beaming with nostalgia, "had our honeymoon in Ireland and London. But, like that couple, we stayed at my mother's house...for five weeks."

"You know what Benjamin Franklin said about guests. . .."

Tara nodded. "After three days guests are like fish— they begin to smell."

———————————

The story affected Tara. Her heart-felt heavy. She imagined her pulse slowing. She felt tired. It brought her closer to her own battle with cancer. She had a wonderful life with John and she didn't want to give it up. She did not want to lose it, nor did she want John and her family to lose her. She thanked God they had twenty-nine years together and thanked him for bringing John into her life—already contented and peaceful, but made more complete with John who co-created with her four fine looking children, their Four Green Fields, whom she loved equally. She remembered telling John, "I can truly say I love each of my children equally. I do not love one more than the other." John concurred.

Love...the essential ingredient that makes happy memories.

# EIGHTEEN

# The Church Fails the Young

When she arrived home, she quick paced up the driveway like the captain of the volleyball team ready to cheer her team to victory. She ate with family and cajoled through dinner. Dishes washed and the kitchen restored to order, she went to the bedroom, thinking how good she had it, especially when she heard the sad story about her neighbors, Joe and Jan Jamison, who hadn't slept together the last three years of their marriage: a marriage without meaning. What price they paid. *A loveless marriage like that is a tragedy.* Seeing them at parties, she never realized they weren't happy. Yet, they stayed together in a house of frigidity in a kind of *Who's Afraid of Virginia Wolf* environment. Many couples like the Jamisons hide their unhappiness by playing a conspiracy game of happy-faced living, role-playing their way through an unhappy marriage by wearing false-faced masks.

She decided to write a letter to her husband.

"Dear John,

"When you say you are lonely, it makes me feel bad. I know you feel lonely and it must be my fault. I love you and as long as we are together I could never feel lonely. I suppose the reason I am not lonely is you are a better and more considerate and loving husband than I am a wife. You give me the same secure feeling I have felt as a child and I doubt if many wives feel this way. I know I take a lot from you without expressing my appreciation.

"I miss you more when you are in school and I am home than I do when I am at work. This is the same way you miss me when you are home than when you are in school.

"It will be much nicer from now on, especially from September, when I come home earlier and don't work weekends. I want you to know when love—you—came to live with me, you raised me up to the heavens where I've lived with you all these years. I think of us as one.

Love,

Tara"

She decided to hand him the letter at Sunday's Mass.

In the center drawer of their bureau, where she kept baptismal records for each family member, she found another old letter from her father and one from her niece.

Her father addressed his letter to her at the Lucy Eaton Smith House for single Catholic girls at Nineteenth and Sansom in center-city Philadelphia. Dated 1959, the year she came to America to meet her previous fiancé, Martin O'Brien. The canceled postage stamp pictured a scene of the Rock of Cashel, the former seat of Irish kings in Irish historiography. When her father had written the letter, she was working overtime as supervisor in the brokerage firm's transit department. Calmly, she reread the colonel's abbreviated note.

"Dear Tara,

"I read all your letters and I am sure your mother and Una keep you informed of all the home news. You should not do too much by way of additional work. Of course, extra experience is worthwhile but one's health can easily suffer from overwork.

                                        Best love as always,
                                                    Dad"

She sighed and glanced at the window into the black night. She felt an appreciation of her years growing up in Ireland and yearned to go home again. She inadvertently tore the letter in half and mended it with cellophane tape. *Couldn't do that with my cancer.* She brushed away a tear. She hoped her guardian angle would help her fly over this dreaded disease.

She found another letter; her niece wrote in consolation of her illness.

"Dear Aunt Tara,

I can't believe it's six months since I last saw you in Dublin. So much has happened in a short time.

"Mum told me about your illness…I know how the Irish skirt topics as cancer; it is part of Irish customs to avoid conversation about one's poor health…and I do hope you are feeling better now. This illness is a personal invasion and does take a while to recover from the emotional as well as physical terms. Scheduled to have a spleen operation earlier this year, I found myself a homeopath who worked with me and with his help and creative visualizations, we have managed to stall for time to date. The guided meditations or visualization techniques have proved a most welcome contribution to my ongoing health and the power of changing a negative thought to a positive one on a moment by moment basis has had its effect."

She went on to narrate her work, travel and future plans. *How typical how the Irish avoid dealing directly with a terrible illness.* She valued her niece's interests in her.

On Sunday, John and she went to the eleven o'clock Mass. Unlike their younger days, when John arose at seven, cooked a full breakfast, serving breakfast in bed to Tara and readying the four children for Mass. Now with their two boys at Notre Dame and Villanova and attending college Masses, they went to Masses with Maura and Thaddeus. College Masses were shorter with no boring hymns and well-prepared homilies with worldly examples college kids relate to. Maura and Thaddeus found Sunday services boring. They went despite boring singing and sermons; they said their own prays. *Ultra conservative prelates are driving youth away from the church. What a family, four children, all educated from first grade through high school, with two in college, attending occasional Sunday Mass. Society beat us on this one.* They had peace of mind that they had shown faith-filled example. They modeled themselves on their exemplary parenting. As Father John McNamee suggested in *The Diary of a City Priest* the Church has not kept pace with the needs of society.

"Our friends are experiencing the same behavior with their adult children," Tara said, as they drove to Mass. "When they get married, they'll come back."

"I wonder."

"I still go to Mass, Ma Ma," Maura asserted.

"I wonder when you leave for Villanova will you continue to attend Mass?" her father asked. "Most young adults don't. Seems they don't trust organized religion."

"We'll see," replied Maura.

They walked up the path to the side entrance of the church.

"Late again," John said. "I get up four hours before Mass and I'm still late for Mass."

Rushing in quickstep, Tara said, "We're on time."

"What? We're late," said Maura.

"No, we're on time. It's three minutes after eleven but we're on our usual schedule - we're not late."

Both looked at Tara and they noticed a twinkle in her eye.

"I've been late for Mass since the children were young," he declared. "In fact, I've been late for Mass since I met you."

"Why did you marry me?" she cracked. "You've never had it this good."

He gave her a look she knew meant: you win.

As they entered church, John smiled proudly and prided himself on how lucky he was to have Tara for his wife. He noticed she radiated in her royal blue suit.

She inadvertently sat in a pew near people who annoyed John either by loud singing or simply those he did not like. She made a half genuflection. She never genuflected with her knee touching the ground. That's just the way she was. At times, he was too rigid, more critical; she, moderate and more flexible. She accepted things as they were. A risk taker, she faced the unknown...unafraid.

The lector led the congregation in the Responsorial Psalm, number 126: "The Lord has done great things for us: we are filled with joy."

A stout man in the pew behind sang louder than anyone else. "Why did you sit here, near this loud mouth?" he whispered into her ear.

"Be quiet, she grimaced. "Behave yourself."

Again, John whispered to Tara as the people, like sheep, blankly repeated the same psalm five times. Irreverently, he said, "Great things he has done for us—he gave you cancer."

Maura made a critical face.

Tara looked at John with a stern expression, the one she showed to an employee who needed a reprimand.

During the second reading from the Old Testament, John found a passage, which he showed his wife.

"Come to me all of you who are tired from carrying heavy loads, and I will give you rest. Take my yoke and put it on you, and learn from me. I am gentle and humble in spirit and you will find rest. For the yoke I will give you is easy, and the load I will put on you is light."

"Believe that," John expressed, "and I'll tell you another one."

She whispered, "Be quiet. Be happy I'm still alive." The ceiling lights shone down on them like stars in an untangled sky of fulfillment and simplicity.

*Cancer is simple: either I'll survive or die.* How easy things are, yet complicated. For her life, he thanked God. For her battle with cancer, John criticized God.

"Dad, stop talking," Maura demanded, the daughter correcting the father.

Tara wondered who was the teacher now, her husband or her daughter. She remembered her father's birthday and mentally offered the remainder of the Mass for him. If he were alive, he would be 104. She didn't pray for a miracle. But at fifty-eight, she prayed for another twenty years. *No sense feeling glum. Can't do anything about it. I need to bring sunshine into people's lives, not misery. No one gets out of this life alive.*

John took a Mass book from the pew holder and handed it to Tara and began to follow the Gospel reading with the priest. Again, he shared the book with Tara.

They read from Matthew, Chapter 15 verses 29-31.

"Jesus left them and went alone to Lake Galilee. He climbed a hill and sat down. Large crowds came to him, bringing with them the lame, the blind, the crippled, the dumb, and many other sick people whom they placed at Jesus' feet and he healed them. The people saw the dumb speaking, the crippled made whole, lame walking, and the blind seeing and they praised God of Israel."

John whispered to his wife. "If Christ healed all those people who never asked to be healed, people who never prayed to him, people who didn't give a damn about him on the cross, why can't he cure you?"

They glared at each other. Tears formed in her eyes. Tears streamed from his blue eyes. For the moment, they fixed themselves on each other's tears, a common bond of the pains of cancer.

He stammered, "Maybe, there isn't any God. Christ—the greatest charlatan. An historical figure after all."

"You know better," she scolded. Often, when she made a point of truth she used few words to express herself.

Then she gave her husband her love letter. After reading it, he said, "Thank you. I love you." His look of affection said much more.

———————

Tara diverted her usual path to Dr. Stein's office and stopped first at the Hallow Hills Mall, one of her favorite places for shopping. She wondered about the two bigoted white ladies she last saw there. *They need more than prayers.* Fingering the fabrics in the racks, she recalled the many times before she, Maura, Thaddeus, John, Sean, Enda and herself went to Plymouth Meeting Mall, the first suburban shopping mall in their area. Inside the mall, they often had dinner in the Harvest House before going their separate ways. Shopping in those days was a family affair. Tara had the freedom to shop while John cared for the two boys. He'd push them in the Hedstrom metal, double stroller to visit pet and hobby shops.

As Tara examined a size eight Kasper suit, she recollected how gorgeous the red and white poinsettia arrangement over the fountain like a Goliath Christmas tree. She remembered how beautiful the mall was during the Christmas season highlighted by Children's merry-go-round and mini train rides along with Santa Claus himself. But, as time moved on, they also moved on to King of Prussia Mall, where the Purple Cow, an ice cream store, was their favorite stop. The area around the Purple Cow had a moat and a short arched bridge, which children liked to walk and run over. *As we all change with age, their ice cream store, the Purple Cow has become a merchandise store.* In time, the moat was filled in with marble slabs. The bridge was no longer there, a central meeting to suite their liking – another thing vanished from their lives. *Like my health.*

Life never passed them by. They changed and stayed equal with the pace of modern times. And when Sean and Enda didn't want to be seen in public with their parents, they went to Montgomery Mall with Maura and Thaddeus. The unbroken family circle remained unbroken. As both parents and children grew up together in family life, they began to go in different directions. No matter how far they ventured, the circle still remained unbroken. In the family circle of events, they repeated the same special events with Maura and Thaddeus. And it all worked out happily like a sculptor cutting out their lives from a block of Vermont Blue granite and coating them with a breathe of life and energy.

Seeing a poster ad of a young couple holding hands, reminded her how pleased John had made her feel with his joy over her love letter. He hugged her in gratitude. It had a deep feeling of truth when he embraced her. They grasped each other for several minutes without a word. She felt his encouragement permeating into her body.

She decided to buy the Kasper suit with a gray top lined in black on the lapels with a matching gray skirt. *Why not pamper myself...go on buy another blue and white Sasson suit.* She bought a second suit.

At the circular walkways from the first to the second level, she visualized herself as a girl playing in Ireland. What fun for her to be a child, growing up in Ireland. Her family was like life-producing marshes, a family formula of interacting with one another with love in a peaceful and contented environment that gave her lifelong happiness. She remembered why she left Ireland. She had come to meet Martin O'Brien, her finance, liked America and stayed. She hadn't missed the cold dampness in Ireland, which penetrated into her bones. Dryer weather in America gave her comfort, especially in the warmth of summer. Stiff winds drove her off the stony Bray beach, but, in America, she loved lying on the Jersey beach at Ocean City, which made life in America more varied. With no affection but with concern, she wondered about Martin, since she broke their engagement.

Fall changed into winter, winter into spring; spring into summer, and summer back into fall, years passing by. O'Brien had married a younger girl and never had any children. He died at forty-seven. Tara thanked God she hadn't married Martin. If she had married Martin, she may not have had children. And the two major items in her life: to marry happily and to have children – both had been fulfilled with John.

She recalled what the fortuneteller told her in Ireland that she would do as well if she stayed in Ireland. John smirked at this story. He had interpreted this to mean he had done only a fair job as a husband. Tara told John he was the best husband, the best father.

Out in the mall parking lot, a tingling paining sensation in the right side of her neck caused her to scratch the area. What now, she feared, and she had a moment ago thanked God for her marrying John. She registered a mental note to tell Dr. Stein. She would not tell John as she often did so as not to alarm him. *The question is what will Dr. Stein tell me?*

# NINTEEN

# Cancer Returns

In her Grand Marquis and feeling stressed, she drove down Walsh Road to Bustleton Pike. She knew stress could lead to distress, causing a negative attitude. She recalled an article by Don Hauch, a counselor, who warned, "Stress is an effect of the fight within ourselves of who we are, the values we have, how we think of ourselves." She considered herself an upbeat person and she wanted to stay that way. She again thought of Earl Nightingale's advice: "As you thinketh, so you are." *Keep thinking happy, positive thoughts.* She thanked God for the happiness in her life. She took a deep breath, focused on calm breathing and pictured herself in a garden of flowers, sitting on a bench enjoying the scent of nature's perfume in the air. She felt relaxed. Advised to take more of these mental practices, she reaffirmed her determination to do so. She promised herself to listen to Irish music before going to bed. Irish music made her feel happy. A man in a Monte Carlo convertible trailed a line of cars a few blocks in front of her. The light changed to red before he reached the intersection. He went through the red light. She reasoned he didn't want to be the car left behind. Road rage. She parked in her usual handicapped space at the front door of the Stein's medical offices. *Handy to have a handicap plate. Thank God for O'Shea's.*

Three people sat waiting ahead of her. Dr. Stein, a kind and understanding doctor, did not overbook and kept patients waiting. He told her, "Patients can be impatient." One patient was a red-faced man. His eyes were as black as the black radiation dots on her chest. He reminded her of Peter Finley Dunne's Mr. Doolan, the Chicago-Irish barman, in Dunne's novel.

Looking at the man, Tara remembered the day she became a citizen, May 1, 1972. *Strange, how the mind works. The man triggered the day Robin Macintosh interviewed her on Channel three, after the Naturalization ceremony at Independence Hall.* Dr. Wade Wilson, President of Cheney University, was the guest speaker. Tara remembered she wore a black and white dotted top with a black skirt. How she liked black skirts. How she championed the rights of Black people. She knew what bigotry had done to the Irish for 800 years as it had degraded Afro-Americans for centuries.

John and two friends, who were sponsors, had escorted her to Congress Hall. After an early dinner, they went home to watch the evening news and Robin Macintosh interviewing Tara on a momentous day. For herself and the benefit of her children, Tara loved being an American citizen. *Too bad we didn't have a camcorder for a visual record for our family history as we have filmed many family events over the years.*

Macintosh had asked Tara how long she'd been in the country. He didn't have to ask her nationality; he knew by her clear Dublin accent. When he asked how she prepared herself, she replied, "I used the booklet given to all candidates and American history books my husband used in teaching."

"How long did it take you?" he quizzed.

"Several months, " she replied to the camera.

Asked about her family, she light-heartedly said, "I've been married nine years and have three children. My husband is with me." Tara motioned towards John and the cameraman showed John who had used a personal leave day from school. The next day, his principal said, "I saw you on TV last night." John thought *it a good thing he didn't use a sick day.*

And this from the same principal who took a sick day to go to the race track and whom did he see but the Latin teacher who also took a sick day to work his part-time job at a betting window. At the window, the principal said to the teacher, "I won't tell, if you don't tell."

———

When paged into Dr. Stein's office, she remembered her mother was born this day and said a prayer to her mother for strength and a cure. Fear becomes a part of life for a person with Stage III cancer.

Dr. Stein observed the absence of Tara's smiling face. "Tara, what's wrong?"

Her cheeks flushed a reddish tint. Her lips quivered. She felt trapped like an inmate in a prison.

Stein squeezed her hand. A *prima facie.*

"There's a lump on the right side of my neck," she stated, fingering a small lump.

Dr. Stein smiled, offering her re-assurance. He felt the right cervical lymph node. His face darkened. He shook his head. "I don't like this," he said. "Relax Tara, we'll help you."

"But what if it's malignant."

"One day at a time...remember your creed...Tara, one day at a time." How's the Jobes machine helping your arm edema?"

"I use the machine and its sleeve, but my right arm continues to swell."

"I'll order a CAT scan and a bone scan for tomorrow. Can you make late afternoon again?"

"Cancer has returned?"

"Let's see," he said, avoiding a direct answer.

Her world – her little world filled with the extensive love of John, Sean, Enda, Thaddeus, Maura—she feared crumbling. She told herself, *I love you, John. I need you.* As she nudged away, she heard the nurse say, "Oh my, the clock stopped working." Her words caused Tara to think about her saying to John: "There's a time clock in all of us. When the alarm rings, it is time to go." *Is the clock about to toll final chimes for me?*

Tara had the required test the next day and spent a quiet, pensive night with family. John wished he could do something. He offered his love and sat with her, talking quietly. Hiding nothing from the children, she telephoned Maura at Villanova University, Sean who lived in an apartment in Philadelphia; Enda who lived and worked in Boston; and Thaddeus at Providence College. She told them Dr. Stein had ordered additional tests for the morning and cancer may have etched itself back into her body. Intuitively, she felt something about to happen. Not afraid, she felt God's presence around her. Alone with no children for the first time since the first year of marriage and with hopes to travel on cruises and European holidays, her spirits sagged with the latest fear that malignant cells had again invaded her body. An upbeat person, she centered in hope and courage. Hope and courage increased her happiness, but now stress again took hold of her emotions and feelings. She didn't want to be plugged into a machine at the end.

"Let's make reservations for the two of us to go to Las Vegas," John encouraged.

"Now?"

"What better time to raise our spirits."

"Our spirits?"

"When you have cancer, I have cancer."

She waved her hand at him. She raised her eyebrows. "Sure," she uttered.

"I feel what you feel. You lead. I'll follow. The person who can't lead and follow creates his own wall."

"You may know what I feel, but not how I feel. I don't tell you all the pains I have. You only know the half of it."

"Why? I want you to tell me everything."

"Not to worry you. You're better off, John, not knowing everything."

They examined each other's face. Moments of silence passed. He gave her a look that only his wife understood.

"I love you, Tara," he said, his right arm around her shoulders.

"It's not often you sit with me and hold me."

"I do it enough."

"Yes. But it's more than a hug you want."

"Tara...I've told you hundreds of times. I fill up with your love when I'm intimate with you. You know you are my flower. Your flower...the flower of your garden...and I'm the gardener with a hoe."

Loving her husband gave her emotional and mental strength. She teased him. "That's a garden of sex."

He had raised her spirits.

"My one track mind gives you much pleasure."

"Mmmm . . . who said," she commented.

They sat on the rap-around sofa, she with her back propped as usual against three end pillows, and he next to her, his right arm still flung across the back of her neck, his hand resting on her shoulders. Silence. Firewood crackled. Flames from the fireplace reflected mysterious and abstract shadows onto the ceiling like giant birds in flight.

"Romantic in here," he said, kissing her left cheek.

"Watch the program," she ordered, alerted for love play.

"I want to tell you a story," he announced.

"Better be good," said she.

"Better," he winked. "It's creative. It's about God and what I'm going to do to him."

"John, what can you do to God? It's he who can do something to you."

"I'd wish he did something for me – and you."

In their marriage, they communicated with their eyes. His eyes told her he meant cure her of cancer. "Here's my story."

"Make it quick. Speak the speech, Hamlet."

He gave her another kiss on the cheek. "Before you start…your kiss reminds me of the note I sent up to you when you spoke at the podium at a home and school meeting. Remember?"

"What note?"

"The note I had a student hand you."

"You mean the kiss note?" said he.

"Yes," she chuckled, "I printed capital K, capital I, capital S, capital S."

He joined her laughter. "That was clever."

"Keep It Short Stupid. Need I write another note?"

"What?" he blurted.

"Whatever your story, Keep It Short Stupid."

"Keep it clean, too," she expressed with an ardent smile.

"I am going to tell Jesus I am creating a wife for him."

"You're weird."

He ignored the interruption. "And I'll tell Jesus here is your wife. Take care of her, provide for her, love her, be happy together, have children."

"You get the strangest ideas."

"In thirty years, I'll go back to him and tell him I'm now giving your wife cancer and you'll have to deal with it the best you can. I won't help you."

She gave him one of those non-verbal communication looks that he was acting strange.

"I'll tell him she's going to die and I'll kill her off. I'll say to Jesus, "Then you'll know how it feels.""

"You're lucky," she said, "he doesn't strike you down dead."

"Let him," replied John. He quickly changed his mind. "Oh, wait. I want you to live. If you die, I want to die. You better live, Tara." His thoughts drifted onto the word MOM and what it meant to him: loving, passionate, self-sacrificing for her children, a great supportive wife, supporter of the poor and downtrodden, a kind caring, human being.

Tara's day of reckoning had arrived. *With cancer, every day is a day of reckoning.* She took one day at a time. Before leaving her office, she rang the owner, Nathan Mountain. He wanted to see her before she drove to hear the test results.

At six feet, three inches, he was a physically fit man who worked out in Doylestown Health Club several days each week. A noticeably black dot sat on the tip of his nose, distinguishing him from about everyone else she knew. He knew the value of health; he knew the value of Tara O'Malley as a refined human being and excellent administrator. From the beginning of her treatments, he made it clear she should take whatever time away from her job she needed to restore her to good health. Tara, in turn, respected him as a caring human being. They worked well together.

She rose to greet him as he came around her desk and hugged her. "Tara, I'm sorry about the lymph node."

She smiled. "Have a seat, Nathan."

"Know…we love you, Tara. My wife and children love you."

"I know, Nathan."

Nathan Mountain often began his sentences with a verb instead of a noun. "Sorry we can't do more."

"You do enough, Nathan. You are considerate and understanding."

"Take all the time off you need."

"I know. You have been gracious enough to tell me many times."

"Have Eleanor take charge when you must see a doctor or take tests."

"I do that," she said, smiling. You are most kind."

"Must take care of you, not only for you being a wonderful person, but also this home has never been run more efficiently."

"Today, I'll find out if the node is malignant. It might be."

"Positive, Tara. Be positive."

"I'm being realistic. When a lymph node can be felt after the cancer is arrested, that's a poor sign."

"Hope for the best."

"I do," she said, looking beyond Mountain at Janet, the first floor aide who appeared at the office doorway. "Excuse me, Nathan."

She addressed the aide. "Yes, Janet?"

"Henrietta has a fever. Thought you should know."

"Thank you. Take her to the nurse."

The aide left the doorway. Nathan said, "You know what to do."

"Common sense, Nathan. A lot of this job calls for common sense."

"Won't keep you from the doctor and x-rays. Let me know right away."

"As soon as I know, I'll ring you."

"Ring me? That's Irish all right."

She smiled as they made their way to the parking lot. A sign on the lawn of a house across the street read: For Sale: 10 ac....In her brain, she added the letters scraped away by someone. *An incomplete sign...*maybe *like her life.*

---

In Dr. Stein's office, she went immediately to the heart of the matter. "Let's hear the results."

"You're being direct today, Tara."

"Yes, on with it, doctor.

He read from a report. "It consists of several disrupted fragments of soft, pink tissue ranging from .6 to 1.2 centimeters. She felt her world collapsing.

She sighed. Doctor Stein placed his hand on her shoulder and kissed her cheek.

"What's next?"

"I'm sending you to Dr. Wiseman and Dr. Johnson. Dr. Wiseman will take a biopsy and if needed Dr. Johnson may recommend more radiation." *More life is what I need, not a Ferriswheel of doctors.*

Tara did not relish going to Dr. Wiseman. He overloaded his schedule again, allowing patients to wait a couple of hours. A pleasant man with a good bedside personality, he was a good businessman. His office often overbooked cancer patients. *And the more people cater to him, the more his head inflates with self-importance.* She laughed to herself.

Tara and John were called into the office. Dr. Wiseman shook hands with John and then said to Tara, "Well, Mrs. O'Malley, you haven't been here to see me in a long time."

"Mostly, I've been seen by Dr. Stein."

"And what brings you to me?" he asked suspiciously, slighted she had not consulted with him regularly, the way you'd ask God for help.

She saw the street lamp on Bustleton Avenue blinking on and off before it finally blew out. *A noxious omen.* "A swelling on the right side of my neck."

"You should have told my secretary Dr Stein sent you."

"Would it have made a difference?"

"Of course. I would have taken you right in and not have you wait with the others," he said. He stood erect, tucking his chin in.

*Does this mean I'd have preferential treatment since I know somebody?* Regardless, she was grateful to him for keeping her alive.

He noticed the alarm in Tara's expression and nervously steered his conversation into a professional manner. "Mmmm. Let's see." he said, studying the ceiling for an answer. He examined the neck and arm areas. Facing Tara and John, he said, "Well, you have edema of your right arm and fullness in your right neck." He paused, placing his hand over hers in a manner of a father patronizing his daughter.

"What we'll have to do is take a biopsy and, if malignant, I'll place an infusaport in your left breast and you'll receive chemotherapy again or radiation or both. Dr. Stein will coordinate this." He paused and noting their drained faces, he said, "Mr. O'Malley, your wife is a strong lady." He looked at Tara. "You've been through a lot."

"Yes," John said, ceiling-gazing, his mind racing through the screen of his brain scanning all the episodes with cancer therapy, treatments, and life and death discussions like a booted up computer scanning its programs before settling on the first step of a new program.

"In the meantime, see my secretary and we'll set up a hospital appointment for surgery."

On the way home, John, the ex-seminarian, quoted Matthew: "And I tell you more: whenever two of you on earth agree about anything you pray for, my Father will do it for you in heaven. For where two or three come together in my name, I am there with them."

Tara sat in silence, tears running down her cheeks, smearing her fresh rouge.

"The two of us have been praying to defeat cancer since 1988 – that's four years ago. Four years! And Christ said, without qualifications 'it will be done for you by my Father in heaven.' The Bible doesn't say if it's good for your soul or God has something else in mind for us. It's a clear statement – 'it will be done for you.' It's all a goddamn fake."

"Don't say that, John." Tara regained composure, dabbing at her tears and drying her cheeks. "We must go on and think and pray positively."

"Why Tara? Why? We've been praying and these lumps continue. God doesn't interfere in the natural order of events as Rabbi Kushner said. It leaves out any chance of a miracle. Christ performed miracles when he was on earth. Why doesn't he act now?" To the heavens he said, "Where are you, God?"

"He took away the spot on my lungs in 1990, didn't he?"

John stopped for a traffic light at Tomlinson Road. He studied her, eye to eye, searching each other for meaning. He sat in a moment of silence. *God hasn't done a lot of things. What the New Testament claims he said he'd do, he doesn't do. Why doesn't he do something? He cured many people. But what about us? Why, for example, didn't he select Arabs, Gentiles, Romans, Egyptians, Jordanians as well as Jews for his Twelve Apostles to show people of future generations how to live in racial harmony. If he had done this, today's world wouldn't be filled with racial prejudice and war.* She turned to her husband and changed the subject.

"It's a smart looking house over there," she said, pointing to the three-story Cape May styled home with a full wrap around porch with wood railings, painted in cream and sky blue—the colors of their home.

"Smart looking?" he quipped. "You're smarter looking."

Her smile told him he had said soft words in a hard situation. He went on, "And the heights of your talents reach the heavens of a bluish sky, the color of my eyes and your genius paints the life of puffy clouds in the sky."

Her smile broadened. "What a line…"

Tara had an appointment at the hospital with Dr. Wiseman for the biopsy. He greeted her with a hug. After the surgery, she planned to meet with Dr. Stein and Dr. Johnson.

"We may be able to treat you without the infusaport this time," Dr Wiseman said.

The room had the smell of sickness, an odor she lived with in personal care homes, the copyrighted smells of a sick room: iodine, antiseptics, wet cotton balls, and disinfectants, used needles, used plastic gloves, discarded sutures, soiled examining robes, and stale blood.

Tara smiled, "I think I'll be fine. I know I'm in good hands."

"We marvel at you, Mrs. O'Malley. How determined you are."

"I am."

"A patient's determinations is part of our treatment and the patient can help us with a positive attitude."

Reading from her medical history, the doctor said, "You have developed a four week history of swelling of the right arm and you have pain in the left shoulder. Your right supraclavicular lymph node is rapidly growing."

"Yes."

"Of course, your workup with the bone scans, liver enzymes and chest x-ray failed to reveal any other malignancy."

"I guess I'll never run out of testing like Fort Knox will never run out of gold. When do we begin radiation?"

He smiled at her wit. "Ah, but do you know all the gold in the world will fit into a single area about 18 cubic yards…? So too your testing will fit into a small amount of time. The testing will stop one day. And, for now, I think you should call me in two days after conferring with the team. I'll let you know."

*I fall into bed like an orange thudding to the ground, with the same thump, to wake up to either the angel of life or the angel of death holding me on a tray—I'm not sure which. How long will I live this way?*

Going out the door, Dr. Weisman said, "And don't forget, Tara, what Thoreau said, 'Success comes to those who are too busy looking for it.' We'll do our best. We're not God. But we'll stay busy on your case."

―――――

Radiation completed, she met with Dr. Johnson for a follow up consultation.

"You're looking better, Tara."

"Thank you, Dr. Johnson."

"But I have lesions all over my body. Possible reactions to radiation?"

Dr. Johnson examined the lesions. "Any new medications you're taking?"

"Yes. Dr. Stein prescribed Megace. *I want grace, not Megace.*

The woman doctor nodded approvingly. "Dr. Stein discontinued tamoxifen?"

"Yes."

"Good. You've had seventeen treatments over twenty-two days for a total of 3060 centigrays. You tolerated the treatment with no discomfort."

"I have more centigrays in me than I have food."

She laughed. "Keep up your sense of humor, Tara. You did have 4600 centigrays so we can't go further with a higher dosage and besides radiation stays in your body for months and continues to react against cancerous cells."

"The pulmonary doctor found no problems."

"A good sign. Your lungs are clear. No fluids have formed, thank God."

Tara remembered when she last thanked God when she felt the swelling on her neck. John fueled his angry at God for not healing her. He wanted a total cure...a miracle.

"One other thing, doctor. I've noticed twitching in my right eye."

"Let's have a look. The entire pupil's enlarged. I'll order an x-ray."

On leaving the parking lot, Tara noticed a bag lady limping along the sidewalk. *God loves her. The poor woman has no money for her care and no means to live in a personal care home where she'll receive proper clothing, food and medications to provide for her comfort the remainder of her days.*

Enroute home, she passed a mansion, next to the beautiful Bryn Athyn Cathedral, built with a multi-millionaire's money. It enlightened her to think the millionaire a good rich person who aided his neighbors and tended to their needs. *Harder for a rich man to pass through the eye of a needle than for him to enter the king-dom of heaven.* She believed this didn't apply to this millionaire.

# TWENTY

## Brittingham's Irish Pub

Early Saturday night, John said, "We need a break. Let's go to Brittingham's."

"Sounds good, John."

"Our favorite singers are there. O'Hanlon and Sheehy."

"They're good, John. They sing good folksy songs."

Saturday night at Brittingham's Irish Pub held a full house of mostly Irish Americans who came to listen to Irish folk singers.

"Guinness please for me and a cup of tea for my non-alcoholic-drinking friend," John told the waitress.

The waitress noticed their wedding rings and smiled.

"Welcome to Brittingham's Irish Pub and particularly to the Nancy O'Shay room where I live most of my life," O'Hanlon said, his eyes filled with expectations for laughter. "I hope you enjoy yourself tonight as much as you are enjoying that stuff you're been pouring in ya."

People tittered and clapped. One man toasted by holding up a pint of Guinness.

"Put your hands together for my partner, Rom Sheehy from County Havertown, the twenty seventh county of the South," he said with a glint in his eye.

Regulars like John and Tara knew Sheehy, an Irish-American. He lived in Havertown Township.

"Do the same, my friends," snapped Sheehy, "for Kerry O'Hanlon who hails all the way from County Donegal."

Warmed up and ready to spend from nine to two in the morning, the popular entertainers began to sing and play Irish tones as "Jamie Mac I'm Nearly Forty," "Irish Rover," "Give Me a Hand" "The Boys of the Old Brigade," "Boston Rose," "Four Green Fields." "Rare Ole Times," and "Sllabh Na Mban, among their repertoire.

A man swayed himself into the men's room. Tara and John watched him exit and, at his seat, he missed his chair as he prepared to sit down. He wore an orange sweater.

"Serves him right," John snapped, "for wearing orange."

"That may mean nothing, John. It may be his favorite color. He can wear what he pleases."

"Maybe, he's actually Murphy. You know Samuel Beckett's Murphy."

"Murphy was a Dubliner."

"Right…killed by a gas fire and his ashes strewn on a pub floor."

"Better to have been thrown into the ocean, don't you think, John?"

"A barroom floor sounds more dramatic."

At intermission, Kerry O'Hanlon visited their table. He gave Tara a hug and a kiss on the cheek.

"How ya feelin' luv?"

"Good, but the cancer has come back. I finished radiation for the second time."

"Good God, I'm sorry to hear that."

"Yes. I've had 4600 centrigrays thus far."

"We're trying, Kerry. The doctors are wonderful."

"And so is your little darling," O'Hanlon said.

John smiled. O'Hanlon made the rounds of his other friends. Cigarette smoke stretched out and ascended to the ceiling fans like pearls in a string necklace.

"Irish music makes me feel good inside," declared Tara.

"Many of the songs are sad about leaving home or dying?"

"Even so."

John motioned with his little finger for Tara to lean across the table. He kissed her gently.

"What's that for?"

"Because I love you. "Can't a guy kiss his wife when he wants to?

Her expression, not her words, said yes.

He pointed to the picture to the left of a pocket-sized stage. "That's Charlestown and it won't be long now for the Miss Mayo Contest."

"Sure won't."

"Remember the expression on Maura's face when she won the Miss Mayo Contest at the Irish Center?"

"I won't forget, John. She paraded on stage with fourteen girls, proud in her emerald green gown."

"She looked lovely – red hair, green dress, freckles . . ."

"The Mayo Ball last November will be among my fondest memories."

"November 2, 1991, is a date to note." Tara coughed from

the cigarette smoke whirling around the ceiling. She wished Pennsylvania would join California and ban cigarette smoking in all pubs.

"Good thing I had my cam-cord" he said. "She won the trip to Ireland for the Miss Mayo contest."

"And now all six of us are going to see her in Charlestown," Tara waved to O'Hanlon and Sheehy as they prepared to continue playing.

"When Molly Murphy placed the crown on her head, I felt great."

"We have Molly to thank," Tara declared. She introduced and instructed her on the contest rules.

"Didn't she look lovely?" Tara said, sipping tea.

The waitress took their order for another Guinness and a tea refill.

"The way she walked down the platform with the people looking up at her – she was truly the queen of the ball."

Tara listened to O'Hanlon singing "The Streets of New York."

John clarified a point. "It's called the Western Rose Festival in Charlestown."

"And I've decided something else, too."

"And what's that?" John quizzed.

"Besides going to Charlestown and touring Galway, we'll visit The Burren, Cliffs of Moher, Kilkee, Tralee, Killarney, Cork, the Blarney Stone, and on to Templemore visit my mother's family. Who knows when I'll see them again? I want to go to Lourdes again."

"Again?"

"The spot on my lungs was cured by Mary. This time, she'll heal my whole body and cure me completely."

"I'm with you, Tara, all the way."

Her smile told him she understood. "I know you are, John."

He motioned for the waitress. He ordered his usual fried mushrooms with a heavy amount of extra cocktail and tartar sauce and Tara ordered fried clams.

"Lourdes is fine with me – your second visit and my first. Let's do Paris as well."

"I wanted to visit Paris, sit in sidewalk cafes on the *Champs Elysees*, sipping coffee and watching people walk by," she smiled, "and talking about the French."

John added, "And the Eiffel Tower, Louvre, Notre Dame Cathedral, Arc de Triumph."

"It'll be my eight or ninth time home since our marriage."

"Not many people can say that, Tara."

"No. But thanks to you, John, I can."

He smiled. "You get all the trips in this house," he joked.

"I'll stay home if you like...."

"That'll be the day." His smile told her not to worry. He thought worry is like sitting in a rocking chair and going nowhere. Worry will get you nowhere. Why worry? Still, he worried for his wife.

"While we go to Lourdes, the kids can go to England." She had grown accustomed to the American way of calling children "kids."

"There was a time you never said 'kids,'" he teased.

"I have an idea. I'll use the Entertainment book. It lists hotels in Paris and London for the usual fifty percent off rate."

"That'll save us money." And with a glitter in her eyes, she said, "and you can give them spending money."

"There's no end to our giving, is there?"

"For better or for worse, remember."

"It's a wonder I have enough money."

"You don't. You have a credit card. A business expense, you know."

He guffawed. "If it weren't for your quick wit, what would I do?"

"You would die without me," she teased.

"I would."

"I wonder if other couples are so open, talking about their deaths."

"At least, we're open about it."

"You're right. With cancer, I feel comfortable mentioning death. You and the children will be better prepared to discuss it openly."

"But you're not dying."

She smiled a look that meant how-do-you-know. *Maybe God wants me to be a saint and suffer all the mental, physical, and emotional pain saints suffer through union with God to become saints. Most saints are priests, brothers, nuns, and they don't experience the joys in life I had during my twenty-nine years within the loving company of John and our Four Green Fields. I prefer to leave the saints to their saintly way of life. I'm doing what God wants me to do in rearing four beautiful green fields – as the Irish song goes – and dedicating our children to God and Mary? Am I not suffering excruciating pain from cancer cells living in my body? Saints are hard to live with. Tara's easy to live with. I'm not a saint, but I am not hard to live with.*

She shot him a look, bringing him back to the realization of the moment.

"If all the books I've read about cancer prevention are right, John...Well, I might live."

She hoped she could say this in twenty years. That would be about 2012, the year the world is supposed to end.

She remembered the many times John had come home from school and played tackle with Sean and Enda when they were youngsters until one day they smacked into him, knocking him off his knees. She recalled John saying, "That's the end of that."

I don't put much faith in the world ending soon, thanks be to God.

# TWENTY-ONE

# A Cancer Reading List

At home and in the shower, she recalled what she said about all the books she read in her positive thinking approach to defeating cancer. John shared in these books as he had shared everything in their marriage. She had practiced the power of mental imaging, which included visualizing non-malignant cells in her body conquering and eating the cancerous cells much like the Atari Space Invaders video game in which the player shot all foreign invaders before landing. She had hopes of shooting down or eating all the cancerous cells before they destroyed her.

Out of the shower and spritzing herself with cologne to make herself more desirous for her husband, she said to John, shaving in front of the medicine closet, "Why is it when we go out, you get tired and want to come home, but as soon as you get into our bedroom, you're always ready for sex?"

"Love," he corrected. "Ready for love." He lathered his face. "You know the first time I loved you, my body got hot. And it's been hot ever since. You know why . . . when I get into the bedroom, I mysteriously wake up—it's you. You're the reason." He stopped shaving and smiled at her. Again, he looked in the mirror and said, "It's a mystery all right."

"Are all men like you – every time they go out with their wives? Do they always want sex . . . love, if you like . . . at the end of the night?"

"I don't know. Ask them. I know one thing. When single, I'd kiss girls good night. Now that I'm married, a simple kiss is not good enough to end the night. I want to feel your closeness. When single, I made love like a single man – kissing; married, I make love like a married man – kissing, fondling, intercourse."

"I'm going downstairs a few minutes. I want to see something in one of my cancer books."

"Don't play that game, Tara . . . delay until I fall asleep." He rolled into bed. The blanket was as soft as Daddle's fur. She passed out of the room like a mysterious shadow.

"Now, why would I do that?" she smirked, heading down the steps, hoping he'd fall asleep. At least this once.

In the family room, she faced the bookcase. With her index finger, she touched each book spine.

She examined a shark-therapy book. She had bought shark cartilage from a health store.

She paged through a book about how thirty people survived cancer. *Will I be the thirty-first?*

She touched the spine of a book that encouraged conquering cancer through mental imagery. *Will I get well, too?* "I'll have a life, too," she said aloud.

A small red-covered book helped her to practice creative imagery.

She felt sad opening a book written by a woman who claimed she had beaten cancer. *Who'd thought she had defeated cancer only to die.*

Another book by a woman, who believed she would live, brought tears to her eyes. *I have hope from her courage.*

Examining a book describing the reasons for good nutrition made her speak to herself, "Nutrition is important and I'm doing my best," she said aloud. Tara found comfort in talking to herself. Hearing her voice gave her comfort.

In looking through a book about alternative treatments, she whispered to herself, "The link between mind and body is also important."

She turned pages of a non-toxic treatment book and said aloud, "Inter-resting About minerals, vitamins, and herbs." *I need a strong strategy to defeat cancer.*

A book stressing prevention against breast cancer prompted her to tell herself, "Well, I must deal with reality if all else fails." *But I won't fail. My risk is in stage three. One more and I'm outta here.* She laughed at herself. *Typical of the Irish to laugh at ourselves.*

Other books sat in her growing cancer library, some she had lent were never returned and still others she didn't like and discarded. All these books gave her hope and stimulus to continue. She read all the books and in each one she found an inducement to pray for healing. *Give me your love and your grace, God... please. I'll take the treatments and you take away cancer.*

She turned off the light. In the dark, she knew where each item of furniture sat and, in the darkness, she made her way to the stairs. In the darkness of her soul, she considered an uncertain future of being cancer-free.

She had been at the bookcase fifteen minutes. She switched on and off the bedroom light and saw John had fallen asleep. John slept on his side of the bed – the window side. *Not in the middle where he would have been if she lay beside him before he fell asleep.* She prayed to God if she should die, her husband would find reconciliation in his bereavement. If she died, she hoped he'd be able to live again, to love again and, if he wanted, marry again. She didn't want him lonely and sad.

She slipped herself under the covers and whispered to herself – "That's one way to get to bed peacefully." However, since John did not have his pleasure, she wondered if he may want a quickie on Sunday morning before Mass. Having intercourse before Mass, a normal experience. She imagined how one of her friends who lived with a divorced Catholic man had sex and went to Mass. Grace for her...but a sin for her friend? She thought not. She wondered about Sunday Mass, a dictum from single priests from the time of the Council of Trent. The Church needed money to exist, single men—priests required Catholics to attend mass on Sundays under threat of mortal sin and to give alms. Funny how clergy, not Jesus, decide what sin is. And who decides if her friend erred in this lonely world. To her, her friend loved the man and thus committed no sin. She concluded her friend a good person who showed respect and dignity to everyone she knew. Love and respect to your neighbor...isn't that the second of the two main Commandments God wants from us? Scolding herself for her fearless arrogance, she fell asleep.

---

Tara visited Dr. Stein again for a check upon the malignant node on her neck.

"I'm going to Lourdes again, doctor."

"You were there last..." he said, staring at the ceiling trying to remember the last year she went, "a few years ago."

"T'was," she said, emphasizing the "t."

He laughed. "For the moment, I thought I was in Ireland."

"My family is going to see our daughter in the Miss Mayo contest."

"Did she win a beauty pageant?"

"She did. It wasn't a bathing suit type of contest. Based on beauty, personality, figure – all judged in one night and each girl wore a gown."

Tara showered a photograph of her daughter. "Beautiful. Where did she get the red hair?"

"My father."

Dr. Stein enjoyed Tara's company and liked talking with her. Over the last four years of treating her, he had come to accept her as a close friend. "Where else are you going in Ireland?"

"John is mapping out a route for us in two cars. We land at Shannon, drive to Galway and to Charlestown where the world competition for Miss Mayo will be held."

"World," he said, raising his eyebrows.

"Girls can come from everywhere. We'll travel to The Burren, The Cliffs of Moher, Kilkee, Tralee, Killarney, kiss the Blarney Stone, see my mother's relatives at Templemore and then go to Dublin. We rented a condominium for two weeks in Dublin."

"Sounds like a wonderful trip."

"It is. The six of us haven't vacationed together since our Ocean City days."

He touched her shoulder and patted her cheek. "You know we're keeping a close watch on the node. Your x-rays revealed haziness in your breasts. The radiation still in your body may clear up. But your lungs are free of fluids."

"I'll ask for Mary's help. We're going to Lourdes, John and I. We'll leave from Dublin, go to Lourdes and stay four days in Paris. The children at the same time will fly to London. And if cancer gives me any trouble, I'll tell it to hump off."

"Hump off...? Interesting. Haven't heard that before.'

"It's an Irish expression. You know...like get off my back."

"Well...your trip sounds great."

Tara nodded.

"Overall, your tumor flowchart is good. All your figures are within range where they should be." He showed her the flow chart.

|  | 5/92 |
|---|---|
| WBC (4.8 – 10.8) | 9.1 |
| RBC (M4.6-6.2) | 4.23 |
| MCV (82-92) | 90 |
| HGB (M14-18)(F12-16) | 12.5 |
| HCT (M42-52)(F37-47) | 38 |
| Platelets | 284 |
| Differential | L-28 |

Pointing to the month of May 1992 and comparing May's results with the normal range in parentheses, he said, "You see, Tara, your tests reveal you are about in the middle area of a low to a high number which is good."

"Encouraging," she responded. She sighed with relief.

"Off with yourself, girl, and enjoy your holidays in Ireland and France. The best is yet to come."

"With the exception of the node in my neck, I will."

He said, shaking her hand, "Tara, remember what Hemingway said: 'There are many good fisherman and some great ones. But there is you.' Bon voyage." The blue sky was powdered with steel white clouds. Her spirits jumped with Stein's warm words. Leaving the parking lot, she noticed a white cloud formation of a French Poodle, which reminded her of FiFi. She envisioned her outstretched front paws, head, miniature body, hind legs extended behind her and her tail. *FiFi appeared happy in heaven.* "I might be with you soon, FiFi," she said aloud. She pushed the Irish tape into the tape deck. A biting loneliness took hold of her. *The lone-liest person in this world is a person who is ill and preparing to die. .* Ah, she told herself, *stop feeling sorry for yourself.*

I need uplift. I need to go to Mayo.

# TWENTY- TWO

# Miss Mayo Contest

Much attention to the trip to Ireland and France. John liked to plan trips. He liked planning for holidays, not leaving them to chance. He prepared trips like a travel agent. Tara's method was to get airline tickets and enjoy herself. She'd contact her sister, Una, buy the tickets and go. She was more direct than John who worked too hard creating schedules and time frames. Tara made life easy. John made life different.

John prepared an itinerary by listing the place visited, the dates of their stay, the time of arrival and departure from place to place. He sent photocopies of the itinerary to the children in college and Enda in Boston.

He ordered six tickets on *Aer Lingus* being sure to include each of them in the frequent flyer program. Advised to save money and fly on a charter, he wouldn't have it. He wanted to fly *Aer Lingus*.

She found another old letter from mammy. Rereading old letters made her feel closer to her mother who, she believed, had received her reward for a good life and now flying all over heaven's skies with her dad. Together again as John and herself would be some day.

Dated Friday, 10<sup>th</sup>, the letter had no year listed. By its contents, it had to be written after Sean's birth, around 1964, twenty-nine years earlier. She read aloud.

"Dear Tara and John,

"I received the photos and letter today. They are lovely pictures. Sean is a lovely baby. You and John look great. We think John got fat, also yourself, but since you're tall you look O.K. However, if you have your health it doesn't matter."

Tara paused and reflected on her current weight of 152—weight increased due to meds intake to kill malignant cells. "But my health, mammy," said she aloud, "I no longer have my health. If you had told me your mother died from cancer, I would have had mammograms every year. Who knows? I'd be healthy today. Prevention may have made the difference. But all this now is a *faiseur de phrases*. Nothing can change the past."

She continued reading:

"The weather here is mixed. You can sit out one hour and have to run in when the rain starts. It's cool at times. Ireland's always cool.

"We have to have a fire in the dining room after 7 o'clock. That's the time we get to sit down and look at TV. I'm writing this in the garden with Una's boys hammering and shouting around me. It's no picnic when they're all together. I hope you will never have six boys. Girls are more useful, although it's a man's world. I think the girls suffer too much bringing children into the world and not knowing how they'll turn out or if they'll thank you for all the care you give them. Of course, if they do, well…it's thanks enough for anyone."

To herself she said, "You're right mammy, it's a man's world all right. If I hadn't married, my body never would have changed and I'd be healthy today. But I'd take all my operations and babies for my married life with John; to be single, childless and alone is unthinkable. Thank God for my life and if cancer is to be part of my marriage, I willingly accept it. Not my will, Lord, but your will be done." She read again:

"Who took the photos? They are lovely. Sean has John's blue eyes. His hair looks fair. You had fair hair until you were 6. I do hope you are not putting black rinse into it now. It looked awful. You had lovely black hair going away to the USA. Everyone said you are getting more like your sister Una every day.

"Your garden and house looks lovely. The flowers are gorgeous.

Love to all,<br>Mammy"

---

On the morning of August third, Sean came home from his apartment in Germantown, and Maura and Thaddeus had already been home from college for summer holidays. And Enda drove home from Boston. Having arrived one week before the contest, Maura enjoyed the festivities. Up early to get to J.F.K. airport in New York on time - about three hours before the 7 PM take-off - they went through all their usual preparation to get everyone on the move. All the motions, John knew, would place them on their usual schedule to be late, a family plague.

Within the ranks of his family for twenty-nine years, John had given up the idea of being on time. On his own, lateness didn't fit in with his lifestyle. Though on time for work, Tara's family and social activities left her late or on time at the last second. John marveled how she could start out late, yet arrive at the stroke of the appointed hour. He considered Tara special; his sincere friend who never criticized him unjustly. She never ridiculed him nor talked about him behind his back. He knew she loved and trusted him. She knew he loved and trusted her. Tara's mother served her breakfast in bed in Ireland, and he continued the tradition whenever possible on weekdays and most Sundays he prepared breakfast while Tara stayed in bed. He simply did not say he loved her; he supported his words with actions of love: attention, conversation, and togetherness. As the kids used to say on the tiny street where he grew up, "Put your money where your mouth is," John put his words of love in his actions. His fiery love ignited like flames in a fireplace, crackling and fulfilling with gentle attention to every part of her body, giving her time and preparation to return his passion in a coil of invisible sparks, which simmered long after the torch-like love act had been consummated. Nothing enhances love, he believed, more than affirmative gestures of pleasing his bride.

There seemed to be one last thing to do, and another, another, and still another – the list went on and on as John did what he thought necessary and Tara made the house perfectly fit to return to. The clothes were washed, carpets vacuumed, closets and bureau drawers put in order, electrical plugs pulled out of sockets, washer and dryer off; the washer hoses disconnected…toilets not running, an endless list. Going out the door, Tara asked John to return to check if the iron cord had been removed from the socket.

Going out the door, Enda kidded her, "Don't forget, Mom, to burn the rolls."

"What?" She smiled, understanding his jest, she burnt the rolls for Thanksgiving and Christmas dinners.

John showed her a thick mass of traveler's checks.

"My goodness, are we moving to Ireland?"

"Looks that way."

"Inter-resting."

As she did with most Americans, she delighted him with her Irish pronunciation. Driving to New York, she remembered her parents' wedding anniversary. They had forty-three years together and thus far she had twenty-nine. With thirteen lymph nodes malignant and fighting cancer in stage three, she realized how tenuous her chances of another fourteen years together. She shivered a frozen rigid feeling as if the gravedigger shoveled dirt onto her casket.

"You know," John said, as they drove on the New Jersey Turnpike, "if we're not going to make it through treatments...how's this sound to you?" John whispered, "We could drive the car off a cliff on one of our Sunday drives or we could both take an overdose."

She gave him one of her serious administrator's faces. "I wouldn't do it to my children – and to myself."

"Enough of that. Another one of your crazy ideas."

"Tara, I love you. If in the end, you'll be spared indescribable pain...."

She interrupted him. "John, I already have had my share of pain – but if I am to have more, I'll have more."

"Trying to help you."

"Thank you. But suicide is for cowards. I'm not a coward."

After two and one-half hours, they arrived at Kennedy. Late, they lost their assigned seats and had to sit in pairs scattered throughout the Aer Lingus Omnibus 747.

———

John videoed their approach to Shannon Airport. Patches of green—light, lighter, dark, darker, Kelly green, budding green, tinted green, seasoned green, herbage green... colors of green he imagined included in the song "Forty Shades of Green." He marveled at stone-upon-stone walls partitioning each fragment of green land; one stone laid on another without mortar. Intermingled with all the greenery parcels of plowed land already seeded for the growing season parceled in sections on Ireland's patchwork quilt. Attractive two story homes and spotted cottages sprung up from the land like outcroppings of welcoming sunlight.

"I wonder, if that is a potato field?" asked Sean.

"Could be anything from this high elevation," responded his mother.

John's first sight of Ireland since their marriage sparked old ancestral thoughts about his grandfather' family. The children had all been to Ireland with Tara who took one, two, and once three children with her on previous trips home.

In two rented stick shift Fords, they drove to Galway for breakfast and a brief center city tour where they visited Kenny's bookstore. "What else?" said Tara, "What can you expect from a teacher?"

Off to Charlestown to the Charlestown Arms, where they planned to nap for a few hours to ease jet lag.

"Mind yourself," Tara told John who equated vacations with passionate lovemaking. She thought it degrading to use the term sex. She cherished his tenderness when they made love.

"I'm too tired," he pleaded.

"Pleasing yourself again," she said, her eyes sparkling.

After a short nap, John awoke and nudged his beautiful wife to wake up. With no wake up call available in the fifteen-room hotel, John knocked on the children's doors.

Get up!" John said through the door. "We'll see you outside."

"Up and at 'em," Tara said, echoing John's voice. "Listen to your father. Get up."

The town had one long main road, the N I7, the main road from Galway to Sligo. The idea for the Charlestown International Rose Festival developed from town's people who wanted to promote County Mayo and Charlestown in particular to boaster the local economy for the five-day event.

Twenty-one Colleens entered the Festival with contestants coming from various counties in Ireland, Manchester, London, Philadelphia, Boston, Australia, and New York.

All ready but not rested, they went outside to watch the car parade. Pairs of "Rose" contestants rode slowly in vintage cars down the long street, waving to locals and tourists present for the Festival activities. Maura rode with the Dublin Rose. *Strange* my *daughter riding with the girl from my hometown.* One thing common to all the contestants: their fresh-eyed, wild beauty.

The main street contained two banks, two food markets, one-quarter the size of a small American supermarket – a series of shops: a tailor, a chemist, owned and staffed by a lady pharmacist, a restaurant, and six pubs, well attended by Festival tourists and local inhabitants.

"This is a typical town in Ireland," Tara volunteered…"with the smell of cows those men are trading off."

Farmers roamed the street with their cows.

"They're not trading, John. They'll sell them."

"Cows in a town street?"

"This is Ireland. You won't see the likes of it in large cities like Galway, Cork, Limerick or Dublin, but here you will. I think it's interesting."

"You mean inter-resting," he mimicked. He smiled and held her hand. Tara liked the way he held hands. He looped each of his fingers between each of hers, their fingers interlocked. Escape impossible. The locked feeling of their fingers intertwined made her feel wholesome, complete, protected. The sun's rays caused heat vapors to rise from the sidewalk like a sea of wavering waves.

Maura's car stopped beside her parents. "Hi Ma Ma. Hi Dadda." Maura beamed. "Isn't this great."

"You're like a queen," said Tara.

"I feel like one."

"You're my little girl, Maura."

"Of course, Dad. And you're my Dadda."

The Dublin Rose smiled. "Dadda?"

"I call my dad that."

"And you call your mother, mom mom?" the Dublin girl asserted her quick wit.

"Not really," laughed Maura.

"When I finish this contest, I'll have trouble with not getting all this attention."

John said, "We'll pamper you. Don't worry."

"You'll have to give me whatever I want from now on."

"Really," noted Tara. "Off with you now."

Everyone enjoyed a feeling of freedom from responsibilities, a sense release from routine, a refurbished holiday. Everyone greeted one another with smiles and pleasantries.

John had an Irish coffee outside Brennan's Pub, where a barmaid prepared drinks.

"How is it?" asked Tara.

"Too sweet. I make them better with Irish creamer and Southern Comfort."

"You don't make Irish coffee," Tara snapped.

He corrected her. "To me, Tara, it's Irish coffee whether I use Irish whiskey or not."

"We should come here tonight. Looks like a nice, lively place."

"Let's," he said

Their three sons joined them. John bought an Irish coffee for each son.

"As good as Boston's," Enda said.

"Great stuff," echoed Sean.

"Authentic, isn't it," stated Thaddeus, the baby of the family. At nineteen, he was under the legal drinking age in the states, but in Ireland he was one year over. Boys become men faster in Ireland.

"We're coming here tonight," Tara said.

"We heard the pub across the street is great. We're going there," Sean said.

"Okay, but now, let's have dinner at the Broadway Restaurant," John suggested.

"Let's sit at the round table by the window," Tara said.

"It's a great seat. It'll be like sitting in a window seat in Philadelphia and watching people go by."

"Sure, Dad," said Thaddeus, "and you can talk about them as they go by. Like you often do."

After dinners of lamb and salmon, John and Tara bid the boys good night and they walked across the street to Brennan's. In the shop next to the pub, a Meet the Contestants flyer in the window attracted their attention as well as passersby. Among the admirers, two different sets of people voiced their choices for the winner: Maura O'Malley.

John and Tara gleamed at each other. As they observed the on-lookers, they spoke not a word. They didn't have to. Joy spread over their faces like the beauty of a multi-colored sunset. They understood each other when their faces or hearts spoke. Their lives together…centered in an open-line of verbal and nonverbal communication.

Brennan's was people-packed, with no seats available. Fortunately, a waitress created seats for them by moving other patrons closer together around the round table. Cigarette smoke curled up to the overhead fans, to the ceiling, to the rear view window, ajar. Typical of Ireland: where there's people there's smoke. It settled in clean glasses ready to be filled with Guinness, in people's hair, on their clothes…everywhere. The taste of smoke made her cough. *Cigarette smoke, a silent killer…you can see it, not hear it. A killer.*

Tara noticed how quaint and ornate the pub was. Many posters, illustrations and photographs adorned the wall. She took delight in pointing out to her husband the illustrations of "The Man, The Maid, The Money," an illustration of James Cagney and Pat O'Brien in military helmets for the movie, *The Fighting 69th*; the old poster listing a football match between Ireland and England at Lansdowne Park in Dublin on Saturday, 4th February. Year unknown.

"Must have been a war," she said, laughing.

"No doubt, they must have refought the war of 1918-19."

John liked the photographs. In particular, he found interest in the picture of Joe DiMaggio, Tony Lazzeri, and Frank Crossetti in and Old Timers Day Reunion at Yankee Stadium, July 17, 1952; and of the Irish boxer, Fitzie FitzRyan.

"Never thought I'd see a baseball picture in Ireland," remarked John. "And they're all Italian."

"Sure, we've antennas on our roofs too," she mimicked him with love in her eyes.

"Smart thing," he retaliated, his face constricted like an orange squeezer, squeezing the last drops.

"Well, people think we don't have TVs, you know."

"The Ugly American idea, huh."

She noticed in the merriment a lone gray-haired lady sat in the corner away from the bar. She smoked Virginia Slims cigarettes and spoke to herself as she sipped coffee. Her face was weathered from cold windy dampness. One of those millions of people throughout the world who are beaten down by day to day living, rarely, if ever, having the opportunity of good luck to come her way. Tara turned away from the woman and faced all the happy faces, enthralled in singing "The Red Rose Cafe."

"What's wrong?" John asked.

John knew what troubled her without her saying anything. "Oh, the woman over there. Why does the poor woman live this way? Why does she not have our comforts?"

"No answer for that."

People drank, endearing themselves to friends and neighbors and joining in the singing with male folk singer. One heavy lady, with her hair tied back, jumped up, raised her arms above her head and waved them from side to side. Her laughter became infectious. Soon, everyone near her waved arms from side to side, with most people singing as well. John and Tara waved their arms. They couldn't carry a tune...but all the same they sang.

"I like the Guinness sign over there, Tara."

"It's a long rectangular mirror."

"Yes. It has Master Brewers since 1759 under Guinness."

"What would you men do if you didn't have Guinness?"

"We wouldn't be here inside Brennan's – and you wouldn't either."

She gave him one of her I know-what-you-mean stares and continued waving.

———————

Mary Robinson, the President of Ireland, visited the Roses and Maura had the opportunity of meeting the Irish President. Tara knew it had to be a fruitful meeting and not like her meeting with a former Irish President, Sean T. O' Kelly.

She recalled she had gone to the front door to answer the doorbell. A man with a top hat and white scarf said, "May I see your father?" She did not recognize the man who gave his name and she asked the man to wait outside while she went to get her father, the president's *aide de camp*. When she told her father the man's name, he jumped up in a frenzy and scampered to the door, saying, "My God, you told the President of Ireland to wait outside."

On the fifth and final day of the Western Rose Festival, the Roses again paraded in vintage cars amidst bands and Charlestown dignitaries. The Master of Ceremonies from Radio Telefis Eireann, Pat Kenny, interviewed each contestant with the same pre-arranged set of questions. He interjected his own dynamic personality and discussed current affairs as five hundred people watched in the athletic facility.

"I think Maura is the best."

"You wouldn't be her father if you thought otherwise," said Tara.

"Dad's right, Mom," Thaddeus said.

"Me too," affirmed Enda. "My sister is the best and prettiest."

"Makes us unanimous." Tara confirmed the family's undivided oneness. Exemplifying the kind of family they were—unified units of love like a good football team that wins as one unified force.

After the interview, each Rose sang, recited poetry, or danced. Maura created a poem in which she saluted her mother and father, praising them the very best parents.

"The runner-up could be a Charlestown girl from Charlestown, Boston."

"A good economic choice," John said, "especially since the Boston group brought fifty people here and have spent a fair amount of money."

"What a thing to say, John."

"Well, didn't they come with people?"

"So what!"

"Sooo."

She gave him a look he knew meant, "give it up."

"And the winner is . . ."

Everyone sat straight and surveyed the M.C.

"And the winner is…" he repeated … is the London Rose, Amanda Sweeney."

Amidst the applause, John proclaimed, "Of all the girls – a bloody blimey limey."

"John . . . she's Irish."

"Well, she lives in London."

"The judges aren't narrow-minded like you."

"Whose side are you on, dearie?"

"Now, who's the limey?"

"You lose, Dad," snapped Enda.

"Temporarily. I'm losing for now, but the game isn't over."

Tara hoped her life wouldn't be over for at least another twenty years. Over her shoulder, she saw a darting black imagine – an *angel of death?* Born into this life head first, she liked not the idea of leaving feet first, at least not at fifty-nine. She recalled the courageous ending of her friend, Fiona. She knew she exited this life in style. She said to her husband when she neared death from cancer, "It's time." She knew she had to go to the hospital to get morphine drip. Time, like the frozen tundra, prepared to freeze her into an eternal sleep.

"Are you sure, Fiona?" her husband said.

"Yes. It's time, dear,"

He collected her coat and suitcase.

She said, "Let's have a toast to a good life."

They had the drinks. She said, "Let's have another."

Then they left.

Fiona died two days later.

She'd remember Fiona's classy exit. Hopefully, not too soon for herself.

Thereafter, they continued their journey along the West Coast, sightseeing through the Burren – limestone pavements, caverns, caves and disappearing lakes. They saw the majestic Cliffs of Moher, the natural saw-toothed rock formation caused over million of years by the Irish Sea pounding the Irish coast, Kilkee. They stopped in a seaside resort with another set of enchanting cliffs. They drove onto the Ferry as the ship prepared to cross the River Shannon for Tarbert, saving a two-hour drive to reach Tralee. In Killarney for three days, they enjoyed the holiday spirit of one of Ireland's main holiday towns and rode a jaunting car. Thaddeus captured their spirits with "I feel like John Wayne and Maureen O'Hara in *The Quiet Man*. They drove to the Rock of Cashel, the seat of former Irish kings, to Templemore where they saw Tara's mother's relatives. Then on to Dublin.

All the nine previous trips to Ireland, Tara stayed with either her mother or her sister Una. This time, they rented a condominium from where Tara and John entertained the O'Shea's, with Tara's siblings and friends.

Tara and her sister, Una, prepared sandwiches.

"Here, John, make yourself useful," issued Una. "Cut the crust off."

"And who told you to be the boss," he responded, taking loaves of bread, the staff of life.

"Mind yourself, Yank. You're in my country."

"Right," Paul said. "Do what you're told."

"And you, my brother-in-law," said John.

"I'm Una's husband first and Irish, too. You're outnumbered. Do what you're told."

"You mean you let Una tell you what to do."

"Mind now," Una answered. "Watch what you say."

"And if I don't?"

"You'll get a rightful smack."

In good humor, John said, "Tara, defend your husband. I'm under attack."

"You're on your own. And don't be daft. You can take care of yourself."

"Daft or not, your smiling sister and her husband are not treating their guest well."

Paul stated, "The trouble with you, John...you mix things up. You're not our guest. It's we who are your guest." Paul enjoyed sarcasm. Verbal jabbing, attacking a person's character, an art form to him, like a fighter pilot stalking the enemy ready for the kill.

"Oh, Paul," declared Una, "There's not much you can do with him."

"Sure there is," John professed. "You can cut your own crust."

"My, my," smiled Una. "A nervy one you are."

"Oh, he's a good boy," said Tara.

"What's he good for?" asked Paul, circling John.

Tara giggled. "He brought me here."

"There you go, Paul. See, I'm good for something." John remembered a proverb a Jewish friend told him: *don't approach a goat from the front, a horse from the back or a fool from any side. Paul might be the fool.*

"I wouldn't bet on it," Paul asserted.

"I would," Tara said.

"Well, well, me wife is defending her darlin'."

"Listen to him," Tara observed. "He's trying to be Irish."

"With a name like O'Malley, I am Irish."

"You're half Irish," Una snapped.

"I'm as Irish as Padraic Pearse. His father was born in England and his mother a Brady and born in Ireland. He was half-Irish, too."

"You know your history," Paul said, continuing to place mayonnaise on the bread John passed to him.

"Pearse was half Irish and so am I."

"Now, don't be comparing yourself with Padraic Pearse," Una noted.

"I'm not. But I am as Irish as he."

In their teamwork, Una took the bread and Paul added one thin slice of Swiss cheese and one thinner slice of ham. "You're not Irish."

"You're a hard nut to crack, Una."

"Don't call my wife, a nut," Paul said, with a smile, which shielded his thoughts of fondness towards his brother-in-law.

John placed his arm around Paul's shoulders. "Oh, you still love me."

"Now, I wouldn't say I love you." He moved his head away.

John giggled. He shot a piece of crust at Tara who returned his prank by raising her hand to her lips and blew him a kiss.

Paul observed her action. "Sweet."

"I remember you two on your honeymoon," Una uttered. "Sweet," she mimicked amidst everyone's laughter. "You slept in our bedroom."

Paul added, "And we could hear the pitter paddle of little feet like squirrels on our roof running across the floor from one single bed to the other."

Tara smiled, as did all.

"Yes," Una inserted, remember the sign we made and put at the end of your bed, Tara?"

Tara's lips widened and her eyes glittered. She placed completed sandwiches on serving trays. "Una, you're a prankster like mammy and John."

"Remember what it said?"

John looked directly at Una, eyeing her with devilment. "GB"

"And you knew what we meant!"

"Getting better," John replied.

Paul echoed. "Has it been?"

"Of course," John said without hesitation. "We have four children to prove it."

"And we have five, John."

"Which means, Una, you're better than us?"

"This conversation's taking a turn . . ."

"Not a bad turn," John injected.

"Like a turn towards a weakness."

"Tara, you sound like one of Hal Roach's jokes when he says his mother took a turn and went into a weakness."

"There you go," Paul mimicked. "Sounding Irish again."

Una joined her husband's biting levity. "Who said you're Irish?"

John ignored her remark and continued cutting crust. He reached for Paul's arm as straightforward as if he scooped up a ball of ice cream from a container. Paul shrugged him off.

"I think we've enough now," Tara stated.

"The baby of the family has spoken," John declared.

"The baby of the family, with cancer, and the one to die first."

"Now, Tara, let's not discuss it," Una said.

*There they go again avoiding my cancer.* During the evening, her two brothers asked how she felt and, after dropping a brief discussion of her illness and treatments, they entered into the evening of social conversation. Delighted for a chance to entertain her family, but, at that time she wanted to discuss her ability and chances of staying alive. But it wasn't what they wanted. The culture of Ireland took precedence.

# TWENTY-THREE

# Lourdes Twice

The children flew to London for three days. John and Tara went to Paris, where they toured the Eiffel Tower, Notre Dame Cathedral, Louvre, Moulin Rouge, and Arc de Triomphe. On the *Champs Elysees* they sipped strong cappuccino and made observations about the French people sitting around them and those people ambling on the thirty-foot wide sidewalk.

"I thought I'd see more fashion on display," Tara observed. "I don't see women fashionably dressed."

"They dress like Americans…jeans and such."

"Well…the French sent us the Marquis de Lafayette," John remarked. "Maybe there's another Lafayette in the crowd," he said, gesturing to the passers-by.

"Young, was he not?"

"Twenty years old when he meet Washington at the Moylan House, a few miles from our home."

"Oh yes. You showed me the house. It's in need of repair."

"Imagine, twenty. And he led men older than himself. And he knew our language. Inter-resting."

"Better than Americans speak."

"Americans can speak English and do. But most speak 'American'—runnin', playin', How are ya, How ya doin', ain't, av for avenue."

"Don't be critical of the country that gave you dual citizenship, Tara," said John.

"I'm not. I'm proud of having dual citizenship. Just making an observation."

After a moment of silence, John remarked, "Besides training Washington's troops as a major general at Valley Forge, Lafayette persuaded the French government to aid the colonists against the English and assisted in negotiations that won our independence."

"Thanks for the history lesson," she smiled.

"From history, we learn our past mistakes and hopefully do the job right in the future."

"Let's get more history. Let's go to Notre Dame Cathedral."

"It'll be like going back to Notre Dame University."

"Maybe," Tara mused.

The Cathedral of Notre Dame rose higher than any other building in the immediate area. The magnificent Gothic church dated back to 1163 with construction continuing for another eight hundred years.

"A restoration project would restore its beauty, John."

From the outside, John studied the front entrance. "The three arched doorways couldn't be built today – too expensive."

"And they might not have the craftsmen to duplicate all the designs, statues, and artistry."

John counted statues and cement spindles. "There are twenty-eight statues of saints…or are they popes."

"Could be either."

"And three sets of seven spindles under the twin bell towers."

Tara observed the circular arches on both sides of the church. She felt her stomach reacting to all her medications and cancer treatments. Her neck throbbed like a vibrator, but she kept silent. "What makes this cathedral magnificent is the arches on both sides. And what a setting on the River Seine."

"The river empties into the English channel about four hundred miles from here."

Inside the 829-year-old church, John noted, "This church was built around the time Diarmuid MacMurrough asked Strongbow to help him win back his wife from Tiernan O'Rourke."

"Hence, the invitation for Henry II to land in Ireland and thus began England's conquest of Ireland."

"More like the rape of Ireland," John said. "And you know who authorized Henry II's coming to Ireland . . .Adrian IV, Nicholas Breakspear, the only Englishman to serve as pope."

"And we've had all our troubles because of a pope, an English one no less."

"Misinformed by English bishops opposed to the Church in Ireland, Henry went after the Irish. Those bishops ill-advised Henry that the Irish lead lives of debauchery and thus Adrian issued a papal bull for Henry to clean up Ireland."

Tara admired the strength of the structure. "I was told the roof consisted of six sections."

"Interesting. The light of day provided light for services, though it must have been gloomy."

"They must have used many candles for evening services, John."

"I suppose. I wonder how many priests or monks viewed ceremonies from the balcony."

"Thinking about going back to the seminary?" she quirked.

He gazed at her, smiled, and winked. "Not on your life."

"And if I have no life? If I die, will you go back?"

"I married you, Tara, forever. You won't die." He thought for a moment. "If you do, I will not go to the seminary."

"Think about it," she encouraged.

Six different tour groups followed guides. Tara listened to one tour guide speaking in French, a language she studied at St. Louis private school in Rathgar. She turned to her husband. "Such large stone blocks to build this church."

"Yes. How did they raise them into position in the twelfth century?"

"Scaffoldings and pulleys."

For some unexplainable reason, Tara recalled the blonde lady at Shop 'N Bag supermarket, the lady who worked the service desk and, during breaks, smoked outside the store. She never looked happy. Worse: the lady had lost her winning lottery tickets. She whispered a prayer for the lady: give her peace of mind, Lord, and contentment; let her not be lonely when she is alone.

"Now we have seen the sights in Paris, isn't it time for God to cure you at Lourdes."

Tara corrected, "Mary and God. I'm asking Mary to heal me. She can do it or she can ask her son to cure me. She already removed the spot from my lung when I came here with Una."

"Like the man suffering from a dreadful skin disease. He came to Jesus and begged for help, like us. He told Jesus he believed Jesus had the power to cure him. And Jesus, filled with pity, cured him. Jesus said, 'Be clean and the man was cleansed.'"    " I f Jesus did so for a believer, he should do the same for you, Tara. The people of Nazareth rejected Jesus. They didn't have faith in Jesus. We have faith to move mountains. Jesus will heal you, Tara. I believe it."

"So do I, John. So do I."

"Ever notice all the cures in the New Testament were performed on people who had or didn't have faith, asked or didn't ask to be cured. He should be able to cure us."

"Me, you mean . . ."

"No. Us. You need to be healed physically. I need to be cured mentally and emotionally."

He grew lonely. He remembered a quotation: Laugh and the world laughs with you; weep and you weep alone. A large knot tightened in his stomach.

"Well, then," Tara said, "off to Lourdes with us believers."

---

Air Intel Flight, 5904, left Paris for Lourdes in the late afternoon. Cloud formations presented an ocean of snowy white cotton balls. Clouds shaped themselves into jagged mountaintops like the Dublin Mountains. *Pushing through clouds seemed like pushing through and reacting against cancer.* Flying at 30,000 feet over geometrically shaped farms, roads, towns, houses, and a river, Tara recalled the trials she underwent in November and December 1988 in dealing with her first bout with cancer. Una had come from Dublin to be with her. Her heart felt heavy remembering those days of depression, sixteen months after having opened O'Shea Personal Care. If she had cancer before July 1987, when she and John bought the large two-story house to be converted into a state licensed, assisted living facility, she never would have bought the place. She didn't want John, who didn't know the personal care business, to be saddled with it.

The river made her recall their many trips to Plymouth Meeting Mall fountain where they took the children for a night out and dinner at the Harvest House restaurant. They left for the mall with several twenties in their pockets and came home with several pennies. Often the case, raising and educating four children as well as dining out, paying for their trips to Europe, drained their family incomes. Regardless, in those days, they had their health, each other, and they loved each other. Now, she didn't have her health. We *have each other and still very much in love, but for how long?*

She, the last born in her family, might be the first to die. She could make no sense out of the situation. *The good die young, people say.* She wanted no part of this cliché. Life, she wanted. She prayed for long life with John. *Oh God,* she told herself as the plane neared Lourdes, *heal me as I've prayed in my rosary Novena. Remember Mary what the Novena demands of you: Thou canst not look upon my gift and fail to see its binding; as thou receivest my gift, so wilt thou receive my petition; from thy bounty thou will give me the favors I earnestly and trustingly see. I despair of nothing I ask of thee; show thyself my Mother, Mary. I want to see my children married, to hold my grandchildren, to be with John through old age. Is it too much to ask? Please give me life.* She squinted from the brilliant sunlight. Her eyes like diamonds cast rays of joy.

"Talking to yourself again?" John asked.

She smiled. No need to answer.

In her second visit to Lourdes, she expected her prayer to live to be answered; she believed Mary, the Mother of God, would not fail her. John's first visit to Lourdes; John believed Tara would be cured. It wasn't faith mixed with doubt. Faith moved mountains.

Tara and John joined in a queue to visit the Grotto, the pivotal point where Mary appeared to Bernadette and proclaimed her Immaculate Conception. Africans, Italians, French, Spaniards, Irish, Americans and Asians conversed in their native tongues. The world's melting pot. Though different in nationalities and language, they professed one common goal – to honor Mary with their pilgrimage of prayer. The clear sky with the sun beginning to set lightened her heart. Warm, humid air carried the scent of hundreds of people huddled together. John wondered how Mary could hear all those people at one time – and how could she give everyone what they prayed for. If they all received what they wanted, the world of trillions of people would stampede to Lourdes and think they should get whatever they asked. This would be impossible…all the same, he hoped, Mary would hear their prayer.

When he told Tara his reasoning, her Irish eyes and cheeks reddened. She clinched her fist. "That's selfish, John. What about all these sick people walking about? They want to be helped, too."

"First things first," he responded. "And you're first."

Tara bought a three-foot candle for forty-five francs. Since all the candleholders had lighted candles, the sign in various languages indicated her candle would be lit at a future time and placed in front of the Grotto. She recalled the countless times she came into the house in the evening with John sitting in the dark with one or two candles lit. "Weird-o," she called him. She prayed for her cure and for the well being of her family. John joined in this intention. He imagined their efforts to reach God shone like a silvery star leading people to the summit of God's attention.

Tara and John lingered in a queue to enter the Baths. With chemotherapy and radiation in her body, she hoped for Mary's intercession, a full recovery.

———————

The spring under Mary's feet when she appeared to Bernadette produced, in time, the practice of submerging one's self in holy waters, hoping to be cured. *Medicine and my faith will cure me.*

John watched his wife enter the baths at 7:40 P.M., 12:40 A.M. American time August 15th, the feast of the Assumption of Mary into heaven. Traditionally, a day for healing, according to popular belief. "Don't take Tara to heaven now," he said to himself.

Later they had dinner with the other guests in the dining room of the Saint Joan of Arc Hotel.

"See the bottle of wine over there on the table across from us," John said. "I'll have the same."

Tara noticed a full-sized seventy-five-millimeter bottle of wine. "It's too much," she said, "you'll get drunk."

"No, I won't. It's about four glasses. Besides when in France, be like the French: drink wine. It's the golden rule."

"What's the golden rule?"

"He who has the gold makes the rule…and I have the gold—you."

Tara touched his arm, "I hope I don't have to hold you up as we walk around Lourdes."

John looked at her. She knew what his eyes said.

John ordered J. Bonnefont's Tricoulet, a red fruit wine. "Look at this. It's marked 'Lourdes'. I'll save this bottle and bring it home."

"And if I die, you'll be able to hold the bottle in your hand and remember our trip to Lourdes and me."

"It will be my *pieces de resistance* at dinner. You're a hard act to forget."

She smiled. "You'll have to tell me when you join me in heaven how did it feel holding a glass bottle in your hands instead of my breasts."

He returned her smile. "I'd rather hold your breasts."

She finished sipping her soup. "You should have found the tumor, you know, since your hands are always on me."

He collected their soup bowls and placed them on the side of the table. He studied the people at other tables. "You're right, I should have."

"Well, why didn't you?"

"Interested in other things."

"You always are," she smiled.

He had finished most of the sweet wine before the entrée of lamb arrived.

"Some day, you'll join me for a drink."

"Do you want me to break my pledge?"

He admired how beautiful she remained, with the additional fifteen pounds she had gained during chemotherapy and radiation treatment over the last three and one-half years. He needed to tell her more often she was beautiful. But, since she knew he knew she was beautiful, he let it go. Husbands make mistakes when beauty is obvious and they don't express appreciation of that beauty. "No, I want you to be yourself. I've never tried to change you. I married you for what you are and I loved you and I love you now the way you are. And, as I've already told you, Tara, I'm with you until the end."

"I know, John."

"Thought I'd remind you."

He drank the last of Tucoulet with dessert of white cake covered with chocolate syrup. "You would think I was frugivorous, drinking all these fruit juices."

John's telling her he loved her prompted a recall of Eoin Sterling's sculpture, *A Tortured face*. She recalled it aptly named: the distorted eyes, shaped like a jagged edge of weather worn stones, the pointed nose, and a mouth without teeth, gaping and opened wide as if it had called out for help to ease its torturous agony, but found no one to ease the pain. The pain of being alone seemed to split its lips apart. Through all the agony there was no ecstasy. With its head raised up to the heavens in anguished sorrow, it seemed to cry out to God in heaven just as Jesus had asked his Father to remove the cup of pain in Gethsemane and heard no answer, it knew it would languish in pain all its days...alone. *Poor John, he'd be desperately alone if I die. All the same, I know failure is not in the falling, but in the staying down. Without me, I hope John will stay up.*

After dinner, they walked back to the grotto. Tara and John sat on a bench directly in front of the statue of Mary. Together, they recited the Rosary Novena... silently. Two months ago, they started saying the twenty-seven days of petition followed by twenty-seven days of thanksgiving. On the eighteenth day of petition of the Glorious Mysteries, they placed roses at the grotto. As others walked near the location from which the spring is said to have first flowed, people genuflected.

At dusk, they waited for the evening processions to begin under banners, which listed various groups' names and locations. Lead by a priest carrying the Blessed Sacrament, they joined in the procession around the concourse behind a marble statue of Mary, which faced the basilica. Many people held rosaries while they walked ten abreast in a sea of people. In their native languages, they sang "Salve Regina" and "Immaculate Mary." The cacophonous roll of their voices rose up to the heavens like the soft rumble of thunder. Everyone held lighted candles with a covering of white cardboard at the base for protection against hot wax drippings. Along the quarter mile circular path, voices leaped to the heavens like a far-off rumbling train.

John whispered, "This is like walking in a gargantuan funeral procession." *How many of the people repeated this exercise from previous visits to Lourdes. Was this a recidivist exercise for them?*

"Shhhhh." The person behind him said. They walked with a group of people from Portugal.

"Why is she shhhing me? She can't understand what I'm saying."

"She doesn't have to, John. You're making sounds."

John motioned Tara ahead, skipping in front of people to avoid the woman.

As various groups walked ahead others joined in behind. By the time the priest carrying the monstrance reached Mary's marble status, the last group had joined the procession. Then a circular ocean of people carrying candles, hearts deep in prayer and hands warm under paper holders preventing melted wax burning their hands. The procession resembled cars on Interstate 95 as they traveled towards Philadelphia with red taillights glowing in the dark. It reminded Tara of her train trip through Horseshoe Curve when seated in the middle of the train, she could see both the engine and the caboose. Above the spirals, a black cloud moved off into the distance.

She concentrated on the singing. The stereophonic sound of hundreds of voices created a unified melody of faith and prayer. She agreed with Thomas Merton in *Thoughts in Solitude*: "We do not pray for the sake of praying, but for the sake of being heard." The flow of soft undulating voices reminded her of monks singing Gregorian Chant, the smoothing, peaceful ringing sounds of church music on the tape she occasionally listened to while driving. In the holiness of the hour, John, said, "It's time, Tara."

The atmosphere contained the aura of burning wax and John's burning love for her.

She said, "Isn't the smell of the wax wonderful? I feel like I'm in a huge cathedral after a solemn High Mass... the whole Church smells of wax amidst the scent and sight of slight smoke from the burnt wicks."

"I've waited all day."

"Patience is a virtue you need more of," she said, "especially at night…in the bedroom." She gazed directly into his blue irises. She said, "If I had eight children, I'd sew your pajamas in front. You know…a stitch in time saves nine. "In a place like this you still think of . . . what a one track mind."

He couldn't help but laugh. "And why not love? This is a holy place and our marriage is a holy union."

She frowned. She smiled, an affirmative smile, which meant she consented.

In reverence, he changed his thinking to the devotion of the many faithful who came to Lourdes seeking a favor. "All those candles represent the body of Christ and the wicks represent the soul of Christ. That's why every Mass is said with lit candles to illustrate the point of the union of the body and soul of Christ being offered at mass and a reminder why we should adore Christ."

"You should have been a priest, John."

"I tried all three vocations – single, religious and marriage. The best one is marriage. I married the best and loveliest lady I ever met."

She didn't say thank you; she didn't have to. The scintillation in her eyes did. John read her effervescent glow.

People blew out their candles at the end of the procession, Tara remarked, "This is like one huge blackout happening all at once in a giant convention room – all the lights going out simultaneously."

Discarding the candles, Tara said, "Okay, let's go now to the hotel."

Laughing, he asked, "You…in a hurry?"

Their room had two single beds. John pushed them together to form one bed. Tara and John undressed. Standing without clothes, he caressed her and standing chest-to-chest, abdomen-to-abdomen, he said "This is like being in the room under Una and Paul's bedroom when we married."

Scratching his back, she responded, "It is that."

As he lowered her to the bed, she felt the arousal of their passion in this holy place where she had come to the healed. She thought every action she and John had performed in their love-making was holy. It had to be. God joined them together when the priest said in 1963 "For better or for worse, for richer or for poorer, until death do you part." *Until death do us part. . little did I know I might die young.*

John's actions reminded her of their honeymoon night in Waterford when they consummated their marriage. *Every time. . like the first time.*

He whispered. "I love you, Tara." She received his love with exultation. She had pleased him. In pleasing her husband, she pleased herself. She had pleased God. She loved him and he loved her. They loved each other twenty-nine years ago as they loved each other in the makeshift double bed in Lourdes. In the holy place of Lourdes, they believed sexual intercourse to be a spiritual and fulfilling act of faith. For John, any place was.

Good together like Jeffrey Gribler and DeeDee Barfield dancing together in the Pennsylvania Ballet's *Swan Lake*. "Remember those dancers at the ballet?"

He thought awhile and finally said, "Yes, they're good. You know, I've heard people saying this about us," he chuckled.

*Yes. . I need to feel great now and when I get home. I don't need this to be my last dance.*

# TWENTY-FOUR

# Looking for a Cure

Returning home from Lourdes, her first trip was to the medical center. She parked in a reserved slot marked handicapped. Her family doctor had authorized a handicap parking license plate because of her congestive heart failure as well as driving residents from O'Shea Personal Care facility to their personal errands. Front door parking provided for shorter walking distance from the car to the door. An oil truck making a delivery partially blocked the pathway. A young high school girl in a checkered wintry top power-walked passed the medical offices. On a cold February day, she wondered, why the girl was not in school.

She hated February. Her mother hated February. Her grandmother hated February. *Must be in the family to hate February with its short days of cold, penetrating snow or rain shooting into her bones.* The dreariness of the season seemed as if twigs splattered across a stony road of leafless trees pricked into her spirit. In December, January, and February, the absence of soft, beautiful scented flowers, green grass and gentle spring or summer winds made life arduous and cheerless, especially for the elderly. A daily routine of seeing gray and black wears on a person. She considered it the psychological series of three. Three straight months of gloomy, cold weather seemed boring, depressing.

She hoped March might bring an early end of wintry dullness. At best, she hoped medical help could be recommended for the swelling in her right arm and hand. The last time she visited her doctors, a tree trimmer had taken down the entire tree except for the bottom section, which contained six branches. She personified each branch as a symbol of each member of her family of six. On this visit, she noticed the trimmer had not returned to finish the job and one branch had broken loose from the trunk and lay on the ground. She imagined herself as the fragmented branch, lying helpless, ready to sink into the grave. With this imagery, she scolded herself for negative thinking.

When Tara shook hands with Dr. Stein, he felt her hand more enlarged than her last visit in January.

"My arm is swelling like an inflated balloon."

"I know. I felt it when we shook hands."

"I'm having trouble holding a pen. I'm afraid of losing my arm."

"There is increased lymphedema in your right arm. And I feel a fullness in the supraclavicular," he said, feeling her neck and breasts areas. "It may be a tumor, I'm sorry to say."

Tara lowered her head. Her heart beat faster. *Help me, Lord. Where are you when I need you?* "Could it be radiation residue? Could radiation have caused the edema of the arm?"

"Well, I'll have you tested for the fullness."

"My breathing remains heavy at times."

"I'm decreasing the Megace to eighty milligrams twice a day from three times a day." *Megace again, not grace.*

She considered Dr. Stein could be her brother, the research

chemist, since she had seen him so many times over the last four and one-half years. Dr. Stein treated her as if she were his sister.

"We have good news, Tara."

"Do I ever need it, doctor?"

"We all do . . . your lungs are clear. The pulmonary tests are good."

"But my arm is not."

"I'm recommending you place your arm on a pump an hour a day. You wear a leather sleeve and the machine pumps air into the sleeve, causing pressure on the arm and hopefully it will reduce the swelling."

"My neck still has a small lump."

"I'm referring you to Dr. Wiseman. He will examine you and determine the way to go."

*Another round of surgery. . oh no.* "I have heard about a doctor in Trenton who does special work with patients with lymphedema. I'll try treatments with him."

"I've heard of him. I can't promise the outcome, but it is vogue therapy today."

"Let's hope for the best. There's one drug we can try, if Dr. Wiseman operates. It's experimental. It's called Taxol. Want to try it?"

"Anything, if it works."

"No guarantee, Tara."

---

On the way to Dr. Wiseman's office, they passed the Hideaway Swim Club. *How many more times will I see this?* An Illuminated statue of a leprechaun decorated the front lawn. It held a lamp. *Either it signifies the light of the world or a "pigs in the kitchen" kind of thing, for all I know people still believe Irish people fostered leprechauns and actually have pigs in their kitchens.* Unlike Dr. Stein, who offered morning and afternoon visiting hours, Dr. Wiseman had visiting hours in the evening since he operated during the day.

Once again, people occupied all available seats in the waiting room when John and Tara entered for the seven thirty visit. They waited until nine thirty before finally being called into an examining room.

"Ah, Mrs. O'Malley. How are you doing?"

She went directly to the point. "I feel lymph nodes again in my neck and my lymphedema is getting worst."

John watched closely as the doctor examined his wife's breasts. Dr. Wiseman pressed his fingers into the right neck side and gently pushed his fingers into both breasts.

John looked away.

"Dr. Stein mentioned Taxol, "John said. The word Taxol hung over the room, like a disease unable to be contained.

"Well, we'll see how it works. Drum up your confidence, Mrs. O'Malley."

On the way out of the office, John said, "I don't like any man touching my wife."

She grimaced. "He's a doctor."

"He's a man. I wonder if he enjoys fondling woman's breasts all night."

"Your mind!" She veered him to the car.

"Anyway, I love being here with you," he said.

"Yes. I like to be kept on top of things."

"Yes," he said, "I like to be on top of everything." His eyes flirted over to hers.

She knew what he meant.

In May, Tara entered the hospital for her first dose of Taxol therapy. The nurse administered the chemical from the bottle to the infusaport. Tara lay on her back for the two hours while Taxol drained from the bottle to her body. She felt aches and pains in her joints. But she believed she'd beat cancer. She wouldn't allow it to kill her.

The nurse smiled, spoke softly, and enjoyed talking with Tara who thought the nurse young, attractive, and motherly.

"We'll do the best we can for you," The nurse said.

"You're a dear," Tara said.

"I'll take care of you as I took care of my husband."

"Was he injured?"

"He had cancer."

"I'm sorry."

"He's better now. When he had chemotherapy as an out patient like you, I gave it to him."

"Inter-resting. How's he today?"

"Fine. Giving me trouble around the house," she laughed. "He's better. There's no sign of cancer now."

"I hope he stays well."

"Like you, he will stay well."

The smell of medications filled the air. A lone fly pestered the nurse who brushed it away. Out in the hall, someone dropped what sounded like a tray of food. The smell of vegetable soup made her hungry. John had delivered her to the hospital on his way to school and would return at three o'clock to bring her home. She wondered would her body be ready? Would the Taxol wipe away all signs of cancer? *Unlikely in a short time...*

She laid her head on the pillow, the nurse changed from feathers to foam due to Tara's allergies. Coupling her hands, she placed them under her head. The infusaport and the Taxol entering her body, sensitized her skin and she softly scratched the area. She saw the fluids leave the bottle and bubble its way into the infusaport under the skin on her left breast. She moved to her side as she felt the Taxol pass out of the plastic bag and into her body. *Will these treatments never end?*

Her mind wandered as she closed her eyes. She recalled all the suffering her father experienced when visiting Philadelphia with the Irish president. He had a heart attack and was hospitalized in the Hospital of the University of Pennsylvania. He had agonizing pain like someone pulling a noose tighter and tighter around his chest. She remembered all the pains of childbirth she experienced in delivering Sean, Enda, Maura and Thaddeus. *All those pains together won't kill me, but cancer will.*

"Are you all right, Mrs. O'Malley?" the nurse said, interrupting her thinking.

"Fine. I was recalling all my pains over the years . . . Funny to think of child births at a time like this."

"Not really, you're relaxed. We think about all kinds of experiences when medication is loaded into the body."

Tara admired the nurse's blond hair. With blue eyes, fair skin, rouge and red lipstick on full lips...she had Maura's features.

"You're a considerate nurse."

"Thank you. I'm considerate when I have good patients like you. I'll be back to check on you soon...and don't worry. Remember, you can't get well without roadblocks. If you have nothing blocking you, most likely it's not worth the effort." After the nurse left the room, Tara reminisced about her operation history. She'd many roadblocks: 1951, Appendectomy; 1964, gall bladder; 1980, Hysterectomy; 1984, Marshall Marchetti; 1986, Blepharoplasty; 1988, lumpectomy; 1988, bladder examination when she had anesthesia, requiring a ventilator. All except the

Appendectomy related to marriage and child bearing. Her medical problems multiplied like hornets gathering around the nest since 1963. She whispered, "I'd go through it again, if I had to, if it meant having my marriage with John and my children. I wouldn't trade these last thirty years for anything. Affluent people can have all the money they greed for. With my family I'm richer."

The nurse re-entered the room and heard her talking. "Ah huh, caught you talking to yourself."

Tara grinned. "Oh, I talk to myself. It helps me hear what's on my mind and I can better put things in perspective when I verbalize a problem. It's what's on God mind that puzzles me."

The nurse took the clipboard from the base of the bed.

"Your records are good, I see here. Your CBC is adequate. Your white count is 3,400 and your platelets 415,000. And you're taking Coumadin."

"Yes, Dr. Stein started it."

"He's one of the best. So is Dr. Wiseman."

"They've kept me alive for five years."

---

Filled with Taxol, Coumadin, Cytadren, Voltaren, Bumex, Synthroid, Lanoxin, Nortriptyline—a melting pot of medication—the infusaport and hope, Tara drove herself to Summit Personal Care. Bristol Road spread out before her like the stalk of a sunflower opened by the sun's rays. Leaf-filled trees ticked past like soldiers standing at attention. Entering the side kitchen door, she greeted Bob, the cook, who proceeded to relate his latest problem with his girlfriend, Janet, the aide who occasionally presented her with questions amounting to what—do-I-do-next in her job duties. Janet didn't know how to work.

Ellie as usual played the piano and Madelene as usual lifted her dress to expose her underwear and saluted Tara with a fanciful wave and a hug.

"You're lovely, dear," Madelene said. "We love you. And we know you love us."

"Of course, I do, Madelene especially, when you keep your dress down." "Oh dearie, do I do that? My word. What kind of woman am I?" Madelene smiled and began to waltz around two sofas.

Tara shook her head, smiling "Hello, Marie. How are you?" A how-are-you-question was a question she should not ask. People unloaded their woes on her. Like priests and counselors, she heard problems of the world. Nonetheless, Tara asked questions and wanted to know residents' joys and concerns.

She waved to Harry, Roland, Henrietta, Sarah, and Susan. "Good morning, ladies and gentlemen. Isn't Ellie's playing lovely?"

They returned the greeting. Harry said, "It annoys me. She's off beat. And when she's not sure of the next key to hit, there's a pause and it makes me nervous."

"Oh, Harry. Be patient. Ellie's doing her best."

The maintenance man, Bill Martel, followed her into her office. Someone usually followed her into her office. As administrator, a resident would walk into the office with her—and she with a coat on and carrying an attaché—the person couldn't wait to give her a problem to solve. But bothered by this morning routine, she wasn't. She was a problem solver? And she enjoyed it, despite her sister Una telling John she should not work. Work and her family: excellent therapy.

"I think Bob is going to be sick today, Tara."

"What? I spoke to him. He told me about the fight he and Janet had. Well, Janet isn't in and he will fake sick and join her."

"About right," Eleanor said, standing in the doorway.

Bob suddenly appeared at the door, holding his stomach. "I feel terrible, Tara. I'm sick." Tara felt like Odette, queen of the swans, under the spell of Von Rotbart in *Swan Lake*. She needed to be rescued by her lover, Siegfried. Nonetheless, Eleanor and Bill looked at one another as if to say, "Here comes the act."

"You have a stomach ache, Bob?"

"I don't know, Tara. But I have to go home. I need rest."

"Can't you stay through lunch?"

"Bill can do it. He's done it before."

"Bill, can you fix the lunch and dinner?"

She studied Bill's face. *It would be a change from fixing things.*

"Of course. No bother."

"I'm sorry you're not feeling well, Bob. Let us know if you're coming in tomorrow."

"Okay. Hope to see you tomorrow." He left twitching his face and holding his stomach.

Bill went to the kitchen and Tara watched Bob leave through her office window. He dashed to his car with arms pumping. "Sick, huh. You're not sick," she said to herself.

"Yes?" Eleanor asked from the outer office.

"Nothing, Eleanor. I'm talking to myself."

Tara made her rounds. On the first floor in room 101, she smelled the strong odor of urine. "Someone wet," she said to herself and making a note on a pad. On the second floor, when she entered room 205, Joan was making the bed. She recalled Joan's attempt to threaten her with the ladies quitting if they didn't receive instant raises. When pushed into a corner, she came out fighting...calm and collected, with a fighting spirit. "Room looks nice, Joan."

"Thank you, Mrs. O'Malley. How are you today?"

"Fine, thank you. You look good."

When you are nice to a person, they return the kindness and away from her audience Joan was a lamb. When she had an audience she acted out, becoming a poor role model for the staff.

On the third floor, she said hello to Martha.

"Are you feeling good today, Tara?"

"Yes, Martha, I am. I'm taking a new experimental drug and, hopefully, please God, it will work."

She went to her desk to write a letter. She had difficulty holding the pen – her hand continued to swell despite the elastic armband and glove and the pump machine. The pen fell from her fingers twice; but determined she finished writing the letter. *I hope this clears up. How can I function if I can't write?*

---

That night, John advised her, he had contacted a priest in Pittsburgh. He was the pastor of a church where Sister Roberta prepared to give a seven-day retreat for the parishioners. Sister Roberta, they knew, was a healer who had the reputation of healing people through the power of God by touching them or praying over them. She wrote a book on healing. John had arranged to call the pastor that night and the priest would do his best to ask Sister Roberta to talk to and pray over Tara. Tara received the news with faith and enthusiasm.

At six o'clock, John rang the pastor, himself an Irishman, as was Sister Roberta. Fortune favored them. The pastor said Sister Roberta would come to the phone.

"Here, Tara, Father is getting Sister Roberta."

Tara took the receiver; covering the phone she said to John, "I heard from Margaret White that Sister Roberta is a wonderful person. She prays before the Blessed Sacrament three hours a day. She herself was cured by Jesus of crippling arthritis."

"Let's hope her prayers are heard by Jesus and Mary."

"Wouldn't it be great?"

Into the telephone Tara said, "Hello, Sister."

"Hello Mrs. O'Malley." The nun dealt directly with the conversation, avoiding pleasantries. She went to the heart of the matter. "Now listen to me as I pray over you."

"Yes, Sister." Tara felt like a schoolgirl again: do what you're told and be quiet.

"Almighty God, hear the petition we request of you this day. Grant through your healing power and in the name of your son, we beseech you to bring peace of mind to Tara O'Malley and give her the grace you offer to all to be able to live according to your holy will. Let her find comfort in these days of suffering and offer her pains to you for restitution for her sins and all our sins. Dear God, we pray and hope in your omnipotent power you will make Tara O'Malley well again, that no trace of cancer remain in her body, if it be according to your divine will. Your son healed all the sick in Gennesaret, and all those sick people who touched his cloak. We ask you to touch the body of Tara and cure her, to touch her soul with your grace to persevere in the days ahead. Reminding you God the Father, in the name of your son, Jesus, of the lesson from the fig tree when Jesus said: 'When you pray and ask for something, believe you have received it, and you will be given whatever you ask for.' We ask this God the Almighty and powerful Father in the name of Jesus Christ, our Lord, your son. Amen."

"Amen," said Tara.

"I hope you stay well, Mrs. O'Malley."

"Thank you, sister. I hope you stay well, too."

"All the best to you and your family. Be brave."

"I will, sister. And thank you again."

Tara placed the receiver on the telephone base. A clap of thunder made her shiver. Heavy rain began to patter against the window. "Well, John, faith can move mountains."

"I believe it. I believe you'll live."

"So do I."

"Let's go to Lourdes again in August."

She examined his eyes. She knew his heart was with her. "I could ask Nathan Mountain for my two weeks vacation."

"Shouldn't be a problem. Eleanor can oversee things until we get back."

"We'll stay with Una and Paul and go to Lourdes one night, two days."

"It'll be my third visit to Lourdes, your second."

"It will show the Lord we are serious believers. You should remind Mary of the Rosary Novena promise. She is bound to heal you."

She went upstairs to shower and prepare for another relaxing night. John followed her.

"This house is too quiet," said he.

"You wanted us to be alone again. And now with no one here...you miss the kids."

"I do. Now, we have time for an extended second honeymoon. I still miss the kids, you're right."

John liked to play pranks on Tara throughout their marriage. At times, he pretended to fall dead to the floor, hid behind doors when she came home from work, hid from the family, faked sickness to draw attention to himself, sing Christmas hymns in an unharmonious voice from *Take Joy!—The Tasha Tudor Christmas Book.*

He called "Sean" into the front bedroom. "Enda" he called down the step to the first floor bedroom, "Maura," he yelled into the middle room. "Thaddeus, where are you?" he yelled into the fourth bedroom.

As he entered their master bedroom, Tara smiled and said, "Look at you. You wanted them out of the house and now they're gone and you're calling them back."

"I miss them."

"You didn't think you'd ever say this, did you?" She knew he wouldn't admit it...until now. *A man thing.*

Out in the hallway, he called out in jest, "Where are you? Everybody, where are you? Come home to mammy and daddy."

She laughed. "They should hear you now."

"Well, maybe they can. Watch me. I'll call Sean in Philadelphia, Enda and Maura in Boston and Thaddeus at Providence College." He cupped his hands at the corners of his mouth and raised his voice, "Come home, all of you!"

"Out with you now. This is my quiet time." She smiled.

"See you downstairs."

With her remaining days numbered, she liked to root though saved letters from her mother. Like eating peanuts, once she started, hard to stop reading old memories. One letter she found was dated Saturday night with no month and day listed. Her mother's last letter before she died.

"Dear Tara,

I received your letter. I'm in bed since Tuesday last and am writing this lying down. Please excuse the scribble. I got an awful dose of food poisoning. I don't know from what, as I didn't take any tinned food. It may be from the new potatoes I ate. I thought my insides had burned up. I feel as weak as anything. It will be a few days more before I get up. Today is the first day I took any food – all drinks with glucose to keep up my strength. I had a little chicken today. However, I have the hard part over, thank God.

"The heat was awful here the first 3 days I felt sick and I took pills, which made me perspire like I lay in a bowling bath. The first chance I got I let the cold tap water splash in my face...a lovely feeling. It's a bit cooler since the rain came."

*That's why I left Ireland—all the rain and dampness.* She shivered as she continued reading.

"Una and Paul went to Salthill for a week before I got sick. But when they arrived, they learned I took sick and had to come back. They waited for a cup of tea and changed and fed the baby. They arrived home at 8:30. Too bad I had to bring them back. They would have had a great time on their own and one week isn't much after working all the year. You know I felt fine up to 11 o'clock. I came to bed and after an hour I got sick. I thought my inside would come up. You see, at my age, I couldn't chance traveling to the USA."

"Well, mammy," Tara said to herself. "I wanted you to come and stay with us. Ah, mammy, I miss you." She sighed as she read:

"I know lots do but not with my stomach. Besides it will be nice for you to get a holiday next year and Sean will be better able for a journey by then, please God.

"I feel fine today, thank God. I don't think I've any more news of interest. I'll have to finish. Seamus came here Friday night – came to go to the Curagh races yesterday. Of course we all know 'Santa Claus' is a sure thing but on this account its money to throw away: 7 to 4 odds. But, as she trained in Ireland, the Irish crowd went mad with excitement. I listened on the radio. Worth 54,000 pounds to the owner.

"No more now. Love to the 3 of you.

Mammy"

She placed the letter in the top dividing section of her dresser. "Seamus what a gambler with the horses you are," she whispered. "And what a name for a horse – Santa Claus . . .Ah, mammy your last letter. It may not be long that I write my last letter." *Off to Lourdes with ya, girl. You're lookin' to be cured.*

# TWENTY-FIVE

# Lourdes, a Third Visit

Unlike in 1992, when the entire family took off for Ireland, in 1993, Tara and John took off for Ireland without the family. Edna bought their tickets as a gift. Other than that difference, everything else remained the same. They flew again on Air Intel Flight, landed in the Lourdes airport and a tour bus drove them thirty miles to the town of Lourdes. They stayed in the same hotel – St. Joan of Arc. They lunched in the same dining room as 1992, when Tara had a slight bit of soup left in her bowl and tilted the bowl away from her. She delivered the spoon to her mouth and sipped from the side of the spoon. John in turn did the opposite. He tilted the bowl and with the spoon moving towards him, he scooped the soup from the front end of the spoon.

"John, where's your manners?"

"What? Oh, you mean I should use the European method of scooping soup – your way."

"It's not my way. It's the correct way. It's proper etiquette."

"All my life, I've had proper etiquette."

"Not if you hold the spoon wrong."

"Snob," he smiled.

She ignored the remark. "Americans should learn better manners."

"You're an American citizen now!"

She smiled and placed her left index finger under her right eye. He in turn returned her "signal"...the recognition signal of the Molly Maguires...by touching his left lapel with his right thumb and index finger. "Oh huh, thought I didn't know the Molly signal of recognition?" Her smile indicated an affirmative reply.

"For dinner, I'm going to have another bottle of wine."

"You'll be drunk."

"Tara, you said that last year."

"Things never change."

"Remember what we discussed," he said, "the last time we were here?"

"Mind yourself."

"You said remember me and my breasts when you hold the bottle of wine you bought home. And I did."

"You did what?" she remarked, her eyes twinkling. She smiled like a schoolgirl in braids.

"I held that bottle," he said, "many times and remembered your breasts, too. The bottle's hard and your breasts are soft and fleshy."

"Your mind again...."

"The similarity in smoothness; both the wine bottle and your breasts are smooth."

She hit his fingers playfully.

They walked to the Grotto. The same basilica, the same statue of Mary at the foot of the courtyard, the same grotto. People recited the same prayers. Seemingly where holy places exist so are vendors out to make a buck. They followed the same paradigm. *I wonder if the candle I bought last year has been burnt or is it still waiting to be lit; will this year be different. Will I be cured? Or will I be the same. . .fighting cancer cells with positive imagery?* She bought another one for fifty francs. A price increase, she realized, of ten francs. John said, "At Lourdes, the Church is out to make a profit."

As Tara and John walked towards the Grotto, the crowds enlarged. Body to body, deep in the midst of hundreds of people. *Are these the same people, too,* John thought? Little old ladies with their arms at their breasts used them like battling rams to push against people's backs to keep the crowd moving.

"Lourdes or no Lourdes, Tara. I'll stop this. Stand still and don't move. If these people push at our backs, hold firm. It'll show them manners."

The ladies pushing ahead, their arms descending on them like hunters with clubs looking for a kill. Finally, the old ladies moved off to their right only to be replaced by men pushing forward.

"Where's the Christian charity of these people?" John asked as pilgrims behind hand-pushed them along to the grotto.

"They forgot their manners, it seems, when they came to this holy place."

"They want favors from Mary while they push and are rude. These people have the same manners as last year's crowd."

Again, John waited as Tara went into the baths. She undressed and wrapped herself in a wrap-around cloth. A volunteer attendant helped her step into what seemed like the same putrefactive water. She emerged herself into the same chilly water, dirtied by other people's body oil. Odorless. The attendant held the cloth and as she prepared to leave the water, the attendant opened the cloth and she again, swung it around her. *Maybe the same man as last year?* The fabric contained qualities, which dried her body by the time she began dressing.

When she rejoined John, he said, "The same water as last year?" He winked at her.

"How should I know?" Holding his hand, fingers intertwined, she said, "Could be, it's dirty enough."

They left the basilica grounds by the exit, which lead to the same narrow street containing all the commercial stores selling holy items, including holy water. People walked in the street but made room for a two-tiered tour bus, inching its way through the crowd. "Isn't it amazing," John said, "how those huge tour buses barely make it down these alleyway streets much less negotiate turning onto other tiny streets."

"I wouldn't want to try it."

She observed two Blackbirds perched on a limb. *They have all they need. They have each other. No need of bank accounts, no investments, no money, no clothes, no utility bills, no entertainment costs, and they have good health. They work for their food and love each other unconditionally. That's all they need: health and love. Like John and me, I believe we will live.* A dog smelled round the statues of the saints, lifted its leg and relieved itself on the base of Virgin Mary.

"What's wrong?" John asked, suddenly noticing the peculiar look on her face, made fuller by chemotherapy, radiation, and all the other medications she had taken since November 1988. Pains and medications weakened her bowels. She gulped the remainder of her words like a glass of milk. "I had an accident. I must go into this restaurant and change." *The same restaurant, but not the same body—it's weaker.*

Saddened, John watched his bride enter the shop and walk to the rear near the toilets. Tara carried in her purse a change of panties and pantyhose. During the last five years, Tara's chin had enlarged. Her cheeks had plumed, her arm swelled to two-times their normal size, her body retained fluids, increasing her weight to the heaviest she had ever been. She lost her hair three times and each time, as precious as Cleopatra's allurement, it grew back as thick as it had been. Her hair defined her femininity. With all this, she filled with an inner peace. Unafraid, she had balance and purpose in life. On her face, she wore contentment. She understood what someone had written: fear makes true what a person is afraid of.

When she returned to John, he saw this angelic contentment shining in her face. In time, Tara's spirits soared above what life wanted her to experience, for she paradigmed her hope-filled life, which she created. Like an artist, she painted life with bright colors, colors sprinkled with white and pink cherry blossoms. It pleased her to create her place on the canvas of live with respect and dignity towards her neighbor, in helping herself as well as helping others. John compared her to Jesus, who, in his lifetime, was the greatest failure, yet, at the same time, the greatest success the world has known, the greatest story ever told. John canonized Tara with his devotion and love. One septuagenarian priest accused John of idolatry, adoring Tara above God. John told the aging priest, "I love Tara above God and anyone else. She is my sole purpose for living, my idol and role model." John cast off the never-married priest as too old to understand.

The priest, a single man who never loved a woman in the spirit and in the flesh, did not comprehend the mysterious nature of a conjugal, powerful and energetic love they experience, itself a mystery...almost as mysterious as Three Persons in One God.

Back in the same dining room for dinner, John ordered another bottle of wine.

"This time, I'll order a white wine."

"How can you drink all that stuff?"

"I don't drink to excess. When in Rome do what the Romans do."

Her smile gave him encouragement as usual. "A bottle of Bonnefont's Tucoulet please," he told the bilingual waiter. "A white wine please."

"I see its marked Lourdes. Good taste, John, white wine. You're like the man who's half-Irish and half-Scotch. He has a problem: he didn't know if he should get drunk or pay the bill."

"That's what I like about you, Tara," he said, laughing, "your sense of humor. Everything seems the same coming back here."

"Except my body. More malignant lymph nodes, Taxol, the loss of using my right hand."

"Yes, Tara, the body's not the same."

"It's worse. But I believe I'll be healed." At Lourdes for the third and John for the second time, they had an archimedean faith she would be cured. Restored, resurrected, regenerated.

"We spoke about this before, Tara. But today, when you came out of the baths, I had a stronger belief that you will live."

"Faith, it's called."

"Well, I believe it, too. Remember what the angel Gabriel said to Mary about Elizabeth six months pregnant.

"I don't remember actually."

"He said, 'There is nothing that God cannot do.'"

"God will cure me?"

"Yes...let's hope, Tara. Let's hope."

After dinner, like last year, they walked in the evening candle light precession among people of various countries while the fluttering candlelight made a kinesthetic picture of them in the flaming light—green white, orange. They walked back to room 303 at the St. Joan of Arc Hotel, the same room as 1992. They made love in the same two beds again joined together by John.

"We did everything this year the same as we did last," she giggled in their embrace.

"The length of stay is different as is your body."

"We stayed two nights last year, didn't we."

He nodded. Lying together, the full moon shone into their room, silhouetting their shadows on the wall. Sounds of young people's laughter along the quay echoed into the room.

Tara observed, "Looks like we're one human being."

"We're always one, my bride."

They held their kiss an extra long time in a clairvoyant embrace. *Is this our last kiss in Lourdes? A kiss of renewed life or a kiss of death?*

---

They returned to Dublin on an Air Intel flight and drove in the rented car to Tara's sister and brother-in-law's home. A fine, gray stucco home with a center hall and five flowery wallpapered bedrooms.

Their living room adjoined the dining room with the kitchen behind this room. "Letting themselves in with Una's key John announced, "Una, Paul . . . we're home."

Coming towards the kitchen, they heard Paul answer, "This is our home, not yours."

Adjusted to Una and Paul's sense of humor over the years, he smiled and patted Paul's shoulder. "Anyway," John said, "it's good to be home."

Una snapped, "But you're not home. You are a guest in this house."

"Have it your way, Una. We're still home."

"Well John," Paul murmured, "you're a slow learner."

Una noticed Tara's arm swelling under the bandages from the wrist to her shoulder. "Oh dear, your arm looks larger. Does it hurt?"

"No, it's uncomfortable, though." Una hugged her sister.

"Our Lourdes visit will help, we hope," John declared.

"What Paul and I think is it's better to stay home and say prayers rather than running to Lourdes and other places."

"Yes," Paul enjoined his wife. "If you're going to be cured, prayer from home should do the job, if prayer will help at all."

"But don't you think, Paul, three visits to Lourdes, one to Knock and Sister Roberta re-enforces with God our sense of faith in him?"

"I think not," Una answered for her husband.

"But do you, Paul?"

"I agree with Una, John."

"I don't." John's lips clinched tight. He looked directly into the eyes of his in-laws. Their behavior depressed him.

"Sit down here, the two of you and have a cup of tea with us." Una made a fresh pot of tea, covering it with a tea cozy for it to draw properly. "You Yanks drive on the wrong side of the street. Yanks think they can do anything . . . except of course draw tea. Yanks think a cup of tea is a teabag in a cup of hot water."

"This arm is swelling. The doctor I am seeing in Trenton has shown me how to massage and wrap my arm with these elastic bandages.

Una volunteered, "Doesn't look like it's helping."

·"It did for a while, but of late, the arm continues to swell and I'm having a great deal of trouble writing with it."

"My dear, girl," said Paul. He touched her arm and her cheek.

"I've already started practicing writing with my left hand," said Tara.

Una pored tea into the cups. "I still think you shouldn't be working."

John clinched his teeth. "The doctors think work is good for Tara. It takes her mind off cancer." He had used the wrong word "cancer."

"Might be better to be free from all the work related stress," Paul agreed with his wife.

John excused himself, went to the toilet and entered the living room. Sorting through Irish history books, he saw the family Bible. Taking it from a shelf, he sat reading Luke at the point where John the Baptist's messengers had asked Jesus if he were the promised Messiah.

John read, "At that time, Jesus healed many people from their sicknesses, diseases, and evil spirits, and gave sight to many blind people. Jesus told the messenger 'Go back and tell John what you have seen and heard: the blind can see, the lame can walk, those who suffer from dreaded skin disease are made clean, the deaf can hear, the dead are raised to life, and the Good News is preached to the poor.'"

To God, John whispered, "You cured all those people. Can't you cure Tara? We don't doubt you. Please."

Becoming angry, he said aloud, "Are you another Dr. Freddie Hamsin, the fake specialist in A.J. Cronin's *The Citadel*? He kicked the carpet like an angry schoolboy.

# TWENTY-SIX

# Darkening Clouds

Back in the states, they settled into work, treatments, and hope—a routine that had become a way of life. On the way to Dr. Stein's office, she thought the car could easily find its way there, after all their numerous visits. A number of dark-colored cars passed them. She knew people preferred dark colors. To her, dark colors invited depression. A yellow school bus rattled by. Swallows chirped in the trees. Sweet fragrance of pumpkins and apple taffies filled her nostrils.

"What's the outcome with Taxol, Dr. Stein?" Tara asked.

"Since you came back from Lourdes, we gave you three more treatments with Taxol." His eyes looked at the floor. Hesitating, he looked into her eyes. Reading from a report, he said, "Your weight is 151, down three pounds. Blood pressure is 150 over 86. And you get nausea and diarrhea for forty-eight hours after treatment."

She listened intently, noticing the sagging lines under his eyes. It wouldn't be long until he retired and she hoped she would live long enough to retire with John.

He settled beside her, his frame shadowing her like a heavenly blanket of solace. "My concern now is with the lymph nodes in your neck. They haven't gone away and have increased in size on your neck. Your spleen, adrenals, pancreas and kidneys remain normal in size. Your bone scan results are good. But since Taxol is not working, I'm stopping treatments. And we'll start you on Cytoxan, Methotrexate, and Fluorouracie. You haven't had these and you can come here to the office. The nurse will administer them."

Tara continued to hold her composure. She remembered what Cagney said in one of his movies, *"I've learned one thing when I hit bottom; there's one place to go—up." Jesus, please help me to go up.*

"Not a good outlook, is it?"

He smiled. He took hold of her left hand, avoiding looking directly at her.

"These other drugs will help."

"I'm beginning to feel I live here, Dr. Stein."

He laughed.

"Life goes on – as people say. And I'm going on with life. Thanksgiving will be here in a few days and I'm preparing for all the children to come home for Thanksgiving dinner. And if I don't burn the rolls, the dinner will be a success."

Laughing, he responded, "You've never lost your sense of humor through all your treatments, Tara. I admire you for your courage."

With a nip in the air a coating of snow was expected.

But I believe I will win in the end. "I don't like the cold. We'll move to Florida. You know John and I are open talking about cancer and death. He kids me saying that if I don't watch myself, I might win heaven. He's not like other men, holding things back, letting things fester like a smoldering fire until one day there's an explosion."

"You can win heaven later. You're too young to win this kind of race."

Centering in on her medical history, he said, "I don't like the large mass of lymphoid tissue in your pharynx. The adenopathy is not responding positively to the OMF we're giving you. And your flow chart numbers are not where we'd like them." He showed her the flow chart.

|  | 9/92 | 11/93 |
| --- | --- | --- |
| WBC (4.8 - 10.8) | 15.0 | 10.1 |
| RBC (M4; 6-6,F4, 2-5) | 4.61 | 4.73 |
| HGB (M14-18, F12-16) | 14.0 | 12.1 |
| HCT (M42-52, F37-47) | 40 | 38 |
| MCY (82-92) | 86 | 80 |
| Platelets | 426 | 406 |

"You can see, Tara, from September, 1992, to now your numbers are down. We've tried Adriamycin, Mexate, and Adrucil radiation with 7600 centrigrays. While all these have helped, the lymph nodes keep coming back and enlarging."

"I keep hoping, doctor," said she, unafraid to face another day.

"We won't give up," said he, equally unafraid to help her to face another day with courage.

"Nor will I."

"Your platelets are down from 426 to 406. Your white blood cells are down to 10.1; your red cells are up to 4.73; your hemotocrit is down to 38. Your numbers are decreasing in all areas except your red blood cells."

"The right arm and hand are hopeless. I have to buy new blouses, sizes larger than normal. My right arm will not fit into my blouses."

"I'm sorry. I know it bothers you."

"My suits I can't wear because of lymphedema. In fact, I can no longer write with my right hand."

"I am sorry, Tara."

She smiled and brought forth a smile from Dr. Stein. "You know me, doctor. I haven't given up. I've been practicing writing with my left hand. It's not bad."

"You are a determined woman, Tara."

"Do I have a choice?"

"Other patients are not as brave and courageous as you."

"Nor determined," she smiled.

"One thing I can count on with you, Tara, is a laugh."

"At home, when I go to Ireland, I can laugh with my family about nothing over a cup of tea."

"John keeps you laughing, too. I take it."

"He does to an extent. But he's too serious."

"Really."

"Oh, he's a good man and I love him, but he can't laugh about nothing. At home in Ireland, we laugh at times with tears running down our cheeks. All about nothing."

"The Irish enjoy conversation and laughter?"

"Of course. Laughter's the life of the soul. Who was it who said, 'Laugh, thy girlish laughter; the moment after, keep thy girlish tears.'"

"A wit, you are."

"Laughter is medicine for the soul, doctor, as your prescribed medicines are good for me."

"I don't remember who said it, but I remember 'with weeping and with laughter,' the story told.'"

"Yes. Just as life and weeping is mixed with laughter." With a glimmer in her eyes, she added, "Let's hope there's an abundance of laughter and a shortness of weeping."

Laughing, he said, "Your wit is the best. You brighten my life, Tara."

"And I'm betting on you doctor, to save my life."

"Ah . . .but remember," he said, "we're not God. We can't forecast the future. We can do our best and let God do the rest. See you after Thanksgiving." The smoothness of her unlined face filled with hope indicated a vibrant peaceful blitheness. Her expression portrayed an ease of manner, like a person about to be canonized. The doctor felt a sense of inner peace in her presence.

---

At night, she sat at the kitchen table typing a letter to her favorite brother,

Seamus. In Ireland, Seamus, acting like a *seanchaidhe*, told story after story and she listened attentively. She flicked on the chandelier light. With a doctorate in chemistry, she respected his expertise in analyzing the chemicals poured into her body.

At the electric typewriter on the kitchen table she sat, facing into the family room. John had placed the typewriter on the table. She no longer could carry heavy items. Reminiscent of a life gone by in her imagination, like a movie camera showing scenes of her life, she thought of her childhood. She observed the crackling fire in the clinker-brick fireplace. The yellowish-rubicund flames hissed as she remembered the many nights in Ireland when her father, mammy, brothers and sister sat around the fire talking. Those marvelous times when time had stood still and when one day seemed to be same as the next and when she thought she would never be twenty-one. At the table, she sensed the same homey feeling, which had been a part of her life for her first twenty-four years in Ireland before she immigrated to the states on Moth-

er's Day in 1959. *Long ago, yet as if it were yesterday, a dichotomy –
with another life of a fulfilling thirty-year marriage.*

She smiled to herself – the log at the base of the fireplace had
become a decorative piece. Her face brightened. Lost in nostalgia,
she examined the four photographs of her four redheaded children – all in chronological order: Sean, Enda, Maura and Thaddeus
– and all of their college graduation pictures and Thaddeus who
would graduate in 1995. *If I live that long. Life.. a dream?* Now,
they were twenty-nine, twenty-eight, twenty-three and twenty;
the twenty something club. John put a picture of Tara in the middle of the fireplace, between the photographs of Enda and Maura.
As the matriarch in the middle of the children she could, she
fantasized, still pull their "strings" and from heaven guide their
lives. She would be their advocate. Defender, promoter, supporter.
*When you die, do you go into the ground and that's it.* "*That's all there
is*" *as Peggy Lee sang.* But she knew better.

She scrutinized the room like a bloodhound on a scent. And
the mugs, the school mugs lined side by side atop the bookcase –
Archbishop Wood, Mount Saint Joseph Academy, Notre Dame,
Villanova, LaSalle, Temple, Providence. *Those mugs costs about a
half million net dollars.* She smiled at her metaphor, took the lid off
the typewriter, placed the paper in the roller, and thought about
beginning a sentence. She sighted two wooden lamps, which along
with the bookcase, she bought at a furniture store where she
worked as the evening office manager. They needed extra money
to support the family. By working, she felt an important contrib-
uting factor in the life stream of their family. She had prepared
dinner and when John came home from school at four, she virtually ran out the door to be on time, kissing John lightly on the lips
without smearing her lipstick. She smiled to herself. The begin-

ning of John's learning how to cook, which he did well. A good husband. A good chef. A good man.

The sliding glass door covered by the flowery drape, the wrap-around sofa, the easy chair, the thirty-five inch television with a picture of John and herself on top, the shellacked college diplomas on squares of wood, trimmed in gold, the clock with tiny shelves—the same clock, which didn't work when she bought it and hadn't ever worked—all set in place under the iconography arrangement. She heard Canadian Honkers gawking their way south.

Still struggling with appropriate thoughts to begin her letter, she admired her choice of reference books in the bookcase: *The World Book Encyclopedia*, the story of Civilization in ten volumes, the *International Family Health Encyclopedia*. She often referred to these health books in raising the children during illnesses and for herself during her fight against cancer. The trophies won by the children in township sports made for conversation when friends visited. Prized trophies. She tried to find anything to distract her from beginning the letter. Her last letter to her brother…the finality of the thing.

In addition to college yearbooks, she cherished Sean's master's thesis "The Effects of Groundwater Pumping on the Hydro-Geology of the Primrose Creek Watershed," which under a hard-bound black cover included Sean's statement "I dedicated this work to my parents, John and Tara O'Malley." *Sean's book, my accolade.*

She recalled the day Lee Harvey Oswald assassinated John F. Kennedy on November 22. Thirty years ago, she remembered where she was and what she was doing. What adult didn't? In the brokerage firm's transfer department, where she supervised ten people. At the bookkeeping machine when over the intercom, the announcement came—President Kennedy had been shot in the head in Dallas. She curled her lips as she remembered the receptionist, a Pennsylvania beauty queen in the Miss America Pageant, saying, "I'm glad he's dead," when a second announcement followed—Kennedy had died.

Collecting her thoughts, she began to type:

"November 22, 1993

"Dear Seamus,

"Since I have lost the use of my right hand, typing this letter is my best choice at this time.

"The visit to your home I much appreciated and the excellent dinner. Nice to see your daughter and her family again. I'm enclosing the information I have received from a cancer clinic located in the Bahamas."

Using only her middle finger of her left hand to strike the keys, she experienced difficulty typing. She patiently went on with her typing. He already knew the facts of her treatment, but she restated her cancer history to refresh his memory.

"Following a lumpectomy in December 1988 and having 22 lymph nodes removed, showing 13 of these nodes malignant, I was in stage three. I received radiation followed by six treatments of chemotherapy with an interval of three weeks between each treatment. (Adriamycin, Cytoxan, Methotrexate, Adrucil). I took Nolvadex 10mg two each day (an estrogen block) and was doing well until I found a malignant lymph node in my neck. I had radiation at the end of May 1992."

She took a respite, flecking her fingers to loosen tightness of holding her middle finger in a fixed position. She watched tropical fish swimming in a ten-gallon tank on a desktop by the sliding glass doors. The mother had had thirty-five babies over the past months and she wondered how to maintain a large population in a small tank. *The Malthusian theory – maybe this would be the answer. The populations will increase faster than the food supply unless there is a war or famine.* Annoyed with herself thinking these thoughts, she said aloud, "What am I thinking. I'm not a Trevelyan who let the Irish famine happen as a form of extermination policy in 1845."

She continued typing.

"All of the above I had on my right side. Around May 1993 on the left side of my neck a group of lymph nodes became enlarged and was assumed by the doctor to be malignant. X-ray shows lymph nodes metastasis through back of chest area. Treatments followed with Taxol, which is a new drug. After three more treatments more lymph nodes increased in size and treatment was stopped. This Thursday I will have my 3rd treatment of 850mg, 5FU, 85 mg Methodtrex. 850 mg Cytoxan along with 250 cc Soline, 32mg Zofran and 4mg Decadron. Lymph nodes are still large. The group I mentioned to you. The Bahamas Group cannot advise. Maybe chemo is not the answer."

She did her best, signing her name with her left hand.

Thanksgiving dinner passed as quickly as the first heavy snowfall of six inches. The Saturday after Thanksgiving, six inches of snow had fallen. Sunday the temperature soared to sixty-seven degrees and under the sun's warmth, the snow vanished. John helped Tara prepare dinner. She appreciated this for cooking with one hand proved cumbersome. Before Christmas, Tara received a reply from Seamus, advising her not to go to the Bahamas. All what could be done in established medical practice had been done.

*Is this the dawning of a new adventure? Holidays create happiness and bring families together. We'll all be together.*

# TWENTY-SEVEN

# All in the Family

Enda and Maura drove from Boston two days before Christmas. Sean would meet them at T.J. I. Friday's Restaurant at the Hallow Hills Mall on Christmas Eve day, the traditional day they went shopping for Pollyanna's, followed by an early family dinner. On Friday John drove amidst snow flurries to collect Thaddeus at the Amtrak Station in Trenton.

Driving on Bridgetown Pike, John clicked on a cassette of Celine Dion, Maura's birthday gift. He listened attentively to "Because You Loved Me." Maura gave it to her father because the words reminded her of her father. The words reminded her of all he had done for her in life…"For all the truth you made me see…For all the joy you brought to my life, For all the wrong you made right, for every dream you made come true, For all the love I found in you . . .."

Reminding him of Tara, the song captured his thought and feelings for his bride still vivacious and beautiful as the day they married June 15, 1963, thirty short years ago. *Fifth year of fighting cancer. Could it be five years?* During their marriage, he placed himself in the background and Tara in the foreground.

On Saturday, Christmas Eve morning, they left for the mall at ten o'clock. To ensure the timeliness of their leaving on time, John performed one of his pranks—he put all the alarm clocks ahead one-hour. When they awakened and saw the time at ten o'clock, they would get up, thinking what harm is there to be late for a trip to a mall.

In actuality, the family was up at nine o'clock – and they left the house on time. For the Pollyanna, John had written each name on paper, folded it and each person took a paper and found the name of his or her Pollyanna. After purchasing their gifts, they assembled at Friday's.

"Thank God, it's Friday," said Thaddeus. "It is T.G.I.S."

"Thank God, it's Saturday," Maura responded.

He laughed. "Quick, Maura. Quick."

"I'm not going to let you guys get ahead of me."

*Guys…the new younger people's way of addressing their elders.* "Woman's rights, Maura," Tara declared. "Remember Maura, you can do anything you want. Don't let anybody tell you, because you're a girl, you can't do what any man can do."

"Remember, girls. We outnumber you four to two," John remarked.

"We're stronger when we're outnumbered, John," Tara said. She put on her administrator's face as a soldier might point his rifle.

The waitress took their drink order – Guinness for the men, one virgin and one non-virgin strawberry daiquiri for the ladies. The O'Malley family had long been a family of children; now a family of adults.

"How's Providence, Thaddeus?" Sean inquired.

"Good. I could use more money," he answered tapping his father's hand.

"Don't look at me. Every time you look at me, Thaddeus, you need more money."

"What else is there but money?"

"Saints and God," Tara smiled.

"Saints and sinners," Enda commented.

"Ah, but we're all sinners, Enda."

"Speak for yourself, mom," said Enda.

"I'm going to get my doctorate in history," said Thaddeus.

Enda, a financial consultant, said, "Get involved with stocks, bonds, insurance plans. You'll make more money. When you get a taste of the green stuff, you'll change your mind."

"Thaddeus will have five month off a year, earn $80,000 and become an *au fait* in his field," John said.

"With time off," Maura said, "he could make money doing what Enda is doing."

Thaddeus finished his Guinness and ordered a second. "I didn't say I wanted to be a financial adviser."

"I know. But you should think about it," John said. "At least, don't teach in a public school system. You'd be better off, Thaddeus, teaching at the college level."

Maura observed the second Guinness for Thaddeus. "We can tell who the college student is…two Guinness to our one."

College students think they're macho by drinking," Tara said.

"How's it going in human resources, Maura?"

"Stable at the moment, Sean. At least, I'm not being laid off."

"Many companies are downsizing. Thank God, mine's not," Sean said.

Tara hoped their children would go to Mass with them that night, the Christmas Eve Mass at 6:30. She fixed her eyes on them like a general observing troops. "Are you going to Mass with us tonight, I hope?"

"We'll go, mom." Sean spoke for them as they nodded yes.

Enda laughed, "Of course. "We're called twice-a-year Catholics."

"Right, " Maura stated.

"Christmas and Easter," Sean said.

"At least you go if it's only twice a year," Tara commented. "Responsibility to your religion is important and you should take it seriously."

The waitress delivered their dinners. "You all look alike," she said. "It's not hard to tell you're a family."

Tara smiled.

"Have you heard of the movie *Cheaper by the Dozen?*" John asked.

She smiled. "Yes, I've seen it."

"Well, my family is called, 'More Expensive By the Half-dozen.'"

———————

They arrived for Mass at 6:10 p.m. "Good thing we're early for a change," John remarked. "The twice-a-year Catholics come early and take seats of us regulars."

"We're not regulars," Maura said, speaking for Enda and Thaddeus.

They approached the front door of the church. "You should be," Tara said, smiling and putting her arms around Maura and Enda. "I didn't raise my children to be little pagans. This is the first Sunday you've gone to Mass in a long time."

"Well, here come the pagans, Lord," snapped Thaddeus, "and we've come to pray."

Sean had not yet arrived.

They settled back, awaiting Mass to begin. John whispered to Tara, "Priests should marry, Tara." She looked at him and did not answer. "Christ called married men his apostles." She remained silent, poking him with her elbow. "Prelates say priests should not marry. Christ never said this."

"Be quiet," Tara said.

John sat against the end of the pew on the main aisle, with a space between him and Tara. "Hope Sean gets here soon. These people may try to take this seat."

Within minutes, the usher whispered to John. "You can't hold a seat with all these people standing in the vestibules."

"We're saving this for our son, Sean."

"We'll seat him if he comes," the usher said, walking off.

John whispered to Tara, "He's an ex-Marine officer. He's used to giving orders."

Tara's light blue eyes, changed from hazel to match the royal blue top she wore. She didn't like tops but she wanted to cover her swollen right arm. He admired her appearance and said, "You are beautiful, Tara."

Her smile indicated thank you. She studied her husband next to her. *Is this the man I married?* He had lost his hair, but maintained his good looks. *If I had it to do over again, I'd do everything the same, thank God.*

Sean still had not arrived. The usher returned. "You must give up the seat."

"If I do, I'm leaving this church and I'm not coming back," John said. John made a move to leave and the whole family joined in the movement. They all rose and made a notion to leave the pew. People behind them and in their pew watched with interest at a scene occurring in a Catholic church, much less on a Christmas Eve Mass.

"No, no," the usher motioned them down. "Forget it. Stay." John imagined the people applauding.

"Won that one," Thaddeus quipped. "Good man, dad."

He whispered to Tara, "We make a living by doing well in our jobs, but you make a happy life by what you give to others. You have to make your presence felt in church. And also, as a anonymous person once said: To accomplish great things one must not dream but act."

---

Once a scene of adventurous stimulation with the children young, Christmas morning…a scene of adults stepping slowly down steps instead of running, saying good morning and drinking orange juice instead of dashing under the eye of the cam-cord to rip open a mass of wrapped presents. Once in pajamas to open presents, as adults, they came downstairs fully dressed and shaved. The impetuosity and anticipation of their youth had settled into a world of sophistication and refinement. With the passing of time, they had blossomed into adults. Presents no longer numerous, were smaller and more expensive. Possibly a check or gift certificate.

Time to prepare dinner under Tara's direction, John prepared the filling— he cut celery into small pieces, sliced onions into mini fragments, causing tears to roll down his cheeks, and melted one pound of butter in the frying pan. He sautéed the celery and onions under a slight flame. He scrapped a hard loft of unsliced bread and placed all ingredients together in two pans and flavored its contents with salt, pepper, poultry seasoning, garlic powder, celery seed, sage and allspice. Maura prepared celery stalks with cream cheese, a round ball of cheese with crackers, baby carrots and onion dip, and peanuts. Together John and Tara cooked fresh carrots, string beans, sweet potatoes, and Idaho potatoes.

The boys watched the Detroit Lions play the Green Bay Packers on television amidst snacking Maura's samples and drinking Guinness and one So Co Man Up prepared for John by Tara. The fire crackled and the flames maintained a bright orange-glow, fueled by logs placed on the fire by the children.

John tied a rope around the twenty-pound turkey to lift it into and out of the pan. Side by side, they spooned the filling into neck and breasts. John closed the two areas with long needled cooking pins. He lowered it into the pan.

"That's that," he said, patting Tara's buttocks.

*What was objectionable when single is acceptable in marriage.* She smiled. He held his hand on her buttocks as they stood behind the counter. From the waist down, the children could not see their actions. Her fragrance had the scent of the morning sun in a wet field of corn. Her hazel-blue irises shone like starlets in the sky. The sky was clear, uplifting.

"Enough is enough," said she, her eyes glowing with life and vigor.

"Never enough of you," he whispered with a smile accented with parenthesis lines at the corners of his mouth. "I can never get enough of you, Tara. You know that."

Unlike many married couples, they never called each other "hon" or "darling." They were too much in love to use tissue-thin, Hollywood terms lacking in sincere emotions and feelings. They used real first names for a real marriage with real love.

"What are you two doing over there?" Maura asked in a definitive tone of voice, indicating she knew.

"Oh, your father's bothering me," she said, with a playful echo in her words.

"Tara!" said he, in equal playfulness. "Don't tell your daughter. She might think I'm a sex imp."

She wiggled herself away from his hand. Never would she admit to him she liked him putting his hands on her, whenever he touched her, especially in bed. It would be against the psyche of a post-war, good, Irish Catholic girl who hid her personal pleasure in sex. A girl had to have secrets. She knew everything about John O'Malley. And she knew he knew she loved him putting his hands on her. Likewise, he knew everything about Tara O'Shea O'Malley. They married to be one and to accept whatever small differences between them. To work out problems and stay together—against the grain of too many modern marriages when confronted with a problem, one says to the other, "I'm outta here."

For the most part, they thought the same, their temperaments the same, their interests and desires the same and their goals and dreams the same. One and the same. Homonyms. In their sameness, they experienced originality, creativity, freshness. Bored with each other, they never were. Both had two lives—one their parents gave them; the other they made better when they married and gave to each other.

As he placed the turkey in the oven he said, "I should call you Tara O. Your single and married names begin with O." Once before, she recalled him saying this…when they were single.

The glow on her face delighted him. "Tara is better," she said, coughing. The abundance of medication caused her to cough. It sounded like the rasp of the Canadian Honkers squawking their way to warmer climates.

"You may have lost something to cancer," he said, "but you have lost none of your wit and beauty. You're still My Irish Rose." He kissed her softly and holding her arms gently, he held his lips to hers. "Hey, what's going on there," Maura jested.

With the brightest smile, Tara said, "Your father's taking advantage of me."

"Doesn't look that way," said Maura, sitting on the wrap-around sofa and in full view.

"He is. He better mind himself or I'll give him a wallop."

Their children did not often see them kiss. They simply did not kiss goodbye in the morning and not always before retiring. They didn't have to. They didn't have to kiss to prove their love. Besides, not kissing in front of people was an Irish thing. Not like couples who had nothing to say about their marriage, they had something to say about their marriage, but kept it quiet in their hearts and actions. John videoed the boys watching the football game, Maura reading a book and Tara in the kitchen.

Throughout the day, Tara based the turkey with butter until finally the automatic pop up timer pushed up and they served dinner with the natural flickering of candlelight. Using Enda's gift, an electric cutting knife, John prepared to carve the turkey when Enda asked, "Is it ready?"

"Sure is, Enda. Time for your traditional stabbing."

Enda guarded the turkey and holding a knife with both hands over the turkey, he plunged the knife into its breasts. "Now, it's dead." His arms held high, he swayed his arms and legs from side to side as Topal did in the movie version of *Fiddler on the Roof.*

From the family room, Sean said, "Enda killed the turkey. Now we can eat. Tradition continues."

"Tis a glorious day," Thaddeus said, imitating a native Irishman, "to be havin' the staff of life, please God."

Maura did an Irish reading to celebrate the occasion. She recited, May the road rise to meet you – May the wind be always at your back – the rains fall soft upon your fields and – until we meet again may God hold you in the hollow of His hand . . ."

Sean joined in. "Tis an Irish Blessing I hear me sister sayin'. Well, me lads and lassies, how's this one – May you live as long as you want, and never want as long as you live."

Thaddeus stammered, "Someone at Providence told me this Irish blessing. 'Grandchildren are gifts of God. It is God's way...of compensating us for being good parents.'"

In her smile, she hid her sorrow. *I wonder if I'll live to see and hold my grandchildren.* "Sounds like we're having an Irish party of sorts," cracked Tara. She looked forward to coherence, directness, and continuity in life. "It's good craic."

"Sure it tis," Enda followed. "There are two kinds of people in the world. The Irish and those who want to be Irish."

The turkey was served on a beautiful ceramic meat tray with a nineteenth century scene of four blue horses pulling an opened carriage filled with six blue people, one blowing a bugle.

"The tray is old, Enda. It's a scene out of Dickens."

"Remember buying it for me when you, Sean, and Dad went to the Kutztown Cave?"

"I do. About sixteen years ago."

"You haven't heard my Irish blessing," said John.

Tara said, "Oh, this will be good. Don't mouth it. Speak the speech, dad. "You're not as young as you used to be but . . .you're not as old as you're going to be. Watch it."

They mixed their cheers with jeers.

John said, "What about you, Tara?"

"I'm the native Irish person here. I don't have to pretend to be Irish."

A family chorus rang out, "Boooo."

She snickered. To John, she said, "Thank you!"

The children saw him slap her buttocks.

"Oh, dad. We saw that," observed Thaddeus.

Tara and John laughed.

At table, John sat at one end, Sean the other. Tara sat with her back to the kitchen doorway for easy access to the kitchen. With their backs to the china closet, Enda and Thaddeus faced Tara and Maura. "Daddy, say grace," said Tara. "Not too long, Dadda," Maura said.

Inspiration came to him like an apparition. "Bless us Lord for these gifts that we give to you. We praise you and ask you to keep all of us safe in the year ahead. We ask you to cure my wife, our mother, and best friend…that we all may have a long life together. Amen."

"Amen," they echoed.

"That was good, dad," Tara said. As they aged together, she called him dad as often as she used John.

From right to left, food plates passed. According to the O'Malley family custom, John collected small portions of food items, filling a saucer plate to his left for the baby Jesus.

Midway through the festive holiday dinner, Enda mentioned the absence of rolls on the table.

"Oh my God!" Tara exclaimed. "I've done it again." She whirled from her chair and opened the oven. An odor of burning filled the rooms. "Oh darn. I've burnt the rolls again."

Maura said, "Oh, Ma Ma cursed." She smiled. "That's the second time I heard you curse."

Sitting down and sipping orange soda from a Waterford Colleen glass, Tara stated, "Oh, I didn't curse. I told you what the man said to me."

A Santa Claus candle burned bright from its centerpiece of a tiny wreath with berries. Two other candles provided enough flickering light for John to video the scene. Tara tottered her left-hand fingers at the camera, as her right hand lay swollen and motionless in her lap.

The Christmas dinner completed, everyone passed their mostly empty plates to Tara who along with John took them into the kitchen. John brought tea and coffee to the table. Tara sliced four pieces of walnut apple pie and two small slices of pumpkin for Maura and herself. The desserts on the table, Tara centered plum pudding in front of her, pouring a portion of Jameson Irish whiskey over the pudding.

"You like that, mom? And you, a tea-totaler," quipped Thaddeus.

"I'm not breaking my pledge, Thaddeus. Whisky is part of the dessert."

"You're bending the rules again, Tara, as you do every Christmas."

"John, I'm not bending any rule. The pudding and whiskey are together. Whatever is cooked in wine, I can eat."

"An Irish lady's twist of the truth, I'd say," said Sean.

"I'll have tea, John."

"Of course, Tara. You'll have a spot of *tay*," he said, thinking this could be Tara's last Christmas.

"Dad's speaking Gaelic."

"I am?"

Tara said, "Dad doesn't know Gaelic."

He held her left hand as she placed it on the table.

"Tay," she continued, "is Irish for tea."

"Of course, Tara, I know."

"In that case . . ."

"In that case, Tara, mind your manners or I'll tell you to hump off."

She gave him her administrator's look that meant, "You're daft."

"No Tara, this serious professional look won't fly here," he smiled.

She returned his smile. "Enda, when are you going back to Boston?"

"Tuesday. I have an appointment on Wednesday."

"And I have to be back in the office on Wednesday," Maura said.

*I'll be in my office, too. Hope my days will be bright.*

# TWENTY-EIGHT

# Dark at the Top of the Mornin'

Snow fell that February day when she drove to the radiologist. Diced snowflakes swirled around her like a group of children running in all directions at recess in a schoolyard. She listened to Tony Kenny sing "Our Lady of Knock" on a cassette.

"And the Lamb will conquer and the woman clothed in the sun will shine her light on everyone," he sang.

*Everyone, I hope.* She prayed the Lamb of God would help her conquer cancer by interfering with the cancerous cells growing in her. "Mary," she said aloud to herself, "You are my archetypal. Shine your light on me, but, I beseech you, with your son heal me from this dreaded disease. Remember my Rosary Novenas. And you are bonded and obligated to grant my request to let me live – hopefully another twenty years, at least. You can do this. And if you ask God the Father, he will deny you nothing. Ask God the Father in your son's name to cure me and he will – I believe this." She quietly regained spiritual energy like flowers budding in a garden.

Last night she browsed through the Faulkner Reader. She liked William Faulkner's ability to write descriptive details, which placed one in the middle of the scene, watching the goings on. She read his Nobel Prize speech. She dwelt on his thought about the human heart in conflict with itself. It captured her feelings about her present state as she entered her sixth year of treatments.

She recalled Faulkner wrote that a writer must understand the truths of the heart – love, honor pity, pride, compassion and sacrifice. She applied this to herself. She understood all those qualities for she practiced them in her daily life, especially with the residents at O'Shea and Summit Personal Care facilities. To those who lived through their end days unloved, she loved. Too those who needed pity, she gave love and attention. To those proud people, she encouraged humility. To those who lacked compassion in their lives, she rendered compassion. To those who had sacrificed much and received blame or mistreatment, she offered, hope, and comfort.

She parked the Grand Marquis in a handicapped space and entered the building. Rubble dust ascended upward as men tore down a Dunk-n-Donut shop a few yards from the medical offices. I hope cancer isn't tearing down my body. She liked Dr. Johnson: pretty, intelligent, personal—she lifted Tara's spirits with her encouraging words of support.

She greeted Dr. Johnson with her left hand. "Excuse the left hand, doctor. I can't use my right hand anymore." Like an ornament her limp right hand fluttered out of her sleeve.

The doctor smiled, took Tara's left hand and led her into a changing room, waited for her to exit and escorted her to the examining room.

"How's your son doing at Providence, Tara?"

"He's fine, doctor. He'll graduate in June of '95."

"The same time as my daughter from Brown."

"I suppose," Tara said, "you've been up there many times."

"Yes. We see her about twice a year on campus."

"We stay either at the Marriott or the Omni Biltmore."

The doctor placed Tara's file on the table. "We stay at the Marriott, too. Parents weekend is in March. We'll be there."

"Ours was last month." Tara sat straight up in her chair, away from the backrest and erect like the tiny Japanese maple tree in their garden, her knees touching each other, her hands folded on her lap. Correct posture came naturally to her. She trained herself to sit erect, a position, which may be uncomfortable for others, but comfortable for her. A lady's position.

Dr. Johnson opened Tara's file. "So far, Tara, with your latest radiation, you have received 4,500 centrigrays...."

"Rods," Tara interrupted, "is the same thing?"

"Yes . . . You've received 4,500 centrigrays in the neck, supraclavicular, axillary, and armpit areas." *Strange.. same number as our love adventures according to John.*

"I have had incisive aches and pains from the treatments as well as skin irritation."

"Let me see." The doctor examined her neck and armpit. "Vaseline Intensive Care Kenalog will help."

Dr. Johnson studied Tara. Her head titled up, in eye-to-eye contact. Tara noticed the doctor's eyes darker than her face. "Unfortunately, Tara, you still have multiple nodules still present in the neck and supraclavicular areas."

"Oh well, we're trying. Is my time running out?"

"We can continue to try and hope. Right now, we'll go along as before."

"I suggest you see Dr. Stein."

"Yes. I will. I'm having shortness of breath. My left arm is beginning to swell." Maintaining her sense of humor, she added, "At this rate, I'll look like a mummy."

The doctor chuckled. "Mrs. O'Malley, you are a delight." She leaned forward and hugged her patient.

"I'll try seeing Dr. Stein before I leave today."

Tara left Dr. Johnson and went up the elevator to the second floor to try to catch Dr. Stein before he left the office. There were no other patients in the waiting room. Dr. Stein greeted her warmly.

"Well, the MRI will be helpful to see about the left arm. I wouldn't worry about it, Tara, but I don't like the sound of your shortness of breath." He paused in thought. "You still have time to have an x-ray of your chest. Go now and have an x-ray in the lab." He wrote an order for an x-ray and gave it to her. Another x-ray. *I feel like a stricken calf of sorts.*

"When should I see you?"

"I'll have the results in the morning. Let's see." He escorted her to the waiting room. He studied the appointment book. "Come tomorrow at three or four."

"Four," she said. *I don't want to take too much time away from the office.*

"Okay, see you tomorrow."

---

The next morning, Tara met Nathan Mountain at Summit Personal Care.

"Nathan, I'm having trouble breathing. I'm seeing my doctor today."

"Trouble with breathing. Can't have that."

"No, we can't. I want to update you."

"Don't let anything happen to you, Tara."

"I won't, Nathan. I want to retire from this job."

"Better not be soon, Tara. We need and want you here."

"I'm having radiation again. The lump is still here in my neck." She felt the insidious lumps.

In keeping with his manner of conversation, Mountain avoided using subjects at the beginning of sentences. "Do whatever you must, Tara. Be healthy."

"Thank you, Nathan. You're a sympathetic and understanding man. For sure," she smiled, "I want to be healthy and stay in this job."

"Always will be your job." With a glimmer in his eye, he added, "The best bargain I have."

"Bargain, am I?"

"You know what I mean," he said.

"I consider this home my demesne."

"Only this place?"

"Well, my home, too. Together they represent my work life."

"Remember, all of us here love you. We care about you."

"I know and thank you for your support."

---

At 4 P.M. the following day, Tara returned to Dr. Stein's office. Dr. Stein held her left hand as he spoke. "Tara, you have bilateral pleural effusions. Your lungs have fluids in them. Both lungs! We think the lower quarter of both lungs is showing fluid deposits. For safety, I am placing you in the hospital. We want to observe closely your progress with the fluids."

"Is this the end?'

A moment of silence followed. He studied her glowing face. "Tara..." he said, his voice cracking, "This will be a difficult time for you. I suggest," his voice fading, "you gather the family together—." He couldn't continue.

She stirred in her seat. She felt the extra weight in both arms, themselves swelling with fluids. She gazed at a painting of a beautiful sunset and beachfront waves. She recalled John once looking and kidding, he talked to a painting and, with people watching, he said, "Where are you, Tara? Come out of there." One of his pranks to make life inter-resting.

"How will you remove the fluids?"

The doctor regained his composure and said, "A pulmonary doctor will take out the fluids. Hopefully, the lungs will stay clear."

"How's this done?"

"More patients should be as inquisitive as you, Tara."

She returned his laughter with a smile, causing him to fill with admiration for his Irish patient. "These days haven't been my *ne plus ultra*. I refuse to let it get the best of me."

"To battle is to win, you know."

His words reminded her of Padraic Pearse, the leader of the 1916 Rising in Ireland, who said at his court martial before being executed. "You think we have lost. We have not lost. To refuse to fight is to lose. To fight is to win." *I'm not a Padraic Pearse, but I am Tara O'Malley and I'm just as determined as he was.*

"To fight is to win is the idea, right?"

"Right!"

She teased him by saying, "But what if I turn left."

She knew by his face he didn't understand. She laughed. "Kidding, doctor. Silly of me."

"To be silly is to lighten the soul."

She repeated the question. "How will the pulmonary doctor take the fluids?"

"Mmmm . . .well, he will use a four inch needle and enter it into your lungs from your back."

"Ugh," she shivered.

"Oh, it won't hurt. You've had plenty of needles to take blood samples. It'll be the same. You will be sitting up and he'll do it from your back."

"How long will I be in?"

"Once he takes it out, hopefully fluids won't gather again, you'll be discharged in a few days."

"And if fluids come back?"

"He'll remove the fluids again and we'll put you on medication."

"Will it stop coming back?"

"We hope."

She paused and folded her hands together. Her stomach gurgled. "Will there be a problem at work?"

"No, the owner is an understanding man."

"You're blessed with a boss like him."

*I need more blessings. I need to live another fifteen or twenty years to enjoy retirement with John when he retires in three years.* After dinner, John wrote to all the children and informed them of their mother's condition to prepare them for Tara's end days. He wrote before he went to bed. He thought *In an open family, parents openly discuss good and bad events with their children. Closed families don't.*

"February 19, 1994

"Dear Sean, Enda, Maura, and Thaddeus,

"I don't want to write this letter, but I must. You must know the facts as I observe them about your mother. I am writing in place of telling you. In writing, I can better reach the point clearly about how you can make Mom's days as content and as happy as you are now doing."

His words burned like acid in his brain.

"Recently, I promised Sean and Enda I'd let you know bad news the moment it is happening. I am advising you your mother is preparing me for living alone – and I'm resisting every effort.

"Rather than write this letter four times I made copies. As your father, you should know what I know—your mother's right arm and hand are twice the size of her left, her neck joints hurt, and her right shoulder area also hurts. Shortness of breath is noticeable, especially in climbing steps, walking, and moving too fast. A short time ago, your mother wore suits. Now, she can't. Her right arm is larger than the sleeve. But we must face these facts to prepare ourselves to help Mom get through these days with loving attention.

"Mom doesn't know I am writing this letter. What you can do is to continue doing what you are now doing – telephone Mom, give her a hug and cheek-kiss, tell her you love her once in a while. There is no need for alarm now to come from Conshohocken, Boston, or Providence, but, as Maura can see, Mom is more tired these days.

"Do your best with your own lives and do your best by your mother. As your Dad, this is what I expect. I know you will.

Love,<br>Dad"

He dropped the pen; he felt he had dropped out of life. Dark thoughts enveloped him like an icy blanket. *How can I survive without my dear bride? Death and bereavement might be around the corner. From personal experience, I don't know how it feels to grieve the loss of my wife. I don't know what will happen to me. I remember the blind beggar crying out to Jesus, pleading "Have mercy on me!" And Jesus ordered the blind man be brought to him and asked the man what he wanted Jesus to do. "To See," the man said. And Jesus said,*

*"Then see. Your faith has healed you." I remember the man was no longer blind.* "Jesus," he said aloud to herself, "by our faith, let Tara be healed." Verbal prayer caused him to remember a friend saying, "Life is either a tightrope or a feather bed. Give me the tightrope." A good choice, but, at that moment, he wasn't sure what he'd chose. He knew someday they'd all be going to heaven. Hopefully.

# TWENTY-NINE

# A Dark Moment

Informed she would be dismissed from the hospital Saturday morning, Tara rang her husband who came for her at nine in the morning.

"They think the fluids will recollect in the lungs, Tara?"

"They're not sure, John. They can't be sure."

On Route 611, they passed the cloistered convent of the Carmelite nuns on Broad Street. John whispered a prayer to save his wife.

*Dear God, what are you doing? Why have you forsaken us? Do you not know we exist? We give you our attention, our love. What is it with you? I'll have to teach you to be kind to us to do unto others, as you would have them do unto you. You told St. Theresa of Avila you send pains to those who are your friends.. no wonder you have few friends. Please make an exception with us. Save Tara.*

"You're not going to die, are you, Tara?"

She searched his face, looking for comfort, her eyes saddened. Would she survive? "Death is a possibility, John."

"You're too young, too beautiful, too vivacious to die."

"Death is still and has been a possibility."

"If I could, I'd take your cancer to let you live."

A burst of sunshine opened up before them like the opening scene of a first-nighter play, sparkling and reflecting off faces of excited actors speaking their lines. Nothing unusual. Sunshine filled their hearts, whether nature-caused or caused by the great love they had for each other, a love, which grew from the dawn of their first encounter at the Drexelbrook Tennis and Swim Club. When engaged, they looked to build meaningful family bonds, which carried them through nights of joy and anxieties like passengers on a luxury liner steaming to its final destination…a ship of adventurers wherein they saw the morning of their dreams merged with the evening of realized goals, breaking open like a placenta and giving birth to a new face, a loving family.

"You can't do it…anyway, if you felt as I do, you wouldn't say. You'd be too afraid."

"You don't complain much about pain."

"I don't tell you half my pains."

"But I want you to tell me."

"No matter."

"If anyone heard us, Tara. They'd think we believed in necrolatry."

"No, they wouldn't. We're not worshipping the dead. We're talking about death."

There's nothing definite as death. The power of its cruel explicitness left him frigid. He clung to her hand, the last tender feel of warmth withering away. Changing the subject, he said, "When you called, I had just begun to paint the carriage house at O'Shea's. I didn't think you'd ring early."

"I did. I want to drive to Providence to see Thaddeus."

"Why?"

"I want to see him."

"You're afraid you're not going to make it?"

"Yes."

Tears filled his eyes. His heart spun like a rotor. He didn't cry when his parents, brother and sister died. He didn't look at her. He wanted to shield his tears from her. His tears reminded him of the time in 1988 when Tara discovered she had cancer and drove home from the doctor's office with tears rolling down her face. It wasn't that he was ungrateful to be Tara's husband thirty-one years. But he wanted more than three decades. A happy quality of life he had during those short years. Now, he needed Tara to live, so his spirit would not die.

When he regained composure, he said. "It's ten now. We'll leave about two. By the time we get there, it'll be seven."

"That's all right. We can stay in a hotel and leave Sunday after we take Thaddeus to dinner."

"He likes Federal Hill and all the Italian restaurants there."

"It's near the Holiday Inn?"

"Right. It's up the street from Holiday."

"Well then, let's get on with it, John. I'll ready the house, buy some things for Thaddeus and ask our neighbors to mind Daddle and Pushky."

Tara prepared the house for their neighbor. *Never can tell. They may give themselves a private tour.*

"I can't have the neighbors talking about me now, can I?"

He sighed, "Why be so particular? They're not coming to examine our home. They're here to feed the cats."

"You never know." She cleared her throat. She inhaled deeply. "As long as my lungs hold out, I'll be all right."

He intended to say, "I want to kill the phantom of death, hanging over them. How weird to kill death." But he said, "You better be all right. First the malignant lymph nodes, the re-occurrences of cancer, all the chemotherapy and radiation and now this: your lungs."

"My lungs. Maybe, I'll die," she kidded, "You can get a new, healthy wife."

He moaned, smiling. "You're the only one. You'll be with me a long time."

"Reality...John."

"I am looking at reality. You're my reality."

"John, with my case history and now with fluid gathering in my lungs, I may not have much time left."

He studied her face. The bright, alert eyes sparkled. Her smiling face had puffed out with all the medications she had consumed. Both her arms, wrapped in elastic bandages, had enlarged. His beautiful bride, Tara...his Irish Rose. Exquisite, enchanting, radiant.

"You haven't much time left," he echoed her words.

"I've heard stories about men whose wives died and they virtually jump into their wives' graves, and, in a few months, they're married again."

He laughed. "Not me."

"Yes you," she smiled. "You'll get married again."

"No, I won't, Tara. I'll never marry again."

"Says you," she snickered.

They left for Providence at two thirty and driving through a light snowfall, they arrived at Thaddeus' dormitory seven hours later, two hours later than the normal time.

"Sorry to be late, Thaddeus," his mother said.

"That's okay, Mom. Must have been a hard drive, dad, with all this snow."

"We took our time, Thaddeus."

"Unlike your father. You know he drives like a race car driver," Tara said.

He moaned in jest. "Tara…I'm a fast driver."

"Dad drives seventy-five or eighty," Thaddeus said.

"Not today. I took my time." He smiled at Tara. "Your mother made me drive cautiously," he lied.

Tara made Thaddeus' bed while John replaced a bed roller in the leg of the bedpost.

"Mom makes me do many things."

"Oh, but your father can be difficult when he wants to."

Thaddeus said, "Seems to me, you both do a lot of sharing." A coin dropped from his hand, rolled into a vent opening, and disappeared. "Never see that again."

She wanted to say, "Like me, someday," but she said, "With your father, Thaddeus, it's not sharing as much as being told what to do. It's about seventy-five to twenty-five, with the seventy-five on daddy's side." She delighted in her humor, telling herself if bees can take nectar from two million flowers to make one pound of honey, she'd have to work harder with positive imagery and more prayers to be cured.

"No, it's not," he quickly retorted. "Our marriage is a fifty-fifty proposition."

"Sure, you're forever telling me what to do."

"Tara-y-y." John faced his son and said, "When we dated, your mother told me one of the things she admired about me was I had asked her to go to a definite place. Other guys, she said would ask her where she wanted to go, whereas I had everything arranged. I was decisive and she liked this quality in a man. And still does."

To Tara, he said, "And now you say I boss you around."

Tara sat on the bed. "Let's go to dinner, " she said, avoiding the issue.

"Now, who's bossing who?" John asked. He noticed the glint in her eyes.

Thaddeus observed the verbal exchange between his parents. For most of his twenty years, he heard his parents forever talking. Together, their conversations seemed as natural as drinking Guinness. "Let's go to Federal Hill, despite the snow."

They enjoyed pasta and fish before returning to campus. Snow had stopped falling. Tara marveled at the majestic sight of snowflakes resting motionless on slender branches. *How can snow collect gracefully on branches?* Telephone wires also held snowflakes atop city streets, purified of oil stains by the snow like a penitent cleansed from sin by a priest in confession. A three-inch snowfall covered lawns, sidewalks and streets. Cars moved silently and gracefully over crushed but still white snow. *A soft, beautiful wintry scene.* She wished she were at home sitting at the fireplace and looking out through the sliding glass doors with the porch light on, illuminating all the whiteness. By the warmth of the fire, she could study nature's snow-covered canvas, sipping a hot cup of Barry's tea.

"Thirty-one years ago, Tara, we sat at the bar of the Waterford Arms and had a drink before beginning our family life."

"Such a night that was," she said.

"A good night, Tara. For you?" she smiled.

"For me. What about you?"

"You're a kind man, John."

"Tara, don't forget. I knew there would be the next night and the next and the next and the next."

She smiled. "Every night is your night." They spoke like that: indirect words with direct meanings.

"What else is there," he said. "But you can relax. My elbows are stiff."

"Guess you're off sex for a while."

"Oh no," he said. "I'm ready. Ready for you, dear girl."

"Don't bother," she smiled.

Sunday, they went to Mass at the cathedral, took Thaddeus to breakfast and lunch. In between, they stayed with Thaddeus, satisfying Tara's need to be with her son for what she considered may be her last visit to Providence College. *Death before graduation!* She saddened at not being present for Thaddeus' graduation, not seeing him marry, or holding his children, her grandchildren.

Upon leaving for home, Thaddeus said, "Great hanging out with you guys."

John winced and said, "Your mother wanted to see you." He avoided telling their son why Tara wanted to see him.

Tara hugged and kissed Thaddeus on his left cheek. John gave Thaddeus a half-arm hug around his son's shoulders. He gave Thaddeus three hundred dollars. He thought, *It wouldn't be a trip to college without leaving money behind. I'd feel strange, if I came home with money in my pocket.*

In the car, Tara said to her husband, "Ah ha...home to Armageddon, for my last scene of battle."

"Tara, you said you believe you'll be healed. Remember, you're playing to win. You said it yourself. Playing to win and playing not to lose is generally the differential between triumph and defeat."

"Doesn't seem like God is listening. When it's your time, there's nothing you can do about it."

"Expect a miracle, then. God can interfere with the natural order of things."

"We're supposed to pray God's will be done, John."

"That's why you say the Rosary Novena. That is binding on Mary to grant your cure." His tone of voice became more intense. "Jesus willed to cure the woman who touched his cloak but yet he won't cure you."

He eyed her and she returned his questioning with a smile. She placed her left hand on his cheek.

Her softness disarmed his anger. "Oh John...frustrations should be laid to rest, not aired forever."

He opened the door and said, "But, Tara," mellowing his tone of voice and opening the door wider, "Jesus told the woman to go in peace. Her faith had made her well. Isn't our faith as strong as the woman's?"

"Didn't the woman suffer from bleeding for twelve years?" to which John dryly replied, "I believe so, for it's a rhetorical question and no need for an answer."

"Her faith was stronger. She prayed for twelve years and, finally, was healed."

"But we don't know this. The Bible doesn't give us this information. We have been praying more than five years – and nothing's happened. Prayer...a game with no results."

"Monica prayed for her son, St. Augustine, to convert for forty years."

"Jesus cured many people in the New Testament. Many of them didn't ask to be cured. Some people had faith, but many didn't. He cured them. Why can't he cure you?"

"I'll ask him when I get up there."

He avoided commenting on her humor. "You're a good person. You have faith. You pray. You believe. You love your neighbor. You do good for people. You help the sick and elderly."

"My, my, you sound like you're on a soap box," she said.

"I wish I had answers to all this. You love God and your neighbor and, instead of getting better, you're getting worse."

They drove interstate 95. In two hours, they had reached the middle of Connecticut as they steered towards the Merritt Parkway.

"All that asking, seeking, and knocking business. If we pray with faith, Jesus said we will receive what we ask for."

"I suppose, John. I might be in my end days."

"No, Tara. You're too young to die," he blurted out.

"I don't want to die."

"If I could, I'd die for you."

"Given a moment of truth, John, if you knew you were going to die, you would want to live."

He considered her words. "If I were to die and about to leave you, I would want to live. If you die first, I'd want to die."

"You wouldn't want to die. The life force in us keeps us going."

"I would. Know what we should do, Tara?"

"What?"

"Drive this car off the road and kill ourselves."

"We had this conversation once before. Why in the world would we do that?" she stated with annoyance. "The children would never live it down."

"We'd go together."

"Hump off, John." This is not part of my plan."

He smiled, placing his hand on her thigh and holding her thigh, he smiled, "Okay, Tara. It's your call."

"You're keeping me warm," she said.

"You're keeping me warm, too, Tara," he quipped with a twinkle in his eye.

She returned his smile and with sensitivity, she looked at the side view of his face. Filled with feeling, she said, "I love you."

"And I love you. I feel, Tara, my life has trapped me like a prison inmate." He wondered about his religion, his God, this man named Jesus. It's a funny religion, he thought: *an evil person commits all the known sins and on his deathbed, if the person repents and wins heaven.*

Momentarily taking his attention from the dual highway, he gazed into her eyes. "There's no one in this world like you, Tara. At school, I couldn't wait to come home to see you and when you come home from Summit, I light up when I see you. When we're together with the family at night, I love being with you and the kids, away from the world, with no one but ourselves. You are my life, Tara."

She jested, "Do you love me?"

The smile on his face she understood to be a yes. He said nothing.

"If I ask you that three times, will you say you love me?"

"Yes. Of course. Why ask. You know I love you."

Outside a dog barked.

He played a John McNally cassette. Tara tilted her seat back, closed her eyes, listening to "The Wind Beneath My Wings." She knew John set her wings and, in her heart, she knew she moved the wind that kept John flying from day to day. *That's what I do— take one day at a time and that's all I can do.* She visualized the Christmas concert given by the St. Joseph's University singers and ensemble. They had performed Johann Sebastian Bach's *Magnificant.* The young baritone, she believed, should pursue singing professionally. The violins, violas, trumpets…all beautiful like the softness of an early morning blue sky blocked-tiled with numerous white clouds formatting a walkway from west to east. *The beauty of the floating sounds and wintry scene could have been brushed on canvas by Edmund Wilson.*

Snowplows had cleared 95, the Merritt Parkway, route 287, the Garden State Parkway and the New Jersey Turnpike. Roads were also clear in Pennsylvania. What had taken seven hours to Providence in the snow had taken less than five on their return, the usual travel time. They decided it was too late to stop at the Montvale Food Court. An aggressive driver, John wished Tara could be cured as fast as he drove. He could do nothing to stop the cancer cells from controlling her body. In a life-threatening illness, aggressiveness meant nothing: a zero, a bubble, soon to burst, a run-away train about to crash.

---

At eleven they arrived home. Once a chamber of human voices, and now a decorative showplace of blue, white and beige walls, but still filled with love between themselves and their children. Her goal to see Thaddeus one last time accomplished, they went peacefully to sleep. In her sleep, malignant cancerous cells worked in her body. Her mind rested. Her body slept. Cancer did not.

# THIRTY

# Maura's Journal

From Conshohocken, where Maura roomed with her friend Peg Boyle, she wrote in her diary about the events. Later in the week, she gave the journal to her father—Dadda, Maura called him. He took the journey to school with him and read it at his desk during lunch.

John read the account with a sorrowful heart.

"Mom was released from the hospital today. She decided to go to Providence to see Thaddeus. She looks great! She couldn't wear suits due to swollen arms. She wore a skirt and white blouse.

"She came home and referred to her list of things to bring while gathering her clothes, medicine, arm wraps, and other items. Her handwriting is wobbly and messy. She lost feeling in her right arm a few months ago. Her mood was vibrant and lively but disturbing to me because she was getting ready to die. She breathed heavily. That makes me nervous. She hugged Daddle and Pushky. She hadn't seen them for a week. I took her picture with Daddle and Peg. Took my picture with her too (in the back of my head I thought this might be the last picture taken with her). Mom said it might be the last picture taken of her, too. I kept up with the movement of getting her hair dyed and the curling iron, but inside I wanted to cry. This is serious. She might not be here in three months. She wanted to bring Hummels for Enda and Thaddeus. I told her, not now. They would be frightened if she approached this weekend as her last visit to them. She wants to give the male Hummels to her boys and me the girl Hummels. She showed me the two she wants me to have. They are in the dining room crystal case. Her mother gave them to her when she came to America. Also, she explained the crystal glasses on the bottom shelf of the case are not as good as everything else. She told me to use those if I have a party. They are not Waterford. Weird! Here she is preparing for her death by telling me what she wants us to have and tips on the Waterford, but she stayed casual about it. She remained full of energy and life. She chuckled and talked about all of this, like she was prepared and ready. She wasn't scared. She is strong. I know mom's strong-minded, but how can a person prepare for their death and be strong?

"When she left, I gave her a long hug. I wanted to hug her for a long time to make sure I will remember holding her. I want to remember how she feels to hold. Her face is soft (her cute cheekies) and warm. She's comfortable to hug. I'm getting ready for her death, too. Every time I see her, I kiss her and hug her before I leave, as if it might be the last time. She seemed like an excited little girl when she left. She did say she wouldn't be back. I wonder if she's not telling us something the doctor told her. She also said it would be better if she had a phone in her car. If anything happened on the way, they wouldn't have to waste time trying to find a phone. Obviously, she's concerned about having a stroke. Again, her whole mood stayed happy and smiley. I kept looking at her as they drove away. She kept waving and smiling. Again, I thought this could be the last time I see her. I want to remember her happy. All day was bad for me. I have a ten page paper due on Monday and I still have to put it together."

John paused, thinking about the term paper Maura had to write for graduate school at Villanova University. Maura let papers go to the last minute, but he knew she'd get it finished on time. Impressed with his daughter's reporter-like instinct for detail, he continued reading.

"I couldn't concentrate at times, and I would start to cry thinking about today. All day, I had sporadic bursts of memories, thoughts, and emotions. I browsed the house looking at her pictures and thinking of her. Peg was concerned about me. I told her my thoughts and how it's weird to see Mom preparing for death and saying what she says. I think about her funeral, but she is still here. Enjoy her now! I can't grasp how death is forever. I will never talk to her again. I can't conceive this. She won't be at my wedding (if I get married). She won't see any of her grandchildren. She won't meet her son-in-law or daughters-in-law. But I can't think about it. She has experienced many other things with us. She's proud of us and we know and she knows we all love her and she loves us and wants the best for us.

"I want to be with her and help her as much as possible. I do not want to tell her I cry and it has been hard for me. Also, I have great friends who care about me. I will tell her again I will take flowers up to Mary at her funeral. I'll also remind her to turn on or off my light at 9:00 P.M. if she's with me. We talked about this a while ago. I made it up in case there is a way for the deceased to get in touch with the living. I will make sure everyone wears suits to the funeral and that she gets a gravestone, not a plate in the ground. She wants that.

"I'm sure she is in pain emotionally and physically. I want to be a support for her. When I cry in bed at night, I think to myself

- why are you crying? It's normal to cry for myself, but I want to cry for her. I laugh at myself, too. I can see Peg saying, "You're funny" if she heard how I cry and then stop and say to myself I cry for Mom. Peg is a great support. She calls a lot to see how I am. She keeps offering to visit Mom in the hospital with me. She admires my strength and how I am handling this situation. She says I get my strength from Mom. I think I am doing well."

John agreed with his daughter. He thought, *Yes Maura, you are doing well. You are a brave girl to write this for yourself. I should do the same.* He readjusted himself in the chair as he continued reading.

"She tells me I'm allowed to cry for myself. I don't think of what will happen or the funeral. I want to spend time with her now and talk to her about how she feels. I want to be strong for her. I don't want to cry in front of her. My eyes started tearing in the hospital the night we found out about the cancerous fluid. She noticed it but didn't say anything. I think she didn't want to get me more upset."

He dropped the journal and held his head in his hands. *I love you, Tara. You are me and I am you.. inseparable.... You are my morning and my night, my breakfast and dinner, my head, heart and hands, my soul, my breath. You are my sense of sight, hearing, smell, taste and touch. Everything I am is you. How will I survive without you?*

He sat at the desk every school day, knowing he had Tara to go to each afternoon. What would he do when he came home and she wasn't there anymore? Life without her, he could not imagine. How empty and lifeless it would be. Extinct. Spiritless inanimate. Nonliving. Blackness and eternal night. Forever alone...and lonely. It would be a lifetime of wintry discontent. Bereavement...what did it mean? Reconciliation...?

Monday morning, Tara drove to Summit Personal Care. She met Nathan Mountain at her office and advised him of her lung condition.

"If the fluids return to my lungs, Nathan, the doctor will hospitalize me again."

"Can't have that for your sake, Tara."

Her head felt like she had been given electric shock treatments. "We'll see. In the meantime, I'll do my best here."

"Do your best, Tara. Whatever I can do to help, I will."

"You are most helpful, Nathan." She pondered the picture on her desk of her four children. She took his hand and squeezed it like a precious gem.

"Never seen you looking better, Tara."

"Thank you, John."

"Bob's doing all right? Heard he faked sick again because Janet was sick."

"Apparently, that's what we think. They both came back two days later."

"A pair they are. Is Bill Martel doing his work all right?"

"Yes. He is. When Bob was out, Bill cooked the meals."

"No complaints?"

"There're always a few complaints. Can't please 121 people all the time."

"The census is 121." He studied the daily report. "Lost three and gained one this week. Millie and Sheldon still have their romance."

She smiled. "Caught them in bed again last week. This troubles me."

"Can't do anything about it, Tara. State regulations provide for their independence and freedom of action."

"I know. Can't dictate morals. But the whole idea is uncomfortable, especially since Millie has Alzheimer's."

Examining the weekly report, he said, "Food bill is up."

"We ordered more fish for Friday. Residents claim they weren't getting enough. Plus, a number of people substituted fish for meat this week. It's Lent, you know and more Catholics will eat fish during lent."

"Like to keep the food costs to about $2.41 per person."

He heard someone playing the piano. "Ellie's playing."

"God bless her. She likes to please people. Henry and Roland are the exceptions. They say she plays off key too often."

"Just did . . ."

"She's not perfect. I like listening to her. She's my background music," Tara said, smiling.

"A wonderful smile you have, Tara."

"And what big eyes you have, grandpa."

"What!" At first, the owner did not grasp her humor. "Oh..." he said. "And what big teeth you have grandmom."

They both snickered. He had lived through the school of hard knocks before managing to buy Summit Personal Care with a small deposit and built it with the assistance of Tara O'Malley into a first class facility. Inspectors brought people from other state agencies to the facility to showcase the operation and performance of a well-run large personal care facility. On a smaller scale and on the administrative mastery of Tara O'Malley, inspectors also toured O'Shea Personal Care to illustrate the operation of a smaller facility. Tara planted seeds of excellence into both personal care facilities.

"Annual inspection will be the first week in March. As usual, we will do well under your leadership."

"My goal is to have no violations, John. But the inspectors have to find something, no matter how small, like a dented can of food. My inspection for O'Shea's is coming up."

"You'll be busy."

"Not really. I have a checklist. I'll be ready for both."

"I know you will."

"I've already started with the file. From my checklist, I know all residents have their M51's for their annual health examinations and the annual screening forms are complete. Contracts are stapled and signed by residents, designated payers and me. If contracts are not stapled, it's a violation."

"A new one. They didn't have that before."

"It is. The House Rules and Regulations are signed as are the Residents Rights forms."

"The Non-discrimination in services?"

"They're all in each file. Signed Volunteer statements, the Inventory of Belongings, Financial Records, and Monthly Fee Statements. Sign out sheets are at the end of each file. Of course, Resident information and Resident Records are there too."

"Transfer sheets?"

"In each file," she responded. "And that's about it."

---

In a large home with 121 residents, the state inspector spent a full day sampling residents' files, speaking to a sampling of residents to establish their feelings regarding the general environment of the home and touring the facility with Tara at the inspector's side. The inspector found only three minor violations—a trash basket missing in two rooms and cracked glass in the basement.

Tara knew the inspector scheduled to visit O'Shea's a decent man who liked people. Tara asked John to excuse himself from school. He wanted to be present during inspection since she had to be at Summit. Tara trained John to be a certified administrator although he was not as experienced and as knowledgeable as Tara.

The gentleman sat in the kitchen where their records were filed in cabinets for each resident. He was a talker. He liked people and enjoyed talking to them as he spasmodically examined each of their ten resident files. His eyes darted through the files like a cat watching its prey. As he began to page through each file, he frequently paused to discuss a resident's progress. Well-liked as an inspector, he treated administrators and owners with respect and dignity. He treated people as human beings. He wasn't looking for violations as other inspectors. Violations, wherever placed, found him. Serendipitous experiences.

In touring O'Shea's, he found one item, though not a violation, that John corrected. A red dot should be placed on the second floor escape plan indicating the exact location where the person stood. Like a Knight Templar guarding The Holy Grail, he knew it a fine facility. John made this correction immediately as the inspector made his observation; he placed a red dot as directed by the state inspector. And in the end, O'Shea Personal Care received a perfect slate with no violations – a feat few homes received.

*In the end,* John thought, *will my lovely wife be cured?*

# THIRTY-ONE

# The Pulmonary Doctor

For the second span in three weeks, Dr. Stein placed Tara in the hospital for the same alarming reason – fluids gathering in the lungs.

"Tara, you need to be watched."

The nurse told John the pulmonary doctor had scheduled her in the afternoon to remove fluids.

John kissed her forehand. "That's for being my Wild Irish Rose."

"Well, Maura was the Philadelphia Rose in the Miss Mayo Contest and now you've crowned me with another title – wild."

"Not really, Tara. You know what I mean."

"You mean you love me."

"If you have the heart, you have everything…and I have everything."

"Then I love you, too."

She took a comb and a mirror and began teasing her hair, a craft she learned by studying the methods of hairdressers who teased and set her hair every week since she could remember. John sat observing the comb moving speedily up and down fibers of hair.

Stroking her hair shot sparks of desire into him like kindling sparks ready to ignite into flames.

"But, how can I forget? After all, at two to three times a week, I estimate we've had intercourse . . ." He paused, eyes set on the ceiling and figuring in his brain. "Let's see now at 150 times a year multiplied by thirty-one years—that equals . . .errr. . .4,500 times in our marriage."

She scowled. "You mean we've talked 4,500 times in all those years."

"A play on words, Tara. You Irish like to play with words."

"Do we? Words are words. True meaning comes from words when words are spoken from the heart."

"Words, words, words." Wordsworth said, "Choice Words and measured phrase above the reach of ordinary men."

"But you are not an ordinary man, John."

"Thank you. But it's a wonder we didn't have 4,500 babies."

She grimaced and the skin under her eyes wrinkled like ocean waves on a calm day. "We need another light in here."

"Ah...you can switch on a light," he replied. "But looking at you, Tara, lights me up."

A volunteer entered the room, carrying mini carnations in a vase. The gray-haired volunteer wore the lightest green cap and uniform, the color of bright green, white and orange carnations.

"Here are your beautiful flowers," she said. "They're lovely. Where do you want them, Mrs. O'Malley?"

Tara motioned to the sink. "Put them there please. If they spill, water won't get on the floor."

"The tri-color – the Irish flag," said John.

"You sent them?" the volunteer asked.

"Yes."

"How nice."

"My husband often sends me flowers," Tara said.

"Often," John responded, "my lovely wife thinks it is a habit and didn't say thank you."

The volunteer giggled as she left the room. She heard Tara say, "Thank you" to her husband.

The pulmonary doctor saw her sitting up in bed. "Here you are again, Mrs. O'Malley. Nice blue nightgown."

The doctor shook hands with John.

"I bought the nightgown," John said.

"Good taste. I think I'll buy my wife a nightgown like this. And I'll tell her you inspired me."

John smiled. "At least, I get credit." He looked from the doctor to Tara and teasing, said, "More than I get from my wife."

The doctor smiled, sensing a spirit of good will and propinquity.

"Oh, my husband's joshing me."

"And she didn't recognize I sent thirty-two carnations."

"Is it a significant number?" the doctor asked.

"Yes. Each carnation represents a county in Ireland: twenty-six from the South and six under English control in Northern Ireland. Together, they're thirty-two counties and the hope is Ireland will once again be an united country. In math, the figures add up to one…twenty-six plus six equals one. United."

"John's more Irish, doctor, than native Irish."

"I'm not Irish, doctor," he said smiling. "I'm American-Irish."

The doctor placed his hand on her shoulder. "Tara, since we've done this before, you know what to expect."

She nodded: "With better results this time?"

"Let's hope. At least, that's the idea. We like you, but we don't want to see you back here."

"I vouch for that, doctor," Tara said, her voice firm and determined.

The doctor, standing behind her, prepared to insert a four-inch needle into Tara's right lung. John moved around the bed and faced Tara. He dreaded to see an instrument inserted into his wife's back. He could not tolerate to see her in pain with the prick of the needle. He recalled the time Tara had given birth to Thaddeus and he had planned to observe the delivery, the obstetrician ordered him from the room when he broke out in a frigid sweat and began to wobble. He watched her suddenly stir when the needle penetrated. He cringed. He held her hand and pressed firmly. She responded with a full-mouth smile, her full kissable lips opened to display white teeth – the lips he had kissed thousands of times with a feeling all was right between themselves, their family, the world. A fullness he had experienced with no other person.

*Ours is a mature love story, like the movie Love Story. Are we like a sinking ship about to be destroyed?*

She looked out the window at the small, round red ball, atop a fire alarm box and watched cars, taxis, buses, and an occasional lorry, she called them in Ireland, silently pass into and out of her life in the flash of an image. Children crammed book bags on their backs. She wondered if the books brought home acted as a showcase to fool parents about their study habits or did they like her children use them at night to complete homework assignments. It had rained on and off during the day, leaving the sky a gloomy gray and as a result vehicles drove with their headlights turned on. She could see people bustling about at the main intersection of a public school and the hospital. People walked, boarded buses, and waited for traffic lights to change. She imagined all those people physically fit, all in good health, and all taking their health for granted. She reflected on how long her health would hold up now that fluids continued to drain into her lungs, the latest threat she had to face in her five year, six month battle with breast cancer. People crossed the street protected inside thick white lines painted on the street. *What protection do I have against this disease? I have no white lines to protect me.* The lines prompted her to recall the Vox Ama Deus concert at Daylesford Abbey during the Christmas holidays. Everything was peaceful. Why wasn't it so now? Funny how life can be peaceful and special at times but disruptive at other times. Of late, nothing had been peaceful, but determined she was to regain a peaceful way of life.

"I'm afraid for you, Tara," John said.

"We've been through a lot, John; we'll get through this, too. This too shall pass."

"Bravura," the doctor said. "You're brave and a brilliant patient."

She grinned. *I came into this world headfirst, and I don't want to go our feet first.* On the road of life, John wanted her first, forgetting no one is ever first on the highway.

The nurse closed the door while the doctor performed the procedure. When completed, the doctor opened the door to be greeted by Peter and Paul Coulter. Coincidentally, the divorced couple met again in the hospital, again arriving at the same time, not knowing each had planned to come the day before April Fool's Day.

Tara and John greeted them as they had done when the Coulters were invited to their house for picnics. Tara considered fate must have been guiding them back together for they seem to chance meet in a hospital.

"April Fool, John! April Fool, Tara," Peter Coulter said, rubbing his chin with his hand.

"My, my Peter and Paula – if it isn't the alliteration twins," John said. "Last time we saw you two in the hospital, was the time Maura was born."

Paula sneered with a shade of annoyance.

"We're glad to see both of you," Tara added. "How long have you been waiting?"

"Not long. A few moments," said Paula.

"It gave us a chance to get re-acquainted," Peter, said, looking askance at his ex-wife.

"Beautiful flowers," said Paula.

"John sent them."

"He's thoughtful."

Peter circled the bed, standing to Tara's left as Paula remained on her right as John stayed between the Coulters as if acting as a referee.

Painted light blue walls lent serenity to the room's atmosphere. A crucifix hung on the wall opposite the bed. Tara found inspiration from the Christ figure. Three wooden armed and leather-covered chairs provided for visitor's comfort. The speckled, blue floor matched the decorum of the room, designed to raise the patient's spirits. But she felt she had fallen into ghastly quicksand, sinking into death.

"Well, Paula, are you still pinching pennies?" Peter asked.

She frowned. "And are you still going to bed with your girlfriends."

"Now, now, Paula. Be nice. We're here to see our friends."

"And to think I use to go to Kelly's on Mole Street with you for fried oysters."

"Oysters? Getting ready for the future?" Paula asked, smirking.

She gave him a darting glance. "As if you needed oysters ..."

Peter centered his attention on Tara. "And what is the problem here with fluids in the lungs?"

Tara propped herself against pillows and pressed the button, raising the bed control button to sit up with ease. "Fluids have been collecting in my lungs. This is the second time I've been here for this."

"Yes, John told me you had been hospitalized in early March."

"I knew, too, Tara," Paula said. "Sorry, I couldn't get here."

"I understand. How are you both doing?"

"I'm doing fine, Tara."

"And I'm doing well in the office," Paula said.

"Well," Peter said, "Paula's doing a little better, especially with the alimony I pay."

Paula glared at her ex-husband with contempt. "He's jealous I live better than he does."

"Good thing I'm in the middle of you two," remarked John, "or we'd have a battle on our hands."

"Peter, why are we saying these things? We're here to see Tara."

"Right, Paula. Why are you saying what you're saying?"

"I thought you two had an amicable divorce."

"We do, but we forget," said Peter.

She and John had a once in a lifetime marriage and had one mild disagreement— not a lifetime shouting match. Whenever they went to bed, she remembered they had kissed, or made love, and went to sleep.

Dr. Stein entered the room; Tara introduced him to Peter and Paula.

"She's a strong girl, Tara is," he said.

"She is," John remarked.

"When do you think, I'll go home?"

"In about a week. We want to stop the fluids from gathering in your lungs. Tara." He paused, took her hand and said, "We can't stop the fluids from gathering in your body."

No one spoke. She looked straight into his eyes, "Thanks for telling me." Sounds of people talking in the hallway rose above the now faceless people in front of her. Faces in the distant corridor. Through the doorway, she saw a person with long blond hair talking to another person with strawberry blond hair. It seemed everyone talked at once and yet she couldn't grasp what they said. She heard but wasn't listening. Her visitors scowled at her with nondescript expressions of emptiness in a world of emptiness. In the distance, she heard a bell ringing. Thoughts of a past life flashed in her brain like darting comets. She thought of Pushky resting on her chest with paws outstretched every morning; she held Pushky's paws. *Holding hands again*, John would tease her. At other times, Pushky patted her cheek with her paws like an alarm clock, indicating time to get up and go to work. *My family's in my blood. So is my heart.*

Regaining focus, she said, "The doctor took two quarts from me today. After that, there can't be much left in me."

He smiled. "Have you urinated today?"

"Yes."

"You still have fluids in your body."

She smiled at his humor.

Dr. Stein left the room. Later, Dr. Wiseman came to see her.

"Busy day today," remarked Paula.

"Why is that?" observed Dr. Wiseman.

"Dr. Stein was also here."

Using his best bedside manner, Wiseman said, "We care about you, Tara."

"If it weren't for you doctors, I wonder where I'd be now."

"Did you speak to Dr. Stein?"

"Yes," she said. "He told me about the fluids."

"We do what we can." He studied the chart attached to the end of the bed. He listened to her heartbeat and took her pulse. "All good here. I'll stop in again." He kissed her on the cheek and said goodbye to the Coulters. She had a vision of extirpation like a beacon of death as he went to the door.

John observed a gray-haired couple visiting a patient across the hall. "When I see older people like those two," he said, motioning to the man and woman, "I get annoyed. I see them at mass; I see them holding hands on the street. I see them everywhere I go – older people in good heath and going on with their lives. We should be the same, Tara," he said, returning to her bedside. He felt like a gray-haired retired man walking along a state park road, lost in thoughts of the day.

Peter and Paula lowered their heads. Tara took John's hand in hers. "I feel the same when I see couples," John said. "I wonder why them and not us."

"You are my life, John. You know that."

"I am you, Tara, and you are me."

"I don't know many couples like you," Paula said. "You're my role models."

Peter said, "You two are always together. You have what too many married people don't have—intimacy in everything."

"Oh, I agree with Peter," Paula stated. "You've had many years of close relationships . . . "

"Thirty-one this June," Tara interrupted.

"Thirty-one years is a long time," Paula continued.

"A short time, Paula," John said. "As I have already calculated it's 11,292 days together, including Leapyear. Not enough."

John's vision blurred. He felt devoid of energy. In his mind's eye, he saw people waving handkerchiefs like flags of surrender. He cut through the maze of the visionaries and saw them as black knights ready for the kill.

"Before I forget, John. Deirdre's birthday is next week as is Margaret White's. Will you get two cards for me? I don't want to forget them. My niece is 43. She was twelve when she was in our wedding. And Margaret – I've been friends with her since our school days."

"Your niece caught up with us."

"She did. She now has four children of her own in Albany."

"Well, Tara, I'll see you soon," said Paula.

"Yes, I guess I better leave," Peter said.

The Coulters said their good-byes. The dead-gray sky hung over a dead-gray environment. Outside, on the gray roadway a gray squirrel lay dead on the road, killed instantly by a driver.

"They seem like they're married, don't they," John said.

"I wonder if they'll ever get back together."

"Peter likes his women, you know. I think he likes it the way it is."

Tara's face beamed. "You'll go out with Paula when I'm gone."

John shrugged his shoulders and shook his head from side to side. "You know better, Tara."

"Never can tell," she smiled. In her heart she wondered if she had reached a nadir.

John put his arm around her and kissed her hand. Suddenly, he sneezed, spraying Tara. The force of the sneeze pushed his teeth into her lower lip, his head knocked against her forehead, snapping her head backward. The irony of the situation gave them a laugh. "Never had so powerful a kiss," she said.

How I dislike this word—"never!"

# THIRTY-TWO

## Letters

Dismissed from the hospital in mid-April, they had a casual dinner at Friendly's. They drove to a state park. A group of mini clouds, like figurines of sheep, dotted the sky in the western sunset. Southern clouds bulged larger and illuminated in a magnificent sun, which turned the sky into a peaceful concentration of a wondrous polychromatic orange—red, gray-blue, reddish pink, yellowish red. Rays of gray-pink formed a kind of protective barrier with streaks of pinkish light like pickets in a picket fence. Two lines of orange appeared from nowhere. The streaking lines traveled westward as if a skywriting plane had released smoke. As the lines lengthened, the smoky clouds widened.

"Must be a phenomenon," Tara said.

"Right, there's no plane in the sky," John said.

"It's beautiful," she said.

"Like you," he said.

She smiled.

The two lines intersected far off in the horizon as they watched a colossal red-orange sun fall behind treetops on the other side of the park.

"Those lines are like us, Tara...always together."

As dusk settled into evening, she projected the imagery skills she practiced to overcome cancer cells in her body. In the distance, over the treetops, she envisioned mountains, blackened by the absence of the sun. Mountains of darkening clouds and dew-like land painted a picture, which she imagined to be a crystal-sparking lake of glistening and twinkling pink and reddish orange. The imaginary scene she had created in front of her gave her a feeling of undisturbed peace. Ready to face what was left of life, she felt drawn to enter the serenity of the lake.

Tara O'Malley continued living one day at a time. She visited her doctors, went to work at the Summit Personal Care facility and often stopped in the evening at O'Shea Personal Care. She and her husband continued socializing at Brittingham's Irish Pub and various restaurants and continued praying the Rosary Novena for her to live to see her children married and to hold her grandchildren. Though early spring, they often lit a fire. Sitting in front of the hissing and crackling flames filled their lives with the warmth of each other's companionship. Not only married, parents, lovers, they were also best friends. They coached each other along.

---

Sitting before the fireplace, they watched flickering flames cast metaphysical shadows on the ceiling and walls, transfixed in each other's web of life. With their pending retirements in 1997, they hoped to travel more than they already had. She would click on the TV, laughing at "The Golden Girls" with him jeering. He remarked the incidents could not happen in life and mocked the background laughter from an unseen audience, which, as he often said, came from a recording of people laughing, not a live audience.

Differences of opinion created variety in their lives, a durable umbilical cord, which bonded them through the hard and good times of their loyal allegiance to each other.

Heavy breathing persisted, causing alarm to herself and John and her doctors. Fluids had gathered again in her lungs. Once again, they discussed the possibility she may not survive, contrary to all their hopes, dreams and prayers. *It's a terrible thing when my life is about to end and my family's life without me is about to begin.*

Her arms were wrapped in elastic bandages and on the right hand she wore a tight-fitting elastic glove. The lymphoma clinic procedures in Trenton had not stopped the swelling, though the doctors and technicians tried their best. Doctors Stein, Wiseman and Johnson had followed established and known procedures to halt the growth of cancer cells. John felt the Master Physician had let them down.

One friend told them, "What makes you think God should treat you and Tara any different from anyone else. Why this week, a friend of ours lost his wife to cancer at forty-eight." *God heard their prayers, but her time*, she thought, *had come and God wanted her in heaven. What Almighty God wants, He gets.*

To this, John had no answer. Tara had stronger faith. Disappointed, she didn't fester her anger on the Virgin Mary or God. Her prayers and three visits to Lourdes would not be in vein. God may have applied them to another person's needs. Bitter she was not. She accepted God's will more than John. *"Burn me twice,"* he told God, *"and you're the fool."* Tara didn't fight God; she accepted what God wanted, though she didn't understand how she could die at a young age. Her acceptance led her to believe firmly in what her parish priest had said about God's will: "Where there's a no, there's never a yes."

She applied her love to her children like a priest applying a sacrament. She notified the children of her status. They came home the second weekend in May and spent Friday night, Saturday, and Sunday together as they had spent everyday together for most of their lives until they went away to college. Her niece, Deidre, a registered nurse, visited her. When she decided to write each child a letter, Deidre offered to take dictation and write it for her, but Tara's determination to type each letter with her left hand gave her courage. The doctors told her the lung condition would cause her to return to the hospital. Before she entered the hospital, she typed her own letters.

John placed the electric typewriter on the kitchen table so she could have more space. She typed one letter at a time. Facing into the fireplace as the flames flickered orange, red, yellow and white, she thought of the colors of the Irish flag – green, white, orange, and began typing first to Sean about the day he was born. Her fingers poised over the typewriter like a priest preparing the host for transubstantiation. *It ain't over 'til it's over, Yogi Berra said, and my life isn't over.*

"April 1994

"My Dear Sean,

"One of the happiest days of my life was the day you were born. May 4, 1964 at 8:06 A. M. and I had been in labor for twenty-four hours. You were a few weeks late (I first realized doctors were not God and not always right) and my anxiety mounted by the minute. Finally, on that beautiful day in May, you were born. A beautiful, little boy with my father's red hair. I was proud and happy. Lucky to have a perfect little boy, I thanked God.

"You started our family and have ever since continued to fill our lives with love and pride. You were a happy little boy. You liked to build everything as high as you could climb. Full of confidence you enjoyed childhood as you should have and I always loved you. You made me proud to be your Mom. Do you remember the time you were lost in the mall? I'll never forget it. One time you lay out on the sidewalk and didn't move until I went out to see what happened.

"I remember the science fairs at Wood. The cross-country running you seemed to enjoy. When you went to Notre Dame I missed you so much. Notre Dame was too far away from home. I feel you do not know the fine, capable and good-looking guy you are. I love you and I will always love you and be with you even after I die. Be proud of your achievements. I know you will continue to achieve great satisfaction in life.

"It is too sad to think of dying. I try not to do that. I don't want to leave you guys but I know it is going to happen. Stay close to your Dad, brothers and sister. Take care of each other.

"God will be there when you need him. Let him know you are on his side. Say a little prayer to him each day. The prayers will be there when you need them. It is hard to pray when things go wrong.

"Have a great life.

With all my love,
Tara (Mom)"

Tears formed in her eyes as she signed with her left hand. "Have a great life, Sean." She whispered to herself. "I'll have a great life in heaven, waiting for all of you to join me."

The next day, John met her at Summit and they went to dinner at Houlihans' Restaurant in the King of Prussia Mall where she bought a new top since her swollen arms did not fit through the sleeves of every suit she had. *No longer will I wear suits.* Outside the mall, an oversized American flag waved rhythmically in the wind, its metal clamps tolling against the four-story flagpole. *My death toll?* When they arrived home, she had forgotten to pull up the weights in the grandfather clock. The weights lay on the bottom. The clock had stopped at ten minutes after eight. *Will my life stop at this time?*

She went to the typewriter still on the kitchen table and typed a second letter to Enda. Daddle sat on the kitchen table; her right paw stretched outward and Pushky sat under her chair as she typed. Images of Enda's life flickered through her thoughts like images formed from quickly turning pages in a picture book.

She felt good and decided to type Enda's letter.

"April 1994

"My Dear Enda,
"July 21, 1965 at 6:15 A.M. was one of the happiest days of my life. Looking at my beautiful baby boy and thanking God for a perfect child, a wonderful time in my life. I had a more fulfilling and richer life because you were born.

"When you were a little boy you didn't like having a haircut or having your picture taken in a studio. Do you remember the Big Jim camper you played so much? You used to set up the camp and drill and park all the cars in their place. I remember you in your baseball outfit – I loved watching you playing baseball. You loved baseball.

" I missed you when you went to Niagara University. When you decided to come back to Villanova University, I was happy. Having left home myself at twenty-four, I understood although I missed you when you went to Boston. We could still be as close though miles apart. You have achieved much and seem happy in Boston. I am proud to be your Mom. I don't feel like you are far away. I love you and I will love you and be with you even after I die.

"You are to be commended for your achievements in life thus far. I know you will continue to prosper. You are a happy and self-confident person. Your good looks and wonderful personality make you charming.

"Keep close to your Dad, brothers and sister. Your Dad has been wonderful and understanding to me during my illness.

"Your religion is between you and God. God wants to know you are with him. He is there when you need him. Driving in your car say a little short hello to God – talk to Him. When things go wrong it is hard to pray. The prayers you have already prayed will help you through hard times. Remember priests are human beings helping to bring God to you – they're not God. It is okay to cry. Have a great life and don't be sad for me. I had a good and happy life.

With all my love,
Tara (Mom)"

Tears flowed down her cheeks. She paused wiping away tears before she signed the letter with her left-hand. She marveled how good her handwriting had become and thought how people and she in particular could do anything, if they tried. She believed, if you were determined, you would reach your goal. Daddle rose to stretch and she fingered the top of the Pushky's head. They meowed at each other. The letter had taken twenty-five minutes to type. *Not bad for a one-finger typist.*

She made a cup of tea for John and herself before taking up the task of typing a letter to her daughter.

"April 1994

"My Dear Maura,

"April 22, 1970 at 5:45 P.M. was one of the happiest days of my life. A beautiful, perfect baby girl was born. I thanked God for my perfect baby girl.

"You were a happy little girl. You loved your brothers and played a lot with them. You loved stuffed animals and live fluffy ones, too. Riding your bicycle was also a favorite sport.

"I enjoyed watching you play softball. The favorite thing I like to see you do is dance. You have a terrific beat. You enjoyed your girlfriends.

"When you went to Villanova, I missed you. I was happy when you decided to live at home after college. You have been a wonderful daughter and friend to me. During my sickness your kindness and love has made my life happy. I love you and will love you even after I die.

"You have grown into a fine young lady, I am proud to be your Mom. You have achieved much already. A pretty girl like you will have a wonderful life. Remember never marry a man who is abusive.

"Keep close to your Dad and your brothers. Your Dad and brothers were all good to me when I was sick.

"Religion is between you and God. Let God know you are on his side. Say a little prayer each day. It is hard to pray when things go wrong. The prayers you say each day will all add up and are there when you need them.

"Have a great life and be happy.

With all my love,
Tara (Mom)"

Weary after dinner, Tara decided to write to Thaddeus the following day. She closed the lid on the electric typewriter, went upstairs, sat in the tub – her doctors told her to rest in the tub instead of having a quick shower – and joined John near the fireplace to watch television. She sighed and in her head talked to herself like a salesman selling a product. In front of the television, her mind wandered to her job at Summit Personal Care. She had resolved herself with the fact she would tell Nathan Mountain she would again enter the hospital in two weeks and her chances of survival slim. She decided it would be fair to him, and he should look for another administrator. Outside, the night was as black as the grave. Saddened by these thoughts, she reflected on the advice she had given to her children: the prayers you have already prayed will help you through hard times. *I hope to follow my own advice in these days of Gethsemane. . to be brave enough to die in peace and with courage.*

# THIRTY-THREE

# Resignation

Enroute to her office along Bristol Road, she understood she had entered the stage of life when you do things for the last time, never again to be experienced. The words *never again* filled her with ambivalent feelings. Many events in life she didn't want to do again, like solving issues between two infuriated employees or drive to work in snowstorms or beat the pain of cancer strangle-holding her dreams. But she would miss what life offered. She loved life. John had called her the happiest person he had ever known—a happy and contented person, a person who found and lived life with meaning. She loved people and dedicated herself to servicing people. She dedicated herself to helping the elderly. She dedicated herself to her family. She found much meaning in her dedications. She didn't look for weaknesses in people nor exploited their faults. She accepted people's strengths, overlooking their weaknesses.

As she unfolded from the car, a Blackbird balanced itself on a wire-thin branch on a tree reaching high into the sky. It balanced itself by maneuvering its wings outward and inward while twitching its tail. Suddenly, it descended in a nose-dive, as if attacking its prey. She walked into her office, greeted the cook, residents and her secretary – all for the last time. She thought how her secretary once appraised her situation... *She's going to die anyway.* She said aloud to herself, "How right you are. This is my last hurrah."

Nathan Mountain held her left hand and hugged her. Her head beside his neck, she felt how thick and warm his neck. He had a football player's neck.

"Coming back in two weeks?"

"That's what I wanted to talk to you about John."

"Back in two weeks. That's all the talking that's needed."

She smiled, taking her seat beside the desk. Mountain eased himself into the armchair and looked over her head. "A fine Irish picture it is, Tara."

"That's Charlestown...where Maura's Miss Mayo Contest was held."

"Must visit the place some day."

"John, I might as well get to the point. This is my last week before I go into the hospital. I won't be returning. Fluids continue to collect in my lungs. My doctors want me in the hospital for two weeks to insert a tube in my abdomen and stomach. They said tubes may drain excess fluids and the screen they place in the walls of my lungs may prevent further fluids from entering the lungs."

His eyes filled with tears.

*Smiles take away tears.* She smiled. "We hope all this will work."

"If not?"

She examined his volleyball sized round face. "It's all over."

"But..." John tried to continue...he feared crying, if he went on. He put his hand under his right eyelid to hold back tears.

"Never get anyone like you, Tara. Never."

"Anyone can be replaced. The next administrator will do well. Besides, the person will have you as trainer."

"Today is my last day?"

Emotion got the better of him. To avoid an emotional outburst, he patted Tara's hands. He froze stock-still like a rabbit about ready to flee for fear of destruction. "See you," he said, quickly leaving the office.

She froze, staring round the office at four pictures of her children, typewriter, pictures of Ireland on the walls, intercom telephone on her desk, at the desk set with her engraved name on the nameplate. "Tara O'Malley, Administrator," she said aloud. She sat quietly, erect in her swivel chair. Sitting erect made her feel relaxed. *I need John to lean on. John to hold and love me. Always John. Always will be. Always into the future. . one day at a time.*

In a small box, she placed her children's pictures, Irish pictures, desk set and nameplate. She asked Bill Martel, the maintenance man, to carry the box. She said final good byes to residents: Harry, Roland, Sarah, Susan, Henrietta, Martha, Ellie, Madelene (who didn't lift her dress this time); and she hugged aides Janet, Joan, and her secretary Eleanor, Millie and Sheldon, the two lovers having a daily affair, and Bob, the cook. In the parking lot, she observed the lot full as she gave Martel a farewell hug. *Lot's full but I'm not.* She felt tired, but not ready for retirement from life. She felt empty, like a car with little gas left in its tank. But she would do her best to maintain the glass half-full to help her carry on during the challenging days ahead.

At home and charged with the emotion of leaving, after dinner she typed her fourth and final letter to Thaddeus.

"April 1994

"My Dear Thaddeus,

"January 23, 1994 at 2:19 P.M. was one of the happiest days of my life. Your birthday and I had my last beautiful baby – the baby I planned and wanted to have to complete our family. A perfect little baby boy you were and we thanked God! Because you were born, our lives were more fulfilling.

"I remember the day you broke your leg. You didn't let the cast put you off doing anything. I liked watching you play soccer – you had energy running all over the field. You played basketball well also. You were a happy little guy and seemed to enjoy yourself.

"When you went to Providence College, I missed you. I missed hearing your laughter from the room downstairs especially when "Coach" and other favored programs were on. I feel we are close to each other when we are apart. I know you like being at Providence and that makes me happy. Knowing I am sick, I have purposely tried to make you as independent as possible.

"I am proud of the way you are growing into a fine young man. I know you will achieve all your dreams in life. I love you and will always love you and be with you even after I die. You are a good-looking, self-confident person.

"Keep close to your Dad, brothers and sister. Talk it out after I die. Cry if it makes you feel better."

Tears rolled down her cheeks. She left the table and sat alone in the living room with the lights out. Pushky followed her and jumped onto her lap. Petting her cat soothed her spirit. She remembered the article she had read on pet therapy – stroking pets reduced blood pressure and helped people under stress. She agreed with the article's author, for she felt calmer. She returned to the table and continued typing.

"Your Dad was good to me while I was sick.

"Stay close to God. God is there when you need him. Remember priests are human beings doing God's work. Say a little prayer to God each day. He wants to know you are on his side. It is hard to pray when things go wrong. The little prayers you say each day will build up and be there for you when you need them. Go away from a situation you feel is wrong or people are taking advantage of another human being. Treat people as you would like to be treated. I am proud to be your Mom.

"Have a great life and be happy.

> With all my love,
> Tara (Mom)"

She finished and to John, sitting on the wraparound sofa, she said, "You know how I feel. This card says I love you. I'll read it to you: 'Day after day, I am able to share my thoughts and activities with you. Night after night, I am able to share the moon and darkness with you. I feel secure knowing that in good times and in bad times, in exciting times and in peaceful times, my days and nights are filled with love. I love you.'" She handed him the card. He kissed her yielding lips. He studied his wife, a dark-haired beauty, now hairless but still beautiful with a well formed round head. Like a hairless mannequin. He smiled. Her once proud bosom now reduced to one breast, which didn't bother him. Her face chiseled in his brain. Her waistline still pleased him. Her character and moral vipers—the makings of one happy, strong-willed and angelic lady! *How will I ever survive without Tara? In time. . .what would happen to me. I will grieve, but will I ever be reconciled?*

Tara's doctor placed her in the hospital in mid-May. Dr. Wiseman inserted tubes into her stomach and abdomen to drain malignant fluids from the lungs. Two containers hung over the bedpost at her feet. Fluids continued to drain into the containers and nurses changed them throughout the day and night. After a week, no improvement was noted. Doctors said there was nothing else they could do. Dr. Wiseman discussed with John the likelihood of assigning Tara to hospice care and bringing her home under the supervision of a nurse who would visit twice a week and aides to assist with bedside chores. A hospital bed would be provided as well as required medications and a commode. The doctor's words unsettled him. He felt he was at Tara's grave. His body quivered.

Since John had already telephoned the children about her lungs, she expected to see them soon. All her life, she went unassisted to the bathroom. *Now I am reduced to sliding off the bed onto a commode. Never again to walk, never again to shop for suits and dresses, a form of tension release for me; never again to work, never again to go to church, never attend my children's weddings nor hold my grandchildren. Never. Now, I will never visit the church; the parish priest will come to me. Never again to visit my children, never again to cook for my family, never again to lie with John in our bed; never again to live again as free as I have lived each day of my life. I dislike the words "never again". Finality.. like death itself, black as a dream in the blackness of night, as black as death.* Unlike many people, she did not take life for granted, she lived life in the present and whatever joy or trouble came her way, she experienced it with an attitude based on common sense that this too shall pass and the following day would be a new start. She started each day with the idea that this day would be the first day of the rest of her life, that God would see her through each day. *Until cancer, every day has been a good day. God-awful days are not part of my vocabulary.*

On May 26, 1994, Tara turned sixty. Her family planned a birthday party in Tara's room 303; the same number as her husband's classroom and the same room number Sean had stayed in St. Edward's Hall at Notre Dame. Tara's last hospital room. *Number 303...a ring of finality.*

John delivered a birthday cake with white icing trimmed in blue "Happy Birthday, Tara." John usually bought a cake with the colors of the Irish flag, but this time he decided to buy a cake with her favorite color – blue. Sean, Enda, Maura, and Maura's best friend Peg, sang happy birthday. Maura and Peg popped open a bottle of non-alcoholic champagne and filled small paper cups for five people.

Tara drank juice. "Well, I've made sixty," she said, her face beaming a glowing smile. She sat straight up, her back away from the pillows. In her sky blue nightgown, she looked spirited and happy. She cooed and smiled shyly like a schoolgirl talking to her first love. Her beautiful face puffed out with fluids. Her swelled body and legs retained fluids. She had gained ten pounds.

"Here's to Ma Ma," Maura said, raising her cup as everyone touched cups and drank.

"How's it feel to be sixty?" Peg asked.

She wanted to say, "I'm too young to die," but instead she said, "Great...but in my condition, I'm okay."

"To Mom." Sean offered a second toast.

"You need a Guinness, Mom," Enda suggested.

"I'd get sick," she reacted.

"A Brittingham's salute," said John, elevating his cup and joined by his family and Peg.

"Mrs. O'Malley, you look great."

"Sure, Peg," Tara smiled. You make me feel good with my wrapped arms and puffing body." She sneezed. She sneezed again. "Always sneeze twice," she said. "I sneeze in pairs. There's one male and a female in my sneeze." Her snicker turned into a smile.

"With all you've gone through, you look great," Peg said, giggling and admiring Tara's sense of humor, footsteps from death.

Tara leaned forward. "Thank you, Peg. You make me feel better." Her family had maintained a sense of humor—the Irish way, smiling and laughing in adversity. *It's a terrible day, thanks be to God, according to Fr. Mike Doyle of Sacred Heart Church in the poorest city in the states, Camden.* A young girl with black hair and long legs walked passed the doorway. The boys noticed. Enda said, "Looks like you, Mom."

"I'm taking a sabbatical, Tara. When you come home, I'll take care of you," John announced.

She smiled, watched a pest control truck turn the corner and said, "I'll be like the pest control truck out there," pointing to the window, "a pest. But thank you, John. I've taken care of the children and now you're caring for me."

"Where would I be if it weren't for you?"

"I don't want to burden you."

"Tara, I love you. I'll do whatever I can for you."

She needn't reply. Her expression told him she grasped his meaning. And she said weakly, "Yes. I know, John. I know."

To all the children and Peg she said, "Since it's my birthday, why not celebrate it at Brittingham's."

"Brittingham's?" Sean asked. "How can we have your birthday dinner without you, Mom?"

"You can if it's my wish."

Maura added, "We'll have a birthday dinner and toast you, Ma Ma."

Tara smiled. All Maura's life, she called Tara Ma Ma like a little girl. "Have one for me," she said. "Have one for the matriarch of the O'Malley clan."

"That we will!" Enda stated.

They each kissed Tara goodbye and gave her a hug. She felt like an uniformed schoolgirl, with her socks rolled down, defiant to the world and all its restrictions and rules of sociability.

# THIRTY-FOUR

# Hospice Care

The school district granted John's one-year sabbatical. If needed, he planned to use his unused sick days for another year.

Maura had given her father additional notes about Tara's health, including the update on Tara's hospital stay. In a quiet moment, he read Maura's notebook.

"Mom went to the hospital this past week. One night, when I arrived, she looked terrific. Mom had her hair done and her lipstick on. No one would know she was sick and in pain. At the end of the night, just before I left, the doctor came in and told her the fluid around her heart had cancerous cells. The doctors wanted to put a window outside her heart. It would be easier for fluids to drain. She has been breathing heavily due to this fluid. The window would help her breath easier. The doctor said she would live about three months without it. With the window she would have up to a year.

"The doctor gave her a brain scan. Today she had severe headaches and pains in her neck. She wanted them to test her, since she never gets headaches. The brain scan came out positive. One tumor is two centimeters long in the cerebellum, another tumor on the top of the brain. I can't believe it. This is happening too fast. But through all of this, she still looks great. She's in great spirits. Of course, she hides her pain when I'm there. She doesn't want me to get upset. She tries to protect her children whenever she can. That's Mom. I love her!

"I visited the following night. Mom told me she went for her first radiation on her brain. That's all they're doing for her now. They are not putting the window in. I don't know why. She told me the nurse wanted to put permanent black dots on her forehead so they would know where to radiate. Mom insisted she didn't want them. The nurse insisted the dots were necessary and Mom being Mom refused them. Mom is a determined woman for sure. She laughed when she told me.

"She wasn't going to get radiation at first. She'd rather live a quality of life for a short time. But she asked Dad what he wanted her to do. He said get it.

"If she doesn't get treatment, she has a great possibility of having a stroke! She would rather die in her sleep. She is taking steroids now to prevent a stroke. I think she thinks she won't be around much longer and she wants to say good-bye to Enda and Thaddeus. When leaving, Dad said to me this was a death trip. They plan to make a will and trust. If Dad gets married again, all his and Mom's money go to us. It protects Dad and us. I've heard about wills, living wills, how much money we will get when Mom and Dad are dead. What topics! What other family talks about death as much as we do? My friends think we are odd talking about this."

Sitting beside the octagonal table, he placed the papers on the table and blankly gazed through the forty-eight squares of window glass. John studied the Japanese Red Maple tree, Tara's Mother's Day present in 1969, less than one year after they moved into their newly built five-bedroom home. He remembered Tara directing him for a proper planting location. She waited at the front door and when he reached the point directly in the doorway's path, she called, "Stop...that's the right place." And he dug the hole to place the infant tree, three feet high. The tree covered the entire front lawn and rose above the roof of their two-story home. The grandfather clock struck five times. *A beautiful clock*. He remembered buying it for Tara as a Christmas present in 1991, the year Maura won the Miss Mayo contest in Philadelphia.

The living room where he sat reflected Tara's taste and personality: off-white, designer shades and light, sky blue drapes edging along the top border and covering the windowpanes. He thought the colors matched Tara's and his personalities – happy and welcoming. The Barbara Weldon's watercolors of a boy in a flower patch and a girl in a flower patch centered in wood squares on each side of the living room windows. A secretary desk filled a corner. Eighteen Hummels decorated the shelves. A square and a rectangular Van Sciver table with glass tops suited Tara's taste for quality furnishings, as did the salmon colored rockers; each placed beside Van Sciver's octagonal. Three Stiffel lamps provided light. The rocker colors blended with the cream-colored French provincial chair and sofa – patterned with soft pink, gleaming blue and dark blue flowers growing out of mild green stems with leaves. A side window looking out onto the neighbor's two-story Evergreen tree matched the styling of the front windows. A family picture, bordered in white wood hung on the wall next to the single window. The blue high-pile carpet completed the decorum of the room and complemented its designer, his wife, his Irish Rose. A photograph of Tara's father with the President of Ireland and New York's cardinal stood frozen in time on the octagonal. A stereo player with two twenty-four inch speakers topped with two plants graced the room.

All was ready for Tara. John picked up a bible beside the photograph and read the gospel of John. He read chapter fifteen. When he read verses six and seven he groaned. He reread the verses aloud. "Whoever does not remain in me is thrown out like a branch and dries up; these branches are gathered up and thrown into the fire, where they are burned. If you remain in me and my words remain in you, and you ask for anything you wish you shall have it."

"Oh God," he blurted aloud, "Why have you forsaken me? Why have you forsaken us? We remained in you and your words remained in us. We had faith in you and we asked for Tara's life and now she's coming home to die. Oh, God, you have thrown us out like dried up branches and you're letting us burn in the fire. Are you an historical figure after all? Is the grave the end? Is this all there is?" He shouted, "Are you like Fang, the overbearing magistrate who sentenced the unfortunate Oliver Twist to prison? Are you a helper of people or a punisher of people?" He held his hands to his face, teardrops surging between the fingers, which held Tara in many acts of love. "You lied to us, to everybody." He grabbed the Bible and crashed it to the blue carpet. It bounced up and hit his leg. *Is this your way, God, of retaliating for my arrogance?*

*That's what you think of me, is it? You're knocking the legs from under me for daring to question you, the great God, the Great Almighty. Adore you? Go to hell! Go adore yourself. If you don't like what I'm saying – good. I'm glad. Strike me dead and get it over with. . No, you won't do this. You won't make it easy on me. You're keeping me here until I'm ninety or more so I will suffer longer, be alone and lonely longer. To bear pain longer. You want me to be fear-*

ful, unmotivated, with no purpose in life, no balance, no contentment, no peace of mind, to live in uncertainty. You like making people suffer, don't you? Yes... right, you suffered the agony of the cross and you want the rest of us to suffer the agony of life – and death. But remember this, God, you suffered a couple of days during your passion whereas human beings suffer throughout their lives. And many poor people suffer every day of their lives. And this delights you, doesn't it? Goddamn you, God. Goddamn you for throwing us to the wolves, for making us pathetic imprisoned people like worn horses tied to posts.

He didn't feel better after this outburst. He felt drained. He cried.

Finally, the ambulance arrived. *May 31st... my day of infamy.* The ambulance men, who looked more like derelicts than medical people carried Tara on a stretcher through the doorway, head first. *Home at last. As Joseph Girzone's Joshua said: "The houses people live in reflect the opinions of themselves"—and I love my house. The next time I am carried through these doors will be feet first and in a zippered undertaker's black sack.* Pollen-drunk bees hummed in an azalea bush. Azaleas, a sign of spring. A symbol of new life. The regeneration of a new beginning. *And here I am, once drunk with the joy of living and now dying the sadness of death.* She remembered Morrie Schwartz and his last days. Schwartz said, "Don't let go too soon, but don't hang on too long." *How long will my long be? My sunset is closer than my sunrise. I've come a long way to die and be buried, 3000 miles from Dublin.*

The hospice bed had been ordered but would not arrive until Monday, June 6, D-Day. *An invasion to free Europe, but for me a day to imprison me.* In the meantime, Tara selected the long end of the wrap around sofa in the family room so she could see the thirty-five inch television. John prepared his wife's "bed." A rare time in their marriage. He cooked a light dinner. Maura visited them after work and stayed until nine when she left for Conshohocken where she roomed with her friend, Peg. John slept at the other end of the sofa, his head resting near Tara's. She had enough strength in her legs to move cautiously to the powder room once or twice a day. She had the use of a bedpan beside her on the floor. *I potty-trained the children and now John has to escort me to the toilet.* Unable to breathe without mechanical assistance, Tara had the service of an oxygen tank with tiny plastic tubes affixed to her nostrils. *At least, I won't live to be old or an invalid or like a little old gray-haired lady, slouched in a wheelchair.*

The long plastic tube grasped her nostrils, chaining her to the oxygen tank, which rhythmically exhaled life-giving oxygen. When she saw the fright on her husband's face, she smiled, consoling him. On the seat of death, she comforted people. Typical of Tara who never manipulated anyone and never sought to make money from the labors of others' efforts. Greed wasn't her God. Always more interested in other people's problems than her own. Love radiated from her, like the radiance of joy on a pregnant woman's face. Not like a saint...but like a decent human being who showed respect and dignity to fellow human beings.

Tara felt she denied John proper rest.

"I'm all right at night, John," said she, with a smile. "I'd feel much better if you slept upstairs."

"You sure," he muttered, "I don't mind staying here."

"No, I'd rather you sleep in your bed."

"It's our bed, Tara," His heart ached, unable to do anything of substance to alleviate their blight. He felt useless.

"Haven't forgotten your sense of humor, have you honey-bunny?"

"Nor yours, dearie."

There was a silence. They decided to go to bed....

Still, John slept a few feet from her on the wrap-around sofa. *Will I see upstairs again and sleep in our bed?*

Friends and neighbors rang and wanted to stop by and talk with Tara. She claimed, "They want to pay their respects, but I don't want them to see me like this. They can remember me the way I was.

With John as a househusband and Tara the patient, they primed themselves for a lifestyle of palatable confinement with the love they shared. When healthy, they had settled into the present and like the sun rising on a new day, they realized the hope they had for longevity had stretched into dusk. He thought their present lives like a deer frozen in the woods, waiting to be killed by a hunter's bullet. They waited for death...from cancer. They knew life for Tara was at an end. *No more waiting*, he thought; *the end was now.* The realism of cancer had caught up with reality.

John prepared a light breakfast of an egg, toast and tea for Tara and a sparse lunch of soup and half a hot dog. John had prepared a full dinner for both, but Tara ate parcels.

He said to her, "I eat dinner the way I make love to you: I start on the perimeter and come to the middle, the flower of your womanhood."

"You never give up, do you?"

"Who would with a beautiful wife like you?"

Maura visited four times a week. Paula Coulter came once a week to talk to Tara and to relieve John for two hours. While Tara and Paula talked, John went for a pint of Guinness to Brittingham's. John and Tara had already asked Kerry O'Hanlon to sing "Rare Ole Times" and "Four Green Fields" at her funeral Mass. *Funeral Mass? I can't believe it.*

On Sunday, Paula made her second visit in two days.

"We're wondering where to put the bed when it arrives,"

Tara said. "John wants me to put it here in the family room so I can watch TV."

Paula had a more practical solution. Practicality...a way of life for some people. "Why here? It's the place where the kids sit and, if you die there, they'll remember you dying in this room."

"I think, Tara, you'd be better off in this room. TV is here, the fireplace; it's cozy here," John said.

"This room," Tara suggested, "has coziness all right but I'm not sure... don't want them to remember me dying in this room when they sit here."

"They will," said Paula, laughing without humor.

"I don't think this room has all the comforts Tara needs. There' no TV in any other room downstairs," John declared. He motioned to Paula to wait a second before saying, "Now, that's a funny thing to say, isn't it?" And he continued, answering his own question, " I said 'I don't think.' Senseless, isn't it. If a person says he doesn't think then he has no opinion on a matter."

Paula gave him a daunting gaze and said, "Where in the world did that come from, John? One of your classroom lectures? To get back to the subject I'd say, try the dining room. A cable could be hooked up in the dining room. There's a great view through the front windows. Besides watching TV, Tara could watch life go by."

"Not a bad idea, Paula. There would be light behind me with the dining room window. "Tara stirred and her face contorted in discomfort. "I have to go to the bathroom, John."

John got up to take Tara's arm and ease her off the sofa. Paula stood to assist.

"All right, Paula," John said, giving her a look, meaning: I'll do this alone, "I'll manage." He smiled at their long-time friend.

"John's becoming a good nurse," Tara said as she moved slowly, being sure each step was secure before taking another step forward. To think I did this so many times without effort," Tara said, about to enter the powder room.

"You'll have to forgive her," he smiled at Paula. "The Irish in her, I guess." John closed the door behind him and assisted his wife onto the seat as she had done so often with the four children. She thought what people often said: *you come in as a child and you go out as a child.*

With John holding her, she paced herself back to the sofa. "Tomorrow, when the bed and commode come, I won't have to do this anymore."

"No, you won't. But if you do," said John, "I'll help you."

Losing her hair three times after chemotherapy it grew back as thick— snow white until she dyed it. This time, the last, she left it white. John told her she was as lovely as ever. "You resembled Sinead O'Connor."

She smiled and laughing said, "I'm like a big baby."

"And you're the kind of big baby, I like, Tara, especially with your soft, tender skin and . . ."

Tara interrupted. "He's thinking such things, Paula."

"Thinking what? I didn't do anything," he retorted.

Tara gave him her administrator's stare—a stare, which told him to give it up.

To John she said, "Hump off." To Paula, she said, "I think, I'll take your advice, Paula and go into the dining room."

"It's your fault, Paula," John kidded.

"It's the best choice," Paula responded.

"I'll call the cable company tomorrow and have a line installed," said John. "But I don't like it."

He noticed a wild flower on the front lawn. "Resembles the Mountain Laurel, our state flower," he said, pointing to the grass.

"People are wild, aren't they," she muttered.

"Like me."

She looked at him and Paula.

Look at me…smiling…with my deathbed on the way.

# THIRTY-FIVE

# Father Mc Bride

A hospital bed, back-up oxygen tank and commode arrived from the hospital hospice health care unit. John and the two hospice men, their boots pounding the floor like hammers, removed the dining room table into the living room and arranged the hospital bed in the center of the room. Flanked by the serving table and china closet, Tara had bought the entire set for a fifty per cent discount when she worked in the evening as the night office manager in a furniture store. John made the bed and pulled the clean sheet tightly at the corners. It resembled an army recruit's well-made bed, taut enough a dime could bounce a foot high. Their home had become a hospital. *I'm entering my deathbed.* Experiencing a lifetime of open-ended communications, they could comfortably discuss death with no holding back one's emotions…it empowered them to laugh at life and death. Death's grip encroached on them with a steel hand. Nonetheless, they continued to talk with the ease and innocence of high school sweethearts.

"You're a "A" student," he told her.

"Better than a "C.""

"Not bad," he said. Harry Truman said, 'Many "C" students rule the world.'"

As John edged Tara onto the bed, said she, "Here I go round the mulberry bush, and into my deathbed." He patted her buttocks as she rolled onto her side. Tara accepted the touch without any acknowledgment. Her heart pounded like a marching band drum.

"Move over," he said, "and I'll come in beside you."

"How can I move over," she smiled "I'm lucky I made it onto the bed."

He slid beside her. Fully clothed, with her on her side, he slithered his arm around her waist. "Now, this is where, I belong."

"In a hospital bed?"

"With you."

She quipped; "I can't go any other place."

He cackled. "Irish wit, Mrs. O'Malley. I love it."

"Somebody has to make us laugh. You're too serious."

"Not always, honey bunny."

"No, not always, but too conservative. Teachers are conservative, afraid to take chances."

"I took a chance on O'Shea Personal Care."

"Because I wanted it?"

"Because you asked me."

She relented a little from their tit for tat. "Yes, John, you were gracious."

"Of course. Whatever you want, you get. You asked if I would re-mortgage our house for the business and I said yes."

"You're a good man."

"At last, I get credit. You get most of what you want."

"But I'm not cured..." She allowed the thought to hang there, to be considered at another time.

"I want you here. I can't live without you."

"You'll jump into my grave and in a few months you'll be married again."

"Tara…you know better."

"I'll be looking down on you. Remember I'll see what you're doing. Mind yourself."

"Oh, I'll be doin' something. Somebody said, 'Those who stand for nothing fall for anything.'" They lay quietly together, not stirring, body-to-body, mind-to-mind, soul-to-soul. Soulmates. United in an oneness they promised and vowed to each other in the wedding ceremony at Rathgar in the Church of the Three Patrons in 1963. Tara peered into the Italian Provincial china closet. She observed the Waterford canisters in the Colleen collection and the large vase she bought at Shannon, returning with Sean to America after her mother had died—pitchers, goblets, drinking glasses of various sizes – all in the Colleen pattern. She singled out the items she wanted Maura to have: the Donegal China and Royal Tara China, along with two Hummels. The gold trimmed desk clock with her name and "administrator" engraved on it anyone could have.

Monday night, John slept on the sofa where he could observe Tara during the night. He slept there for the remainder of Tara's life. Prior to their going to sleep, Daddle jumped into an empty cardboard box of Trout Apples, which John used to store materials for school projects. A white, blue point Himalayan Persian, Tara accepted her from a friend who moved to an apartment that would not permit cats. Daddle was one year old when she came to the O'Malley home. Never liked by their first cat, Pushky, Daddle faced a disadvantage. The previous owner declawed her. Since Pushky had arrived before Daddle, the black cat ruled the roost. Pushky sat on the edge of the bed and Tara waited for Daddle to join them. Daddle jumped out of the box and onto the bed. Immediately, Pushky went for the white Persian. Clawless and defenseless, Daddle leaped onto the serving table. Tara watched Daddle. *Daddle…better watch yourself. She's a girl and as Eleanor Roosevelt said: a woman is like a teabag. You don't know how strong she is until she gets into hot water.*

"Pushky," Tara warned in a firm voice. "Leave her." The black cat sat quietly on the end of the bed as the white cat rejoined them, sitting at the other end of the bed. At times, the two animals sat near each other, but for the most part, Daddle lived on guard against possible attack. Planning for the best, preparing for the worst, taking whatever comes along. Daddle feared this traumatic experience unlike a female teacher John knew. The teacher feigned Agoraphobia and said, "I have ways to get what I want." Pushky used bullying tactics on Daddle, the picture-perfect identical twin of the Persian cat on the label of Fancy Feast cat food. Tara missed her two dead poodles, Fi Fi and Puff.

In humorous playfulness, John claimed the black Pushky didn't like Daddle. Since the Persian was white, John called it a race war. Tara frowned on the idea.

In the morning, John rang the rectory and asked Father McBride, their pastor, to visit Tara, hear her confession, give her viaticum, and anoint her.

The priest arrived Wednesday morning. Father McBride was a cheery man in his sixties. He wore a blond toupee covering the entire top of his hairless head. A glossy, lustrous hairpiece it looked like it contained a legion of tiny silk fibers. McBride, according to the curate, cherished the hairpiece. He thought it made him appear younger and hence more in tune with young people. A round, moon-shaped face, and with royal blue eyes, he was a handsome man, the spiritual leader of 5,400 parishioners.

"Father, I have a short time to live."

"And you have breast cancer."

"Yes. It's spread to my lungs and brain."

"I'm sorry." The priest placed a crucifix on the serving table. A brilliant stream of light illuminated the cross, casting shadows in four directions: north, south, east, west. Tara believed Christ was near. She wondered where she would be in a month's time. *Soon, I'll see the light of Christ.*

"Doctors have done their best."

"How long have you had cancer?"

"Five years, eight months."

"You've had a battle, haven't you?"

"John and the children have been good throughout it all."

"I bet they have."

John sat opposite McBride on a chair beside Tara's bed.

"She's a good patient. A little turbulent at times," John said, waving his right hand side-to-side and smiling.

She held her hand to her forehead, her eyes alert and luminous. "What I'm trying to do," she said, "is to live every day as if it's my last. And one day, I'll be right."

McBride roared. "Your sense of humor is amazing."

"Ah, Father," said John. "You can't beat her humor."

"Seems so."

"Did you survive the rain yesterday, Father?"

"I did."

Tara chimed, "When it rains, it's an overflow from heaven's kitchen with the ladies being annoyed having to wash dishes and in frustration they spilt water on the men still living on earth."

McBride laughed, touching her head.

Sitting up in bed, a position she had grown accustomed to, Tara jeered, "Well, I'll tell you this. When I get to heaven, I'm not going to wash dishes for any pope. He can wash his own dishes."

"I can't believe this," McBride said. "Your sense of humor is remarkable." He noticed she smiled as warm as a sky-blue spring day with puffs of cotton-like clouds. "I'm use to people in sad states in situations like this."

"And I'm not in a sad state, Father."

"Sick, yes. But not sad," McBride answered.

"How do you do this, Father, seeing death in front of you?"

"Remember, Tara, we see death all the time. I love helping parishioners."

"Doesn't it bother you to see death every day?"

"No. It's part of the job. I see it all the time."

"How long have you been a priest?"

"Thirty-five years."

"You're about ready for retirement."

"We don't retire. We fade away," he smiled. "I love what I'm doing."

The priest noticed two puzzles on the dining room table in the living room. "Who makes puzzles?" he beamed, admiring the patience of someone to sit hours contentedly placing piece after piece of a thousand-piece puzzle.

"Our daughter, Maura," answered Tara.

"I love puzzles. I haven't seen anyone doing puzzles in years."

John excused himself as the priest heard Tara's confession and gave her the sacraments. He knew Tara and thought he could recite Tara's confession. She was a good person. Her confession: *Bless me, Father for I have sinned.. but I have nothing to tell you.* Other than a sly remark about nuns, he knew of no serious sin she had committed in their marriage.

Father McBride left, begging off on lunch for work in the rectory. John prepared Tara's lunch of soup and half a tuna sandwich.

Tara watched "The Price is Right." A runner jogged by the house. Staring out the window, she observed a ten wheeler dump truck swish out of her view, a pick up truck carrying lawn mowers, a red plumber's truck, a maroon and gray van. Birds fluttered onto and away from the Red Japanese Maple, as a red Honda, a darting black compact, a soft water van passed by the picture windows. *I wish I could flutter away from cancer.* Whizzing, dashing, bounding into and out of her life. *Life, what was left!* She timed the traffic for one minute. Six vehicles passed. *One every ten seconds ...a busy street.*

To her left, she placed four pictures of her children she had removed from her desk at Summit Personal Care onto the serving table. A small plastic battery-controlled globe-shaped clock was stationed between Thaddeus and John's photographs. A tiny scale wooden grotto of Lourdes with a candle beside Maura's picture. Directly behind her, a full view of the town of Lourdes and another picture captured the actual grotto. The Lourdes pictures reminded her of her three trips to Lourdes to seek a healing. *And to no avail now that I'm bed-ridden and about to die. Lourdes often mispronounced in the plural—the word ended in 's.' But I gave it my all. And that makes me happy.* She remembered John and herself in the hotel St. Joan of Arc. How he ever drank a full bottle of wine on each of their two visits amazed her. She always admired the pictures of the Blue Boy and the Blue Girl that hung beside the china closet. Each child wore reddish tennis sneakers. The Blue Boy read from a book with his sneakers laced. Uncharacteristically, the Blue Girl ate cookies and pondered a glass of milk; her laces unlaced. She reasoned girls are the most serious and the boy should be eating with unlaced sneakers. She guessed a man, a chauvinist, painted the originals.

A reproduction of Notre Dame Cathedral in Paris – where they visited – hung on the wall near the doorway to the kitchen. Six, six inch by four-inch bronze frames darkened by age, hung facing her on the wall. On her left was a mirrored clock. Another tiny mirror stationed itself between the two children. In the right corner, nearest to the living room, a large glass container held several hundred pennies she had collected for years. Out of the container rose four feathered stems. The carpeted living and dining rooms had hardwood floors. If she lived, she planned to bring the floors up to present day decorum by removing the carpets and having the hardwood floors refinished.

With a sparkle in her eyes, she told John she wanted to arrange her funeral. He rang up Frank Cherry, the funeral director, who had buried two residents from O'Shea Personal Care.

"I don't trust you, John," she bantered him. "You'll put me in a box and bury me."

His face lit up. "Hump off," he chuckled. "Well, you know me. I don't believe in the American way of death—all the glitter and waste."

Her face wrinkled. "You'd have one of Sean's friends make a wooden box for me," she remarked, frolicking.

"Right. I'd make it myself to avoid wasting money on a funeral."

"Cheap."

"No, Tara," he said in their give and take conversation. "You know all I want when I die is to be buried in a wooden box and buried in the back yard."

She laughed. "And I'd have the township after me."

"Let them. Funerals are a waste of money."

Pointing her index finger at him, she rattled, "Show respect for the dead and bury me properly."

"You know I will."

"But if I died first, Tara, bury me in a box."

"I won't be here to bury you."

"Who knows? I may die of a heart attack tonight."

"No, you won't. You're in good health."

"People die suddenly," he blurted out, smartly.

"If you died, I don't know what I'd do . . . First thing I'd do is sell O'Shea's."

"Keep it for the kids."

"No, I'd sell it. I couldn't do it without you."

"You're the administrator!"

"But you do everything. I'm not able for this anymore."

"Yes, you are," he said, hugging her.

"I love you, John."

He leaned over her, kissing her softly. "I love you, Tara."

"When was the last time we said we loved each other?"

She hesitated. "The last time we made love?"

"Maybe. Remember what I told you about dying—if you die first."

"You're weird."

"Aha," he laughed, "You remember. I'll have them open your casket, drop me onto you, face down and close the lid. We will be locked in intercourse for eternity."

"You're so weird."

"Simply showing my love for you." He rose from the side of the bed.

"Now, go answer the door. Should be Frank Cherry."

*My first and only visit from an undertaker.*

# THIRTY-SIX

# Dying Graciously

"Frank," Tara said, "I want a dignified funeral, not the kind John wants. He's cheap. I want a proper funeral."

Frank Cherry laughed. Her humor was unexpected at a time like this. He had red hair with a plethora of freckles on his ruddy-faced complexion. His ancestors had come from County Down in Northern Ireland. An Episcopalian and friendly with Father McBride, he gladly accepted funeral referrals from Father McBride's parishioners. McBride, a Catholic priest, was a decent Christian who didn't penalize people for not being the same faith as his pompous, rigid priests friends.

"No disrespect to you, Frank. But you know how I feel."

"I know. We talked about this when I buried a couple of people from your personal care home."

"Pay him no mind, Frank. He's a cheapskate." Tara repositioned the pillows behind her and pushed the blue button on the hospice bed. She rested her head against the pillows. Their frankness and light-heartiness impressed Cherry. He didn't expect such a light atmosphere. Not many of his clients approached death with such high spirits.

"I won't, Tara," Cherry said.

She felt a sharp pain in her back. She moved her body, but showed no pain on her face.

John went into the kitchen to prepare tea.

Tara studied the casket spec sheets, delineating various caskets and prices.

"This blue one looks good." She felt like an immigrant scuffing to board the last boat.

"It's all steel with the finest quality of silk coverings. This one is $6,900."

"A bit much." Cherry sat beside her, touching her hand. "And this one?" He pointed at a casket. "This one is all steel with fine silk coverings. It's $6,000."

"And this one?"

"That's mostly steel with fine silk coverings."

"The price?"

"It's $6,000."

"I'll take this one," she said. She chose the middle of the road, one pleasing to John and herself. The most expensive item didn't mean the best to her.

"Do you prefer a dress, suit, or one of your dresses?"

"I have a pinkish dress. I'll wear it."

"Your husband can drop it off anytime." John passed out cups of tea and sat at the end of the bed. She twisted her body like a tulip in high-speed photography, coiling itself to reach for sunlight.

John said, " You like suits. Wouldn't you prefer a suit?"

"I've decided to wear my pink dress."

" Well, I like your navy suit."

"John, You're not dying. I am."

Cherry snickered. He enjoyed this conference. It wasn't morbid like most.

"Will my wig be set?"

"Yes, Tara. I'll need a picture of you."

"You mean when I die and look a fright, you need to see what I looked like to reconstruct me?"

He roared aloud. "This sounds like a comedy routine...." He smiled. "We need a photograph."

She laughed at herself. "I must look right. You know. People will talk about me if I don't." Her smile glowed like the early morning chirps of a Robin.

"I'll need earrings and under garments," Cherry said.

"I'll bring them with the dress," John said.

"Do you want to write your death notice?"

"Yes."

"If not, I can write it from an information sheet."

"No. I've already prepared one, showing him a typed notice. How does this sound?"

Cherry read aloud: "Tara O'Malley of Hallow Hills died June_____. ('I'll put the date in later,' he said and continued reading) "at home. She was 60. She was the wife of John O'Malley. Born in Ireland and the daughter of the late Col. Sean and Mary O'Shea. She was a resident of Hallow Hills for the past twenty-six years. Along with her husband, Mrs. O'Malley was the owner of O'Shea Personal Care Facility and administration of Summit Personal care in Chalfont. She was a member of St. Richard's Church. She was a member of the Personal Care Providers Association. Surviving besides her husband are three sons, Sean O'Malley of Conshohocken, Enda O'Malley of Boston, Thaddeus O'Malley of Hallow Hills, and daughter Maura O'Malley of Conshohocken, two brothers, Dr. Padraic O'Shea and Dr. Seamus O'Shea, both of Ireland; and two sisters, Una O'Day of Ireland and Meaghan O'Shea of England.

A Mass of Christian burial will be celebrated at 10 A.M. on_____." ('I'll put in the day,' Cherry added and continued reading) "at St. Richard's Church."

Contributions may be made to her church or the Cancer Institute Memorial Fund, Bustleton Avenue, Philadelphia, PA."

"Is it unusual to write my own death notice?"

"No. Many people prefer to do their own."

John said, "Mine will be easier, Frank, I'll have a wooden box with cheap wood and I'll wear a bathing suit—nothing else."

They shared a laugh. Cherry left their two story colonial home, thinking the next time he left the house he would be carrying Tara out in a zippered bag feet first. Tara remained in silence. She watched an elderly man taking his early morning walk. Two ladies power-walked by the windows. *Never again will I walk. Instead of feeling sorry for myself, I'll switch on the TV.*

Her sister Una rang from Ireland. "I'm feeling fine as can be expected, Una."

"Are you sleeping well?"

"Yes. John is with me at night as well as during the day. He sleeps on the sofa."

"Hope all is well."

"Yes, Sean and Maura visit often. Enda came home to see me. Thaddeus is still at Providence."

"Paul sends his love. Has Padraic or Seamus given you a ring?"

"They have. Meaghan also rang me earlier today."

"I haven't seen her lately, but we talk on the telephone."

"I am thankful, Una, I have a sister like you. Your leaving your family on Christmas to take care of me when I was diagnosed with cancer was wonderful of you. John thinks so, too."

"You're my sister. You would have done the same for me."

"Yes. But I wanted to thank you again—before I die," she said, tears falling onto her nightgown.

"Is John holding up?"

"He's doing a good job."

"What do you do all day?"

"Watch TV, nap, talk to John, nap again." She chuckled. "We met with the undertaker. My pastor has given me Holy Communion and holy oils. We will meet with the cemetery salesman soon."

"Well, you're kept busy."

"Paula Coulter, a concerned friend, comes over regularly to talk to me and gives John a break to go out for a few hours."

"You haven't been out?"

"No, I can't walk…Well, I can make it to the powder room…sometimes. But John helps me. I get tired easily."

"Try to get as much rest as possible."

"This is about all I can do, Una, is rest. I take one day at a time."

"I'll ring you again, Tara. I love you."

"I love you, too, Una."

When she put the receiver down, she realized at a time like this people tell each other they love them. *Dying brings us expressions of love that otherwise might be left unsaid.*

Maura came and lay beside her mother. Tara had pictures of Sean, Enda, Thaddeus, and Maura and other family members, also photos from her mother's childhood and family in Ireland. Maura separated pictures to arrange photo albums for her three brothers. She knew Tara had wanted to do this, but she didn't have the strength. Maura told her mother she would prepare the albums. However, she needed her to identify some of her relatives before she died.

She thought of all the stories her mother told them. The one she remembered the most the day she came to America to meet her finance, Martin O'Brien. Maura wanted to remember those stories in great detail so she made some notes. She didn't want to forget them. She remembered her mother came to America on Mother's Day, May 10, 1959. And she remembered when her Ma Ma's father died…Mom had missed the funeral. Her family told her not to come home. An obedient Irish daughter, she obeyed. But in a few days the trauma of missing her father's funeral caught up with her, causing slurring of her words. A doctor told her to go home to Ireland and to rest at home—and grieve with the family. Maura remembered her mother telling her at first she disliked American food, especially Italian food. She lived in the Lucy Eaton Smith House for Women in Philadelphia. Maura had planned to go to dinner with Peg and other girls. She felt guilt…any day could be her mother's last. But her mother insisted she should join her friends. After the hospice nurse left, Maura went to dinner.

Tara wanted to arrange for a burial plot in St. John's Cemetery and John had the salesman come to the house. Like an angel of death the man was. Tara had hoped to visit the cemetery to pick out a location of her choice but her health prevented this.

Tara had been home on hospice care fifteen days. Dr. Stein finally told her how long she had to live. Never before would he answer this question during her five years, eight months of battling cancer, begging off on the fact he wasn't God. But now, with cancer in her brain, breasts, and lungs, he told her "About six weeks at most." The day before their wedding anniversary, she met with the cemetery salesman to select her grave. He was a gaunt man with shoulders stooped forward like an arc on a bridge support. He appeared on the verge of death himself. He reminded John of Digger O'Dell, the friendly undertaker on the old radio program, "The Life of Reilly," which he listened to, as a boy. The man's face was like fallen autumn leaves laid over into winter and, if touched, they might crackle and crumple.

"I want a plot with a headstone." She sounded like an army officer discharging orders to his men under siege at Dunkirk. She remembered thinking about serendipity and the time she decided to take one day at a time without looking for a long happy life. A long happy life would find her.

The man said, "You'll have enough space for six people."

John said, "Tara, the kids will marry and won't be in the area when they die."

"All right. I want a headstone with my name on it—like my Mom and Dad's."

"But we need space for two—us."

The salesman didn't want to lose the sale. He rightly assumed Tara's position. She was his customer and represented his sale. . "A good idea," he said, feeling a sense of closure.

Determined, Tara added, "You can only fight a good idea with a better idea. I want the plot for six and my name on the headstone."

"But we don't need six, Tara."

She shot her husband her cold administrative stare. "John," she said slowly, her index finger pointing at him, "you don't respect the dead. If you don't want to honor my last wishes you disrespect me."

"End of discussion," he said, "You win. Whatever you want. But we'll be lonely down there, the two of us."

She smiled a caring glance. "You're all I need."

The salesman, observing their conversation, smiled faintly. John noted the man's face did not crack. John and Tara signed the agreement with the salesman. John gave the salesman a check for a deposit and the man left.

# THIRTY-SEVEN

# Death Philosophy

The next day, Wednesday, June 15, 1994, they celebrated their thirty-first wedding anniversary. Tara remembered the sunny day in Dublin thirty-one years ago. *How beautiful I was in my white satin wedding dress with a lace design around the thigh and chest areas. How my life has been enriched in those thirty-one happy years with John, four children, our home, our business, my career, the ten times I went home to Ireland to see my family.* John gave her a kiss and a spring-like arrangement of long stem roses in a vase. She met his lips eagerly. A kiss was all they needed, a simple touch of their lips, re-awakening their marriage vows, a simple touch of their lips sparking the oneness they gave each other in the Church of The Three Patrons—oneness in mind, oneness in soul, oneness in body and the intimacy they shared in all facets of life.

They passed time watching television, talking on the telephone with family, friends, relatives, communication—the number one reason why good marriages get better. Without stating it, they waited...waited for death. Outside, life moved on. Inside, life flew out the window. Hospice care meant as much care possible while waiting. Waiting for Godot. "Aren't we born to die?" she once told John, long ago. "From the moment of conception we're dying, as we're growing."

They had a past. Their past had happened over and over. Their past was only the present—with the claws of death ready to clamp them into submission. *Doesn't this happen in life? The past catches up with the present. . and the present passes into eternity.* The future, they placed on hold. Normally, one's past mixed with the present helped create a future. Not for them. They lived in and for the day, one day at a time. For all their 11,300 days (John had calculated), they had a past. But no longer. Their past was about to fade away. Their present and future bore down on them from the grave, dark and threatening like the blackening skies before a tornado, a storm forever changing life into death, joy into grief, contentment into bereavement. Everyone dies, but not many people worked towards death, waiting for the final breath to snap off a too-young life, pre-maturely completed in the bearing of healthy children, but incomplete in not experiencing the fulfillment of their children's goals and dreams. Death's shadow lived at their door and each sundown caused them to think the night could be their last night together, their long day's journey into death and each sunrise the last they would spend together as man and wife, the lover and the loved, the pursuer and the pursued. After sixty years and out of the land of the living, Tara's life had grown into her death. And John would soon to begin to learn how to live without Tara. Unlike Christ, she would not resurrect herself to show herself to her family. John told her he was pre-determined in this world of determinism to live alone and be lonely, to have no peace of mind, no balance, to live in fear, to bear life in the land of the living without his wonderful wife.

John showed her driver's photo license, which had arrived in the day's mail.

"Think I'll need it?" she quizzed.

"No," he said, his eyes downcast, morose, heavy. He didn't lie to her; he never had. No need to start lying at the end. Unafraid to show Tara his feelings, he showed her tears. Tears for a life together...soon to be no more. Tears of joy for having lived a short lifetime together. *The impossible was about to become possible.*

Her brothers rang her regularly. They touched base with the baby of the family and the first child to die in their family. In the course of the human chain of events, life normally follows a pattern of first to the last. *Negating the chain of events, I was last to be born in my family, but the first to die.* People told John and Tara, "God takes the best first." Meaningless chatter. People said this, not God. John knew Jesus had said, "The Father will give you whatever you ask of him in my name. Ask and you shall receive, seek and you shall find. Knock and it shall be opened to you." They had asked, sought, and knocked with a faith strong enough to move mountains...nothing happened. Tara didn't believe this; in his grief, John did. All positive requests met with denial. *Maybe the entire Bible, both Old and New Testaments, is a titanic lie, a mere fairy tale as his in-laws claim. I don't want to believe this. Tara doesn't; she believes in living while dying.*

During the sleeping hours, Tara's breathing had become more spasmodic. Her breath twitched in her lungs, heavy gasps like someone crying after hearing of the sudden death of a loved one. During the night, John awakened often and turning on a light in the living room, he watched for Tara's irregular breathing patterns, as she lay asleep on the hospice bed in the dining room. Her chest swelled and she made grunting sounds. Occasionally, John rose from the sofa and watched over his wife and listened to her breathing. Watching laborious breaths, he imagined he viewed her death mask. At times, Tara gasped sucking for air though she slept with the oxygen cup attached to her nostrils. Never again, John knew, would his wife breath without mechanical assistance. Without the oxygen tank, she would have died in the hospital.

Standing over her, he considered whether he wanted her to live this way—confined to bed with an artificial breathing device—or was she better off dead and away from an existence she tolerated only to be with him and the family a trifle longer? *I don't want her dead. I love talking to my best friend all of our thirty-three years together, including our courtship. Neither do I want my wife to live struggling for every breath in pain or discomfort. Thirty-three years: a Christ symbol. Christ died at thirty-three and after knowing Tara thirty-three years she would die, too. At least, she will be spared the pains of old age—as she more than once told me. She found positive aspects to difficult situations. She made difficult situations livable, by taking a bad experience and turning it inside out until she found the good. But at the same time, I don't want to see my vibrant and energetic wife living a non-existence, one she does not want.*

In his all-embracing and all-inclusive love for his "Little Irish Girl," his Irish Rose, he selfishly wanted Tara to be with him, no matter what. Conversely, he didn't want her to suffer and hoped for a painless and quiet death. *Is this happening?* He tried to face their situation as she did—bravely and realistically. But would he be brave without her? He thought not. But what did he know? How could he know what life would be without Tara? How could he know what he had not yet experienced? During one of her hospital confinements, he wanted her to know he would be with her until the end. He knew she knew it; he wanted Tara to hear it again from his own lips. "I will be with you until the end," he told her. And Tara predictably answered, "I know." Some men, he had heard, left their wives when they had cancer and terminally ill. He wanted Tara to know he would take care of her as best he could until the end.

After a breakfast of soft-boiled eggs, toast, and tea, she told her husband, "John, I don't want to leave you with bitter memories about my cancer and about God. Begin to think now about letting go. Live life to the fullest. Don't hang on to me when I'm gone. I'm leaving you with life, the most important gift God can give you. Life is for the living. Death is for the dead.

"He didn't help, did he?"

"John, it wasn't to be."

"It should have been."

"We both believe what will be, will be."

He nodded. He knew she was right, but he wouldn't admit it.

"It wasn't to be. Don't be angry with God. Anger will make you an embittered, unhappy man."

He wasn't angry with Tara. *How can a just God murder his own creation? God was taking away the joy of my life and I will be left alone.. unhappy, punished, cheated. What kind of God is this who tortures his friends?*

"Anger will destroy you. Let it go, John. I told the children to rely on God. And now, I'm telling you."

"God said in the Bible he would cure people who had faith and asked for help. We had faith and asked for your cure and he didn't help. He failed us."

"No, he didn't," said she, reading the sorrow in his heart. "You don't know what good you can do after my death."

"Good from your death? I don't want to know any good coming from your death."

"You know better. You're a self-made man. In difficult times, you rose to the occasion—no matter how bad—and took on the challenge."

He didn't know what to say. So he said nothing. He looked at the Japanese Maple tree on the front lawn, the tree he had given Tara as a Mother's Day present twenty-five years ago. He said, "I can't help it," tears welled in his blue eyes. "You're right. But I can't help it."

She read his sad expression. She read his soul. "Yes, you can, John." She repeated her words with more warmth. "Yes, you can. I know you can."

"Like 'The Little Engine That Could.'"

She smiled at his humor, causing a broad smile on his face, accentuated by wide parenthesis lines at the corner of his mouth. She brought out the best in him. "Yes, like 'The Little Engine That Could.'" *Let's see what today brings. Maybe a solution. Solutions lead to resolutions, satisfactory or unsatisfactory. Information with hope leads to at least living with whatever life brings.*

"But what about Lourdes, the Rosary Novenas, the Masses, prayers...."

"God must have something else in mind." He wanted to know what's on God's mind.

"But he outright said, 'Ask and you will receive; seek and you find; knock, and the door will be opened to you.' He doesn't have us on his mind."

"I can't answer for God."

" I can. He said the door would be opened for anyone who knocks. He's a damn liar!"

"You must let go, John."

" He lied to mankind."

"Yes, I've thought at times he wasn't listening, but now I'm dying...."

"You don't look like death."

"But I'm dying. I hope where I go I'll be able to help you and the children."

"Help us by staying here?"

"How can I? I've no say in this."

"I have."

"No, you haven't, John. You will be more at peace if you realize this? You'll go through bereavement and reconciliation."

"What peace can I have without you, Tara?"

"Let go—for me, John. I want you to be happy."

"How can I be happy, without you?"

"Try."

"I've tried and look what's happened: you're going to die and I'm left behind."

"Try. The two most important commandments, remember, are to love God and the second is to love your neighbor as yourself. John, if you don't do this, you will become an empty old man with no friends and no meaning in your life."

"I've tried. God hasn't."

"You can't go through life with these feelings of blaming God."

"Life will be miserable."

"It doesn't have to be."

"Tara, what you are, I am. You are all I know. You're my total happiness."

"I love you, too, John. But for you, life goes on."

"In a cell of misery?"

"The more you're angry, the more you will be angry at others. You're being angry with yourself. Anger will wither you up.

You will dry up if you continue to stay angry. For you, life goes on."

"You sure you can help me after death?"

"No…but the children need you. Live for yourself and them."

"They're all grown now. They don't need me anymore."

"Life has problems and they'll continue to need you with their problems."

"Promise me, you will try to live your best."

"Promise that—without you?"

"Promise," said she in a pleading tone of voice and with an angelic face.

John lowered his head and standing beside the bed, he said, "I'll try. But with no guarantees."

"Life has no guarantees. The important thing is you will try to live alone."

"I'll try it."

She smiled and kissed his hand. He reached over and kissed the fullness of her lips. "There you go again," he said. "Another kiss without lipstick."

He rolled half onto her chest and kissed her again. They found something indefinable in their embrace, her lips on his, his lips on hers. Sealed.

*They listened to the silence. How can I describe listening to silence? Guess one has to experience it to understand.*

# THIRTY-EIGHT

# Stillness

As Tara watched television, John sat at the kitchen table trying to write her eulogy. He knew he'd have no time to do justice to her life when she died. He feared being an emotional wreck. He wanted to capture the beauty of her life to portray how admirable she was.

On Wednesday, June 22, Father McBride again visited for confession and viaticum. He commented on how upbeat they looked, and he said he would never forget her comment about not washing dishes for those men up there in heaven. By evening, her breathing became cumbersome, but she showed no sign of imminent death: no skin discolorment, no bluing on the lips. She had a light dinner of small portions of chicken, green beans, and mashed potatoes. John's specialty—mashed potatoes, something he couldn't get enough of. Like Tara…he couldn't get enough of her love. He realized there would be no more triumphant twangs of the bedspring.

John awakened at five thirty, but lay on the sofa watching Tara's labored breathing. She waddled in the sheets like a newborn baby. In exhaling, she released short rattling breaths. The left side of the nightgown lay flat against the chest since the left breast had dissipated from the radiation and chemotherapy treatments. Those lovely breasts he had so often reverently held—like softballs she called them—all those many nights.

She awakened and said, "Good morning." Tara smiled, her upper lip straight across her face while the lower lip curved in a half circle. She had a wonderful smile John labeled "My kissable protractor." Her bald head was as smooth as a lightbulb, bright enough to send light where there is darkness.

John served French toast and tea on the serving tray, which straddled her. He sat on the bed beside her eating. Maura and Sean had stayed overnight, she sleeping on a mattress in the living room, and Sean slept on the sofa in the family room to be near their mother.

"The kids and teachers are getting up," said he.

"Would you rather be in school?"

"Of course not."

"I think you don't want to do this."

"You are my wife. I'll care for you." Her words papercut into his heart. *How can she question my complete devotion to her?*

"Tara, why are you asking? You should know better."

"Tell me the truth now," she said, pointing her finger at him, a gesture she rarely did. She was like Christ telling Peter "The rooster will not crow tonight until you have said three times you do not know me."

"There's no other place I'd rather be." Hurt shot through him like a rocket. He wished she had never asked him.

"I think there are times you'd rather be in school."

"No."

"Well, sometimes this gets boring."

"There is no other place I'd rather be."

Kissing their mother good-bye, Maura went to the gym. Sean went to work and John went to the kitchen table to pay bills while Tara fell back to sleep. She awakened at ten o'clock, watched Phil Donahue, and rang her brother Padraic, her favorite brother. *Often, I stayed at his house and he took me with him to the Fairytown Races when I was a young lass.*

Tara had a pill dispenser, a Sunday to Saturday container she used for each day of the week. Tara...the organizer. She kept asking what day it was, and scolded John not to confuse her by putting in Tuesday's place what should be in Thursday's slot. He kept his composure. Each felt the hurts about Tara's sickness and the affects it had on them. She had been hallucinating the past week.

On the way home from the gym, Maura stopped at the Seven-Eleven store to buy a pina colada slurpee for her mother. The store had no pina coladas. Maura thought this a bad omen.

At lunch, John and Tara ate hot dogs. She wanted hers cut into tiny pieces while he served his on a roll. She only ate three pieces.

"I don't feel hungry, John. I can't eat." She coughed up mucus. Subterhuman pains gripped her face.

Near one in the afternoon, Tara went in and out of delirium.

"Una," she called out, her eyes glassy. "Una, I need you."

Maura had returned from the gym and she and her father stayed at her bedside. Her eyes seemed centered on an unknown person or object as she peered straight ahead. John placed his hand on her leg. He wondered if she knew he was beside her. The sun flashed a radiant glow of brightness, as if showering intense joy on God's people. As if God joked with his children in need.

She turned to him and said lucidly, "Oh, I don't know what I'm saying. You'll have to forgive me." Her eyes turned liquidly.

"There's nothing to forgive, Tara."

John held a small yellow plastic cup to Tara's mouth. Again, she coughed up mucus. He recalled the time they met at Drexelbrook Tennis and Swim Club. A slender dark-haired Irish beauty, like the Madonna radiating loveliness for all to behold. Mucus seeped from under her eyelids. John handed the cup to his daughter who sat with Tara. Maura asked her dad to call the nurse, but he knew the end had come. Tara moaned from the pain in her brain, her lungs, and her breasts. Helpless, they gathered near her. She had taken all possible medication to ease pain.

"Maura, don't leave me," she pleaded.

"I'm here Momma. I'm not leaving you."

Emotion flowed into Maura's heart as if arrows had struck her heart. Maura had told Tara she loved her. Maura felt if she didn't express her feelings this time, she would regret it. "I love you, Ma Ma."

"I love you, too." Tara spoke her last words…words of love. Conceived in an act of love, she left the world with love.

In the moments of silence, Maura's tears seeped down her face as Tara closed her eyes.

Tara opened her eyes and said, "Thank you."

Maura thought this an odd thing to say at the moment. "Your welcome," she said as John re-entered the room.

Tara knew. She knew she had entered the last stage of life before death, the last time she would see John, the last time she would be with her children, the last time she would be in her home. The last time! Finality. Her head kept bobbing. She went in and out of consciousness. Tara had the angel of death at her side. She couldn't move her arms and her legs, but in her spirit she reached out to someone or something. Maybe God…an angel. John straightened his wife's legs on the bed. He told her he loved her. He didn't think to say he was sorry for anything. He didn't need to. There was nothing he didn't do for her in their marriage. He devoted his life to her and she gave everything of herself to him. No regrets...for either.

Maura remembered the night O. J. Simpson was on the run on the highway with six police cars after him. She had been watching a video with Peg in the family room when Tara called, "Come in here. Quickly. Watch O.J."

They sat one-half hour and watched Simpson's Bronco drive along the highway. She remembered this was the weekend Enda came home from Boston and spent everyday with her. They watched the Ireland-Italy soccer game in the World Cup Tournament.

Maura made dinner from a friend's cookbook—baked pasta. She had tentative plans to go to the Aztec Club with Amanda and Peg. She remembered her mother telling her the night her father had a heart attack she went to a dance. Looking back on it, Tara told her daughter she couldn't believe she did it. Maura decided not to go.

Tara's face looked pale and drained. Her eyes seemed glassy. They were puffed out with mucus. They bulged out of her head. John, Sean, and Maura were shocked and frightened, helplessly watching Tara's life fade away like early spring snow. John rang the nurse. The nurse, after listening to John's description, told John these were the last hours. John could not speak. Maura came to the phone. In an unconscious state, Tara remembered the dream she had when a man in a snow-white gown extended his hand to her. *Guess, it's that time.* She tried to lift her hand to greet him, but hadn't the strength. In her subconscious, she was ready for her end day.

The nurse said, "Your mother is unconscious. If you speak in her ear, she will hear you. Hearing is the last of the senses to go." When Maura hung up, she told her father and Sean.

Maura said, "We're here Ma Ma. I love you. We all love you." Strange, Maura remembered her mother telling her if she were dying, she didn't want Maura to put her hair near her. It bothered her. Maura imagined it was the scent of the hair spray. Maura made sure not to have her hair too close to Tara's face.

"I love you, Tara," John whispered. "You are my life. You are the best mother and the best wife a man could have." Crying, he moved away to the side as his son came to Tara.

"I love you, mom. There's no one like you," said Sean. He saw his mother's life fading as the sunlight blinked over their garden trees on a June evening, settling into the western sky.

Maura remembered her mother being testy those last few days. When she asked her mother how her make-up look, Tara said, "You need more." Never before did her mother tell her to put on more make-up. "You need more lipstick and more eyebrow pencil."

The children never before saw their father cry. In his tears, John rang Enda and Thaddeus. Enda was on his way to pick up a date when John rang his son's car phone. John started crying again, but he managed to talk to Thaddeus who waited for a ride. No one knew how long Tara would remain in a coma before dying and they hoped Enda and Thaddeus arrived home.

The nurse suggested diapers, so John had asked his daughter to go for Depends. She did not want to go to the pharmacy. She feared Tara might die and she wanted to be near her mother when she did. While John drove the two miles to Thrift Drug Store, Maura continued to talk to her mother and held her hand. She felt her mother's thumb move quickly like a muscle jerk. At first, she thought it a muscle spasm, but she wondered if Tara tried to communicate to her by finger movements.

Maura remembered when her mother's friend died with cancer. The daughter sat beside her mother's bed talking to her. Her mother tightened her grip on her daughter's hand when she told her mother she would miss her. Maura believed Tara could hear her. Tears flowing, Maura felt the end had come. Sean sat at the end of the bed and started crying. He held his mother's hand like a sacred relic.

Tara's breathing had slowed from loud quick breaths to almost nothing. Maura and Sean sat in silence and waited in dreaded anticipation. Frightened, they watched Tara's chest. Tara's chest swelled. Tara gave three short breaths. The little Irish girl became still.

In tears, Maura checked her watch: 8:10 P.M, the time the clock had stopped in the house the day before Tara came home from the hospital one last time. She hugged her mother, holding back her own hair so not to disturb Tara. Maura wanted Tara to put her arms around them to comfort them as she often did in life. Maura looked at the ceiling, thinking Tara in an out of body experience, gazed down on them. Misty-eyed she waved at the chandelier hoping Tara watched and smiled upon them. Maura believed her mother the happiest person she had ever known.

Strange to think, Maura compared her mother's breathing and facial expression to a fish—quick breaths and blank face. Within seconds, she turned whiter. A death mask. Within moments of Tara's dying, John came back from the pharmacy and immediately thereafter Mrs. Coulter arrived. Paula hugged Maura. Everyone cried. Maura felt sad dad had missed the moment of Tara's death.

"Are you all right?" Maura asked her dad.

"I'm all right. I'm glad you and Sean were here."

Between sobs Maura told Tara, "I love you. You are the best. I'll always remember you. And how good you were to us."

Maura remembered Tara told her, "You are our only daughter, our princess, Maura, and I will always love you, too. I'll help you in any way I can with God's help. Have a great life. Remember when the light flickers I am beside you."

John, standing beside his daughter, said, "Remember, Tara, how much I love you. How I live without you is my burden. I await the day I join you in heaven, that is if God forgives me for all my criticism."

As John suggested, Tara heard him and in her brain, she responded, *No other man has been as wonderful to his wife as you, John. You put the children and me first, seldom asking anything for yourself. And even though the children playfully criticized you for wearing dorky clothes, you were the best husband and father. God will guide you.*

Sean leaned close to Tara's ear, whispering, "I love you Mom. Thank you for all you've done for me."

Maura was glad she saw her mother at the end. She would cherish the moment she sat with her mother in her hour of need. Maura felt a sense of inner peace for doing all she could.

Father McBride came over and sat with Sean, Mrs. Coulter, and Maura.

John rang Enda, "Mom died. She died before you left Boston." He lost his ability to speak. His heart ached and tears rolled down his cheeks as he left to collect Enda at the airport. He looked like a corpse from an unwritten novel called *The End of Life*.

Enda had hoped to see his mother one more time. He too cried.

Thaddeus' ride didn't materialize. Heidi, his girlfriend, was with him, adding comfort to his sorrow. Thaddeus, the baby of the O'Malley family, would come home in the morning. Maura felt frightened. She looked into the dark dining room and studied her mother's white and bald head. They removed her wig. She looked good without it. The family believed Tara looked "cute" without it. Not to hide the inevitable from her children, she lived life indoors with no wig. They grew used to seeing her round and firm head. Maura feared Tara would pop out of nowhere. Tara's body, Maura decided, symbolized her fear of death.

Frank Cherry, the funeral director, placed Tara in a black, canvas zippered bag as Tara had foretold and carried her out feet first. John watched. *How right, Tara, you are: you come in headfirst and go out feet first.* Maura thought the assistant, Frank's son, cute. They watched in disbelief—their mother leaving her house the last time inside a black bag. The reality of the shocking scene impacted on them: their mother and wife who countless times had entered and exited the house unassisted, left the house assisted...lifeless.

John and the children, minus Thaddeus, sat on the porch, discussing their mother's life, planning a route to take to continue life without their standard bearer. John said it best: "From death springs life, and in heaven mom begins a new life as we must begin anew." *How will I do it? I don't know.*

---

In bereavement and on the morning of the funeral, John exited their home and stepped into blinding sunlight. His emotions black, his heart black, and his mind darkened, he saw the birth of another, new day. He imagined a brilliant sun, rising up from behind the Dublin Mountains in Ireland...my *beloved Irish*

Rose's homeland. From my bereavement will I one day awaken reconciled to a new life? I know the dictionary definitions of bereavement
and reconciliation. With resistance to reality, I now understand the
personal, emotional meanings of these words. Tears knotted his vision. Will I ever have reconciliation? I don't know.